the Kiss *on* Castle Road

A LAVENDER ISLAND NOVEL

the Kiss *on* Castle Road

A LAVENDER ISLAND NOVEL

Lauren Christopher

Published by Montlake Romance, Seattle
www.apub.com

Amazon, the Amazon logo, and Montlake Romance are trademarks of Amazon.com, Inc., or its affiliates.

ISBN-13: 9781503949706
ISBN-10: 1503949702

Cover design by Laura Klynstra

Printed in the United States of America

For my parents:
Happy fiftieth wedding anniversary!
Thank you for being such great parents always,
and for being such
wonderful role models of true love.

CHAPTER 1

Natalie Grant edged around one of the jutting rocks of the Lavender Island headlands behind her seven-year-old niece, trying not to let the slapping ocean get as high as her tennis shoes.

"Lily, slow down!" she called, but her words were swallowed by the sound of the crashing waves.

Normally she wasn't afraid of things—normally she was like Lily was right now: fearless, giggling, scampering to greater and greater heights. But at this particular moment, and from this particular position—teetering over the cold Pacific with a child in tow, desperately gripping a four-foot slab of slimy bedrock—she was feeling nervous.

"Lily! Seriously."

"He's right over here." Lily pushed her pink-rimmed glasses up her nose and continued to scuttle over the next set of rocks. "We're almost there."

The little girl—shockingly lithe on these rocks, her tanned legs strong and sure—dodged around the next bend with no effort at all. Natalie adjusted her snap-brim hat, threw her thick braid over her shoulder, and resolved to keep up. She used to be the "cool aunt." She couldn't believe she was now taking shaky breaths and yelling "Slow down" like some kind of schoolmarm.

She slid her body around the next bend, stepping carefully around the tide pools. She was officially there on LA's Lavender Island for the next three months to keep an eye on her niece, since her sister Olivia was on bed rest until the end of her pregnancy. Olivia's husband, Jon, was serving his last tour of duty, which would end right before the baby was due, and they just needed a few months of help.

When they'd proposed the idea, Natalie had agreed immediately. She was between boyfriends and jobs anyway. She'd tried not to be hurt that she was the last one they'd asked—she'd heard they'd asked her mom and her other sister, Paige, first. She'd assured Jon and Olivia with an enthusiastic yes, pulled out her well-worn duffel bag, and jumped on the next ferry to Lavender Island, determined to show her whole family she could be the über-responsible adult they never seemed to think she was.

Lavender Island was a great place to escape for a while anyway. She and Olivia and Paige had spent many childhood summers here, visiting their grandmother's cottage as young girls. It had surprised the whole family when Olivia inherited the cottage. And surprised them even further that she'd wanted to make it her permanent home. Natalie had loved Lavender Island as a kid, but as an adult she couldn't imagine how Jon and Olivia could stand it there full-time. With only three thousand residents, it was a little stifling. Plus, there was a serious shortage of twentysomething men, which was why she and Paige usually bowed out of invites, preferring their nightclub-dense Los Angeles.

But three months was doable. Helping Olivia for a short time would be good for her. Natalie needed to escape her life for a bit anyway, and especially men. In fact, the lack of twentysomethings could work in her favor. No temptations.

"Lily! Slow down!" Natalie hoisted herself over the next row of rocks, glancing once at the water. Was the tide rising? She didn't think it had been quite that high before. Lily was used to these tide pools and rocky headlands—the little girl had made this stretch of beach her playground for nearly two years now, ever since Olivia and Jon had taken over Gram's cottage—but kids didn't always think about rising tides and time of day.

Natalie glanced overhead. The sun was already setting. They'd have to hurry.

She pulled herself up and over the next set of rocks, which looked like a lava flow—thank goodness she did all that rock climbing with her girlfriends back home—but, dang, she had to stop and catch her breath. She was only twenty-seven, but lately the increasing number of candles on her birthday cakes was starting to bother her. Maybe she was already over the hill when it came to "scampering."

She shoved the wisps of hair out of her face and tried to get some air into her lungs. Another wave crashed below her, and a family of seagulls did a flyby near her head.

"Lily!"

At the top of the next ridge, her niece stilled. She perched atop a flat granite rock, peering over its edge.

"Here, Aunt Nattie," Lily called.

Natalie scrambled up and over the next ledge. There, in a deep, horseshoe-shaped cove that was rimmed in the island's signature sea lavender plant, were three little sea lions, all wriggling on their sides.

"There was only one before," Lily said, tiny lines of concern etched between her eyebrows. She looked out at the tide coming in, as if another cluster of animals might come ashore with the next wave.

Natalie nervously watched the ocean, too, then slipped over the rocks and moved past Lily. The animals didn't look well. Natalie didn't have a lot of experience with sea lions, but she remembered them from her summers here. The ones she was used to seeing were a shiny acorn brown and seemed to weigh nearly five hundred pounds. These were sort of a faded tan color and probably weighed less than fifty. On one, she could see ribs outlined.

Natalie started to shuffle down into the clearing, but Lily touched her arm.

"Aunt Nattie, we're supposed to stay away. I think a hundred miles."

"Do you mean a hundred feet?"

"Maybe." Lily's eyebrows puckered again.

"We're about fifty feet right now," Natalie said gently.

Lily's fingers came up into the air to count off steps. "We need to stay back and call the rescue center if they're in trouble."

"How do you know all this?"

"Brownie Scouts. Will you call, Aunt Nattie? They said an adult has to call." Tears suddenly brimmed behind her thick lenses.

"Oh, sweetie, it's okay." Natalie reached out for Lily. *Oh jeez.* It was her first day on the job, and Lily was already in tears. Dang, this child-care thing was harder than it looked. Thank goodness parenting wasn't on her life's agenda.

But being an aunt was already special. She settled her hand on Lily's shoulder and gave it a quick rub. "How do we know if they're in trouble? Don't they sometimes come up onshore to sun themselves?"

The waves crashed along the rocks below them, splashing the sea lions' flippers. One little pup made a pathetic attempt to squirm back into the ocean but landed on his side, then simply laid his head down and closed his enormous brown eyes.

Without taking her eyes off the scene, Natalie reached into her back shorts pocket for her phone. She slapped her other pocket. Then the front. Then . . . *Damn.* Where was her phone?

She whirled on the rocks, looking back over the terrain they'd just traversed.

"What's wrong?" Lily asked.

"My phone. I don't know where it is." Natalie scooted down the rock behind her. Could she have dropped it on the way? The back pockets on her favorite shorts were a tad small—not exactly designed to scale headlands with a small Brownie Scout. She'd have to start dressing more appropriately for this nanny gig.

Lily followed, looking into the rock crevices herself, but her face soon crumpled into panic. "We have to help them, Aunt Nattie! We have to call!"

"Yes. Yes, of course. We will. We will definitely help them. Okay. Let's . . ." Natalie scanned the cliffs below. "Let's go back. We'll find someone with a phone."

Lily gave an uncertain nod, then glanced worriedly at the animals.

"Let's go, Lily. We need to hurry. It looks like the tide's coming in."

That's all she'd need: to get poor Lily stranded out here in a cove with three sick wild animals. Jon and Olivia would definitely regret asking her then. Or fire her. First day on the job . . . Damn, she really didn't want them all to be right about her.

"This way, honey!" She motioned with her hand.

Lily hesitated at the top, still staring at the sandy beach that held her three sick charges, but she finally followed.

Natalie let her pass so she could keep an eye on her while they crawled over the same rough terrain all the way back.

The tide was, indeed, higher. Waves splashed Natalie's tennis shoes, and her hat fell off her head. She adjusted it quickly, then hurried to keep up with Lily. As they made their way gingerly back around the tide pools, she glanced around for her phone. That thing had cost her *three paychecks* from her last measly job.

Once around the last of the tide-pool rocks, they scaled one more ledge, then landed with thuds in the sand. Natalie reached for Lily's hand. "Let's go find someone to call for us."

The sun hung low, casting the whole beach in a beautiful sherbet orange. Lily's pale skin reflected the sunset's peach hue, her blonde hair now fiery gold around her worried face. Hand in hand, they hustled along the shore.

They wouldn't have much time. Jon and Olivia's cottage was still a mile away, and the rising tide would make any kind of animal rescue difficult if they waited much longer. Certainly they would find a jogger or beachgoer with a phone? But Natalie knew the chilly April beaches could remain empty. The only people who might be this far out by the headlands in April were the handful of home owners who lived along the C and D Street cottages with Jon and Olivia, maybe out on an evening stroll.

"Does Dr. Johnson still live up there?" she asked Lily, nodding to the nearest path, which switchbacked up a hillside covered in the bulbous green vines and leaves of dormant beachside ice plants. Dr. Johnson had been the local vet during the years Natalie had summered on the island. He'd helped her patch up a bird she'd found once, and also helped her rescue a rare marine turtle when she was eight.

"No, he moved," Lily said.

"Who lives there now?"

"A weird guy with a telescope."

"Why is he weird?"

"He wears funny hats."

"Funny how?"

Lily shrugged. "They look like fishing hats, but he never fishes. He just sits on a beach chair and reads books."

"Is he old or young?"

Lily shrugged again. "Old, I think. He wears glasses."

Natalie took a deep breath. Personally, she liked funny hats. And reading books sounded pretty harmless. And old and bespectacled didn't sound like someone who could give them any trouble.

"Do your mom and dad ever talk to him?" she finally asked.

Another little shrug.

"Think he has a phone?"

Lily nodded, and the two of them went hand in hand up the narrow ice-plant trail.

First day on the job and she was already out of her depth . . .

Elliott Sherman balanced the two dinner plates carefully as he rounded the corner of the still-unfamiliar dining room in his rental, then laid them gently on the table, squinting to see if there was anything he'd forgotten.

"This looks delicious," his date said.

He nodded absently, still inspecting the mounds of spaghetti. *Pepper? Salt?* No, his sister had laid those on the table in fancy little bowls with tiny spoons she'd brought over about two hours earlier. *Basil?* No, he'd remembered that. *Cheese? Yes!*

"I forgot the cheese." He made an attempt to grab the edges of both plates again, ready to swing back into the kitchen, but his date put her hand on his wrist.

"This is fine." She directed him back to the table. "Where did you learn to cook, Elliott?"

Elliott tried to focus on her. He blinked the dryness out of his new contacts. Her name was Caren (with a *C*, she'd said), although he kept wanting to call her Carrie. She was pleasant. She had soft-looking hair. And he liked how she smelled—like pencils and sharpener dust. But he found himself continually distracted, idly glancing toward the bedroom.

"My sister," he answered.

"Nell taught you well," she said. Another kind smile.

He returned a polite expression and resisted another glance at the bedroom door.

Not that he was thinking of taking her there. It would be nice, of course—he'd been in quite a drought—but he'd been raised a gentleman and was much too shy to figure out how to seduce this woman anyway. Caren, with her buttoned-up blouse and carefully combed hair, looked too smart and no-nonsense for first-date fumblings. Plus, his sister would kill him. Caren was the second date Nell had set him up with this week, and his sister's intention was to help him meet a nice, agreeable woman he could settle down with, not hop in the sack with. Nell just wanted to leave for Italy with her new husband and baby and not have to worry about him anymore. He found her fussing unnecessary, but she'd looked at him with increasing concern over the last couple of years. They'd been through a lot together, though, ever since they were kids, so he was trying to cooperate.

"Nell's always been a good cook herself," Caren said.

Elliott rubbed his eye. These contacts were ridiculous. Nell thought he should "show off" his eyes, wear trendier clothes, put gel in his hair, switch his waterproof watch for something with style. He'd followed all her advice, but these contacts, and these dates, were killing him. Especially this week. Of all weeks for her to have set him up with a date every night. He was *this close* to pinpointing a new strain of bacteria that might be affecting Lavender Island's seashore—the reason he'd been ferried over here by Nell's husband in the first place. And he'd had an important thought as he was ladling sauce over Caren's spaghetti. It was all he could do not to rush back into the bedroom, where his laptop was, to search for any precedent for his latest hunch. But Nell had made him promise he wouldn't be the obsessive, absentminded scientist he usually was on these dates. She'd said he'd had a decade of that since he'd graduated from college, and look where it had gotten him.

He dragged his gaze back from the bedroom for the fifteenth time and turned, instead, to Caren.

"So, how do you like teaching junior high?" he asked.

He tried to concentrate on her answer. The pencil scent swirled around her every time she shifted in her chair, and he tried to focus on that, on her smile, on her delicate hands, on her kind-sounding voice. But the mutations in new isolates from beached sea lions kept shoving their way into his mind . . . *Had the organism ever been detected in terrestrial wildlife reservoirs?*

"Elliott?"

"Yes?" His head snapped back up.

"Do you?"

"Do I what?"

Her smile took on a forgiving nature as her eyelashes lowered. "I'm not holding your attention very well, am I?"

"No, no—it's not that. I mean, *yes*. I mean, yes, you are. I'm sorry. I just keep thinking about this—"

A frantic knock rattled the back sliding door in the living room.

Elliott leaped to his feet. His hand shot out to Caren's, and he shook his head. This could be dangerous. The slider faced the ocean and very public property. Anyone could wander up to it. When he'd rented the beach house for the year, Dr. Johnson, the old vet, had warned him that the occasional drunk or vagrant might stumble to the back door.

He slipped around the corner into the darkened living room and reached for a golf club out of a dummy set Dr. Johnson kept there for decoration.

Belatedly, he remembered that Nell had suggested he open the blinds in this west-facing room. To let in the sunset because it would be romantic, she'd said. And it would help him avoid looking like the hermit he was becoming. Too bad he hadn't listened. As it was, he couldn't see a thing.

He crept through the dark, knocking his shin against a coffee-table corner. As he got past the grand piano, past the last of the three oriental rugs, squinting through his lame contacts, he positioned the club in front of him. Just before he leaped, the figures outside came into full silhouette.

He took a deep breath and lowered the club.

It wasn't a vagrant.

It was a little girl.

And, if his contacts weren't deceiving him, a very sexy woman with long, tanned legs in very short shorts, who snatched an old man's snap-brim hat off her head to lean into the glass with her hands cupped around sharp, beautiful eyes.

His full attention was finally captured.

CHAPTER 2

Natalie almost face-planted through the slider when the dark glass opened, but her trajectory was stopped by a youngish man with a golf club in one hand.

From Lily's earlier description, Natalie had been expecting a Carl Reiner sort—maybe softly shaped, with a bucket hat and a smart, grandfatherly grin. Kind of like Dr. Johnson. But this man wasn't out of shape at all, nor was he bespectacled or fisherman-hatted. And he certainly wasn't "old." Maybe to Lily anyone over twenty was old, but this guy was late twenties, tops, with a long, lean face and startling blue eyes. He had a swath of sandy hair that fell over his forehead and an embarrassed, playful look that belied his serious chinos and button-collar shirt. A stuffy sweater added about ten years to him, though.

He gripped Natalie's elbow, where he'd caught her fall, and frowned into her face, seeming concerned and awed and baffled by her all at once, as if he were looking at a unicorn.

"Doyouhaveaphonewecanuse?" she burst forth, still a bit breathless from the climb up the hillside.

"Are you okay?" He glanced at Lily. "Is someone hurt?"

"Not us. Some, uh, sea lions. Down there. We need to call. I lost my phone. The tide's coming in, and we're hoping someone can come—"

Before she could finish the sentence, he stepped past her to the patio and scanned the beach below. "Sea lions? Where?"

"They're behind the rocks, just past the tide pools."

"They look distressed?" He already had his phone out of his pocket.

"Yes."

"How many are there?"

"Three."

"What makes them look distressed?"

"They're very small and rather discolored, and—"

"Hi, Jim?" he said into his phone. "We've got three down here, right at the tide pools . . . Yeah, just north of my place." His eyes went back to Natalie, but any unicorn-gazing he'd had in them before was now replaced by Sea Lion Emergency mode.

"How big were they?" He squinted at Natalie.

Natalie held out her arms to show him.

"Color?"

"They looked kind of . . . whitish."

"Yeah," he said back into the phone, turning away. "Let's get someone down here. Come in around from the north. I'll meet you."

He slid his phone into his back pocket and, without a backward glance, began gingerly climbing down the hill among the ice plants. The vines tangled almost all along the hill, and he carefully stepped around the bulbous green buds, making his descent awkward at best.

Suddenly, he stopped. "Oh," he said to himself. He turned abruptly and inelegantly climbed back up.

Landing on the patio in front of Natalie and Lily, he motioned toward the house. "Could you tell—"

Whatever he was going to ask was interrupted by the arrival of a neatly put-together woman who stepped out of the darkness of the house and through the patio door. She looked about his age—or maybe a little older—and had the patient, wide-eyed face of a kindergarten teacher.

"Is everything all right?" she asked, glancing at Natalie and Lily.

"Caren! Yes. I, uh . . . I have to go. I'll be back, but there are some sea lions stranded, and I have to . . ." His hand swept back toward the tide pools. "Do you want to come?"

"No."

He looked momentarily confused by her answer, then a bit desperate. "But I have to—"

"Yes, go," she said.

A look of relief washed over his face.

Natalie peered over the edge of the patio, watching him sidestep the plant vines a second time. The vibrant hot-pink flowers of the ice plants were still closed, shivering on the edge of readiness for their annual spring debut, which would create a vivid carpet of color. But now they were just a mass of bulbous green being protected from the scuffed dress shoes of this determined man.

Lily's little shoulders relaxed, and Natalie was able to let out a relieved breath herself. The sea lions would be fine.

As she watched the stuffy young man take off running, she couldn't help but wonder why he was so quick to respond to such a strange request. And why he seemed to have the rescue center on speed dial. And why he'd seemed to have forgotten she existed as soon as she'd said "sea lions." With a stab of embarrassment, she realized that seconds had ticked by and she was still staring at the chino-clad backside of this woman's husband or boyfriend or *something*. She turned and forced a polite smile that had a bit of an apology in it.

"Does this happen often?" she asked into the uncomfortable silence.

"All in a day's work, I think," the woman said. She stepped inside the dark house and closed the slider on Lily and Natalie with a nod good-bye.

Well. So much for that. Natalie turned to Lily with a shrug. People on Lavender Island were usually friendly, but there were some exceptions. She reached for Lily's hand. "I think we did okay, kiddo."

"Can we go watch?" Lily looked up hopefully, bouncing on her toes.

"It's getting late. I think your mom will be worried."

"I want to see him rescue the sea lions!"

Natalie glanced at Nerdy Awkward Guy, who was now running nimbly toward the tide pools. He kicked his shoes off about ten yards out and carried them as he continued at an even more amazing pace. The orange sun sat on the horizon. It was probably seven or so. The tide would be too high for them to follow him and get back over the tide-pool rocks without getting trapped. She wondered how he was going to do it, but then she realized that might be why he'd told "Jim" to come from the north—there was another opening on the other side of the cove where they could probably drive a golf cart or use nets or cages or whatever they did.

It would be fun to see how it happened. She was a little curious about Nerdy Awkward Guy, too, and his ability to help. He had a bit of a Clark Kent thing going—shy and stuffy on the outside but then looking like some kind of superhero once he took off his shoes and hit the sand running. But she needed to make the responsible decision for Lily. Turning new leaves and all.

"I think we need to get back. It's getting dark."

Lily gave her the exact look she remembered from her own childhood—that expression of exasperation kids gave adults who wouldn't let them have the fun they wanted.

Natalie tamped down the surprising realization that she was now on the other end of that look and averted her eyes.

"C'mon," she said. "Let's get back to your mom."

She continued to avoid Lily's gaze all the way back down the succulent leaves of the dormant ice plants.

Damn, being responsible kind of sucked.

Elliott dragged himself up the steps to his place hours later.

He entered the back kitchen door, half hoping Caren would still be there so he wouldn't have to report to his sister that his dating behavior had been as deplorable as ever.

But then he half hoped she wouldn't be there so he could escape to the bedroom, where his notes were.

He didn't usually get to see the rescues—ever since becoming the youngest microbiologist on the West Coast to win the Harbor Fellowship, he'd been a specialized scientist who shuffled from center to center and typically saw pups once they were in the ICU or starting recovery in pools. But now that his buddy and brother-in-law, Jim, had called him to Lavender Island to help set up the new sea lion rescue center during the next year, it was all hands on deck. And he got to actually *see* them sick in the wild. And help.

It was exhausting. But exhilarating. For the last three years, Lavender Island and the rest of Southern California had been seeing epidemics of dehydrated sea lions washing up on shores in the spring, and the regular veterinary centers couldn't handle the large numbers. No one knew what was causing the epidemics, but Jim, as a veterinarian, knew that Lavender Island needed a center of its own to provide rescues. And he knew Elliott could help him with the scientific research through the Harbor Fellowship. He'd called Elliott down from Monterey to see if he wanted to build the center with him, and Elliott had leaped at the chance. He'd published a series of papers on bacteria in marine environments, and this would give him the opportunity to work with the animals right in the field. Not to mention be near family again. For at least three months anyway—before Jim and Nell moved to Italy. After his fellowship year was finished, Elliott figured he'd take one of the many jobs waiting for him at the National Institutes of Health or the Centers for Disease Control and Prevention.

Tonight, though, had reminded him how much he missed field-work. It had been just Jim and young Garrett and him, since the call had come in so late. But it had been so rewarding getting those tiny pups rescued.

Not to mention he'd had the pleasure of meeting the Good Samaritan.

He ran his hand down his face, embarrassed that his thoughts had gone there for at least the fiftieth time that night, especially because he should be thinking of poor Caren and her cold spaghetti with no cheese.

But he couldn't stop thinking about Hot Citizen.

He wondered if that was her little girl she was with, if she was married. He'd forgotten to look for a ring. And he should've asked for her name. He'd seen the little girl before, but he'd thought she belonged to another couple who lived up the beach. But, then again, he wasn't very observant about such things. People didn't interest him as much as his work did.

Except some people.

Like beautiful, long-legged, fiery-eyed Good Samaritan people.

He sighed.

As if he'd ever get a woman like that to look at him.

It had never happened before, and it sure wasn't going to start now, according to his sister. Especially as he got older and "weirder," Nell said. A twenty-year-old college guy could get away with a bedroom filled with stacks and stacks of scientific journals, she said, to maybe attract an equally nerdy, nice college girl. But a nearly-thirty-year-old man would just spook a woman—any woman—if he kept his shades drawn all day and used his bed to hold reams of notebooks of scratchy handwriting and gene sequences. And regularly let his mind drift to equations instead of the woman sitting in front of him.

His best hope, Nell said, was to meet someone soon, someone equally cerebral, maybe a professor or another scientist, definitely someone over thirty. Nell was pleased that the island had a shortage of twentysomethings, telling Elliott that he should set his sights on older women anyway. She was disgusted by the young spring-break crowd, which Elliott still managed to get swept up with. They'd taken one look at him, one look at his rented beach house, then nuzzled up to him long enough to get him to invite their sorority sisters over on the ferry to party in the house overlooking the Pacific. It had happened twice already. The first time he'd managed to get Dr. Johnson's house robbed of two irreplaceable vases before the women left in the morning. He'd mailed off a check to Dr. Johnson the very next day. The second time he'd at least gotten laid, but it had also required $1,500 worth of alcohol and hors d'oeuvres, taken from his new inheritance. And he'd managed to pass out afterward to boot. He was a smooth operator, all right.

He sighed and entered the dark house, glanced at the table still set with his and Caren's uneaten food, and barreled past it to the bathroom, where he took out the torture lenses—worse now with saltwater spray aggravating his eyes—and changed into his more comfortable running clothes. He tore a new notebook out of the cellophane wrap and found a pencil that had rolled onto the floor.

He fell onto the bed and propped himself up to write:

April 16, 7 p.m.: Direct observation: three sea lion pups found alive, washed ashore in Diver's Nook, north side of Lavender Island. Displaying standard behavior of dehydration. Will continue to observe over next few weeks.

He stared at the paper, tapped the eraser against his bottom lip, turned the page, and then added, for some strange reason:

April 16, 7 p.m.: Direct observation: met the woman I want to marry. Probably Nell's worst nightmare.

CHAPTER 3

Natalie brought her sister a steaming mug of tea and a plate of unbuttered toast, setting them on the coffee table in front of Olivia's new couch/bed setup, then returned to the kitchen to pour Lily a bowl of cereal.

"Is this all you have?" she whispered to Lily, scanning the selections of fiber-filled and whole-wheat circles and shapes. "Nothing good, like Fruity Pebbles?"

"I can hear you," Olivia called from the couch.

Natalie held up each of the disappointing choices for Lily until she got a nod of approval, then rummaged around the fridge for some strawberries, for at least a little flavor. Olivia and Jon were already turning into nutty island health-food types.

"So, what are your plans for the day?" Olivia asked.

"That's up to you," Natalie said over her shoulder. "I can take Lily to school, then come back and help you with"—Natalie glanced back at Olivia, who was staring at her unbuttered toast—"whatever."

Olivia sighed. "This bed-rest thing is going to kill me. What am I going to do all day?"

Natalie had no idea. Bed rest sounded like the worst possible thing in the universe. She poured milk into her and Lily's bowls. "Want me to buy you some magazines or something?"

"Maybe I'll design some baby announcements." Olivia stared at her laptop on the fireplace hearth and sighed again. "I do need to go through Gram's boxes in the back room. Maybe you could drag them out here, and I can look through them throughout the day?"

"Sure, I can do that."

"Then why don't you just explore today?" Olivia said. "I could definitely use your help picking Lily up from school, but other than that, just have some fun. I'll come up with more of a schedule starting tomorrow."

"I do have to find a new phone." Natalie served Lily her cereal. She was crushed about the extra expense. It would set her back several weeks, and she was already behind financially as it was.

"Can we visit the sea lions after school?" Lily bounced in her chair with her pretty-please grin.

Natalie leaned against the kitchen counter and took up her own bowl.

"Lily, you have a Brownie Scout meeting," Olivia reminded her from the couch. "Maybe tomorrow?"

Lily slumped into her chair as if she'd just been told Christmas was canceled. But Natalie nodded to her, and her silent smile returned.

Natalie herself had been obsessing about the sea lions since last night, wondering if they'd all been safely rescued. And, if she wanted to be honest with herself, she'd been thinking about Nerdy Awkward Guy, too. Last night, when they'd entertained Olivia with the story of their adventure as they'd unpacked Natalie's things in the guest room, Natalie had tried to press Olivia for details about her new neighbor. She wasn't sure why she was so curious, but something about his Clark Kent persona, the sincerity of his eyes, the way his passion had lit up about the sea lions as soon as she'd mentioned them, the way he was so young but in Dr. Johnson's old house—it all intrigued her. She'd caught a glimpse inside the darkened house of columns, a baby grand, and elaborate furnishings that looked as if they'd been there forever. Were they Dr. Johnson's things? Nerdy Awkward Guy seemed awfully young to have amassed all that. And he seemed too absentminded to have such good taste. Maybe the kindergarten teacher look-alike had decorated for them.

And, if Natalie was really being honest with herself, maybe her interest was partly because he didn't seem interested in her. It was kind of a novelty to have a man's eyes never land on her breasts, to not stare at her as if he was thinking of eight different ways to get her into bed. Nerdy Awkward Guy definitely didn't seem as though he'd know. And there was something kind of sweet about that.

Natalie had tried to slip in a few sly questions, but Olivia didn't know much about him. Said he'd been there only a few months. When Natalie threw in the phrase "and his wife," Olivia had frowned. "I'm not sure he's married," she'd said.

Although all Natalie's synapses began firing at that comment, she'd concentrated instead on hanging her favorite hats along the guest-room wall.

"Where would they have taken the sea lions?" she asked now, focusing on scooping tasteless wheat circles into her mouth. She had to buy some better cereal. And get Nerdy out of her mind. But she did want to see the animals again.

"Probably the Friends of the Sea Lion center," Olivia said. "It's a new little rescue place on the south side of the island."

"Do they allow visitors?" Natalie asked.

"I think so. They have a full veterinary hospital and outdoor pools where you can see the sea lions that are healthy enough to be released back to the wild. You should check it out."

"Take me! Take me!" Lily bounced.

Natalie smiled at Lily and put her bowl in the sink. She might. It embarrassed her that she half hoped Nerdy would be there, too.

What was the matter with her? She'd barely gotten rid of clingy David of the Broken Motorcycle in LA, and now her mind was already wrapping around someone *else*? She was supposed to be on a "man-cation"—no men for at least three months. She just needed to step back, reevaluate her life, and figure out why it had stalled at twenty-seven. Growing up, she'd always pictured herself having, by this age, a strong career, a decent apartment, a well-stamped passport, like-minded friends, and a fabulous boyfriend. Marriage and kids had never been on her life's agenda—the phrase *settling down* had always made her feel rebellious—but she did hope to have some kind of exciting, forward momentum by now. A purpose. A goal. A life philosophy. Instead, all she had was a long string of disappointing dates, three pink slips, two eviction notices, five engaged girlfriends who could talk of nothing but wedding dresses, and a constantly packed suitcase. Which was now at her mother's house. Under her childhood bed. Waiting for the next move.

"What street is the center on?" she found herself asking anyway.

"Canyon Road."

Natalie nodded. She would go just to see the animals. She had to stop thinking about Nerdy. He wasn't her type at all. Her type was much tougher-looking: facial hair that formed sharp, dangerous-looking angles, longer hair, tattoos. She tended to gravitate toward mercurial, dramatic Los Angeles types, although she didn't know why. They were exciting for about five minutes, but ultimately they never worked out. And when they didn't, they became unbelievably hard to shake.

"C'mere, Lily," Olivia said from the couch. "Let me braid your hair. Are you done with breakfast?"

"Almost." Lily scooped the remainder of her cereal into her mouth like a kitten.

Natalie rinsed the dishes while Lily scrambled onto the couch so Olivia could work two braids to her shoulders. Lily had on one of her EMT costumes from Halloween. She'd been a fireman, an ambulance driver, and then an EMT in rapid succession, and Olivia always let her wear the costumes to school if she wanted, as long as the school didn't complain. Lily wasn't allowed to bring her plastic fireman ax, of course, but she never whined about that.

Natalie smiled now and handed Lily her pink-rimmed glasses.

It would be relaxing to just hide here in Lavender Island for a bit with Olivia and Lily. She needed a vacation from her life, from her crappy apartment, from her go-nowhere jobs, from men. All her girlfriends were now getting married, making her feel as if they'd abandoned her, or abandoned their agreed-on mantra that they would be independent, successful career women first—at least well into their thirties. It was a mantra her mother had murmured into her ear when she was sixteen, and Natalie had carried the flag happily, moving from man to man, job to job, city to city. But now—with constant invites to wedding showers and friends "settling down" enough to not want to travel anymore—she was starting to reevaluate and question every decision she'd ever made. It would be nice to be on Lavender Island—away from all the advice, the voices, the opinions—and just be able to think for herself for a few months.

"I'm inviting Paige over tonight," Olivia called over her shoulder.

"Paige is coming?"

"Yep, on the five o'clock ferry."

"She didn't give you one of her usual excuses?"

"Not this time. I told her you might need some cheering up."

"*Me?* What makes you think I need cheering up?" Natalie couldn't quite keep the irritation out of her voice.

"The 'mancation' and all—I thought there might be more to the story."

Natalie sighed. There was. But she didn't feel like going into it right now. Her sisters were always on her about the serial dating. Not to mention the terrible boyfriend choices and her inability to stay at one job. Although Natalie felt as though their mom encouraged "experimenting" and finding where you felt comfortable, she was the only one who'd taken it to an extreme. And, as nice as it was to be invited to live Olivia's life for a while, she really didn't feel like doing it if it meant coming under criticism.

"Well, I don't need cheering up. You're the one on bed rest. I think you're projecting."

Olivia laughed in her good-natured way and tugged on Lily's braids to let her know she'd finished. "You might be right."

"Either way, I'll be here tonight to join you and Paige," Natalie said. "Let's get going, kiddo." She reached for Lily and guided her into the back bedroom to get her shoes on.

In a half hour, Natalie and Lily were both out the door with an almost-forgotten library book, a Hello Kitty backpack, a pink-and-orange lunch box with a toy stethoscope in it, a construction-paper poster Lily had to turn in about flowers, a list of four things Olivia needed from the grocery store, and the address of the Brownie Scout meeting after school. They piled everything into Olivia's golf cart—the only mode of transportation allowed on the island—and began bumping along one of the back roads toward the school.

"So can we go see the sea lions soon, Aunt Nattie?"

"Let me call and check on them first, okay?"

Natalie wanted to make sure all the pups had survived before bringing Lily by. Plus, she had to decide what to do about Nerdy Awkward Guy. Would he be there? Did he work there? She might have to do a little more research.

She was only two days into her mancation, after all. And thinking this much about a normal guy couldn't be normal.

Natalie pulled into the dirt parking lot, her golf-cart tires popping over gravel. Leaning forward, she peered from under the brim of her fedora through the open windshield. Was this the right place?

She didn't normally come down Canyon Road—these back areas had always been a little mysterious to her, even as a kid. Lavender Island was twenty miles long and eight miles across at its widest, but almost the entire population lived in the three-square-mile town shaped like a *D* that faced the harbor. The wealthier families lived in the coastal homes, plus in the hills that rose up along the curved part of the *D*, while the worker families and middle class lived in the center, in the C Street through G Street cottages. Although Natalie's grandmother had some property up in the hills, she'd always made her main home on C Street, and the girls mostly stayed there when they visited. They knew all the shop owners on Main, which intersected the town and catered to tourists all summer. When she was small, Natalie had loved running to the candy shop, the ice-cream shop, and the toy shop that lay between E and F. Some of the original owners were still there.

But Canyon Road rose off the back of the town, leading up toward the island's interior, which was sparsely populated. The only things back there were the Castle, which was a high-end hotel and bar; the island's only airport, which was run by the odd Mason family; and three herds of free-roaming bison, which had been brought to the island in 1952 for a movie and never removed.

Natalie peered farther through her windshield, and—through a row of massive oak trees that bordered a tiny stream—she could see a small red barnlike building set well off a dirt road. She set the cart's emergency brake and took a deep breath.

The April sun fell gently through the oaks, dappling the brick walkway with delicate shadows as she chose her steps up the uneven path in her high-heeled espadrilles. Natalie didn't dress up much—today, in fact, she was just in cargo capris and a T-shirt with one of her beloved fedoras shading her eyes—but she loved wearing high sandals. The height, added to her already tall stature, always made her feel brave.

In the distance, she heard barks that sounded a bit like dogs but had a sharper, hoarser upswing on the end. Seals. Or sea lions. Dozens, it sounded like. She quickened her pace through a small wooden gate and came upon another walkway that led to a large brick courtyard with four fenced pools, shaded behind a tall stand of silver-leafed eucalyptus trees and a few palm trees. Before she got to the first fenced pool, a silver-haired woman in a half apron and bright-blue T-shirt with "I'm a Friend!" across the front came hustling over.

"Hellooooo!" the woman said in a cheerful soprano. "Are you here for the tour?"

"No, I'm just stopping by to see the three sea lion pups that were brought in last night—I found them in Diver's Nook and wondered how they were doing."

"Oh! We love when people follow up! Let me check on them for you. Don't you look cute! Are you a model?"

Natalie shifted uncomfortably. Her modeling days were long over. "No. I—"

"Do you know who brought them in and what time?" The woman had already moved on.

Natalie breathed a sigh of relief and nodded. "Jim, I think. About seven p.m."

"They might be in ICU. I'll go check. Have a look around, and I'll be right back. My name is Doris." She pointed proudly at the name pin attached above the friend proclamation.

"Thank you, Doris."

"We have a tour coming in five minutes. You should join them. We take them all throughout the facility." She cupped her hand near her mouth like a whisper. "You can slip in in the back."

Natalie slid her hands into her cargo pockets. "I might."

"And here." Doris pulled a flyer out of her blue half apron and shoved it at Natalie. "Be sure to come to our Bars and Barks Event. It's the last Saturday of every month, and it's a fund-raiser for the sea lions."

While Doris shuffled up one of the cement walks toward the barn-like building, Natalie read the flyer. Lavender Island sure had a lot of events—it seemed as if every weekend there were three or four charity events to choose from. The problem was, unless it was tourist season, they were mostly populated by senior citizens. Or sometimes thirty-somethings with small kids, like Olivia and Jon. Although Lavender Island might have been magical for her when she was a child, it just wasn't a fun place to hang out as a single young adult.

She tucked the flyer into one of her pockets and followed the sound of barking sea lions to one of the four fenced pools, which had five two-hundred-pound animals swimming around inside, with two additional ones sunning themselves on the sidelines. They looked healthy and shiny brown, their wet coats glistening in the sun. One stretched his neck up toward the sunshine, wriggled it back and forth with seeming appreciation for the warmth, then slid back into the pool and dove out on the opposite side. He seemed to like that spot better and turned his whiskered face toward the sun again. He gave a contented bark.

In the next pool, five more sea lions, a little bigger than the last set, acted rowdier. Two were arguing over their position in the corner, while another three swam in circles together, then all leaped out the other side in a wet, blubbery slither. They barked at one another, as if to get out of the way, then finally settled on a comfortable dog pile, overlapping one another, to enjoy the dapples of sun.

The third pool had a different mammal—smaller, with lighter-brown bodies, more doglike faces, wrinkled furry necks, and larger eyes like puppies. Three of these creatures swam together and let off higher-sounding barks, leaping over one another in the water like a game of leapfrog before slithering out to the sidewalk for some sun.

"Those are baby fur seals," came a deep voice behind her.

Natalie whirled. There, not twelve inches away, was none other than Nerdy Awkward Guy.

"What are you doing here?" Her voice was embarrassingly breathless. She had the brief, horrible thought that she'd somehow conjured him from the unthinkable number of times today she'd hoped to see him again, then remembered her mancation and hoped not to see him again.

"I work here." The corner of his mouth quirked up. "What are *you* doing here?"

"I came to see . . ." The words escaped her. Her hand fluttered in the direction of the buildings.

Men didn't normally make her clam up. Especially intellectual-looking guys like this. Today he actually had a lab coat on. And glasses. Her usual guys had antiestablishment glowers, not curious expressions. And motorcycle jackets, not lab coats. Yet for some reason she couldn't stop staring at this guy and his soulful eyes. He peered at her as if he were studying her under a microscope—not in the leering way most men did, but in an intense way, as though he were looking at the unicorn in his living room again.

"Did you come to see Larry, Curly, and Moe?" he asked gently.

"Larry, Curly, and Moe?"

"The rescuer usually gets to name them. I thought I'd go with something cheerful."

She finally had to look away. She knew what to do with leers, with suggestive smirks, with half-lidded eyes that dropped to her breasts. She'd been enduring those since puberty. But this . . . she didn't quite know what to do with what looked like sincere curiosity. Or such a kind, no-expectations smile.

"They're in the back, if you want to see them," he said. "They're still in ICU. We usually don't let visitors back there, but if you—"

"Dr. Sherman! Dr. Sherman!" Doris tottered through the court-yard, a deep look of concern on her face. "What are you doing down here? You don't need to be out here. We'll take care of the guests." She grabbed his lab-coat sleeve and tugged him toward the walkway.

"It's all right, Doris." He slipped out of her handhold. "I know this guest."

She looked at Natalie with a new sort of appreciation. "You didn't say that. Well, I found the three patients you mentioned from last night," she said, turning toward Natalie. "They're still in ICU. We don't let guests back there, though, but if you want to come back in about three days, they'll probably be on their way to a great recovery."

Behind Doris, Dr. Nerd dropped his gaze to the ground and seemed to bite back a smile. He glanced up at Natalie, his eyes begging her not to reveal that he'd just been inviting her to break the rules.

"Thanks, Doris," he finally said.

"Or, you know . . ." Doris winked at Natalie. Her hand came up again to channel her whisper between girls. "Slip into the tour."

Natalie suppressed a smile and nodded.

Doris headed up the path. Once she was out of earshot, Dr. Nerd slid her a glance. "Want to sneak around the back to see them?"

"Doesn't Dr. Sherman get to do what he wants around here?"

"I'm just a visiting scientist. The lead vet is my friend Jim, and he runs a pretty tight ship around here. Elliott Sherman." He held his hand out.

She shook it. "Natalie Grant."

He frowned while he held her hand too long, as if perhaps he was concentrating on her name. "I like your hat," he blurted.

"Thank you."

When she finally wrestled her hand back, he cleared his throat.

A small silence welled. Natalie was normally good at filling these—usually with a smart-assed comment or inane observation—but for some reason, she didn't want to take any chances with this man. She didn't want to risk saying the wrong thing. Turning toward the pool, she gripped the fence, concentrating on the baby fur seals. Shifting her focus felt like a self-preservation tactic.

"Thanks for your rescue last night," he finally said. "You really should have named the pups instead of me. Or your daughter should have named them."

"She's not my daughter." She didn't mean to look back at him, but she did.

He gave another of those thoughtful nods, seemingly waiting for her to fill in.

"Niece."

The nod continued, became more thoughtful.

The nudge from her gut, or maybe her heart, told her to move away.

"Sherm?" Another lab-coated man shouted from the barn-building doorway.

Dr. Sherman turned.

"Seizure!" the man yelled.

Nerdy turned back to Natalie. "Domoic acid," he mumbled.

"What?"

"Sorry. Nothing. I've . . ." He made a motion with his hands back toward the building but looked at her with entreaty.

"Yes! Go!" Natalie said. Seizure? Did sea lions have seizures?

"I'm sorry." He seemed distraught. "Can we . . . ? Or can you . . . ? I know you want to see the sea lions you helped rescue."

"No, go!" Natalie said.

He lingered for what seemed like too long, frowning at her, and then jogged up the walkway.

Natalie watched the perfect crease in his chinos that fell from beneath his lab coat, noted the natural step in his dress shoes as he jogged up the bricks, and knew she had never in her life been attracted to such things.

And yet here she was.

Attracted.

She frowned and turned back to the baby fur seals.

The feeling of self-preservation returned.

Elliott hustled up the steps and ran a few curse words through his head at his stupidity.

I like your hat? Had he seriously just said that? That had to be about the lamest line in the universe.

At least he got her name. And found out the little girl wasn't hers. And saw that she wasn't wearing a wedding ring.

But damn, what good did all that do? She looked like a supermodel, with that wide smile, perfect body, and all that shiny braided hair. And a smart supermodel at that, with those fierce brown eyes. She probably had guys hitting on her all the time. Cool guys. Guys with moves. Guys who said things that were a hell of a lot more clever than "I like your hat."

He groaned and decided to banish that line from his memory forever. He'd never think about this incident again.

"Room two?" he asked Jim, who was waiting for him to pass through the big door.

"Yep. It's Mr. Warbler. We thought it was the leptospirosis, but looks more like domoic acid poisoning." Jim slammed the door behind them and lumbered after Elliott. "We might be back to ground zero. I was going to administer an injection but thought you might want to take a look at him first."

He did. Jim was great about letting Elliott view everything as a scientist, which most centers didn't. The results were inconsistent and confusing: Mr. Warbler had seemed as if he was suffering from leptospirosis, but now a seizure indicated domoic acid poisoning; the three pups that came in last night—Larry, Curly, and Moe—were not fluttering their flippers over their midsections in the manner expected of an animal with leptospirosis. They were exhibiting dehydration, similar to the frightening number of sea lion pups that had been washing up on California coasts since March. It was only April, and they were already showing record numbers.

"Thanks for letting me take a look." Elliott jotted everything down on his notepad, then turned the gurney with Jim and they both rushed Mr. Warbler down the hall. On the way, Elliott almost ran right into the Colonel, whose five-foot-five frame lingered near the doorway. He wrung his gloved hands, waiting to assist with the gurney. He was one of the center's oldest volunteers at ninety-five—a veteran of World War II who'd lived on the island since the 1940s. He looked as if the wind could blow him over at any second, but he was still strangely intimidating and smart as a whip.

"Sorry Jim had to interrupt you out there," the Colonel's gravelly voice drawled. "We didn't know you had such pretty friends."

"She's not a friend."

"Doris said she was."

Elliott blinked. "How did Doris get in here and already say that?"

"She came gallivanting up here and told us. We were watching you through the window."

They pulled the gurney into place, and everyone grabbed a pair of gloves.

"Sorry, Sherm," Jim said, snapping his on. "I don't mean to be such a lousy wingman. I was planning on being better at setting you up than my wife."

Elliott waved off the apology and helped Jim and the Colonel contain Mr. Warbler from his seizure. He took a few more quick notes as Jim drew blood. The three of them held Mr. Warbler down while Jim gave him injections of antiseizure medication. It didn't work for all the sea lions—about half still died—but it worked on many. It was the best they could do until they figured this out.

Elliott left his hand on the sea lion's fur as the seizures slowly subsided, offering gentle strokes. He was going to have to work faster.

And stay focused. And stop chasing model-looking women like Natalie Grant down brick walkways.

He was embarrassed he'd told Doris he "knew" her. He simply *hoped* to know her. He'd hoped she'd return to see the sea lions she'd helped rescue. And when he'd seen her from the window, he'd thought for a second she was some kind of mirage, with her stylish, funky clothes; her braid shimmering in the sunlight; and the menswear fedora that reminded him of something *he* might wear from the box of hats his granddad had given him.

But he'd been his usual lame self and had bored her away.

Story of his life.

When the animal finally calmed and drifted into a tranquilized state, Elliott helped Jim and the Colonel move Mr. Warbler back to the recovery room.

"Do you think he's going to be okay?" the Colonel asked, tugging off his gloves.

It was always interesting to see what types of people became attached to the marine mammals. The Colonel was a sharp-tongued, martini-drinking, orders-spitting man, who'd probably been a hard-ass in World War II, but he'd become attached, for whatever reason, to Mr. Warbler, along with several other mammals at the center. He spent every Monday, Wednesday, and Friday there with other senior volunteers, like Doris and Marie and George.

"I think so," Elliott finally assured him, slowing a little with the gurney so the Colonel could keep up. Mr. Warbler was completely tranquilized now.

The Colonel gave a sharp nod and seemed to slip back into colonel mode. "She's pretty," he barked. "Didn't know you had it in you, kid. You've come to every Bars and Barks Event solo, so I thought you weren't much with the ladies."

Jim, at the other end of the gurney, laughed. "He isn't, Colonel. My wife has been torturing him by forcing him out on blind dates all week."

Elliott shook his head. He was used to the ribbing. He and Jim had known each other since college—they'd gone to the same Ivy League school together and had roomed together for two of the four years, until Jim had gone to veterinary school and Elliott had branched off into microbiology. But they'd stayed best friends. At one of their homecoming parties, Jim met Nell, and it had been love at first sight. At the time, Elliott couldn't believe it. But it all seemed to make sense as he saw it unfold, and he was pleased to have been the best man at their wedding two years later. It had been Jim who'd told him about the idea for the new center on the island, putting out the word that Elliott was the most brilliant microbiologist there was in marine study, despite the fact that he wasn't yet thirty. Elliott couldn't let him down.

"Who does she have lined up for you next?" Jim asked, his voice suddenly taking on a gentleness that seemed laced with pity.

"I think an . . . Alice?"

"I DATED AN ALICE ONCE," the Colonel shouted in his gravelly voice. He was hard of hearing, too. "Nineteen forty-seven, I think. A real looker."

They slid Mr. Warbler into one of the recovery rooms, where another volunteer took over and set him up with some of the other sea lions that needed to be watched as they came out from under sedation.

"Who's your Alice?" The Colonel shot a frown at Elliott.

"I don't know her yet," Elliott admitted.

He was already dreading meeting "his Alice." His sister was arriving at six to help him set up for the new date tonight. Caren had bowed out of a second date—no surprise there. But he'd work harder to comply with Nell's rules. He'd go through the motions. And not get dragged back into work. He'd meet the teachers, the professors, the scientists, and the fellow introverts who were more in his league.

Jim kept glancing at him with a note of apology on his face. Or maybe it was blame. Maybe he just wanted Elliott to hurry the hell up and figure out what was wrong with these sea lions.

As the three of them sauntered back down the hall, past one of the windows, a figure outside caught his eye. Natalie was still there, hesitating on the periphery of a tour group. He stopped and marveled at the strange sensation in his belly—one he was used to feeling when on the verge of a discovery or on the edge of a major breakthrough, but one he was unaccustomed to feeling in relation to a person. He tugged at his lab coat and stared.

"I say keep your eye on the prize, young man," the Colonel said.

When Elliott turned toward him, the Colonel winked and continued down the hall.

Elliott nodded to himself. He wasn't 100 percent sure what that meant, but the Colonel probably meant Alice was the prize—the surer thing, the one in his league.

Stay focused, man.

Stay logical.

He glanced down the hallway where Jim and the Colonel had disappeared and willed himself to follow. He needed to work up some clinical samples.

The world he felt comfortable in.

Alone.

CHAPTER 4

When Lily was finally in bed, Paige broke out the merlot and poured herself and Natalie large goblets. Olivia skipped because of her pregnancy and requested a glass of ice water.

"I'll pour it in a wineglass so you can pretend," Paige said. "So, what's in that box?"

Natalie pushed another of Gram's boxes toward the end table, then scooted her bottom closer as she finger-combed the ends of her damp hair. She kicked Paige's duffel bag out of the way, which Paige had arrived with, saying she was staying the whole week.

"I think this box just has some old material and sewing items."

"We can donate what's still good," Olivia said.

Olivia began pulling items out one by one to inspect them while Natalie started on her usual braid.

"Why don't you wear it down?" Paige asked, taking over the most comfortable chair in the room.

"Tired of it."

"It's so pretty, though," Olivia added.

"Thanks, but I'm still tired of it."

"We always want what we can't have, right?" Olivia asked.

"You wanted my hair?"

"Always."

"Me, too," chimed in Paige.

Natalie looked at both of them in disbelief. She'd always felt mousy around her older sisters until she hit her teens. The year she was thirteen, she grew taller than both of them, and her mousy brown hair took on a sun-kissed, auburn sheen and shimmied down her back in a glossy waterfall. Which drew lots of compliments from women. And—of course—she got a figure. Which drew lots of stares from men.

Their mother, who'd run a modeling agency in those days, had been putting Olivia and Paige in beauty pageants since they were golden-ringleted tots, but suddenly she abandoned all that when she noticed the dropped jaws Natalie was getting in the grocery store. She decided Natalie was her best hope of passing down a modeling career.

But Natalie, unfortunately, had no interest. Men's stares unnerved her. When she was thirteen, she told her mother she "quit," although she'd been to only one group photo shoot. That had been enough. Instead, she began wearing boyish clothes and hats and the most shapeless shoes she could find. Her mom finally acquiesced about not pushing her any further into modeling, but the stares continued, became more leering. Natalie covered up more, wore even more boyish clothing. Her mother would watch her walk out the door in another pair of ripped jeans, Converse sneakers, and a menswear-print fedora, and would let out one of her infamous martyr sighs.

But Natalie's legs grew longer still, making her taller and even more noticeable over the heads of her peers, and despite the baggy clothes and visored hats, she continued to draw attention from the male species. Mostly it scared her, especially when she was thirteen and fourteen. It scared her how men would follow her, how they'd catcall her when she just wanted to get a soda from the dispenser in front of the grocery store, how they'd back her into corners when she was riding her bike, how they'd let their eyes roam.

The day after the air-conditioning repair guy had lunged at her in the living room, she'd sheared off her long, auburn-highlighted hair. The day after the grocer, Mr. Antonello, had cornered her in a back alley and tried to reach inside her shirt, she'd pulled her baseball cap lower over her face until she could hardly see.

But she never told her mom. Or her sisters. She somehow felt the unwanted attention was her fault.

Finally, by the time she was in her midteens, she'd simply gotten used to it. She adopted the "independent woman" credo their mother liked to tout. She learned how to fend off loudmouthed men with an edgy veneer. She'd planned to get a row of tattoos across her shoulders to look tougher, much to her mother's dismay, but she couldn't commit to a design, so she simply collected possibilities in a box on her dresser. She still wore the baseball caps, the snap-brims, the Converse sneakers. She discovered that if she went out with tough-looking boys, leering men wouldn't mess with her. And she perfected her smart-ass attitude.

She continued this way all through high school and into her twenties. She learned to shoot daggers at men who disrespected her. She learned to swear like a sailor in bars and even how to throw a punch. She dated bikers. She quit jobs if bosses got too handsy, like Simon at the pet photography studio. And life became tolerable.

Except she was *tired*.

So damned tired.

All the time.

But here, with her sisters, she could just be herself. It felt good to shed the layers of sweatshirts, the hats, the attitude, the armor, the bravado. Each layer came off and made her feel lighter still. She closed her eyes and lay back on the shag rug, her arms out, her braid only half done, the rest of her hair splayed along the floor.

"Look—it's Gram's USO cap!" Paige pulled it out of the box.

"Definitely put that in the 'save' pile," Olivia said.

"So what's this I hear about a mancation?" Paige shot over to Natalie as she dug farther into the box.

Natalie gave Olivia a hard stare.

"What are you looking at me like that for? She *asked*," Olivia said. "By the way, do you want me to replace your lost cell phone? I know they're expensive. I can help with a new one."

Natalie shook her head. It was tempting. She'd finally had to leave the phone store earlier that day empty-handed and overwhelmed, wondering if she could max out her credit card. But if she didn't figure out how to stand on her own, she'd stay in the role of the irresponsible, helpless little sister.

"No, thanks," she said. "I'll figure something out."

"I could list it as a job expense for you—I truly need you to have one if you're going to help with Lily."

"It's okay, Olivia. I'm a big girl now."

Olivia gave her a dubious look, then glanced at Paige. It bothered Natalie to no end that they had no faith in her.

"So spill," Paige said, coming to the bottom of the box. "What's a mancation?"

"Olivia has bigger problems," Natalie said. "Let's start with her. Ask her about her bed rest."

Olivia leaned back on the couch cushion and closed her eyes. "Yes. I'll admit it. It's bad. I'm never going to make it through three months."

"We can fix that," Paige offered. "We'll find you some projects. How about creating some books for Lily? You know, like 'You're a Big Sister Now' kind of books. You could write them, and we'll print them out for her."

Olivia nodded absently. "That's not a bad idea."

"Or photo albums. You have all those photos on your laptop. Why don't you get professional albums made online for all of Lily's firsts, or all her birthdays, or something like that? Then you'll have the template set up for the new baby."

Olivia nodded again. "I like that."

"And if you show me some ideas for what you like, I can set up the baby's room," Natalie offered. "I'll run around and get whatever you need."

Olivia nodded but didn't say anything to that—Natalie was sure her sisters didn't think she could decorate either. But she was interested in it. She had a good sense of space and arrangement and a decent sense of style. Her mom had been pushing her to get into event planning with her—their mom now ran a famous event-planning company for celebrities—but Natalie wondered if her mom was just placating her. She wanted to do something on her own.

"Let's take a break from boxes," Paige said. "We've been going at this all night. Come here, Natalie—let me brush your hair."

Natalie crawled into their typical position from girlhood: Paige leaning against an easy chair, her knees up, and Natalie leaning against Paige's knees. The scent of baby shampoo wafted with each stroke of the brush and helped spin the cocoon of their past.

"Why don't you guys move here with me?" Olivia asked.

Paige rolled her eyes. "Because there's still a shortage of dateables."

"It's getting better," Olivia said.

"I doubt it."

"There's John O'Donnell, and that new guy named Tag Tagalieri, and I think another guy they might have just hired for the new bar."

Paige shook her head. "John-O is arrogant, Tag is too much of a womanizer, and this new guy is probably a figment of your imagination and hopes because I haven't seen *anyone* new here in the last six months."

"What about Garrett?"

"Olivia! Garrett is eighteen!"

"Is he really? Okay, well, there's Adam."

"Adam *Mason?*" Paige's voice went an octave too high. "Remember him?"

Paige stalled. Natalie was about to turn around to see what was wrong, but Paige pushed at her shoulders and started to brush again. "Isn't he at least thirty-five by now? I picture him as some old man already on the top of that hill at the airport."

"You might be surprised," Olivia said, a strange smile curving her lips.

The three of them all sat in silence for a minute, sipping their drinks.

"Oh, there's the new science guy who lives in Dr. Johnson's old place," Olivia suddenly said. "Natalie met him."

Natalie snapped her head up.

"I don't know who that is," Paige said. "Is he young? Cute? Single?"

"What do you say, Natalie?"

Natalie swallowed a gulp of wine and put her glass down carefully on the table. "He's young," she said cautiously. "I'm not sure about the single part."

"Cute?"

Natalie shrugged. For some reason, she wanted to keep her feelings to herself. Somehow she thought they'd tease her. Maybe it was just being back on the island that was stirring old behaviors. Maybe it was the relaxation of having her hair brushed, or the comfort of her sisters' familiar smells. Or it could have been the one and a half glasses of wine. Whatever the reason, it tempted her to regress. She wanted to prove to all of them that she was an adult now, but being here, like this, in Gram's old cottage, made it hard.

"Huh." Paige took a deep swig of her wine and seemed much too lost in daydreams about the new scientist. Natalie almost wanted to tell her to back off. But that was silly. She wasn't claiming him. Her hyperawareness of Dr. Nerd seemed senseless and strange. Just because a smart-looking man had approached her with a degree of interest rather than with a trail of drool didn't mean she was necessarily a more valuable person. Plus, he might be married. Plus, she was taking a break from men.

"I finally dumped David," Natalie announced abruptly.

"Is David the one with the '67 Harley?" Paige asked.

"No, that was Devlan."

"David's the one with the broken motorcycle," Olivia said from the couch. "And no job. And he makes that weird sound when he's drinking."

"And he looks like a troll when he yawns?" Paige asked.

"No, that was Mike," Olivia said.

"Ah. Mike. I can't believe you broke up with that guy because of his yawn."

Natalie shrugged. At least she didn't try to change the men she was with, like Paige did. She just accepted that everyone had quirks and moved on.

"Didn't you break up with Joey Piccolo because he separated all the food on his plate and ate each item one at a time?" Paige asked.

Natalie couldn't help but giggle. Her normal reaction might have been to bristle. Her sisters' teasing could easily be taken as another poke at her. But the wine had loosened her up, the strokes of the hairbrush felt lovely, and she had to admit those had probably been her exact words. The absurdity of her constant breakup decisions all bubbled to the surface.

Her giggles caught on with Olivia and then with Paige. Next thing they knew, they were all laughing into the pillow cushions for no reason at all.

It felt so good to laugh for so long—to let her abdominal muscles tighten, to let her cheeks hurt, to just look at her sisters and send one another into another collapsing fit of laughter. It was just like when they were girls, relaxing into the moment where you could be silly with the people who loved you most.

"So who's next in Natalie's Dating Carousel?" Paige finally asked, wiping tears from her eyes.

"No one. I'm taking a break. That's the mancation."

"*No* one? I can't imagine you without a guy, Natalie. Despite your fear of commitment."

"Fear of commitment?" Natalie leaned out of the hairbrush's reach to turn and look at Paige. "What are you talking about? I'm always with a guy. I'm not afraid to commit."

"Oh, please. Just because you're always with a guy doesn't mean you know how to commit." Paige turned her shoulders back so she could continue brushing. "Commitment is something deeper. You go through guys like eyelash extensions."

"I don't wear eyelash extensions."

"Even worse then."

Natalie rolled her eyes. "I'm not afraid. I'm just not ready to settle down."

"I respect that—I'm definitely not either," Paige said. "But for me, it's a choice. For you, I think it's fear."

"I'm not *afraid* of commitment."

"Natalie, you break up with guys because they wear tightie-whities instead of boxers or because they floss their teeth after every meal or because of the way they use 'literally' in every sentence."

"What about Ted with the restraining order, or Milo with the wife?" Natalie threw in.

"You do have some legitimate breakups. My point is, you don't differentiate. You look for reasons to break up, whether they're legitimate or not."

"Maybe I've just met terrible guys."

"Or maybe you *know* they're terrible, or unavailable, and that's why you date them," Paige said. "So you can have your fun, but you know there's an out for you in about a month, when you can break up and say things like 'He didn't have a job' or 'He had too many tattoos' and no one will fault you."

The truth of that philosophy floated before Natalie's eyes for a second, drifting back and forth, back and forth, like a feather that Natalie wanted to watch until it fell at her feet.

The brush went softly through Natalie's hair three or four times in silence.

"Well, my mancation is to step away from it all," she said. "I just want to get to know myself a little better, figure out what I really want." It sounded silly when she said it out loud, but she squared her shoulders to bolster her resolve.

"You won't last a week," Paige said.

"Paige!" Olivia lifted her head from the couch.

"Sorry, I think it's true," Paige said. "But I'd love to be proven wrong."

"I'll prove you wrong."

"How long is this mancation supposed to last?"

"Three months."

Paige burst out laughing.

Natalie could feel all her defenses coming up around her again. The soft euphoria of their senseless laughter earlier was now falling away, replaced, unfortunately, with the sharp edges of jealousy and irritation. She'd always been close to Paige, since they were barely a year apart, but they'd also always fought like cats.

Olivia met Natalie's eyes and shook her head. "Don't let her get to you. I think it's a smart idea, and you'll do great."

"I'll bet you three hundred dollars you won't last three *weeks*," Paige said.

"I'll last three weeks!"

"Three hundred and fifty." Paige held out her hand. "I need some new clothes."

Natalie shook Paige's hand without thinking. It was what they did. They'd been betting each other since junior high, sometimes Paige winning and sometimes Natalie. But as soon as she shook on this one, she had a brief panic. Could she last three weeks? She certainly didn't have an extra $350. But she could, right? She was on an island, for goodness' sake, with a shortage of twentysomethings. What could be the problem?

"I'm going to take a walk," she suddenly announced. She stood and started looking for her hoodie. She needed to take a few gulps of fresh air and clear her head before letting her hurt feelings come between her and Paige.

"*What?*" Paige said.

"A walk. Down by the beach."

"Now?"

"Yeah, a little nighttime stroll."

"Not now, Natalie. That's crazy. It's dark."

"I can see."

"Are you angry? About what I said? I'm sorry. I didn't mean to hurt your feelings. We don't have to bet if you don't want—"

"No. That's silly. I just want to take a walk." Natalie tugged on her velvet hoodie jacket and adjusted her favorite brimmed beanie on her head. "I'm fine. I'll be back in an hour. I don't get to take walks alone in LA, so I'm taking advantage of it while I'm here on safe Lavender Island."

Paige looked at Olivia warily, but Olivia finally nodded. "We'll have your wine waiting for you here. Be safe." Olivia waved over her head.

Natalie nodded and zipped up the hoodie.

Elliott watched Alice saunter out the sliding door with her wineglass in her hand and followed with a certain degree of nervousness.

They'd had a nice dinner, which Nell had helped him order in so he could work until the date started. But now—as far as he was concerned—the date should be over.

He and Alice had talked. He'd worn his contacts again. He'd tried to stay focused. He liked her lips, though he was unsure about all the pink gloss she had on because it sometimes looked silver, like some kind of alchemy metal. She talked about geometry. She had five brothers. He thought she might have said she was from Ohio, but he'd already forgotten a few details like that. She may or may not have had a cat . . .

He felt as if he'd processed a lot of information on this date, and they'd had their dessert, and now . . . Well, now his eyes were itching and he was sort of done here. He hadn't planned on having sex on any of these back-to-back dates—these were just the "meets." He got that. So what was left?

And why was she wandering out to the patio?

Maybe he was supposed to follow her with the rest of the wine. Is that what Nell had meant about "Try to be romantic"? But that might extend this date into oblivion, wouldn't it? A sheen of sweat formed across his forehead as he splashed another few sips into his glass and followed her like a prisoner toward the gallows.

Maybe she wanted him to kiss her? She'd been looking at his lips all night, and now she was walking outside and staring at the ocean and stars over the patio railing with a weird, dreamy look on her face. He tried to remember the last time he'd made out with someone, like teenagers, when there was no endgame of sex expected. He tried to remember the moves. He'd been such a geeky kid in high school; he hadn't had a lot of experience back then. Plus, he worried she was getting a little drunk. And he didn't see things going anywhere with her anyway, despite how nice she was. And he needed to get back to his work. Mr. Warbler's seizure today and Jim's uncertain glances weren't slipping from his memory, despite the good wine and the pout of shiny, silvery lips.

Another gulp of wine felt like fire going down his throat. He tried to focus on the moonlight, focus on the sound of the waves, think of what to say . . .

"Your view is delirious," she said.

He smiled, but wondered at her use of *delirious*. Wouldn't *she* be delirious? *At* the view, right? He didn't want to be responsible for getting her drunk. The bottle hung heavily in his fist.

She held out her half-empty glass.

"Maybe we should quit now," he ventured.

She gave him a little pout and flung her hair over her shoulder while she peered over the patio railing.

"Let's go down," she said.

Before he could put everything together, she'd slid around the patio railing and was scampering down the ice plants, her almost-empty glass raised slightly over her head.

"Wait, no. Alice. No." He set the bottle and his glass down on a nearby patio table and followed—it was so easy to get tangled and slip down that hillside. And damn, she was crushing the flower bulbs. "Alice, wait," he called, gripping the vines to lower himself as fast as she was.

But she'd taken off.

He continued to carefully scale the sandy decline, the bulbous vines of the plant leaving a sticky sheen across his dress shoes, but she'd really taken off. And now she was . . . *taking off her clothes?*

He landed with a thud in the night-damp sand next to her sweater. Next to that lay one high heel, and next to that . . . He was afraid to look up.

When he finally did, she was skipping through the dark, barefoot, toward the sound of the crashing waves, her wineglass silhouetted in the air against the moon.

"Do you ever skinny-dip here, Elliott? It's like your own private beach!" she yelled, right before she disappeared behind the lower dune.

Damn.

This was probably not what Nell had in mind.

And this was definitely not a private beach.

He followed anyway. Of course. (He was a man, after all, and there was possibly a naked woman on the other side of that dune.) But all he could think of was that something was going to go terribly, horribly wrong here. His shoes filled with sand on his way down.

The familiar scent of the ocean hit him full in the face and grounded him, giving him a chance to think. At the water's edge, Alice watched the cold water rush around her ankles, squealing with cold or fear or delight—he couldn't quite tell—and holding her wineglass high enough to avoid sea spray. The ocean air was damp and salty. Before he could get his contacts to fully focus, her dress dropped into the ocean sand, and she stepped out of it, standing there in only her underwear. No bra. Sexy black-lace underwear. But no bra.

Elliott gulped. "Alice?"

"Join me!"

He stepped carefully toward her, having no intention of joining her in skinny-dipping but fully prepared to whip off his shoes if he needed to go in and save her.

She kept wading in.

"Alice, wait."

His heart rate picked up. His shoes came off in a whoosh, and he sent them sailing behind him. His socks followed. He rescued her dress from being rushed back out in the sea foam. What if she fell? What if the ocean swept her away? He didn't know her well enough to know if this was normal behavior for her.

He rolled up the pant legs of his dress slacks and hesitated. Should he follow her in and save her? Did she need saving? Did she just want to play? She was wading in steadily and was already in to her waist. Tentatively, he took another step toward her. The water was freezing.

She lowered herself into the next wave with a loud whoop at the cold, her wineglass over her head, then turned, suddenly, and splashed water at him. She laughed and began trudging back up the wet sand, extending her glass for him to hold. Her body glistened in the moonlight.

He tried not to look too much—suddenly she seemed too drunk and vulnerable for words—but he had a hard time getting around the fact that a very pretty woman was walking, dripping, toward him, almost naked.

"Elliott, *please* join me."

She handed him the glass, which he took, dumbly. Then, before he could think, she threw herself into his arms, dripping ocean water down the front of his pants.

"Dr. Sherman?" he heard from behind him.

His brain couldn't quite wrap around everything that happened in the next split second, but somehow he grabbed the naked back of the very-drunk Alice, dropped the wineglass, turned toward the voice, and caught sight of Natalie Grant standing on the shoreline, gawking at him with her mouth slightly open as if he were some kind of serial killer.

Alice slid to his feet.

CHAPTER 5

"Is she okay?" Natalie asked.

She stepped closer and watched the half-naked woman slide sloppily along Dr. Sherman's legs.

Dr. Sherman sure didn't seem like the kind of guy who would harm a woman—he wasn't even the kind of guy who harmed ice-plant bulbs—but you never knew. As a fellow woman, Natalie wasn't the type to turn away when someone was naked, alone with a man, and so drunk she could hardly stand up on her own. And this was definitely a different woman from the one last night. What was going on here?

"Yes, we're fine." Dr. Sherman pulled Alice up toward him. "Right, Alice?"

Alice's legs seemed to grow sturdier beneath her, and she leaned into him. She had black-lace underwear on—cut to her thigh—and no bra. Dr. Sherman was holding her as if she were a bomb about to detonate, carefully placing his hands in strategic places.

"Yes, thank you, Elliott," she slurred, low, into his collarbone. Her hand went into his hair in a half hug, half dry-hump against his chinos.

Natalie adjusted her hat and tried to avert her eyes.

Alice giggled and turned toward Natalie as if her ligaments were made of rubber bands. "We're skinny-dipping!" she said. "I can't get this cutie to loosen up, though." She made a clumsy dive to unbutton his pants.

Dr. Sherman caught Alice's hand as best he could. "We're uh . . . heading back."

Natalie noticed Dr. Sherman's shoes and socks in the sand, and heat raced through her cheeks as she tried to imagine all that might have gone on here. Skinny-dipping? *Dr. Sherman?*

The cold night wind whipped up from the ocean. Natalie tugged her hoodie tighter around her middle and told herself to walk home now. But wow, Alice must be freezing.

"Wait!" she called.

She yanked her jacket off and held it toward them.

"Thank you." Relief crossed Dr. Sherman's face.

He began dressing Alice, murmuring things into her ear while the waves crashed loudly behind them. Alice fought him for a minute, seeming upset that she couldn't press her naked breasts into his thin shirt anymore, but eventually she gave in and poked her arms through the sleeves.

Natalie forced her attention toward the surf, and a brightly colored floral item caught her eye in the moonlit sea foam. Alice's dress.

She jogged toward the ocean to snatch it up, then bent and caught Dr. Sherman's shoe, then the upside-down wineglass, then a sock he didn't seem to realize had fallen.

"That's not necessary!" he yelled down to her as he finally got Alice zipped up. He turned and guided Alice back up toward his house.

Natalie grabbed the rest of their clothing and followed anyway. She tried to stay a reasonable distance behind them to give them privacy, but she just wanted to make sure Alice was okay.

At least she thought that was why she was following them.

Near his hill, Natalie spotted what must be Alice's high heels and cardigan in the sand—where their escapade must have begun—and snatched them up, too, trying to ignore the heat flushing her face. She followed them both to a staircase that wove up through a vast hillside of the island's sea lavender—the tiny stalks always reminded her of purple coral reef reaching toward the sky.

"We can take it from here," he said from the first stair. "I'm just going to get her into something warm and take her home."

"You don't have to explain to me."

"It seems I do."

She ignored the reprimand and followed them up. Once inside Dr. Sherman's kitchen, he ushered them past countertops filled with take-out bags and boxes, then moved Alice through the dining room. The rooms had the imprint of Dr. Johnson on them—old-fashioned sconces, heavy oak furniture, a china cabinet filled with dishes and stemware. Only in a couple of places did young Dr. Sherman shine through—a pair of earbuds on the kitchen counter, a set of keys on a college lanyard near the door, a few T-shirts haphazardly folded and set near the hallway, stacks of papers that had formulas written all over them on the entryway table.

The dining table was still set with what must have been the date dinner—plates scattered across one corner, candles recently blown out. The food was dished out onto what must be Dr. Johnson's old china, which warmed Natalie for some reason. Dr. Sherman seemed to try so hard.

In the enormous living room, he lowered Alice into a velvet chair, then dropped to his knee in front of the fireplace, quickly kindling it.

"How long have you lived here?" Natalie asked, glancing at the gold-leafed lamps that sat on either side of the tufted sofa.

"Three months."

Alice's legs came off the edge of the velvet chair in a sloppy *V* and sprawled across the oriental rug.

"Are these Dr. Johnson's things?" she couldn't help but ask.

Dr. Sherman got the fire lit and turned to see what she was referring to. "Yes. I'm renting. Did you know him?"

"I spent lots of summers here on the island. He was my grandmother's vet."

Alice was all but passed out now, and Natalie reached over to cover her underwear with the front of the hoodie.

"I'll get her some clothes," Dr. Sherman said gruffly, taking off for the bedroom.

Natalie watched him fly out of the room.

"He's the sweetest," Alice whispered with her eyes closed, and then giggled.

Dr. Sherman came back with a pair of sweats, a thick pair of socks, and a wrinkled "Dolphin Dash" T-shirt, which he handed to Alice awkwardly and then stole away again.

Alice yawned and started to slink down farther in the chair, but then sat up and sleepily unzipped Natalie's hoodie. She handed it back and let Natalie help her get the warm clothes on. The fire created a peaceful snapping sound.

"How long have you been dating?" Natalie whispered, her curiosity getting the best of her. She reached down to help Alice with the socks.

"This is our first date."

Natalie's hand stalled. She couldn't help but gape up at Alice. But she finished her task. This was none of her business. Alice was none of her business—now that she knew she wasn't in danger. And Dr. Sherman, especially, was none of her business. Not how he managed to get a first date naked by the ocean, not whether he enjoyed skinny-dipping in the black Pacific, not why he had two different dates in two nights, not why he was renting this old-person-furnished ocean-top mansion. And definitely not the cute, perplexed way he looked at Alice from beneath the bangs that fell in his eyes.

"Here you go." He came back into the room with a steaming mug of something, a glass of water, and an aspirin, then put them all on the fireplace hearth for Alice, backing away as if he were feeding a feral cat.

Natalie reached for the mug and helped Alice drink a few sips of whatever it was, since Dr. Sherman didn't seem to want to come closer. It looked like tea. Alice grimaced but took a few gulps anyway.

"Would you like anything?" he asked Natalie.

"No. I should be going. Could I use your phone again? To call my sister?"

"Sure. Do you want a ride home?" His face seemed to light up at that. He really had beautiful eyes.

"Looks like you've got your hands full already."

"No, I can take you home. It's the least I could do." His hair fell into his eyes again as he seemed to search for keys.

"They're over by the door. But, no, really. I'm close by. I just need to call my sister first. I'm staying with her."

"Where does she live?" He handed her his phone.

"About ten cottages that way. We're on C Street." She motioned with a nod outside his windows, with their incredible view, and punched in Olivia's number. "Liv?" she whispered into the phone. "Just me . . ."

When she handed the phone back, Dr. Sherman was staring at her from beneath his bangs; the firelight played along the side of his face.

"Thank you," he said. "You seem to have a Good Samaritan gene."

"I just wanted to make sure everyone was okay."

"My point exactly."

"I'm sorry if I interrupted your . . . plans. Or . . . date. Or whatever."

They both looked at the slumbering Alice.

"Yeah, I'm a great date," he deadpanned.

Before any more flashes of Dr. Sherman on a date went through her head, Natalie whirled toward the sliding door. "Can I go out this way?"

"It might be slippery through the ice plants."

But she was already halfway through the door. "I'll be fine."

Once her feet hit the sand, she wrapped the damp hoodie around her front and jogged back up the beach, eager to get away.

Dr. Sherman was not her type.

And she was on a mancation.

And he was on a date.

The ocean air felt good against her face, calming her foolish, thundering heart.

By the time Elliott got Alice into his car, drove her all the way home, came home, got the torture lenses off, cleaned up the dinner, and called Nell, it was close to three a.m. He definitely wouldn't get any work done tonight. And he couldn't stop thinking about Natalie.

"Are you kidding me?" Nell asked into the phone. "That's not the Alice I know!"

Elliott sat on the edge of his bed, exhausted. He ran his hand through his hair. "Well, that's the Alice who was here tonight."

"Elliott, I'm sorry. That's not the kind of person you should be with. You need someone who will take care of *you*, not the other way around."

"No one needs to take care of me, Nell." He scanned his bedroom desk. Maybe he could get a few notes in if he stayed up until five or so. "Look, maybe we should cancel the rest of the dates. I don't want to do this dating thing. I have so much work to do, and—"

"But that's part of the problem. You work too much. You need to poke your head out and look at the world around you."

"I'm looking at the world plenty, at least where it concerns me. And right now, the sea lions concern me. I don't work more than Jim does."

"You most certainly do!"

He sighed. He could hear his baby nephew cooing near the phone. Nell often nursed at two or three in the morning, and if he texted or called, she'd sometimes pick up, as she had tonight. Plus, they were both hopeless insomniacs.

"I need to help at the center and put in some time to figure out what's going on."

"It's only a few more dates, Elliott. Please. I think these next women might be just right. Let's find someone who will keep an eye on you."

He pinched the bridge of his nose to stop the headache from coming on. "I don't need someone to keep an eye on me."

They'd had this argument a million times, but Nell was getting more and more desperate as her Italy departure loomed. She'd always looked out for him—always saw it as her responsibility, ever since that terror-filled night when they'd sat huddled in the closet.

"Just a few more dates," she begged.

He sighed and let the familiar sense of guilt overwhelm him. He'd been seven, and Nell had been ten. The gunshots had woken them first. Their mother's screams had shot ice through their veins second. Elliott had frozen, barely able to move, clutching his stuffed elephant to his chest. But Nell had been fast and clearheaded, and she'd whisked them into the tiny closet behind the laundry chute, where they'd crouched in their pajamas, listening to the intruders stomping through the house and flinging open doors. He'd tried to keep his ragged breaths from being too loud, tried to keep from moaning in fear. Nell had held his hand. The terror of waiting for the intruders to leave—listening to them upturn every blanket, every drawer, every door to find them—was second only to the horror of discovering, two hours later, their parents shot to death in a sea of blood.

"How many dates are you talking about?" he asked into the quiet of the room. Only his clock ticked gently in the background. He liked to fall asleep to the sound.

"I have three more set up."

Elliott groaned.

They'd gone to live with their granddad and grandmother after that, far away in Kansas, sometimes being shuttled to various aunts and uncles in Illinois or Wisconsin for a month or two when either of their grandparents' health was bad. When their grandmother died, it was just him, Nell, and his granddad, trying to make things work in their strange little family of three. He and Nell had switched schools frequently. Elliott had never made friends well. He'd been paralyzingly shy, and Nell had always tried to protect him from bullies, always tried to watch over him.

"Maybe I met someone on my own," he finally said into the phone.

"You did?" He heard his nephew gurgling and cooing again. "Hold on, Elliott."

He waited while Nell switched sides, or switched phone ears, or whatever she was doing. He was happy she was happy. Her new baby and Jim were long-overdue lights in her life. She'd lived in dark clouds for so many years, always haunted by fear, always afraid of potential danger. They were both spooked by the dark, by scary sounds, by anyone approaching them the wrong way. Although their parents' killers were caught almost immediately, they'd lived forever with the unthinkable images they'd stumbled across that morning. They'd lived forever with the nightmares. Nell had lived forever with the need to protect Elliott. And Elliott had lived forever with the memory of how he'd frozen. If it hadn't been for Nell, he knew he'd be dead, too.

"So, who is this woman you met?" she asked between coos to his nephew, Max.

"I don't know her, per se, but . . ." He let that trail off. He didn't even know what he was talking about. He was thinking of Natalie, but he was just conjuring this up now. Natalie probably thought he was some deranged lunatic, abandoning dates on his patio or getting them drunk and letting them wander, naked, into the freezing Pacific.

A wave of mortification had gone through him when he'd realized that Natalie had doubted Alice's safety. He'd seen her eyeing Alice warily when she'd first approached. But once that disturbing realization had passed, he'd taken a deep breath and admired the gesture. Most women—or even men, for that matter—would probably have let the whole scene slip right past them, assuming it was what it was: a date splashed with too much alcohol and going a bit awry. But, in truth, admiration swept over him that Natalie hadn't been afraid to intervene and possibly come to the rescue of another woman. Which was why he'd let her come inside and analyze as much as she wanted.

"Well, what does she do?"

"I'm, uh . . . I'm not really sure."

"Where does she live?"

"A few houses down, I think, on the beach?"

"How old is she?"

"I don't know. Maybe my age?"

A deep sigh sounded. "Elliott, this sounds like someone you *saw*, not someone you *met*. Please, let's just get through the next three dates. Trust me. These are good, caring women. I saved the best for last."

"Nell, let me take care of my own dating life. I need to get back to work, and—"

"If you wait until you have a break in work, you'll never meet anyone. *Please*, Elliott. Just these last three. I already set them up. After that, I promise I'll back off."

Elliott ran his hand through his hair. "Really?"

"I'm that confident."

"Okay."

Having Nell finally back out of his business would be a relief. Maybe then she'd just go to Italy with Jim and live the life they were meant to live. And he could stop feeling guilty for being such an albatross around their necks.

"Three then," he said. "But I have to work until seven tomorrow." Beautiful visions of quietude to study his slides danced before him.

"I'll make you reservations at a restaurant so you don't have to do the whole thing at your place. How about eight o'clock?"

"All right."

That might be less stressful. He could pay the check when they were done and leave. The whole thing could be contained to just an hour or two.

"Good night, Elliott. Don't stay up all night . . . Sunrises."

He smiled.

"Sunrises" was what he and Nell used to say to each other when they were kids to get each other through the night. She'd told him to always picture the sunrise, to know it was coming, to conjure it behind his eyelids, and to watch as it came up over the ocean. It had worked. It had gotten him through two decades of nightmares.

"Sunrises, Nell."

He clicked off the phone and turned to his notes, where he always felt safe.

CHAPTER 6

Natalie spent the next day trying to be a mini-Olivia. She waited with Lily in front of the red-tile-roofed first-grade classrooms until the first school bell rang, and chatted with the other moms; she arranged with another mother to drop Lily off for a playdate after school; she popped into a cute little craft store on Main Street to find foam letters for a Brownies project and met the woman who owned the shop. She picked up Olivia's dry cleaning and chatted with Mr. Hale the dry cleaner, then stopped at Jon's post-office box to pick up his mail, where Mrs. Conner, the post-office worker, asked all about Jon and Olivia.

The only kink in her day came when she had to take the midmorning ferry all the way to the mainland to look at phones again. After the two-hour trek, she stood at the kiosks, staring at possibilities.

"What can I help you with?" asked the phone technician. Young guy, kind of geeky like Dr. Nerd. Only he didn't look at her intensely. Or with curiosity in his eyes. His empty gaze went straight to her breasts.

"I'm just looking for a replacement phone," she said. "I'm trying to decide between these two."

He pulled himself together and explained the features. His voice had a condescending note to it, as if she didn't understand pixels or SIM cards.

"I'll think these over," she finally said. She needed one more day to weigh everything. Two-year contracts made her break into a sweat. But she had to do something.

As she rode the ferry back, she found herself breathing in the salt air along with a sigh of relief as she came upon the welcoming, palm-tree-lined roads of the island. Lavender Island did have a cozy, accepting feel about it. Natalie adjusted her earbuds, turned up the Jack Johnson tunes on her MP3 player, and leaned over the ferry railing.

Okay, here's what she would do about the phone: She'd borrow *half* the money from Olivia. But she'd pay her back. They'd write up a contract and everything. It was a step in the right direction, at least. Or a half step . . .

She hustled off the ferry and over to the golf cart, then gunned it up the hilly, winding road out of the harbor. She was proud of herself for looking straight ahead, not even glancing at the road that led to the Friends of the Sea Lion center, not even letting Dr. Nerd enter her thoughts for more than ten seconds this time.

She spotted the entrance to the island's only supermarket and pulled over sharply behind a large wooden wagon filled with fresh flowers. She'd pick up a few groceries before heading back to Olivia's. First up were some Froot Loops.

As she wandered through the aisles, basket on her arm, she heard two women giggling. She turned the corner and ran almost basket-first into none other than Doris, who was standing with another woman, heads bent over a row of paperbacks.

"Have you read this one?" Doris was asking. "It's not quite erotica, but I love it anyway. The hero is a cowboy, and he rides the heroine like—oh! Natalie!" She made room for Natalie in their semicircle. "Hello! It *is* Natalie, right?"

"Yes. Hi, Doris."

"I was just telling Marie here about this hot, sexy novel. Marie, meet Natalie. She's the beauty who came to see Dr. Sherman yesterday. Natalie, this is Marie. She volunteers at the center, too. Do you read Madame X?"

The last question was directed at Natalie.

"No, I—"

"I highly recommend these!" She threw a copy into Natalie's basket, then turned to get another one and shoved it toward Marie. "Your boyfriends will thank me!"

The other woman—at least seventy, like Doris—nodded.

Books were not in Natalie's budget when she was scraping pennies for a phone. She pulled it out of her basket.

"Doris, thanks for the recommendation, but I can't afford this right now."

"Oh, honey, are you coming upon hard times? Let me buy that for you."

"No! No, I don't need you to buy it for me, but I'm just trying to stay on a budget these days. I—"

"I understand! This economy is so hard on you young people. Are you looking for a job? I know of at least two openings."

Natalie's head snapped up. A *job*? That could give her the money she needed for the new phone without having to rely on Olivia. Maybe she could work extra hours while Lily was in school. And, coming from Doris, maybe this job was even at the center? She tried to ignore the little flutter in her chest.

"Is it at the center?" she asked, trying to hide the embarrassing lift in her voice.

"One of them is. But that job requires a yearlong commitment. Will you be staying here a year?"

Natalie felt as if she physically shrank an inch. A yearlong commitment? Who knew what she'd want to do in a year? In six months? In two months, even? And who could live on an island for a whole year? Well, besides Olivia and Jon, of course.

"What's the other job?" she asked.

"The other is better paying," Doris whispered behind her hand, as if it were a big secret there on aisle four. "It's at the retirement apartments Casas del Sur, where Marie and I live."

Marie's coif bobbed in agreement. "Ooooh, she'd be perfect for that. Do you Zumba, dear?"

"I—I don't think I've ever actually—"

"They'll train you!" Doris interrupted. "They need a part-time activities assistant. But one of the activities is driving the volunteer golf cart to the Friends of the Sea Lion center, so it's the best of both worlds."

Natalie perked up at that. "I can drive a golf cart."

"But the biggest part of the job is that they need someone to help us plan the big Senior Prom in three months. Like an event planner of sorts."

"I'd be interested in that. My mom is an event planner, and I've learned a lot from her. You think they'd hire me without showing a portfolio?"

"I could get you hired." Doris waved her hand.

Natalie frowned.

When Doris caught her puzzled expression, she shrugged. "I have some pull with the director. I taught him when he was a boy. If I recommend you, he'll hire you."

"Oh. Well, I would love that job. Right now, I'm watching my little niece every day, but she's in school from eight until two, so I'm free then."

"Perfect!" Doris scribbled a name on a piece of paper and handed it to Natalie. "Here's his name and number. If you're free right now, you should go down there and meet him. I'll text him and tell him you're coming."

Doris whipped out an impressively new phone from her oversized leopard purse and texted with both thumbs like some kind of teenager. "Done!" She threw the phone back into the cavernous purse. "Now, let me buy you this book. Marie, I'll buy you one, too."

Doris whirled toward the counter and began marching forward with the two books tucked into the crook of her arm.

"Doris, really, that's not necessary," Natalie called.

"Nonsense! My treat. Now, you go do your shopping, and this book will be waiting for you up at the counter. Have a great day, dear."

She and Marie left the aisle in a swirl of Shalimar and Jean Nate.

Natalie wandered up the sidewalk to the Casas del Sur, feeling as if she were heading into some kind of Hollywood movie gala. The luxury apartment building was high on a hill, at the very southeastern tip of Lavender Island, and boasted an incredible view of the ocean. A long red carpet led up a flagstone porte cochere, all ringed with palm trees. Inside was a three-story, metal-and-glass lobby.

Natalie approached the glass-fronted reception desk. "I'm looking for"—she glanced at the paper Doris had handed her—"Mr. Stegner," she told the receptionist.

Once buzzed back, Natalie shook hands with Steve Stegner. He was middle-aged, rather plump, prematurely balding, with a host of gold-rimmed picture frames on his desk featuring a pretty wife and four blond, smiling, elementary-aged children.

"Doris said you'd be perfect for this role," he said, sitting back at his desk. "She seems to think you'd be great for the rescue center tours.

Or the marina. Or Zumba. Or any of our activities. We do a lot of picnics on the beach, tide-pool visits, that kind of thing. Do you have any experience?"

Having changed jobs at least three times a year for as long as she could remember, Natalie always knew the answer to this question.

"I'm a fast learner, and eager to expand my experience into new fields."

Steve Stegner looked at her over the top of his glasses. Apparently, he could see a line of BS coming a mile away. "Well, Doris highly recommends you, so I'll go with her gut. This is a part-time job, with mornings preferred. The seniors like doing their activities primarily before noon. What's your availability?"

"I'm available from eight thirty, after I drop my niece off at school, until two, when she gets out."

"Perfect." He reached behind him and grabbed an application off his desk. "Fill this out, and we'll get you started."

By eight that night, Natalie had a second job, a month-to-month phone plan, a phone in her hand after an hour-long negotiation with the eyes-on-her-breasts kid back at the phone store, and a DVD for how to Zumba. She tucked her purchases back into her tote bag in the pleather-lined booth of the Shore Thing bar and lifted the laminated menu between her and Paige.

"You look like Donna Summer gone wrong," Paige said.

"You look like Richard Simmons gone wrong," Natalie said.

They both smiled through the dim lighting, casting giggling glances at each other over the tops of their menus. Paige wore a bright-yellow afro wig and Natalie's was hot pink. The wigs were for 1970s Night, which Olivia had somehow talked Paige and Natalie into, right after she talked them into standing in for her and Jon on their dart league. Paige had capped her look off with blue-shaded John Lennon glasses sitting on the edge of her nose, and Natalie wore heart-shaped wire-rimmed ones with pink shades.

"Your ass looks amazing in those bell-bottoms, though," Paige said. "You should walk around the bar more. Besides, Olivia wanted you to meet Tag." Paige looked over her shoulder. "I hope he's coming tonight."

"I don't want to be set up, Paige."

"Not a setup. Just a meet."

"No men. I'm just here to play darts. Let's focus on the game."

"I'm sorry, by the way, for teasing you about your mancation. I didn't mean to hurt your feelings. I've just never known you to be without a guy. Maybe I'm just jealous."

"Jealous?" Natalie laughed. "You definitely don't need to be jealous of me."

"Well, we don't need to do the bet."

"No, I'm good for the bet."

"It's okay. It's not right."

"What's not right?"

Paige suddenly seemed to find the menu unduly interesting.

A slow heat moved up Natalie's face. "You're thinking it's not right that you take my three hundred and fifty dollars, aren't you?"

"I know you don't have much money right now."

"I'm not going to lose!" Natalie sat back in the booth. Wow. Her sisters really had *no* faith in her.

"Of course. But we don't have to—"

"Paige, stop! This is nonsense. I wouldn't have made the bet if I didn't think I would either win it or be good for it. The bet's on. End of discussion."

Paige shrugged. "Suit yourself."

"Now let's talk darts. Or you can help me with this phone. What is *this* thing?"

Paige took the phone out of Natalie's hand to see what she was pointing at.

Although Paige could be critical of Natalie's dating decisions, she never criticized her intelligence, which Natalie always appreciated. As smart as Paige was, she always made Natalie feel smart, too, and called her the "brains of the family." They all seemed disappointed that she'd never extended her education like Paige and Olivia had. But Natalie had wanted to get on with her life—not spend another four long years learning about it.

"Here are your gimlets, extra lime," the waitress said.

"Thanks, Cynthia," Paige said. "Are Cody and Tom playing tonight?"

"No, I think they had business on the mainland they both had to attend to."

"Cool." Paige sipped her drink. "Olivia said they're our toughest competition." She grinned at Natalie over the rims of her blue-shaded glasses.

"So do you want your usual?" Cynthia asked.

"Yep. Double everything, though. My sister eats a lot." Paige tucked the menu back into the holder.

Several of Olivia's friends seemed to know they'd be there and came over to their table to introduce themselves and say hello. Tag wasn't one of them, much to Natalie's relief. She knew Olivia was trying to set her up with friends to lure her out here—trying to show off how awesome Lavender Island was and get Natalie immersed in her community and lifestyle. And maybe lure Paige out here, too. But Natalie didn't want to be lured. She didn't want to settle down. Especially not on an island— she didn't like the idea of everyone knowing everyone else's business. It all sounded so suffocating.

When the last friend left, Paige leaned over the table. "Tell me about this new job."

While Natalie explained it, their appetizers came, and they both dove in as Natalie finished her story about all the famous people who apparently lived at Casas del Sur. When Steve Stegner had given her the tour, he'd told her that four previous Rose Parade chairmen lived there, a former Los Angeles Rams owner, a trumpeter from Les Brown and His Band of Renown, the woman who'd invented the No Lines girdle in 1960, and two former state senators.

"How fun," Paige said. "Sounds like it could be a great opportunity for you."

"I'm not looking for 'opportunity.' I'm just looking to make a little money while I'm here."

Paige's eyebrow lifted.

Clearly Paige wanted to say something about that, but Natalie avoided asking and sipped her cocktail instead. The 1970s jukebox in the corner fired up—Joe Jackson's "Is She Really Going Out with Him?"—and Paige's silence lengthened. Finally, Natalie couldn't stand it any longer. "What?"

"Nothing."

"What did you want to say?"

"Nothing."

"Yes, you did. Tell me."

Paige gave a long-suffering sigh. "I'm just thinking that maybe that's what you're missing. You're missing the opportunities that are floating in front of you. You're so focused on avoiding boredom and staying in motion that you're missing some wonderful possibilities that could pan out if you just threw some energy behind them."

"I don't want a lecture, Paige."

"You *wanted* me to tell you!"

They both shook their heads and sipped their drinks at the same time. It was their long-standing argument. Paige the workaholic and Natalie, who avoided sticking around.

After a few seconds of sulking, they both smiled at each other, which was their way: quick to snap, but quick to forgive. Paige leaned forward and ducked her head conspiratorially. "Speaking of opportunity, I wonder if that's the rest of the dart league."

Natalie turned to see the most recent crowd pushing through the bar doors, then sucked in her breath a little when she saw Dr. Nerd himself. Arriving with another pretty blonde.

Elliott made his way across the terracotta tiles of the Shore Thing bar, to the scent of hearty beer and the loud strains of Joe Jackson on the jukebox, hesitantly guiding Lynne at the small of her back. She'd told him right away—when he'd met her on the sidewalk—that she didn't like to be touched, so he moved his hand away as soon as he remembered and glanced through the dim lighting.

He frowned at the strange sea of tie-dye and adjusted his glasses, which he'd worn tonight instead of the contacts, despite Nell's warning. Those contacts were killing him. Lynne would just have to deal.

They shuffled past a white-leisure-suited John Travolta look-alike and a woman dressed as Elvis in the *Aloha from Hawaii* special, and Elliott frowned again, desperately searching for a table. He was still confused about why Lynne had wanted to come here. When Nell had told him the date was set up for the Shore Thing, he'd tried to change that plan. The Shore Thing was fun and all—he'd been there exactly twice, both times with Jim for a quick after-work beer—but it was a bar, not a restaurant, and he'd thought first dates should probably happen in a restaurant, right? Nell had argued that first dates were wherever the woman wanted. Elliott had just shrugged and said, "Let's get it over with then."

"There's a booth over here," he said to Lynne, resisting the urge to guide her again.

Lynne was aggressively pretty, with carefully lined red lips and heavily black-lashed eyes. She looked a bit too pretty, actually, and he had a moment of disbelief that Nell thought she was right for him. Plus, she seemed a little too much into primping. She'd already checked her purse mirror three times, and they weren't even at their booth yet.

She looked around before she slid in, then frowned at the sticky tabletop, lifting her elbows off the brown table and tucking them into the sides of her sundress. Her dress was attractive—it gave him a nice glimpse of her shoulders; a pretty, tanned collarbone; and even a tiny bit of cleavage where her top began to dip. He waited for the little surge of lust that normally accompanied such a view, but for some reason it wasn't happening here. Maybe he just needed more time. Maybe if he got to know her first . . .

"Are you sure you don't want to go to Figaro's?" he shouted.

"No, that's okay," she said.

He looked around at the crazily dressed patrons. "You think it's sixties night or something?"

"Seventies," she said.

Of course. He reassessed some of the costumes. "Maybe we should have dressed up."

"It might have helped," she said.

"What?"

"Nothing." She pushed her hair over her shoulder and pulled her phone out of her purse, scrolling through a few messages. It struck Elliott as rude, but he decided not to say anything. Maybe it was an emergency or something.

He scanned the menu and let her finish her messaging, then tried to engage her on what sort of appetizers she might like. She delicately picked up a laminated menu from the chrome salt-and-pepper holder.

He ordered a beer, and she ordered water, and he asked her a ton of questions about herself, but she gave him only brief answers, her eyes still darting around the bar.

"Can you take off your glasses?" she suddenly asked.

Elliott blinked back his surprise. "Take them off?"

She nodded.

"Why?"

"Nell said you had pretty eyes." She threw a little smile into that line that looked vaguely flirtatious.

Elliott quickly removed his glasses and laid them on the table. He could barely see her now. But he thought she might still be smiling.

"You do have pretty eyes," she said. Or at least that's what he thought she said. With both his hearing and vision impaired now, he suddenly felt flustered and wasn't sure where to look next.

"I'm going to run to the little girl's room," she announced. He thought she was holding up a finger.

"Do you want me to order for you?" He squinted at the menu.

"No, I'll be right back." She slid out of the booth before he could say anything else, dragging her huge purse behind her.

A disco song lit up the jukebox—Gloria Gaynor, he identified— and the bartender grabbed a microphone and announced round one of a dart tournament.

Elliott turned in his seat. He'd always liked darts. He shoved his glasses back on and watched the teams assemble. Eventually, he switched to the other side of the booth so he could have a better view.

A hot-pink-wigged woman in bell-bottoms on the dart team captured his attention, and he found himself leaning forward at the table, staring at her stance as she practiced her aim. She had good form. And *a* good form. His eyes made a quick assessment of her shapely behind as she leaned over a bar stool and laughed lyrically at something one of the other players said. He didn't stare at women often—his granddad had taught him to be respectful—but this one held his attention. Her joyful laugh, her confident movement, the way she didn't seem flattered by the fact that every guy in the bar was checking her out—he found himself peering much too long over the top of his menu. Damn, he didn't know what was happening to him here on Lavender Island. He was on a *date*, for God's sake. With someone Nell thought was in his league.

Stay focused, man . . .

He tore his eyes away and scanned the menu again while he tried to think of what else to talk to Lynne about.

A buzz on the booth seat caught his attention, and he glanced down to his left. It was Lynne's phone. It must have fallen out of her purse. He didn't mean to zero in on the screen, but the message flashed clear and blue: Hey, sorry he's a loser. I'll call you in five and you can make your excuses.

Elliott blinked at the display a few times. He read it again. Then another time. Then, as realization slowly dawned, he moved back to his side of the booth and removed his glasses with a sense of defeat.

When Lynne returned, she gave him a placating smile, then saw her phone.

"Here it is! I thought I lost this."

She slid back into her seat to the sound of Rick Dees singing "Disco Duck" on the jukebox. She started to throw her phone into her purse when it buzzed in her hand.

"Hello? . . . Oh no." She glanced up at Elliott and gave an Oscar-worthy performance—complete with hand over her mouth.

He pretended to study the menu.

"I'm so sorry—that was work. It seems there's a late thing I have to go in for." She stood abruptly, dragging her bag up over the table, and knocked his glasses to the floor. They skidded to a halt right behind a huge crowd at the bar.

He swung forward to pick them up, and she bent at the same time. The crowd at the bar moved back just an inch until the terrible sound of crunching glass somehow drifted through the disco-duck quacks.

"I'm so sorry, Elliott!" She gave him a ridiculously exaggerated look of disappointment.

He always had a hard time acting and couldn't even come up with an appropriate expression of surprise. He simply nodded and collected the broken pieces of glass in his hand. "I'll walk you to your car."

"No! No, that's okay. You stay. The calamari is good here. I'll catch you soon, okay? I'm so sorry about your glasses." She was already on her way toward the door.

He shuffled to the bar to enjoy the last of his beer and pay for it. He'd just sit for a minute, listen to this next song by Earth, Wind & Fire, and then find his way home and tackle some gene sequencing. At least the sea lions needed him.

As he waited for the bartender to come by—studying his glasses to see if he could find a quick fix, trying to concentrate on how he'd expand his notes on the sequencing—his mind kept drifting to what he'd done wrong. He wasn't cut out for dating. That was the bottom line. He wasn't cut out for marriage either, truth be told. He couldn't imagine giving all his attention to someone else when there was so much work to do. He should call Nell and just cancel this ridiculousness. These dates were excruciating for all parties involved.

A figure to his left crowded him, and out of his peripheral vision, he caught sight of the hot-pink wig. It was the sexy woman in the bell-bottoms. She leaned over the bar, directly at his elbow, and asked for a gimlet. His body reacted to her before his brain could. He felt the heat from her polyester blouse, smelled a spicy scent from some kind of exotic perfume. His heart began pounding. He tried not to look directly at her and scooted away—why torture himself with reacting to gorgeous women when he couldn't even make a date last? But she turned toward him ever so slightly and closed the gap between them just as he was trying to elongate it.

"Whoever your matchmaker is, she's doing a terrible job," she said, her voice drifting toward his ear during a brief instrumental from Earth, Wind & Fire.

He turned his head over his beer and—in disbelief—met the feisty brown eyes behind pink heart glasses that had been part of his dreams just last night.

"Natalie?" he breathed out.

Damn, chemistry was a funny thing . . .

CHAPTER 7

Natalie had seen the whole debacle.

Dr. Nerd's latest date—who Paige had told her was dental assistant Lynne from Main Street Dental—had given him the classic Have-a-Friend-Call-You-Away brush-off. And had even managed to get his glasses trampled as she'd practically flown out the door.

Natalie had watched the whole thing over the rim of her pink glasses, between dart throws and sips of her gimlet. She'd had to look away at the end, trying to remember if she'd ever employed that ruse herself, and instantly felt bad when she realized she had. Although she'd done it because she'd thought she was in danger from a three-hundred-pound biker in LA. Not faced with a kind man like Dr. Sherman. And she certainly would have offered him a ride home after breaking his glasses. *Sheesh.* Sometimes her own kind embarrassed her.

"So who's your matchmaker?" Natalie asked, leaning farther toward him and deciding she needed to get to the bottom of this issue with Dr. Sherman and his revolving door of dates.

"How can you tell I have a matchmaker?"

"These just don't seem like women who suit you."

"Ah." He lifted the beer bottle to his lips and eyed her over the rim. "Thanks for not mentioning the alternate possibility."

"What's that?"

"That I don't suit *them*."

She took in his soulful eyes, his sexy-messy hair, his tanned wrists, his long fingers, and thought she might be able to think of a few women he'd suit just fine. But she shrugged the thought off and leaned more casually against the bar top.

"My sister is my matchmaker," he finally answered. "She's set me up on dates every night this week. I'm on date three, and zero for three, I think."

Natalie cocked her head and leaned a little closer. The next song came on the jukebox—"Werewolves of London"—and she took her heart-shaped shades off so she could see him better. Dr. Sherman had really remarkable eyes—a sharp, crystalline blue, seeming to take in everything, with the most ridiculously long lashes. He kept inching away, which kind of hurt her feelings, so she backed off a little.

"Maybe I can help," she blurted. As soon as the words left her mouth, Natalie questioned their wisdom. She didn't even know where that idea had come from.

He turned more toward her, though, which made the comment feel like a success. At least she'd finally gotten his attention. "And how is that?" he asked.

"I can coach you." As she said it, the idea began to take shape. It would be fun to spend time with him. She could still be on a mancation. And his matchmaker was obviously throwing him to the wolves. "How many dates do you have left this week?"

"Two." He winced as if the very idea hurt.

"Where?"

"Tomorrow night's is at the art walk downtown."

"Oh, the Wednesday Art Walk. I'm going to that anyway. Where is the other one?"

"Thursday's is at the new restaurant next to the pier—the tiki one?"

"The Wanderer?"

"That sounds right."

"Maybe we'll run into each other and you could secretly sign to me how things are going. I'll see if I could lend you some tips."

"Why would you do that?"

She took a sip of her drink. How much could she admit here? Could she say he sort of fascinated her and she just wanted to spend time with him? She didn't want to act as though she were coming on to him.

"You seem like a nice guy," she said instead.

He looked at her skeptically.

"You're good with the sea lions. But I know women. And I know Lavender Island women in particular. And I know dating. Trust me, I've got this."

B. J. Thomas came on the jukebox next with "(Hey Won't You Play) Another Somebody Done Somebody Wrong Song," and Dr. Sherman glanced into the mirror behind the bar, then stared into his beer. "I'm not a charity case."

"You sort of are."

He shot a look her way, his eyebrows raised, but then eventually laughed. He had a low, sexy laugh—deep and reluctant, as if it was a gift to anyone who cared to pull it out of him.

"Maybe you're right." He took a swig of his beer and looked at her sideways. "So, what are you doing here tonight, and who am I stealing you away from?"

"I'm here with my sister, but I'm sure she's not missing me. We're playing darts, and she brought me here to apologize."

"Apologize for what?" He took another drink.

"For laughing at my mancation."

He choked a little and brought his bottle down. "Is a 'mancation' what I think it is?"

"It depends on what you think it is."

"Sounds like it could be either a vacation to find men or a vacation *from* men."

"Which do you think?" she asked.

"Well, I doubt you need a vacation to find men, so I'll guess the latter."

"Yep."

"I don't think I've ever heard that one before," he said. "How long does a mancation usually last?"

"I had planned three months, but my sister bet me that I couldn't keep it going for three weeks."

"And she was apologizing for . . . ?"

"For laughing that I couldn't last for three weeks."

"Ah. So you know dating, huh?" Dr. Sherman asked.

"I'm pretty good at it."

"You like to date?"

"I used to."

"What's different now?"

"I've had some bad experiences."

He nodded thoughtfully. "Hence the mancation."

"Nice hypothesis."

He smiled at that. The dart crowd erupted into a cheer, and they both looked that way. But Natalie soon turned back to Dr. Sherman. She scooted a little closer—he smelled so good, like sandalwood and earnestness. And she liked the look of his sinewy forearms along the bar—it reminded her of the way he'd had them wrapped protectively around Alice last night.

But he casually sidled a little farther away. She sighed.

"Plus, my sister invited me here to play darts," she added, her disappointment hopefully covered up by her voice.

"Ah. Yes. I noticed you earlier. You have good form." He cleared his throat and pushed at his cocktail napkin with the beer bottle.

"Do you play?"

"I do."

Somehow she'd guessed that. "Do you want to play with us?"

He studied her, then pushed a bill across the counter to the bartender with a wry smile. "I think I've embarrassed myself enough for one evening."

He picked up his broken glasses, then gave her a quick nod as he tried to move out of the small gap she'd left between them. "But I'll see you at the center Thursday, right? As Doris said, Larry, Curly, and Moe should be out of ICU then. You could bring your niece by." A piece of his sandy hair flopped into his eyes in the cutest way, and he swiped at it.

"Oh! Yes!" She was surprised he was leaving so abruptly. Did she say something wrong? "You know I—" She tried to move away as he politely stepped around her. She wondered if he didn't like her. Maybe she came off as too aggressive. She'd cultivated a long life of being aggressive when necessary, but she needed to learn to back off when faced with situations that didn't warrant it. Or men who didn't warrant it. "I um . . . I got a new job. And it might be at the center some of the time."

He stopped and snapped a look back at her. "Where?"

"At Casas del Sur. I'll be driving the seniors around—and sometimes to the center."

"No kidding?"

"No kidding."

A crowd right behind them let out another loud cheer and clattered bottles together in a toast as Dr. Sherman seemed to think over her news. "I might see you sooner then."

"Yes. And maybe you'll let me help you with your date tomorrow?" she asked.

He gave an embarrassed laugh. "Why don't we talk about that if you come to the center tomorrow? I might've had one too many beers to agree to that right now."

"How many have you had?"

"One." He squinted toward the door, as if trying to figure out where it was, then headed toward the exit sign.

"Wait—you probably can't drive with your glasses like that." Natalie glanced at the mess in his hands. "Would you like me to drive you home?"

But he'd already shoved his glasses and his hands in his gabardine slacks and was making a beeline for the door.

Natalie sighed.

Maybe smart, kind men just would never be attracted to her.

Elliott pushed his way through the crowd, which was spilling out into the street.

It would be a pretty long walk home, but his glasses were a bit beyond hope right now, and his driving through the night, even in a golf cart, would be reckless at best.

But there was no way he was going to accept a ride from Natalie Grant.

He was just too nervous around her. Gorgeous women could do that to an introvert.

Best to get her out of his mind. Or at least out of his mind as someone he could date. She'd laid it out pretty clear with her mancation story.

Of course, she did seem to think of him as a charity case, so that was an option, he supposed, if he wanted to be fully pathetic. He could be her pet project and let her help him with his dates.

But no. As much as he liked being near her, he had to draw the line somewhere between his testosterone and his pride.

He shoved his hands deeper into his trouser pockets and squinted at the busy street, trying to remember where the back canyon road was on this little island. He knew there was a path leading the back way to his house—he'd even run it once—but now, in the dark, without being able to see clearly, he couldn't quite locate it.

He walked another two blocks, following the sound of his beloved ocean, and then pulled his glasses out of his pocket and peered through the shattered left lens at the street sign. *Ah, Oak Lane.* That sounded right.

He glanced back over his shoulder to make sure no one from the bar could see his goofy self, then shed his shoes and socks, shoved the lens back into his pocket, and took off in a cross-country-style gait toward the trail he was pretty sure would lead back home.

He'd forget about Natalie. He'd just get through these next two dates for Nell, then refocus his life on the sea lions. He would probably leave Lavender Island as soon as he could.

He was striking out here.

Story of his life.

CHAPTER 8

Natalie awoke the next morning to a hangover and a general feeling of sadness she couldn't quite identify. She slammed the alarm clock until it bounced off the nightstand, then groaned, caught the ringing cacophony, and snapped it off with more force than necessary. Rolling over, she sighed and drifted back into consciousness. Vignettes of the previous evening floated before her—laughing at Paige's wig, winning the dart tournament, meeting a huge guy with cartoonish muscles named John-O who'd flirted with her the second half of the evening, and then . . . Dr. Sherman . . . hightailing it out of the bar, seemingly wanting to get away from her.

The source of her vague sadness was identified.

She rolled off the bed as her head throbbed in protest, and instantly wondered if she could talk Paige into taking Lily to school. Natalie definitely needed another hour of sleep, not to mention an aspirin and a few glasses of water.

But then she remembered the new leaf she was turning and forced herself into a standing position. This was her job. Lily was counting on her. And so was Olivia. Plus, she was starting her second job today. And she might get to see Dr. Sherman. And maybe she'd help him on his date tonight, if he didn't keep running away from her.

She steadied herself against the nightstand. She'd just have to cut her nights shorter, and drink less, if she was going to do this early-rising thing. As she snatched up her clothes to head down the hall to her shower, a wave of admiration swept through her that Olivia did this every day.

The shower and some coffee did her well. By the time Lily was swinging her legs under the table and humming into her Froot Loops, Natalie felt 75 percent prepared to face the day. She even made Olivia some plain toast and coffee and brought it to her in bed, telling her not to get up this morning—she and Lily would be fine, and she'd do Lily's hair. By ten minutes to seven, Lily had on her fireman costume and a flashlight in her backpack, and Natalie cheered up the last 25 percent.

Or maybe 23 percent.

There was still a 2 percent tug of sadness every time she thought of Dr. Sherman and the way he'd kept sliding away from her at the bar.

By nine thirty, she was taking her second, more detailed, tour of Casas del Sur, her new name tag secured to her blouse underneath her braid and her new pink "Casas" cap pulled low over her eyes.

"And this is the movie theater," Steve Stegner said, sweeping open a heavy metal door to a dimly lit room with sixty red-velvet seats in six rows and a small aisle down the center. Like the library, dining room, computer room, and exercise room, the space was rich and luxurious, with flashes of gold in the curtain tassels and carved chair handles.

It also was not empty.

"Colonel!" Steve said. "What are you doing in here?"

A small, hunched man—not much more than five feet tall—side-stepped slowly from the front of the stage to face them. He had an ocean-blue three-piece suit on, neatly trimmed white hair along the base of his skull, and a rose stem in his hand.

"Ah, Stegner, my favorite person," he said in a gravelly voice. "I'll bet you graduated least likely to smile."

"Colonel, you shouldn't be in here when no one is—"

"Balderdash!" he barked. "I'm just setting up a little surprise for Marie. Leave me be. I'll be out of here in a minute. And excuse my language, young lady." He bowed at Natalie. "Stegner, you're dismissed." The man shuffled back toward the stage and resumed his bony-fingered arrangement of the rose with a card and envelope near the stage steps.

To Natalie's surprise, Steve backed out of the room, motioning for Natalie to follow, and closed the door behind them.

"The Colonel is one of our tough customers," he said. "Pretty much always gets his way."

Natalie bit her cheek and nodded.

"Let me show you the second-floor dining room and ballroom. Then I'll take you outside and show you the activities shuttle cart. You'll be driving one, and John-O will be driving the other."

"John-O?"

"John O'Donnell. He's the other assistant activities director."

"Big guy?" She held her hands out from her shoulders to indicate the Popeye-looking muscles she recalled from her flirter last night.

"Yes. You've met already?"

"I believe so. Socially. Unless there are two John-Os on Lavender Island built like tanks."

"He's the one." Steve hit the elevator button. "He'll be driving the volunteer crew today, and you'll be driving the ladies to their harbor walk."

The elevator doors closed as Natalie tried to remember John-O more clearly. He'd seemed nice enough. But as she frowned and tried for better recall, her mind drifted instead to Dr. Sherman, sitting with his knee up at the edge of the bar, his sexy, tanned forearms on the edge, twisting his beer bottle . . . She quickly pushed the new image out of her mind and stepped off the elevator with Steve.

The ballroom was gorgeous. Parquet flooring shone across a fifty-foot expanse, taking up almost the entire second floor. Floor-to-ceiling windows ran the length of one side, showcasing a palm-tree-and-ocean view, with a row of round tables set all the way around. Five crystal chandeliers ran down the center, their beads reflecting the sunlight as it came through the windows.

"It's lovely!" she said, a little breathless.

"We just finished it," Steve said proudly. "One of the things we need help with is planning the Senior Prom for the last day of spring. It'll be our first event here. Our last part-time activities assistant left abruptly, with many of the plans undone, as well as with half the ticket money." Steve shook his head. "But we can recover. Our seniors are excited about it, and we have a volunteer prom-planning committee, but they need someone to help them with some of the particulars. Are you up for that?"

"Yes, sure."

"We'll need you to stick around." He turned to face her. "I don't want them to be disappointed again. Can I count on you?"

An instinctual panic began to set in at being asked to commit to a time period, but Steve's face was full of so much entreaty. She could do this. Steve wanted to count on her. And Natalie wanted to be the type of person who could be counted on. And it was only three months.

"I promise," she said.

Steve broke into a relieved grin that made her heart do a funny flip. It felt like something she hadn't experienced in a long time—something along the lines of pride.

As they walked back through the ballroom between the sun's pretty rays across the parquet, she straightened her spine and felt a lift in her chest. It was the best she'd felt in eons.

At ten thirty, just as her tour with Steve was ending and she'd seen the pool, the pool house, and one of the apartment rooms, Natalie ran into her first snafu.

"Where *is* he?" Steve asked the front desk.

"He left with the harbor-walk ladies," the young woman there said. "Hi, I'm June Lee." She held out her hand toward Natalie. She also wore one of the Casas del Sur name tags and collared shirts.

"Natalie Grant."

"Natalie is the new assistant," Steve said. "She was supposed to take the harbor-walk ladies today, not John-O."

"It was rescheduled, and you two weren't here, so John-O took them."

"We can't just have willy-nilly schedule changes like that, June."

June glanced at Natalie with a barely suppressed eye-roll. "Well, they're gone. Natalie can take the other cart with the volunteers for the center."

"The center?" Natalie asked hopefully.

"The Friends of the Sea Lion," Steve mumbled.

Natalie couldn't help the little soaring in her chest when she heard him mention Dr. Sherman's center—but it was followed much too quickly by a flutter of butterflies.

She couldn't remember the last time a man made her so nervous—and it was probably from a job interview, not a date. Maybe she wanted to impress him. What was she saying? She wasn't trying to *impress* Dr. Sherman. Her type didn't impress brainy PhDs. Maybe she just wanted to help him—make sure he didn't feel bad about his dates and do better on the next one. Or maybe she felt as if she had to apologize for her species—women like Caren, Alice, and Lynne shouldn't treat shy men like Dr. Sherman that way. All he needed were a few smooth lines and a way to deliver his honesty, to show these women what a wonderful man he seemed to be.

June handed her the ignition keys, and she and Steve went out to the parking lot so he could explain the shuttle's bells and whistles. It was called the Concierge—a six-seat, open-air, tram-style golf cart with a soft-top roof that had scalloped edges hanging down. It had larger tires than most of the other golf carts she'd seen, probably designed to handle the hills of the island. All except Castle Road, Steve said, which was too steep even for the Concierge.

Just as Steve finished and ducked his head out of the passenger-side seat, an elderly, rotund woman came down the sidewalk ramp, yoo-hooing in her blue "I'm a Friend!" shirt.

"I'm Sarah. But you can call me Sugar," she said in a sexy Southern drawl.

"I'm Natalie." Natalie hopped out of the shuttle to help Sugar into her seat, just as Doris and Marie came arm in arm down the ramp.

The women wriggled into the shuttle as two gentlemen made their way down the ramp—the Colonel, who she'd seen earlier with the rose and the three-piece suit, which he still had on, and another elderly man who was taller and looked to be younger—maybe eighty—who still had a shock of thick white hair and whose "I'm a Friend!" T-shirt stretched tightly across a barrel chest and belly.

"Why, hello there, young lady. Aren't you pretty. I'm George." He thrust out his hand.

George climbed into the back of the shuttle as the Colonel walked around front to the passenger seat. He swung himself inside in an impressively lithe move that reminded Natalie of the way he might have entered a cockpit decades ago.

"Full speed ahead," he ground out.

The Colonel proceeded to bark directions to her the whole way there, drowning out the soft female voice of the GPS, while George flirted with Sugar in the backseat, and Doris and Marie began chattering in the middle seat about the fact that someone named Veronica Stevenson was really too young to be Senior Prom queen.

Natalie couldn't help smiling to herself.

This was going to be an interesting three months.

Elliott stood in the back room, working up the blood samples he'd taken that morning and blinking back the dryness in the contacts he'd been forced to wear until he got his glasses fixed.

He hoped to find a correlation of some sort between how sick the sea lions got and a presence of a certain gene. Another four sea lion pups had been rescued that morning—usually they got four or five calls a month, but now they were getting four or five a day.

The three samples he was testing were from Larry, Curly, and Moe, and he hoped he'd be able to help the little dudes out. They were taking a while to recover because they were some of the youngest pups the center had seen yet, but this morning all three seemed to be on an upswing. But, as excited as Elliott was about this new work, he was surprised that his mind drifted for the fortieth time to Natalie Grant.

Heat formed around his collar at the way he'd run from her inquisitiveness at the bar, and he had to put down the culture tubes he was prepping to lean against the counter and think for a second.

He took a deep breath and told himself to concentrate. He snapped on the Bunsen burner and reached for the vials of blood Jim had helped collect.

He probably wouldn't see her again. She might come to the center to drop off the seniors for her new job, or maybe check on Larry, Curly, and Moe, but she wouldn't seek him out, even if she did say she wanted to help him on his dates. Surely that had been her gimlet talking.

He imagined a more likely scenario would be that she'd stay in the main periphery by the pools and wouldn't even think of him. He was sure someone else could take her on a tour of the sea lions she'd helped rescue. He'd mention it to Doris.

He inoculated each tube with blood from a different animal and tried not to think about her anymore. Eventually, Jim banged through the door.

"Hey, keep that door closed, would you?" Elliott said over his shoulder.

"Your new girlfriend's here to see you."

Elliott tried to keep the samples delicately balanced as he brought them to the incubator. He frowned. Normally he might find Jim funny and try to figure out who he meant—his next date tonight, perhaps, courtesy of Nell? What was her name again? Stephanie? But he had to concentrate for a second. He'd lost too much time this morning daydreaming about Natalie; he couldn't lose all these samples now.

"Did you hear me?" Jim asked.

"I did."

"I said your new girlfriend is here."

"Working here, buddy."

"She says her name's Natalie."

Elliott nearly dropped the tube rack.

Natalie stood at the top of the brick walkway and glanced nervously at the laboratory door as she waved to each of her charges. Doris, Marie, Sugar, George, and the Colonel all seemed to know where they needed to be and had told her she could drop them off right at the gate. But she'd parked the shuttle out front and accompanied them all the way up the bricks. She was proud of them and wanted to see where they all worked.

"Bye, honey! We'll see you in a few hours," Doris said.

Natalie waved.

And, truth be told, she wanted to see Dr. Sherman. She was embarrassed by her interest, and her hands were already getting clammy, but she glanced at the door where the man named Jim disappeared.

Sea lions barked in the distance while she watched the shadows of the oak trees play along the side of building. Finally, when neither lab coat came through the door, she adjusted her cap and turned on her heel to leave. Maybe he was busy. Or just didn't want to see her. Or, most likely, just wasn't interested. Intelligent, business-minded men, like Dr. Sherman the scientist, would always see her as just some pretty bimbo. She might as well accept her lot in life. She wiped her hands along her cargo pants and shuffled quickly down the walk. She didn't know why she was obsessing over him anyway.

"Natalie?"

Dr. Sherman was walking toward her, his tousled hair glinting in the sunlight, blinking back at her with those long eyelashes she could see clearly again today. He must not have been able to fix his glasses. He had his hands thrust into his lab coat pockets and a hesitancy about his step, as if he couldn't figure out if he wanted to hurry toward her or turn back around.

Her hands grew clammier. Any bravado she'd found last night to talk to him dissipated. In the light of day, with no alcohol in her, Dr. Sherman looked intimidating again.

"Hi! Dr. Sherman!"

"Please—call me Elliott. Doris calls me Dr. Sherman, but it sort of embarrasses me."

"Why does it embarrass you?"

"The PhD thing is still a little new—maybe I'm just not used to it yet."

She nodded, but she wasn't sure she could think of him as "Elliott" yet. But she would try. "Elliott then. How are your glasses?" *Stupid. Stupid question.*

He motioned toward his eyes. "Contacts today. Glasses are getting fixed."

"Ah." She waved her hand toward the building where Doris and the others had disappeared. "I dropped the seniors off today."

All her normal sassy lines flew out of her head, and her heart picked up a ridiculous rhythm that she didn't recognize at all. She strove to think of something smart to say, and nothing would present itself.

He watched her expectantly.

"I just wanted to say hi," she finally blurted. "And uh . . ." She scrambled to remember their conversation last night. What had she committed to? Behind her, doors banged at the top of the walkway. "Oh, and see if you needed any help for tonight?"

"About that, Natalie." He shoved his fists into his lab coat and took another few steps toward her. She liked the way he said her name—softly, with a tenderness around the edges that she wasn't used to hearing from men. "I don't think that would be a good idea. It's cool of you to offer, but I don't need—"

"WHAT do you not need?" the Colonel bellowed down the walkway. He was peering down at his jacket lapel, seemingly trying to fasten something there.

"Hi, Colonel," Elliott said. "I was just telling Natalie here that—"

"Can you help me with this, doll?" The Colonel stepped past Elliott and close to Natalie. He only came up to her chin, but he still had a commanding presence. He handed her the pin he was trying to attach. It was a white-and-blue "I'm a Friend!" name tag shaped like a sea lion, with the name *Stanley* written across the center.

"That's my real name," he grumbled. "Anyway, these blasted name tags always poke my thumbs."

Natalie brought her face close to his lapel and carefully secured the tiny clasp.

"So, what is this you don't need from Natalie?" the Colonel asked.

"Just her help with something that came up last night when—"

"Hi, kids!" Doris sang out, heading down the path and adjusting her half apron; she had a fresh stack of bookmarks and brochures in two front pockets. "How is everyone today?"

"Sherm was just telling us he doesn't need Natalie's help with something," the Colonel said. "Whatever it is, I'm suspicious. She seems to be good at everything." He slapped his name tag in satisfied thanks.

"What is it, dear?" Doris asked Elliott.

"Nothing." Elliott's neck seemed to be turning a deep red.

"Spit it out, son. We can lend a hand. Doris and I do have a few years of experience."

"It's just . . ." Elliott took a deep breath and glanced at Natalie, then seemed to give something up that he was fighting in his head. "Natalie and I were talking last night, and she offered to coach me on the next few dates I have that my sister set me up on."

"We can do that." The Colonel slapped him on the back. "Is this the Alice date?"

"Uh, no." Elliott glanced up at Natalie again and cleared his throat. "This is the Stephanie date."

"What happened to Alice?"

"She didn't work out."

The Colonel shook his head. "You need our help, all right. Stand tall, Sherman. First, you need to start with a proper date pickup. None of this 'I'll meet you there' crap. Pick her up at her door."

"Well, my sister, Nell, is handling that part, and Stephanie wanted to—"

"Would you want to be picked up at the door?" The Colonel looked at Natalie.

Elliott turned toward her, too.

She blinked against their intense stares. "We're not talking about me here."

"Just asking for reference purposes," the Colonel said.

"Oh. Okay. I guess it would be sort of old-fashioned and maybe romantic," Natalie admitted. "But most women these days prefer to meet their dates at the location. They don't want to end up with stalkers who know where they live."

"ARE YOU GOING TO STALK THIS WOMAN?" the Colonel barked at Elliott.

"Of course not. But—"

"Then pick her up at the DOOR. Shows you care that she arrives safely and gets home safely. Plus, it gives you a few extra minutes with her. Kids these days don't even know the beauty of the at-the-door good-night kiss."

The Colonel and Doris exchanged a knowing nod. Elliott turned another shade of red.

"Next, women love when you bring them flowers," the Colonel continued.

Elliott glanced at Natalie again with a raised eyebrow. "Is that true? In this day and age?"

"DORIS?" the Colonel yelled. "Would you like it if a date showed up at your door with flowers?"

"Yes, that would be lovely."

"Marie?"

Natalie hadn't even noticed Marie coming down the walkway, but there she was right behind the Colonel. Marie nodded her agreement.

"What about you?" the Colonel demanded of Natalie.

Natalie blinked harder against everyone's stares, especially Elliott's, and tried to picture it. She blushed a little at how cute that would be. "It might be a bit old-fashioned, but I guess I would think he had gone through all that trouble for me, and I'd be flattered."

The Colonel turned to Elliott with a smug grin. "See? It works. Shows you care enough to spend a little on her—money *and* time. It's good form."

Elliott looked at them all skeptically. "All right. What kind of flowers?"

"Nothing serious. No roses," Doris said.

Elliott addressed Natalie. "What do you think?"

Natalie found herself blushing again. "I agree with Doris—no roses. Something unassuming."

"What's your favorite flower?" Elliott asked.

"Me? It doesn't matter what I like."

"I'm just asking."

"I sort of like gerbera daisies."

Elliott scribbled on a piece of paper that he seemed to pull out of nowhere. "All right, what else?"

"DRESS NICE!" the Colonel yelled.

Elliott smiled. "You don't like how I dress, Colonel?"

"You do all right," he grumbled. "At least you know how to wear decent trousers, and I've seen you in a tie. But for God's sake, don't wear dungarees."

Elliott and Natalie both stared at the Colonel blankly.

"BLUE JEANS!" he barked. "Disrespect. If a man wants to show respect, he wears nice clothes, neatly pressed, shined shoes. He puts some effort in, shows her she's worth the extra time. Sets you on the right course to a good relationship."

Natalie couldn't remember the last time a man wore anything but jeans on a date. Let alone picked her up at her door. Let alone brought her a bouquet of flowers. She just went out with guys when they asked to "hang out." She watched Elliott scribble more notes.

"As soon as you see her, tell her how nice she looks," the Colonel added. "Agreed?" he asked Natalie.

She nodded. She tried to remember David of the Broken Motorcycle and then Devlan and realized they'd never told her such a thing. At least when she had clothes on.

"THE FIRST THING YOU NOTICE!" the Colonel continued. "Her hair, the color of her dress, her eyes. Don't say anything about her body! I know that's what you'll notice first." He cuffed Elliott lightly near his ear. "Stay focused on something she took time for. Women spend a lot of time getting ready, and we should let them know we appreciate it."

Elliott jotted down more notes.

"Like Natalie here. What did you first notice about her?"

Elliott looked up at Natalie like a deer caught in headlights. "Um . . ." His gaze made a swift move across her body, but he snapped it back up to her face. "I, uh . . . I like her hats."

"He did tell me that when I first met him," she told the Colonel.

"Good!" the Colonel said. "Proud of you, boy. What do you like about her hats?"

"They, uh . . . they remind me of my granddad's hats—the snap-brim and the fedora—I have some of the same ones from him. She looks a lot better in them, though."

"You're better at this than I thought you were, son," the Colonel said. "So what else did you first notice about her?"

Elliott was still gazing directly at her. "She, um . . . she has beautiful eyes. Intelligent."

The Colonel nudged him out of the way and looked up to see Natalie's eyes himself. But she was too busy staring back at Elliott over the top of the Colonel's head. Elliott bravely held her gaze, seeming to infuse the comment with all the sincerity he could muster. Natalie felt a blush rising up through her cheeks and swallowed hard. No man had ever told her she had intelligent eyes before.

"Nice," the Colonel said, nodding. "Now tell her something about a body part not connected to her torso."

Elliott frowned a little, as if confused by such a specific command. "Uh, not connected to her . . . ?" His eyes swept downward again, and he struggled to bring them back up. "Yes, okay. Um . . ." He seemed not to know where to look, but he finally settled on her face. Once there, he slowly took in every feature. His intensity caused her whole body to tingle. "She has pretty lips."

"Something not used during sex."

A deep red rushed across Elliott's face. "Okay. Uh . . . she has beautiful hair."

"C'mon, you can do better than that. What does the color remind you of?"

"Sea lions, actually. When they're healthy and shimmery."

The Colonel cuffed Elliott on his shoulder. "SEA LIONS? Son, girls don't want to have sea lion hair! Think of something else."

"Okay . . ." He took his time studying Natalie's hairline and the braid going down her front. "Acorns."

"Acorns?" the Colonel asked. "That's pretty good. Where do you see acorns?"

"The acorns behind my granddad's house. I used to find them when I was a kid. I used to collect them in jars on my desk in my room at his house."

A silence fell as they all stared at Elliott. Natalie thought that might have been the sweetest compliment she'd ever received.

"There we go!" the Colonel said. "You've got the compliments down pat. Now for the drop-off at the door. Can you handle a good-night kiss?"

Marie and Doris all turned toward Elliott, who finally broke his gaze away from Natalie. "I think I can handle a kiss, Colonel."

"Let's make sure. Now, you don't want to move in too close, to where she feels crowded out or intimidated." He moved Natalie into Elliott's reach.

"Colonel, really," Elliott said.

"When's the last time you kissed a girl good night at her door?" the Colonel barked.

Elliott thought that over.

"Just as I suspected," the Colonel said. "What's the last time you got a telling good-night kiss?" he asked Natalie.

Caught off guard, she scrambled to think of her answer. *A telling good-night kiss?* She thought of all her biker dates, and the MMA fighters, and the football player she "hung out" with for a week, and couldn't think of any first kiss that wasn't just part of trying to get her into bed. "Um . . ."

"Oh, good heavens. Have you *ever* received a good-night kiss at your door?" The Colonel sounded angry.

"I don't think I have."

He blew out an exasperated breath. "You young people today are ruining dating, you know that? There's an *art* to it. The good-bye kiss is part of the *art*. It tells you how interested you are and how interested you want to be. Now here." He positioned Elliott and Natalie closer together. "If you're not that interested when the date's over, just give her a polite kiss on the cheek and say thank you right afterward. She'll know that you're sincerely thankful—and you'd better be, young man—but that you're not interested in moving much beyond that. Here, try it."

"Colonel, I don't think I need to practice. I can just—"

"*Try it.*"

Elliott looked startled, but he stepped forward and kissed Natalie lightly on the cheek. "Thank you," he said right into her eyes. His thanks seemed to be more about enduring this coaching than anything.

"Good!" the Colonel said. "I bought that. Now if you *are* interested, what will you do?"

Elliott swallowed hard. "Well, I would kiss her better."

"BETTER?" the Colonel barked. "*More thoroughly* is the answer. Kiss her *more thoroughly*. Natalie, do you mind if our friend Elliott practices on you?"

"Colonel!" Elliott seemed irritated now. "This isn't necessary."

"He can practice on me!" Doris piped up.

"Or me." Marie smiled.

Natalie grinned and shook her head. "I don't mind."

Four sets of eyebrows raised.

"There you go," the Colonel said. "Now, first—and Natalie, you correct me if I'm wrong—but first, I think you want to reach out and put your hand in her hair. Yes? Marie? Doris?"

The two women bobbed their updos.

"Natalie, do you like it when men put their hands in your hair?"

Another heated blush chased up Natalie's face. "Yes."

"Show Elliott where to put his hand."

Elliott still looked a little startled, but he finally lifted his hand near her ear. Natalie moved it slightly—he was almost right.

He stepped closer. "Here?" he whispered in a voice only she could hear.

She nodded. Her breathing picked up at his nearness, at his masculine scent, at the feel of his forearm, which flexed when she dragged her hand across it after positioning his. She could feel his breath across her temple, his fingers in her hairline. His eyes darted around her face, as if asking if this was okay. It suddenly didn't feel like playacting anymore.

"Now kiss her like you're never going to be able to kiss another woman for as long as you live. That's how we kissed during the war," the Colonel said.

Natalie meant to smile but couldn't. She couldn't seem to muster any frivolity right now. All she could concentrate on was how good Elliott smelled and the crazy pounding of her heart.

"Can I get him off my back and show him I know how to do this?" he whispered.

She simply nodded, staring up into his long eyelashes.

The feel of his lips surprised her—velvety, soft, cautious. She didn't remember ever feeling lips so soft before. But she also had never been kissed this way before. Elliott wasn't being aggressive, pushy, moving things along so he could get to the better part, like most of her dates did. He was kissing her thoroughly, carefully, trying to please with just this kiss. His lips moved languidly across hers; then he sucked hard on her bottom lip until her toes curled. Tingles shot out through every one of her extremities. Slowly he backed away.

"That was *great!*" The Colonel's bald head popped up almost between them. "You've got it in you, boy." He slapped Elliott on the shoulder. "I was worried there for a minute, but I think you've got this down. Now, where are you going to take this date of yours? What's her name? Stephanie?"

Elliott didn't seem to hear the question at first, concentrating instead on Natalie's face. But finally he broke the gaze, removed his hand from her hair, and stepped away. "Yes." He cleared his throat.

Natalie pressed her lips together to make sure her jaw hadn't dropped. She tried to get her breathing under control, not sure where to look next. Not at Marie or Doris—both women seemed to be grinning at her giddily.

"Okay, Sherman, you've got this." The Colonel clapped him on the back again. "C'mon ladies—let's get to work. I see visitors coming in."

He motioned for them to follow, and all three headed down to the pools to begin their volunteer presentations.

"I should go, too," Natalie said into the silence they left.

She wanted to say something like, "Where did you learn to kiss like that?" or "Can I have another one of those?" But that would be inappropriate, especially since Elliott was already turning back toward his lab office and looking as if he didn't know what had just happened either.

"Of course." He shoved his hands back in his lab coat, staring at the bricks.

"So I might see you tonight at the art walk?" She began stepping backward along the pathway, trying not to think about how her body had just lit on fire because of this nerdy lab-coated man. "Good luck on your date. Although I think you got some great advice there from the Colonel. The flowers would be a nice touch. And I think you've got the rest . . . pretty down pat."

Natalie turned and tore down the brick walkway.

The sea lions all barked—or maybe they were laughing—as she ran to the golf cart.

God, she was a mess.

Some mancation.

CHAPTER 9

The art walk was pretty full. Elliott twisted his shoulders and ushered Stephanie through the doorway of the Kublai Khan Gallery. He'd never been to an art walk before, but everyone on Lavender Island seemed to be at this one. The cobbled sidewalks of Main Street teemed with young and old who walked in and out of the galleries, small paper cups in their hands filled with wine. Quartets played at the backs of some of the galleries, oozing jazz into the night. The scent of mushroom-laced appetizers mingled with wine and perfume, wafting through the galleries on a breeze of ocean air. Local artists were on hand, sitting in directors' chairs near their pieces and answering questions.

"What's this piece?" Stephanie wandered deeper into Kublai Khan and peered around the corner at a large sculpture made of tin.

She was pleasant. Elliott could find no fault with her, even though his reaction was lukewarm. He didn't get to pick her up at the door, as the Colonel had suggested. Nell had said exactly what Natalie had—that Stephanie was among the modern women who preferred to meet blind dates at the date location. Elliott could understand that. You never knew who you were going to get.

But he had tried the flowers. He wasn't a fan of cut flowers, preferring to keep all organisms living, so he found some potted ones outside the little hardware store on Main Street. He asked the elderly clerk for gerbera daisies, since that's what Natalie had named, and got some in bright pink. They looked just like Natalie to him. But he tried to ignore that fact and bought a small pot for Stephanie. The clerk had kindly tied a bow around it for him.

Stephanie had seemed shocked when he'd handed them to her—not excited, exactly, but surprised. And now she was sort of wondering what to do with them, he could tell. He probably should have stuck with the cut flowers.

"Do you want me to hold those for you?" he finally asked.

"That'd be great." She shoved them back into his hands.

The event was a good idea for a date, though. Nell had set up this particular date for Stephanie because she was into art. Elliott followed her obligingly, nodding at the information she gave about each piece. He loved when people had passions, like he had about the ocean. Stephanie escaped behind another gallery wall and crooked her finger at him to follow.

He tried not to look around for Natalie. Knowing she was there, somewhere, among the crowd, was hard. Every time he saw a flash of acorn-colored hair, he found his heart racing and his palms getting sweaty. He really needed to reeducate himself on how to focus. He'd been a straight-A student all through school because of his laser focus, but Natalie was keeping him strangely unbalanced.

And, stranger still, he sort of liked it.

His mind kept drifting to her kiss that afternoon. And the cute way she'd ducked her head during the Colonel's questions about what she liked on a date. She'd seemed embarrassed to admit her preferences, but Elliott had noted them all with interest. He now knew she would think it was romantic to be picked up at the door; she liked gerbera daisies; she liked a man's hand in her hair, right underneath her earlobe;

she'd never been kissed good-bye at her door; and, damn, she had the softest lips.

He'd been embarrassed when the Colonel set up the little "practice" for the two of them. Especially for kissing. That was the *one* thing Elliott felt confident about when it came to women. Every other element about what women wanted—touching, sex, foreplay—sort of baffled him, but kissing was fun. Maybe because he'd actually been told in high school that he was a good kisser. Twice. Despite his geeky status. So the Colonel had rattled him to no end this afternoon. But once he'd had his hands in Natalie's hair and was staring into her eyes, he couldn't resist going through with the "practice" anyway. There was no one in the world he'd wanted to practice on so badly.

And those lips of hers had not disappointed. One bit. He'd already been partly turned on with the Colonel's ridiculous questions that made him think about dating Natalie for real. But when their lips met, and all her beauty and promise unfolded right before him, he'd gone hard in an instant. Thank God for lab coats.

"Elliott, come look!"

Stephanie. Yes. He needed to focus.

He had to think about Stephanie right now and how to make her happy on this date. Natalie was not part of the bargain. She'd made it clear last night with her mancation story that she had no interest in dating. Which meant no interest in dating *him*, he was pretty sure. So he needed to get her out of his mind and enjoy the one he was with. He'd make this work out for Nell. Stephanie was one of Nell's better friends.

He focused on Stephanie's well-toned body, on her short hair that made her look sort of playful, and on her glasses, which he usually liked on women. He wished she smiled more, but he could maybe get into that. He concentrated on her intelligence, her passion for art, her seriousness—

"Dr. Sherman?" he heard behind him.

The voice—which he instantly recognized—sent a quiver into his stomach. Joy. Nervousness. Anticipation. It all funneled forward in a heady feeling he didn't remember ever experiencing before.

"Natalie! Hello."

She had on another one of her hats tonight—this one a feminine thing, though. Sort of a 1920s-looking bucket hat with a flower on one side that for some reason made her brown eyes look even more huge and beautiful. It was a soft berry color—the same color as her lips, which he couldn't stop staring at now—the same color as the ice plants on the side of his house that led down to the ocean. She had on a dress that also made him think of 1920s flappers, but she filled hers out better. A lot better. Only a healthy dose of fear and years of his granddad's reprimands kept his eyes off her breasts.

"Where is she?" Natalie whispered, glancing around.

It took him a second to jolt his mind back to reality and make the connection. "Right around that corner."

"How's it going?"

"It's going okay."

"You went with live flowers?" She eyed the pot.

"Was that a bad move?" He smiled. "I just like things to stay alive."

"I feel the same way. The cut ones die so quickly. Potted ones you can enjoy for some time."

"Exactly."

"Why do you still have them?"

He lifted them lamely. "She didn't want to hold them, I guess."

A disapproving frown crinkled Natalie's face. "Do you like her?"

"I, uh . . ." He tore his gaze away and looked in Stephanie's direction. "Yeah, she's okay. I like her well enough."

"Do you need any help?"

"Help? I—no. I think it's going okay."

Natalie looked over his shoulder, her eyes widening just enough after a second that he knew Stephanie was coming their way.

"Stephanie, this is a friend of mine, Natalie Grant. Natalie, this is Stephanie."

The women nodded politely at each other. Elliott faced both—his new date and his new crush—and wondered what the hell kind of universe he was in right now.

"Are you having fun?" Natalie asked her.

Dr. Sherman's date was cute and small. She had short dark hair, layered into a pixie cut that shimmered as she bobbed her answer yes. Her smile was reluctant, almost invisible. Maybe shy. She had glasses on that made her look especially smart.

"Yes. I love the art walk. I come every month if I can," Stephanie said.

Natalie nodded and stepped back, suddenly feeling as if she was looming over this tiny thing. Natalie had admittedly dressed a little more feminine tonight, but she still felt masculine standing next to Tinker Bell there. Or, scratch that, she'd dressed a *lot* more feminine. Paige had been laughing at her since six o'clock, saying she couldn't remember Natalie wearing a dress since second grade. But Natalie had simply been feeling so comfortable on the island that she'd wanted to shed some of her usual layers. The dress felt light and fun. And knowing she was only going to be among friends tonight, she thought she'd try this one that Olivia had in her closet.

"So you're a good docent for Dr. Sherman tonight," Natalie said from a foot away.

"*Elliott,*" he whispered so only she could hear. He followed the reminder up with a private wink.

"I hope so." Stephanie looked around at the art.

Natalie watched as Elliott looked down at Stephanie—just a quick glance, filled with no clues whatsoever—and yet Natalie felt a twinge of jealousy. She pictured him giving Stephanie those gerbera daisies tonight. Maybe they'd look for a place at her house to plant them . . . Maybe Elliott's hand would find its way into Stephanie's short, shimmery hair. Maybe he'd lean down slowly, watching her eyes, and kiss her at her door with one of those amazing kisses.

Natalie looked around desperately for the exit. She needed air. And wine. Wine would be good.

"Which way are you headed?" Elliott asked. "We're heading north. I think next up is—"

"South!" Natalie all but shouted. "I'm heading south. I'm going to go now, in fact. I have to find . . ." She waved her hand to let them fill in whatever they wanted, but really she had to go find her sanity and rational behavior. And that wine.

Her face heated up as she fled toward the door; a jazz saxophone wail seemed to follow her as she squeezed through the crowd. Her low shoes made quick time as she snaked across the cement floor, where she joined a cluster of art-walkers around the front table and waited patiently for her Dixie cup of wine, taking deep inhalations of the ocean breeze that came through the front windows.

Damn. What was wrong with her?

She was not the type to feel jealous. She couldn't remember ever having those kinds of feelings sweep over her. But, she consoled herself, it wasn't the man she wanted; it was just the kiss. Somehow that made her feel better, although she knew she shouldn't examine her logic too closely.

She snatched a cup off the card table and downed it in one gulp. As she crushed the paper in her hands in a very unladylike way, she caught a glimpse of John-O and Doris across the gallery. In seconds, she was at John-O's side, laughing at something he was saying, touching Doris's shoulder, offering thanks for their compliments on her outfit tonight, gazing up at the Kublai Khan art, and hoping to avoid seeing Elliott and cute Stephanie exit together. She felt bad that she wasn't helping him on his date as she'd promised, but he'd said he was fine. And with that mouth of his . . . She shook the image off and tried not to imagine his lips.

He'd be fine.

As soon as she thought the coast was clear, she exited Kublai Khan and headed south.

She truly had been going north, but she could head down to her bicycle and leave now. She didn't need to stay.

Although she hated the idea that she was letting a man chase her away from a good time.

She forced herself back into a few more galleries she'd been in already and ran into a surprising number of people she knew. Olivia hadn't come tonight, of course, but Natalie recognized a lot of Olivia's friends. Plus, she ran into Steve Stegner, George, Sugar, Marie, and even Mrs. Conner from the post office, who was dancing to some techno tunes in the Futuroso Gallery. Paige came late and finally introduced her to Tag Tagalieri. He was cute, but Natalie simply shot Paige a warning look and mouthed "the bet" at her.

As the night wound down, Natalie peeled off her shoes and wandered toward her beach-cruiser bicycle in the lower parking lot. She inhaled the salty, familiar scent of the cool ocean air as it tossed tendrils of hair across her cheeks and blew her dress around her legs.

As she threw her shoes and purse into the front basket, a figure sitting out in the sand caught her eye. *Is that . . . ?* She squinted harder through the dark and headed in that direction. The sand was cold beneath her bare feet as she drew closer.

"Elliott?"

The wind swept his hair in front of his eyes as he turned his head. "Natalie! We keep running into each other."

"What are you doing here? Where's Stephanie?"

"We saw her ex in the Kokopelli Gallery and they . . . uh . . . rekindled, I guess. Behind one of the Chinese tapestries." The moonlight bounced off the ocean and illuminated his sad smile.

"Oh, I'm sorry." She bent her legs beneath her and sank into the sand beside him. "That sucks."

"It's okay. I wasn't very interested in her anyway." He threw a piece of driftwood out toward the water. "Maybe I'm off the hook."

The waves crashed wildly in front of them. Natalie glanced at the ocean. The beach was always peaceful at this time of night, the water so dark it seemed a black hole for secrets that you might want to whisper and be absolved of by morning. The only sounds to interrupt were the waves rolling forward and hissing back, and some crickets chirping in the distance, up by the sidewalk.

She swept some of the sand to the side and relaxed beside him. He had his arms wrapped around his knees, his ankles crossed. His shoes sat in the sand. The pot of daisies lay pathetically nearby, getting sand blown into them.

"Oh!" She rescued them and shook some of the sand out. They were a gorgeous, vibrant berry color. "Stephanie didn't take these at all then?"

"No. Do you want them?"

"Oh—I couldn't. You should bring them home."

"Honestly, I might forget to water them. You take them."

"Really?"

"Absolutely."

She tucked them into her side. It was cute that Elliott didn't like cut flowers. She'd always felt a little sad about them, too. These live daisies would look pretty planted outside the window of Olivia's new nursery.

"So, you weren't really smitten with her?" she asked.

"Not really."

"What usually causes you to be smitten?"

He looked up at her, as if surprised by the question. "I haven't felt smitten in a while."

"Do you date much?"

"No."

"Why not?"

"Work."

"You'd rather work than date?"

He gave a little smile at that. "It's easier to figure out gene sequences than to figure out women."

Natalie smiled back and watched the ocean for a minute. "What exactly do you do, Elliott?"

"I'm a microbiologist," he said. "I study virulence factors in pathogenic bacteria."

Natalie blinked. "And that's easier than dating?"

"Infinitely." The smile grew sexier.

Natalie cleared her throat. "So what does 'studying virulence factors in pathogenic bacteria' mean, exactly?"

"Virulence factors are molecules that tell you about the bacteria, so you can study them and make correlations. Like if the sea lions that have a certain gene are getting sicker or not responding to meds. There's such a huge outbreak here, so I came to have a lot of samples to study. But my friend Jim is . . . well . . ." He slumped back and stared out at the ocean.

"Jim is what?"

"Never mind. I've got to knock this off."

"Knock what off?"

"Talking like this. My sister told me to stop talking like a geek. Especially on dates. This can get boring very quickly."

"We're not on a date."

"Of course." He winked. "Mancation."

"Yes."

Natalie didn't want to admit how cute he looked right now. Or how many times she'd questioned her mancation already. Because of him. If she admitted any of that to herself, the bet was over. So she dove back into denial and tried to ignore the small flutters in her stomach.

"I find you interesting," she suddenly blurted.

He lifted an eyebrow.

"Or, I mean, *it*," Natalie stammered. "Your *job*. I find your *job* interesting." Why was she blabbering? This wasn't going to help her denial at all. At this point, denial might require a zip for her lips. Or a blindfold. Or an ejector seat to jettison her butt out of there.

Amusement played along his features as he looked at her more carefully. "Seriously?"

"Seriously."

"So you think it's okay that I talk about my job on dates then?"

She took a deep breath. "I think your sister is wrong on this one. I think you should be able to talk about what you love and feel passionate about, and if they don't find it interesting, then maybe they're not right for you."

The waves crashed into the blackness again as he contemplated that.

She shook a little more sand out of the flowers so she wouldn't have to meet his gaze and be befuddled by that quirk of his mouth.

He nodded slowly. "Thanks."

"So who's your next date?" she asked with as much enthusiasm as she could muster. Denial also demanded that she stick to her plan of helping him if she could.

"I think her name is Betsy. Or Becky?"

"Becky Huffington?"

"Nell didn't say her whole name."

"Science teacher? She's writing a paper about the telescope on the hill?"

"That sounds right."

"Huh." Natalie stared out into the ocean.

Becky actually *would* be a good date for Elliott. She was one of Olivia's friends—smart, kind, funny. Her long-term boyfriend had died in a scuba-diving accident two years ago and everyone had been encouraging her to move on. She was in her midthirties—maybe a little old for Elliott—but Natalie could picture them perfectly together. She took a deep breath and ignored the twinge of jealousy that shot through her.

"If it's Becky Huffington, you'll do fine," she finally admitted. "You can probably talk science all night long, and she'll gobble it up."

"Is that right?" Elliott turned his shoulders toward her. "Nell said she saved the best for last."

"Yeah, definitely . . . I could see that."

"Do you think she'd like all the things the Colonel mentioned? The flowers, all that?"

"Um, yeah, actually." Natalie thought about how Becky had always had an old-fashioned gracefulness. "I think she would. Here—give her these." Natalie thrust the flowers back at him. Suddenly she wasn't in the mood for them anymore. Becky would take her new flowers, her new friend. He would probably tell *her* she had intelligent eyes.

"No, you keep them." He pushed them back. "They reminded me of you anyway. I asked specifically for gerbera daisies."

Natalie raised her eyebrow. "Really?"

"I figured you had good taste."

"I think all women love gerbera daisies." Another competitive streak flashed through her, and she tucked the flowers closer to her hip. She shouldn't take them, but now she wanted to keep one thing from Elliott before he met Becky. Which didn't make sense, but there it was. "Thank you."

He was looking at her intensely. "Should I pick her up at the door? Do you think she'd be amenable to that?"

"Yeah. She's rather traditional. Plus, then you get to bring her home and offer one of those good-night kisses." Natalie tried to throw a friendly grin into that one, but it came out feeling a little lopsided.

Elliott shot her another grin. "Sorry about that earlier. The Colonel can be a little pushy. I didn't mean to make things awkward."

"I don't know if I'd call it awkward, exactly. You definitely know what you're doing in that department."

Elliott wouldn't meet her eyes, but she thought she saw him smile.

"Anyway, I think Becky will be in good hands with your first-date skills. And the Colonel's advice. But she's old-fashioned enough that you probably shouldn't push past the front door. I don't know if Becky would sleep with anyone on the first date."

"Oh, yeah. I would never . . ." Elliott shook his head.

Natalie turned more toward him and marveled at his clear discomfort at the topic of sex. This guy was adorable.

"You don't sleep around on first dates?" Natalie didn't know what was propelling her to push this conversation, but suddenly she was intensely curious.

"I . . . uh . . . *no*." He shook his head. "I have um . . . firm . . . uh, instructions. Firm instructions. I'm uh . . . no. No sex on these blind dates. Instructions from my sister."

"Well, that's smart. Too close together? Too many girls?"

His ears were bright red now, visible even in the moonlight. "Um . . . yeah. Too uh . . . too many of her friends . . . It would just be . . ." He pulled out his phone and looked at the time. "I should be going."

Natalie swept her feet underneath her and hastily followed Elliott to a standing position.

She didn't really want to leave. Sitting out here with the ocean crashing in front of them, holding berry-colored gerbera daisies that Elliott said reminded him of her, and watching him blush while he stammered about sex was more charming than she cared to admit, but she probably should be getting back. She swept sand out of the lace on her dress.

"Let me walk you." He scooped up his shoes.

"No, I have my bicycle. Plus, I should check to see if Paige is ready to leave, too."

"Are you sure? I'd love to walk with you."

She looked up at him—at the way the wind was whipping his hair into a mess over his eyes, at his hand casually in his trouser pocket, relaxed now that the topic of conversation was off him—and thought she truly would like that.

But . . . mancation, Natalie.

Maybe Paige was right to laugh at her. Maybe she couldn't last three weeks.

"That's okay. Good night, Elliott," she finally said, turning to walk away up the dune.

She thought about turning back, to see if he was still looking at her. It was the first time she'd ever hoped for such a thing. All her life she'd hidden under menswear and clunky clothes and men's hats, hoping to *keep* men from looking at her. But those were men who weren't seeing her for who she was—only for what she looked like, and what they might like to do to her. But this man—this man was different. He thought she had intelligent eyes. Her hair color reminded him of a place where he grew up. He might want to be her friend. He didn't sleep with women on the first date. He wanted something more. And the idea that he might find "more" in her thrilled her.

And she hoped he was looking right at her.

As her bare feet pulled through the sand at the very top of the hill, Natalie thought once more about turning to check.

Then her hope and confidence slid away. She resisted looking back. Because she didn't want to know he was already turned toward the ocean, probably thinking of "the best for last" Becky.

She put the daisies that weren't really hers in the basket of her beach cruiser, knocked her kickstand with her bare foot, and—although she could almost feel his eyes on her—pedaled away before she could check.

Because disappointment sucked.

Elliott watched Natalie all the way up the street, her 1920s dress flapping in the wind behind her, her hips dipping heavily left, then heavily right, to pedal her bike in her bare feet.

Damn, she was cute.

And incredibly sexy. He couldn't remember the last time he'd sat so close to a woman he'd found so sexy.

Maybe Ashley Thomas? In tenth grade? Ashley had sat next to him in English class and once asked for a pencil, and he'd spilled his lunch all over her—homemade by Grandma—including the gravy packed for his cold chicken. He'd scrambled to clean it up, accidentally touched her thigh, and she'd shrieked and pushed him away, yelling "Pervert!" at the top of her lungs. He'd never been able to look at her since. He was so glad when he'd switched schools a few weeks later.

Or then there was the time he stood by one of the Notre Dame cheerleaders at a football game and—in his gawking—hadn't realized he'd put his sweatshirt on inside out. She'd smiled at him, checking him out, and he'd thought it was because she liked his build. When he'd gotten home and had seen the inside stitching in the mirror, which looked like some kind of insane heart, he'd realized why she'd made such a quick getaway.

But Natalie didn't make him feel like a misfit. He had to give her that. Even with all his stammering through an unintelligible admission about how little dating he did and how little sex he had—had he seriously admitted all that?—her expression had managed to look like one of interest more than pity. And for that he'd be forever grateful to her.

Thoughts of her kindness carried him all the way back to his place. And then they mingled with one or two sexier thoughts of her that he allowed himself for brief interludes. The sexier thoughts mostly involved the glimpse of a beautiful thigh he'd caught when she'd stood up from the sand, along with the hint of some lacy underwear, and how the curve of her bottom had made him almost hyperventilate.

But she deserved better than to have him lusting after her. She was trying to be a friend, and the least he could do was respond in kind.

He forced himself back to work. And back to thoughts of his sea lions. And one or two brief thoughts about how he'd approach this date with Becky tomorrow. When his thoughts began drifting toward Natalie again, as they inevitably did, he forced himself back.

It was best to stay grounded in reality and logic.

CHAPTER 10

When Natalie woke the next morning, the first thing she saw were the berry-colored gerbera daisies on her nightstand, and she wanted to smile and roll back and think of Elliott giving them to her, but she didn't.

Because he hadn't really bought them for her.

And she wasn't his date.

And she was on a mancation.

And he was going out with Becky Huffington tonight.

"Aunt Nattie!" Lily bounded on her bed as the springs groaned their dismay. "It's time to get up!" Lily had come along with four stuffed animals and a soft Elsa doll, all tucked under her arms. "Guess what day it is?"

Natalie rolled over. "What day?"

"Sea lion day!" A few more squeaky-bed bounces confirmed her joy.

All Natalie could do was groan. She'd have to go to bed earlier to get used to this schedule. It wasn't even Friday yet of the very first week, and she was already crushed from this nanny gig.

"All right, let's get ready. School first."

Natalie dropped Lily off at school with several oohs and aahs at the fifteen crayon drawings Lily had done of the three little sea lions, then multiple promises that they'd see the pups after pickup today. Then Natalie drove through the canyon in Olivia's golf cart to her other job.

It was Zumba day at Casas del Sur. Steve Stegner explained that the ladies had lost their usual Zumba instructor, Cheryl, who was getting married and moving to Tahiti, and they wondered if Natalie might fill in.

She rushed down the hall to the ten a.m. class.

"I haven't had time to study the DVD yet," Natalie told Doris, who met her in the doorway.

"It's okay, dear, we know the routine." Doris patted Natalie's arm as she pulled her into the room. Tiny bells—lined all the way around Doris's brightly colored belly-dancer skirt—jingled as she took each barefooted step. "We just need you to help us with the music equipment. I can handle my phone, but those MP3 players confuse the heck out of me."

The room was filled with twenty senior citizens, about seventy years on up, who all wore jingling scarves around their hips and colorful dance clothes. They were all shapes and sizes, and they all moved at different paces—some practicing slow, simple samba steps in the corner. All were barefoot.

Natalie found the music they were looking for on the MP3, connected the speakers through Bluetooth, and adjusted the volume for Doris, who took her place at the front of the room and shouted out instructions. "Now salsa, ladies! Now merengue!"

Doris was impressive. Although she moved fairly slowly, she seemed sure and steady in her bare feet, knocking her hip out at all the right moments, moving her limbs as if they were made of water. Natalie found herself staring and wanting to dance along.

After the last song, the women whooped and high-fived. The energetic activity seemed to have taken ten years off each of their flushed, smiling faces, and they all moved toward the door with their water bottles, hugging one another and giving more high fives.

As Natalie turned the system off and wound up the speaker cord, Doris and Marie approached from the side, dabbing at their foreheads with embroidered hand towels.

"Thanks, dear! I couldn't figure out how to operate that thing," Doris said.

"But you sure do a mean Zumba," Natalie said.

Doris waved her hand as if to flutter the compliment away.

"Were you a professional dancer, Doris?"

"I was, dear."

Marie glanced adoringly at her friend. "She's too humble. She was the founder of Madame Zora's Studios."

"The national ones?" Natalie asked.

"Yep."

"*You* were Madame Zora?"

Doris actually blushed. "One and the same. I danced with the Boston Ballet for ten years, then started the studio when I was twenty-seven."

"Wow," Natalie whispered. Twenty-seven? That was Natalie's age. As she watched Doris nodding her thanks to all her friends, Natalie thought about what lifetimes these women and men had lived before moving here. The *Boston Ballet*? Then starting a studio that went national and had been on late-night commercials Natalie's entire life? And the Colonel and his years in World War II? And their friend Trummy playing with Les Brown and His Band of Renown? They must all feel as though they've lived nine lives. But they'd committed to their passions early on to build rich lives for themselves.

Doris and Marie scooped up their belongings, the speakers, and the MP3 player, then shoved half of it into Natalie's hands.

"We've got to get out of here. The poker class is next, and they need to cover the mirrors. Did you have fun last night at the art walk, dear? I thought I saw you talking to Dr. Sherman."

Natalie juggled the speakers in her arms. "Yes, but he was on a date."

Doris tsked, waving the thought off. "That didn't seem like much of a date. That tiny Stephanie isn't right for him at all."

Natalie slid her eyes over to Doris. "You don't think?"

"Not at all. Dr. Sherman needs someone more outgoing. Smart but a little wilder."

"Really? He's so shy himself."

"Exactly. Opposites attract, you know. Let's go this way. We need to bring all this stuff up to June at the lobby entrance."

Natalie hoisted everything in her arms and followed Doris, still thinking about the opposites comment. "But you don't want to meet someone too opposite," she said. "I mean, Dr. Sherman's so shy he might not like to leave the house. And Stephanie seems sort of the same. Maybe he needs someone like her."

"No." Doris shook her head fiercely. "He's young. The younger you are, the more opposite you can handle. And the more opposite, the better. Right, Marie?"

"That's right," Marie said.

"Marrying your opposite brings you to the center," Doris said.

"The center?" Natalie asked.

"Where the balance is. No one should go through life being too shy or too outgoing. Or too conservative or too liberal. Or too stingy or too much of a spendthrift. Being in the center is where it's beautiful and where you can finally find your peace. So meeting your opposite, and learning from each other, brings you there. And the sooner you get there, the happier you'll be."

"I don't know," Natalie said. She was young, but if she met someone who was that opposite of her, she might want to rip his head off.

"Trust me, dear. I know these things."

As they neared the next corner, bells jingling, they were almost sideswiped by the Colonel coming around the corner of the hallway, heading toward the lobby desk.

"Hello, ladies," he said. "I was just coming to find you."

"What's going on?" Marie asked.

"I got a call from the Friends of the Sea Lion center. Apparently they're seeing another increase of sea lion rescues this week, and they want us to come in today and start extra training."

Steve Stegner hustled over from the lobby counter, where he'd apparently overheard the exchange. "No, no, we have to stick to the schedule, Colonel."

"Schedule, schmedule," the Colonel growled. "I'll drive."

"Colonel, your doctor said you shouldn't be driving anymore," Steve said.

"AT NIGHT. My doctor said no driving *at night*. I can drive during the day." The Colonel looked back at Natalie. "He's just jealous because my cart's souped up to go faster than his."

"How will you get back, Colonel?" Steve asked from behind them. "It'll be dark."

The Colonel stretched to his full height, and his face took on a fierceness that looked like something that would have made soldiers shiver in their boots.

But Natalie put her hand between them. "I'll drive. My own cart. I'm off in fifteen minutes, and I have to take my niece there this afternoon anyway, so I'll take as many as will fit."

Steve opened his mouth, but Natalie guessed his argument. "And I'll drive them back," she added.

Steve closed his mouth and barely hid his glare toward the Colonel. Then he finally shrugged. "If you're sure it's okay."

"All systems go!" the Colonel said, turning and pointing over his head toward the entrance. At the rate they were moving, Natalie would probably beat them to the parking lot.

But she wondered about Elliott and Jim and the sea lion influx.

This should be another interesting afternoon . . .

Elliott followed Jim around and listened to all his instructions for how to handle an influx: put extra towels down in the incoming room, make sure formula was being made, call for reserve volunteers. They'd risen from four incoming sea lions per day, four times a week—already a high number—to five incoming sea lions per day, five times a week. And Jim was looking nervous.

"Any ideas yet on what this is?" he asked Elliott as they moved eight baby sea lions from one room to another. They didn't have enough crates or gurneys to go around, or enough volunteers, so the two of them were simply lifting the animals in their gloved arms and hauling them from one room to the next.

Elliott wiped a line of sweat from his hairline and blinked against his salty contacts. A crew of newer volunteers had already been promoted to rescue team, and they'd been out almost all day, responding to calls all over the island. A smaller crew was inside, handling intake and feeding. In this room, Jim and Elliott were lifting each pup onto a table to have a symbol shaved onto its belly so the crew could identify the pups while they were in the center. The whole team was exhausted. They'd been doing this all morning.

"These four were all found near Fruit Hill, so let's call this one Bananas, and those ones Apple, Pear, and Peachy." Elliott pointed them out to the young vet-in-training who was doing the shaving. She wrote each name in her ledger, next to the Greek symbol she'd shave on their sides to correlate with their names. Elliott held Bananas's flippers aside so the vet could do her work. Normally Jim did this part, but Jim had headed for the front room, busy on the phones trying to get additional loads of sardines and anchovies brought in, plus trying to find a night crew who could blend the fish into formula for the dehydrated pups. Jim was smart to plan ahead and get all the right people in place this early in the season.

"Dr. Sherman! What are you doing in the intake room?" Doris tottered to where Elliott was still holding onto Bananas and reached for her own pair of gloves, presumably to take over flipper duty. Behind her trailed the Colonel, George, and—much to Elliott's surprise—Natalie Grant and her little niece.

"I brought a whole crew for you," the Colonel growled from the back. "Where do you want us?"

"I see." Elliott had a hard time tearing his eyes away from Natalie. She had on her cargo capris, with a strappy pair of sandals, and still wore her Casas del Sur T-shirt, which hugged her in all the right places. A sporty ball cap sat on her head; her long braid escaped from underneath and fell heavily down her right breast. She gave him an intimate smile, and his whole soul seemed to settle.

"I, uh . . ." He tried to remember what question he was answering. "I think Jim has plans for all of you. I think he needs help on the phones today." He nodded to Doris, who was good there. "And he might need help here, doing intake." He glanced at George.

Elliott hoped Jim would put Natalie with him, wherever that was. He'd love to have her assist him in anything he did today. Although . . . *Come back to reality, man,* he chastised himself. Natalie's niece probably just wanted to see her three intakes.

"Are you here to see Larry, Curly, and Moe?" he asked the little girl.

She was so cute—she had little braids, just like her aunt, and thick-lensed glasses like he'd always had.

She shoved the glasses higher on her nose and nodded enthusiastically, bouncing her knees against a small plastic case that looked like a toy doctor's kit.

Elliott came to his senses and realized he should probably get her out of this particular room, where the incoming sea lions hadn't even been tested yet.

"Let me take you to see them." He hoisted the pup Bananas into his arms and inclined his head in the direction they needed to go. "Follow me," he said, glancing down at Natalie's niece.

He sure hoped her aunt would follow.

Natalie tucked Lily into her side and trailed behind Elliott into the next room, where she couldn't seem to tear her eyes away from him. He carefully lowered the baby sea lion he was holding like a sack of potatoes, his biceps straining all the way to the ground.

"We had to start a new room because our usual rooms are full," he said, surveying the surroundings. "These guys will get bottle-fed next, and then we'll draw a little blood so I can study it."

He turned toward Natalie, but he seemed to remember that Lily was in the room. "But your three rescues are doing great," he told her. "You got them to us just in time. Let me take you to see them."

Elliott didn't have his lab coat on today and instead wore cargo shorts, flip-flops, and a T-shirt, as if he'd just come off the beach. Large yellow rubber gloves stretched up along his muscled forearms. Having not seen him in so few clothes before, Natalie hadn't been aware of what upper-body strength he had.

"They're in here." He opened a large windowed door for them at the end of the hallway and ushered them both inside.

The room held a small aboveground pool on one side, surrounded by wet concrete and a fence, where seven small pups lounged in a dapple of sunshine that came through a west-facing window.

"That's Larry, that's Moe, and that's Curly there, over on the side. These other pups have been here longer, but Larry, Curly, and Moe have almost caught up already." He squatted down on his haunches beside Lily next to the fence. "They're still recovering and still a little weak, so they're not as active as you might be expecting, but they're definitely doing better."

They did look fuller than Natalie remembered finding them, and not as gray. Their coats were turning a healthy brown.

"They do look better," Natalie said.

Lily frowned and took her stethoscope out of her doctor's case. "Can I check them?"

"Oh—no, they're wild animals," Elliott said. "I know they look cute, but we like to keep them wild, and we try to minimize their involvement with humans. That's why we wear these." He held his gloves up. "If we get them too used to human touch, or human care, they won't be able to take care of themselves in the ocean, and that would be bad for them." He made a cute sad face to Lily, but she was having none of it. Her sad face was for real.

Natalie stepped closer and ran Lily's braids through her hands. "They have to learn how to live with other sea lions, hon."

Lily looked as if she was going to burst into tears.

"But you can still help," Elliott added. "Do you want to make their formula?"

Her face cleared, and she bobbed her head energetically, looking at Natalie once for approval.

"Sure. You can do that," Natalie told her.

"I have to warn you—the formula's made of fish. It doesn't smell very good. But you get to wear an official volunteer apron."

Lily nodded again with enthusiasm.

"Follow me."

Elliott set Lily up with a volunteer who outfitted her in an apron and gloves, and Lily looked as though she was going to lose her mind with joy.

Natalie watched them both, not sure which one she found most amusing. But she definitely knew which one she found most alluring: Elliott's confident movements, his backward grins toward Natalie, his patient explanations to Lily, and the way his arms were flexing were suddenly making her heart quicken.

She finally had to look away.

"She's quite a little helper," he said, coming toward the back counter where Natalie stood. They both leaned against the stainless-steel top.

"She wants to be an emergency volunteer of some kind."

He nodded.

"Are you ready for your date tonight?" she blurted out. She didn't know what made her say that, but a tiny thread of jealousy was winding its way around her heart.

Her question was enough to sever the small connection he'd seemed to be trying to make. His smile became distant and forced. "I suppose," he said.

She wanted to kick herself.

"Are you excited about it?" she asked anyway. She'd become a glutton for punishment.

He watched Lily for a few seconds, then glanced at her with half-lidded eyes. "Are you still offering tips?"

The jealousy quickly faded into the background as a sexual jolt sent a shiver down her arms. Damn, what temporary lunacy had ever propelled her to offer such a thing? One should definitely not offer to help a man whose biceps one was starting to notice.

"Sure," she squeaked. "What do you want to know?"

"The pressure's on about my appearance now. Nell says Becky's really sophisticated and knows fashion. I have a feeling I'm doomed on this one." His smile let her know that he wasn't that worried about it.

"Becky is into fashion, yes." Natalie wondered if she should also mention Becky's tendency toward low-cut necklines and the exaggerated Southern drawl that she pulled out for sex appeal, but she decided against it.

"The Colonel says no 'dungarees.' I've got that." They both laughed. "Nell says wear contacts and leave my *Star Trek* watch at home. And—"

"You have a *Star Trek* watch?"

"It's a nice watch—I mean, it's not plastic or anything. I—"

"Is it one of the collectibles?"

"It is, as a matter of fact."

"It's not the TAG Heuer one, is it?"

He smiled. "It is. I won a his-and-hers set on a game show."

"You were on a game show?"

"*Twenty-Nine Questions*. All my dirty laundry is coming out now."

"Oh my God, that's great."

She watched the ruddiness take over his neck again and stared at the cute smile he had when he was embarrassed. Becky was a lucky woman.

"I think you should wear what you want to wear, Elliott. And forget about the contacts. If these women can't accept you for who you are, or have an appreciation for a collectible *Star Trek* TAG Heuer, then they're not worth your time."

He nodded. "I like the way you think, Natalie Grant."

The cool air from the sea lion pools warmed up just a little as Natalie let the coziness of that comment settle within her.

"Would you like me to give you my cell number in case something goes wrong and you want to call me for tips?" she asked. It wasn't the best reason to give a guy your phone number, but it would do. She wanted to lengthen their new connection in any way she could.

He gave her another of those sexy sidelong glances. "I don't expect to be calling you for advice from my date, Natalie."

She nodded. Of course.

"But I'll take your number." He pulled his cell phone out and punched in the new number she dictated.

It felt like a bridge was crossed—she and Elliott were now officially friends.

When she and Lily left a bit later, she tried to keep her eyes off the forearm muscles she was noticing too much and focus again on their new trust.

"Good luck tonight," she said at the door.

"Thanks." He stared down at her curiously with a strange smile on his lips.

She grabbed Lily's hand and headed down the brick walkway, trying to ignore all the duplicitous feelings ricocheting around her heart.

She really liked him. But she couldn't date him. And she wanted him to be happy. And he very well might be happy with Becky. But she couldn't help feeling stabs of jealousy . . .

Clearly, she still had a ways to go on this selfless-female-friend thing.

But she knew she could do this.

CHAPTER 11

Elliott approached the tiki-style restaurant at fifteen minutes till eight and made his way through the crowd that was spilling out onto the sidewalk, looking around briefly for a single woman who looked as though she was on a blind date. But she probably wasn't there yet.

He was surprised he was so early, given the fact he'd stalled as long as possible to have Natalie around. After enjoying every minute of showing her and Lily the center, while still handling two more intakes, he'd rushed home and showered, changed into his date clothes, irrigated his eyes with some lens cleaner, and flew to the Wanderer.

Now he slid through the crowd sideways to get to the reservation desk.

"Reservations for two?" he said. "Elliott Sherman."

The receptionist looked at her tablet. "You're early. Would you like to wait at the bar?"

Elliott found an empty bar stool at the long bar, which ran down the side of the room, and tapped his fingers on the wooden top. He ordered a Maker's Mark, neat, and sat and waited, looking around at the various couples. His mind had kept drifting to Natalie the whole time he'd been getting ready. *Does she like to eat shellfish? Did she grow up with both parents? Did she spend a lot of time on the island? Does she like the smell of aftershave?* Now, though, he needed to focus on at least giving this last date a chance.

He glanced again at his *Star Trek* watch. He'd decided to wear it. Because Natalie was right. He was tired of thinking he had to alter himself so dramatically for a woman to like him. If she liked him, she liked him. If she didn't, she didn't. Once he'd presented what he thought was his best, most respectful self—he'd even worn a tie tonight, but only because he liked ties—she had to accept him from there. He would have gone back to his much-more-comfortable glasses, too, but he still had to get them fixed. He'd bring them to the shop tomorrow. People were just going to have to accept him the way he was.

Another ten minutes went by, and Elliott asked the bartender for a pen so he could take a few gene-sequencing notes on a cocktail napkin to relax himself. When a full twenty minutes had gone by, though, Elliott began to think that Becky clearly couldn't be good for him. Who came twenty minutes late to a first date? Plus, he wanted to get home and compare the formula he'd just jotted down with one he'd read about in a journal the other night.

Just as he was taking his last swig, ready to swing himself off the bar stool and maybe give up for tonight, a woman walked in who could only be Becky Huffington.

She wore a sparkly low-cut dress and wriggled her fingers in hello from across the bar. She held a pale-pink bag over her elbow that had a Chihuahua poking out the side.

Although he didn't know what kind of person brought a Chihuahua to a bar on a date—and twenty minutes late at that—he took a deep breath and bolstered his reserve.

This was starting to feel like a challenge.

And Elliott decided he wanted to win.

Natalie curled up on the love seat in her flannel pajamas and told herself how relaxing this was.

Lily was in bed. Olivia was in bed. Paige had fallen asleep on the couch. And Natalie was planning on getting caught up with a few romantic comedies she'd wanted to see. She clicked the remote and repeated to herself that this was yet another wondrous advantage to being on a mancation—catching up on her Netflix list.

It was good to have a little mancation pep talk with herself. She'd started slipping this afternoon. (A man with roped forearms could do that to a gal.) But she needed to pull herself together. The twinges of jealousy she felt every time she thought about Elliott out with Becky right now were not becoming. Or appropriate. Or even healthy. Was she really as weak as Paige suspected? Not quite able to handle a full mancation, so clinging to any scraps of attention she could get from any man at all—especially one she wouldn't normally look twice at, and one she supposedly only wanted to be friends with? And was she desperate to have *this* man pay attention because he was so uninterested in her? Pathetic. She needed to reset her priorities and remind herself that she could certainly survive three weeks without a boyfriend.

She found a Reese Witherspoon movie, pulled out some notes and her laptop, and jotted down a few ideas she'd had for the Senior Prom. It had been eons since she'd brought work home. It felt good to be so excited about something again. She called up an old spreadsheet template she'd seen her mother use and organized some of the details the seniors were struggling with. She spent an hour looking through catering plans, then another hour planning a music list.

By the end of the night, she'd almost entirely dismissed Elliott's forearms from her mind.

And almost, even, the fact that they were likely wrapped around another woman right now.

Elliott hesitated in Becky Huffington's doorway and watched her saunter in ahead of him as she corralled a bunch of tiny dogs that were yelping at her happily. She moved them toward a side room and motioned for him to come inside, heading down a hallway that looked as if it might lead to some bedrooms.

For a second, he hesitated. An image of Natalie leaped to his mind. But that was ridiculous. Natalie was not his. Natalie would never be his. And this date with Becky might actually have a future. So even though his heart wasn't 100 percent in it, he stepped over the threshold and glanced around the corner to see Becky's swaying hips heading back his way into the living room.

"Would you like something to drink?" she asked, moving toward a crystal decanter set up on a wet bar by the window.

"No, I'm good." Elliott sneezed.

He'd had a nice dinner, although he'd seemed to be allergic to the candle on the table. But other than that, he'd had an okay time. He'd learned a lot about her by the second course. She seemed perfect, really—pretty, sexy, smart. She threw a Southern drawl into the conversation from time to time, which seemed to come out of nowhere, but he could maybe get used to that. The dog coming along was weird, but he'd learned his name was Chip, and Becky was just genuinely into dogs. She volunteered at a rescue center, which Elliott found admirable. He kept trying to crack jokes, and they kept falling flat. But he'd survive. He'd thought of how Natalie would have laughed at his cell-interfusion joke, but then he'd rubbed his itchy eyes, forced Natalie from his mind, and had tried to focus again.

By the end of dessert, Becky had given him directions to her place, and he'd followed in his golf cart to her house high on a hill on the far side of town.

At her door, she'd asked him inside and had yanked him playfully by his tie. There was no denying her intent.

"Are you sure you don't want something to drink?" she asked. "I have gin, scotch, and vodka, and I can make you anything."

"I'm good for now."

"All right then, I'm going to change into something more comfortable," Becky said with enough coo and innuendo and weird Southern lilt that no one could mistake where this was going.

He watched her sashay around the corner, and his heart went into overdrive. His throat felt as if it was closing seriously now. He'd never thought of himself as the type of guy who did things like this—slept with one woman while thinking of another. He usually didn't have that many options, or that many women in his periphery.

He rubbed his stupid itching eyes, coughed to open his throat, and finally caved and poured himself a scotch from her decanter.

The scotch didn't do much for his closing throat, but it did still his nerves for a second. Enough to lean casually against the wet bar and enjoy the lights of the city for a second. And then to sneeze again. And then to swallow around what felt like a fur ball in his throat. And then to see a little dog that came wagging around his feet. And then to come to the gradual realization that . . .

Oh damn.

He was allergic to these Chihuahuas.

He tried to swallow again, then gripped his throat. He had to get outside. He fumbled with the lock and frantically threw himself into the fresh air. The cold hit him in the face, but he sucked in as much freshness as he could, willing his throat to open back up.

When Becky finally came into the living room in an elegant, loungy-flowy pants thing, she took one look at Elliott through the glass and came flying out beside him.

"What's wrong?"

"Do you happen to have an antihistamine of any kind?" He squeezed the words out. He was holding on to the balcony rail, trying to balance his highball glass and taking deep breaths.

"No, I don't think I do," she said, rubbing his back.

He tried to move out of her grasp, because it really wasn't helping, and then rolled off a few brand names that he managed to squeeze out of his windpipe, but she kept shaking her head.

"Call Natalie!" she finally said.

"Natalie?" Elliott wheezed. Although the name had been on his mind all night, it felt weird hearing it come from Becky's lips right now.

"Yes, Natalie. You said you knew her here on the island. She's probably staying at Olivia's cottage, Olivia has one of the faster golf carts, and Olivia always has things like that. Lily has lots of allergies."

"No. I can just stop at a drugstore or something. There's one down near my place. I'll just—"

"Mr. Gurley closes the drugstore at midnight. He's gone. Here, I'll call her!" Becky twirled toward the door, but Elliott shot out his arm and stopped her. Last thing he needed was for his date to call Natalie Grant for help.

The least embarrassing path seemed to be calling her himself, although he still didn't know what to say. Maybe he could somehow make his allergy attack sound smooth. He reluctantly shuffled his phone out of his pocket and dialed.

"Elliott?" Natalie whispered worriedly into the phone. "Is everything okay?"

He wheezed out his predicament, asked if she had any antihistamines, and felt heat rise around his collar when Becky grabbed the phone and asked Natalie in a panicked, shouting voice if she could deliver them quick.

He grabbed his phone back. "No!" he said. "It's late. I'll come to you. I feel better already."

"I'll be right there." And she hung up.

Elliott was sure his embarrassment couldn't get much worse, so he concentrated on taking deep breaths, already feeling better out of the dander-ridden house, and leaned against the balcony. "I'm sorry" was all he could squeeze out to pretty Becky in the flowy pants. He just wanted to be swallowed up by the sagebrush surrounding the house, but instead he made his way across the balcony, leaped over the rail, landed in the brush, and walked around the side so he wouldn't have to walk through the dander house again.

Becky met him at the front with a bottle of water and sat with him on the porch. He took a gulp to make sure his throat was still working and immediately felt better, although he sneezed twice when Becky got too close. She said she'd go inside and change.

He begged her not to bother. "We'll do this another time. I'll be more prepared."

"Thank you for dinner, Elliott. And for an eventful night. I'm so sorry about the dogs." She kissed him on the cheek and headed into the house.

A second later, Natalie came bouncing up the driveway in her red golf cart, then ran toward him with her arm held out, ready to drop the antihistamines into his waiting fingers. "Did she leave you alone out here?" she asked incredulously.

"I'm fine. I feel much better outside, and I kept sneezing around her. You didn't have to come all the way out here."

Seeing her again solidified his embarrassment. She'd changed into pajamas—flannel-looking things with cartoons all over them—and he was sorry he'd called her out of bed. Or maybe not. He couldn't stop staring at her, even in an oversized, man's-style top and pants, and huge floppy slippers.

"Are those pieces of toast?" he asked, inspecting the cartoons more carefully.

"I like toast."

He downed the antihistamines with the bottled water and inspected the toast more carefully. He couldn't get over her. She just made him want to smile.

She seemed to ignore all that and furrowed her eyebrows, directing him back to her cart. "Here, let me take you home."

"Natalie, seriously, I'm much better now." Although it felt good to have her hands on him, he was uncomfortable with her treating him like an invalid. He warred over whether or not to move out of her reach. He didn't want to. He liked being so close to her pieces of toast, and thinking about the fact that only one thin layer of flannel lay between him and her body. But . . . ultimately . . . his pride won out.

"I'm fine." He moved away from her babying.

"Let's just let the antihistamines do their work for a minute; then I'll let you go. You probably need fresh air. Do you want to walk a little?"

She pointed to a trail that ran from Becky's driveway and seemed to wind down the mountain. The surrounding trees and fresh night air looked appealing, and Elliott led the way, each step farther from Becky's house giving him more strength.

"I see you went with the *Star Trek* watch," she said.

"I did."

"It's really nice."

"I appreciate that you appreciate it."

She laughed as they reached a small outcropping with a large flat boulder in the center. Natalie climbed up, wriggling to the top in her floppy pajamas and slippers. Elliott hauled himself up the rock and sat beside her. It felt as if they were on top of the world, the wind whipping their hair around their faces, overlooking all the twinkling lights of the tourist town.

"Isn't everything beautiful up here?" she asked breathlessly, peering over the side of the hill.

He took in her flannel pants getting buffeted by the wind, her hair that was barely held together in a hasty half braid that looked as though she'd thrown it together before running out to the cart, the loose tendrils of auburn-brown flying about her temples, and her makeup-free face that had spots of color where the cold was touching her cheeks.

"Sure is," he finally said.

CHAPTER 12

Natalie tugged at her pajama-pant leg, crisscrossed her legs underneath her, and smiled back at Elliott.

He was so cute. She liked taking care of him. She could keep this mancation under perfect control when she was reacting to him as a sincere friend instead of a potential new boyfriend. And that she did. When his call came, her first instinct was to change into something presentable before hopping in the golf cart—her old way of thinking. But Elliott had been in serious trouble—she could hear the wheezing. So she'd simply grabbed the antihistamines, jumped in the cart, and came to help him without even glancing in the mirror. Without thinking of how to impress him. Her only thought was how to help. It was freeing.

Plus, he was on his dating quest, and she wasn't part of it. Just because his date ended in a semidisaster didn't mean Becky was finished with him. Becky's slinky pajamas that Natalie had gotten a glimpse of solidified that.

No, Natalie needed to stay focused on simply being Elliott's friend. He looked as if he could use one now.

"Aside from the ending, how did this date seem to go?" she finally asked.

"I don't expect a call soon."

"Oh, I do."

"The fact that I just stumbled through her bushes out her back patio because I'm apparently severely allergic to her dogs, which she rescues and loves more than anything, isn't a deal-breaker?"

"It could be. But the fact that she invited you over, invited you in, and had on her Sophia Loren lounge clothes makes me think it was going pretty well. How did she invite you in?"

"She just kind of . . ." Elliott waved his hand back toward the door. "I don't know, exactly. I didn't know what was happening."

"Lust, maybe?"

Elliott glanced up at her, looking almost ashamed. She didn't mean to make him feel bad. What man wouldn't follow sexy Becky into her bedroom if she asked?

She sighed and reminded herself to be a good friend. "I think you're doing great," she finally admitted.

He blinked up at her.

His phone buzzed loudly. Natalie stared at his trouser pocket. "That's her," she said confidently.

"No, it's not."

"It is. Check."

He pulled the phone out and lifted his eyebrows. A small grin made a dimple appear. "You're right."

"What is she saying?"

"She says, 'Had a great time'—*great* is in all caps—'and hope to see you again soon. Next time we'll go to your place.' Huh." He looked up at her, the surprise evident on his face. He gazed out across the vista as he tucked the phone away, clearly lost in thought about a possible next date. Natalie pushed aside her gut reaction toward jealousy and told herself she was being a better person if she could help Elliott out here.

"Okay, you can do this," she said. "I could tell she was interested in you. What's your next plan?"

"I don't have a next plan. I didn't even know I was moving to a next plan."

"Well, what's your standard second-date plan?"

"I, uh . . ." His hand flew into the air in exasperation. "I don't know. You tell me. What's a good plan?"

She forced herself to look at this selflessly, and to forget about how sexy he looked with his tie loosened around his neck like that and the start of a five o'clock shadow across his jaw. "Okay, she mentioned your place, so she's clearly ready to move things along. I think maybe dinner in, like you did for Alice and Caren. And serve a sexy dessert."

"A sexy dessert?"

"Something like strawberries and cream."

"You find strawberries and cream sexy?"

"It doesn't matter what I think. It's kind of a standard message. Strawberries equals sexy."

"Do I do something with the strawberries?" His mouth quirked up on one side.

"You could do something with the cream," she snapped.

His smile slipped a little, and his Adam's apple bobbed in a visible swallow.

What was wrong with her? She didn't like making him feel uncomfortable. But she also didn't like the slimy jealousy slithering through her veins right now and didn't know how to handle it. But she could. She was determined to be selfless.

She took a deep breath and tried again.

"And feel free to touch her throughout dinner."

Elliott glanced back up at her. "Does this involve the strawberries?" He cleared his throat.

"No. Touch her body, I mean. Her hand, her thigh. Depends on what you have access to during dinner. It sort of starts the whole foreplay process early."

"During dinner?"

"Of course. How good are you at foreplay?"

Elliott took a nervous swig of bottled water and looked away.

"Elliott?"

He shook his head.

"Are you okay?" Was his throat closing up again?

"I'm okay," he choked out.

"Is foreplay not your forte?" Natalie moved across the rock so she was positioned in front of him. If they were going to be friends, she could put this all on the line. It might be nice to speak for all womankind, actually, and instruct at least one good man on the art of dating and sex. She tucked her pajama legs underneath her. "It should be easy. Women have many erogenous zones, and you can touch any of them—some during dinner, and then . . . Well, some you should wait until you're naked."

Elliott swallowed again.

She crossed her legs tighter against her body. "Do you need me to tell you where they are?"

"I could use a refresher," his voice rasped.

"You're not going to get this kind of help from the Colonel, you know."

"Thank God."

"Do you want the during-dinner ones first, or do you want to skip right ahead to the while-naked ones?"

"We'd better start with dinner."

"Are you a pretty quick study?"

A wicked smile slowly turned the edges of his mouth. "I always ruined the curve."

Now it was her turn to catch her breath. She gulped and finally got hold of herself. "All right then. Wrists." She pointed. "Inside elbow." Pointed again. "And behind the knee. You can touch those spots during dinner. Try one, and if she doesn't pull away, feel free to try one more. Don't go with more than two or you'll seem desperate. Wrists are easy. You can gently stroke while you're talking to her at dinner. Kind of like this." She grabbed his hand and positioned it on the rock as if it were on a tabletop, then rubbed her thumb across it as she looked into his face. "See? You don't even have to watch what you're doing."

He stared at her fingertips. "Women like that?"

"Some do. Erogenous zones are different for everyone. If that doesn't get you far, you can try behind her knee, although this works best if you're sitting side by side, like watching TV or something." She scooted around so she was next to him and put her legs out in front of her. "Like this." She grabbed his hand and pressed his fingertips into the back of her knee. This was one of her personal favorites that no man seemed to ever get, so she was pleased to share the knowledge. For womankind and all.

"Here?" Elliott pressed once, then stroked gently, then . . . *mmm.* Natalie had to force herself to move away as his strokes began sending tingles through all her nerve endings. He definitely got it.

She cleared her throat. "Mmm, okay. Very good. Then. There we go." She moved farther away and took a couple of quick breaths. "Okay, then there's kissing, too. With clothes on, you can still kiss those same places, like wrists again." She held hers up. "Or back behind the ear, or along the back of the neck." She moved her braid and pointed.

"Should I try that?" He was staring at her neck.

"Now?"

He nodded.

"On me?"

He nodded again.

She glanced up toward Becky's house and was certain Becky couldn't see them from here. And she wasn't flirting, exactly. Was she? She wanted to be a good female friend. She didn't want to lose her bet with Paige. She was just teaching, right? Certainly, if she'd wanted to flirt with him tonight, she wouldn't have stayed in her toast pajamas. "Okay . . ."

Elliott turned toward her. Next thing she knew, he had his legs bent on either side of her and had her sitting between his knees. He gently moved her hair. She could feel his breath on her neck, right beneath her pajama collar, and she waited, holding her own, shivering a little in anticipation as he leaned closer.

"Here?" he mumbled.

He placed a delicious kiss at the slope of her shoulder, and a large shiver went straight into her scalp. *Damn.* Dr. Sherman had some kissing skills. "A little higher," she choked out.

Another kiss followed the first, this one at the base of her neck. Goose bumps covered her arms and ran up to her neck, but she hoped he couldn't see them in the dark.

"Here?" he mumbled again.

"A tad higher," she managed to squeak.

A third kiss landed in just the right spot—her favorite spot—right at the hollow behind her ear. The kiss was warm, with just enough tongue to make it almost seem like a lick, and enough to send goose bumps all over her body and a pull into every sexual nerve ending she had. She couldn't help but close her eyes and enjoy it this time, and she fought the moan that wanted to escape her throat.

"Good?" Elliott asked softly.

"Yes." Her answer came out breathless and embarrassing, and Elliott rewarded her—or maybe punished her—with another kiss, right there, in the same spot: warm tongue, cold night, his fingers pushing her hair aside, his breath along her neck. Her shoulders came up this time in a reluctant shiver, and she pushed herself away abruptly, holding him at bay.

She was almost afraid to meet his eyes, completely afraid to address the sexual awareness between them, afraid that she'd initiated it but he'd felt it, too. But when she finally lifted her eyelashes, he looked completely guileless.

"Was that okay?" he asked.

Unable to speak momentarily, she simply bobbed her head.

He pulled back, looking at her expectantly, waiting for the next instruction.

She took a couple of deep breaths.

"Okay then," she finally managed to say.

"What's next?" he prompted.

"Yes, yes, of course. Maybe . . . um . . . maybe we should continue this tomorrow? How are the antihistamines working, by the way?"

"Perfect. I feel much better."

"Good! Good. That's really good." She slid off the rock into the sage, rubbing her pajama arms against the wind that came up over the mountaintop. Or maybe against the goose bumps that still remained from Elliott's skillful kisses. Or maybe against the awareness that she wanted him *now*. Whatever. All she knew was that she needed to get the hell out of there before she knocked him down right on the rock and kissed the living daylights out of him. If he could kiss good-night like he'd proven yesterday in front of the Colonel, and kiss her neck like he'd proven just now, she couldn't imagine what other wonders he was capable of with that tongue.

"How about if we maybe do this tomorrow?" she asked. "I have to, um . . . get home and . . ."

Another shiver had her sprinting toward the carts. "I've got to go now, Elliott. I'm glad you feel better," she yelled over her shoulder.

He followed behind her, thanked her as she started her ignition, and lifted his hand as she rolled down the driveway.

Natalie floored her cart to its full twenty miles per hour all the way down the mountainside.

Elliott hung his hands on his hips and watched Natalie power toward the first turn on the mountain, dust swirling around all four tires.

He didn't know what, precisely, had just happened, or why she was running away, but he knew he was ready to break into a smile from ear to ear.

Because Natalie Grant had moaned.

Or hummed.

Or some kind of sound. Right beneath his lips. And it was positive. So positive, in fact, he'd kissed her again.

Of course, the second kiss was when she'd all but fled off the rock, but Elliott still considered it a positive sign. He'd made Natalie Grant moan.

Or hum.

Whatever.

The important point was that, whatever happened for the rest of his life, he'd always have that little moment of success.

He'd probably dream about it for the rest of his livelong days, in fact.

As soon as she turned the corner, he ran a hand through his hair and glanced up at the stars. This night had turned out to be not as bad as he'd thought.

He hopped in his own cart and concentrated on keeping his itching eyes open for the rest of the drive home.

At the base of the mountain, just before his driveway, he felt his phone buzzing again, and he pulled his cart into his garage, almost knocking down a set of bicycles and golf clubs the owner kept along the side. He scrambled to get his phone out, hoping it would be Natalie.

"Hello?" he said eagerly.

"Elliott, it's Becky."

His chest fell.

"You can put this number into your phone if you'd like." She gave a low, sultry laugh. "I was just calling to say I'm sorry again and hope you're feeling better."

"I am." He got out of the cart, carefully sidestepping the golf clubs he almost just ran over.

"Well, if you're feeling better, I was wondering if we could have a repeat date? This time it's on me. I'll be sure not to bring Chip, and I'll wear something that hasn't been near the dogs. We can go to my favorite Mexican food place right by the tourist dock—El Farolito? How about Saturday?"

Elliott stepped inside the house and flipped on the lights. He didn't really want to do this. He didn't need a repeat date with Becky. He'd rather work. Or be with Natalie. And then there was . . . Oh damn, the seniors' fund-raiser Saturday.

"I have to work, Becky."

"Nell said you work too much. Just take one Saturday off."

"It's not technically work. It's a fund-raiser. But I go every month. It's the Bars and Barks Event."

"What's the Bars and Barks Event?"

"It's a bar event that the seniors put on at different bars each month to raise money for the sea lion center. It's at the Shore Thing this month."

"We could go together."

He sighed. He didn't want to go with Becky. He almost hoped he'd see Natalie there. But . . . well, what the hell was he thinking? He wasn't seeing Natalie. Despite that delicious moment of kissing her neck on a mountaintop above the island, she was still on her mancation. Which she'd made clear to him multiple times.

He might as well go out with Becky again. It would give him a rare second date, probably make the evening go by faster, fulfill his obligation, and then he could tell Nell he was done with dating for a while. He needed to get back to work.

"Okay. We can go together."

"We'll just meet there," Becky said. "So you don't have to be near the dogs."

"Sounds good." Elliott wondered what the Colonel would have to say about not picking her up on a second date. "Around seven?"

"I'll see you then."

Elliott clicked off the phone and dragged himself into the bedroom to finish some of his notes.

And tried to think about the right woman.

CHAPTER 13

Natalie woke Saturday morning completely thrilled—no taking Lily to school. She'd slept in until eight, then shuffled her slippers into the front room, straightened her pajama top, and glanced up to see Lily already awake, eating Froot Loops at the dining table.

"Lily, sweetie, how did you—"

Blonde hair caught her eye to the right.

"Paige! What are you still doing here?"

"Thought I'd catch a different ferry out."

"You're staying?"

"I guess I'm having fun. I thought I'd stay one more night and go to Bars and Barks." Paige put her own cereal bowl in the sink and started the coffeepot. "And, actually, I offered to come every weekend from now on while you're watching Lily. Olivia and I agreed that you need weekends off. How did it go last night?"

Natalie smoothed her hair down and rummaged for a coffee cup. "What do you mean?"

"I mean, I saw you leap off the love seat and grab something out of the cupboard and fly out of here. Whose rescue did you come to, and how did it go?"

Natalie didn't know how much she wanted to admit to. She arranged her coffee cup, then dug back into the cupboard for a bowl. "I thought you were sleeping," she said with as much innocence as she could muster. "Did you leave me some cereal?"

A slow smile slid across Paige's face. "I thought so."

"You thought what?"

"I thought it was a guy. Did I win the bet?"

"Paige, you don't know what you're talking about. I went to see a friend last night."

"And was this friend a guy?"

Natalie slammed the cupboard and went to find a spoon. "If you must know, yes. But I'm not dating him. And you didn't win the bet. He's a friend."

"I didn't win *yet*."

"Ever. You won't win this one. I'm almost one week in now, and only two to go."

"But that blush creeping across your cheeks tells me everything I need to know. And you're not going to last two more weeks. Who is it?"

"It's none of your business."

"John-O?"

"No! And that's all I'm saying."

"Steve Stegner?"

"*No!*" she let slip. Paige was too good at egging her on.

"The new guy at the post office?"

"Paige, I'm not engaging with you anymore."

"Tag? Oh, tell me it's Tag! He's really cute."

"We're not doing this."

"It's the sea lion man," said Lily calmly as she continued coloring with her crayons.

They both looked back at Lily; then Paige turned toward Natalie, her eyebrows up in her bangs. "A sea lion man?" Another slow smile stole across her face. "Where did you see the sea lion man, Lily?"

"Paige, knock it off. It's not the sea lion man . . . Well, it *is* the sea lion man who I went to help last night, but I'm not interested in him. And his name isn't Sea Lion Man. It's Elliott."

Paige lifted her coffee cup to her lips and smiled at Natalie over the rim. Natalie knew she'd lost this round.

But she wasn't losing this bet.

She made two cups of coffee with harsh movements and walked one back to Olivia's room. "Some sisters are nice," she snapped at Paige.

When she came back out, Paige and Lily were sitting at the table, both coloring. She decided to skip the cereal and instead take her coffee out to the balcony, where she could breathe in some fresh ocean air and forget about how much Paige irritated her.

She leaned against the balustrade and stared at the beautiful ocean just fifty feet away. A young couple looked peaceful walking their dog along the water's edge, a do-gooder woman was picking up trash with a long pole and a large bag, and behind all of them a male runner was sprinting at a pretty good clip in the damp sand. Natalie took a sip of her coffee and enjoyed him for a minute. He had his shirt off, a lean torso with clean molded muscles across his chest and shoulders, muscular legs flexing at every long stride, and—

Natalie almost spilled her coffee over the balcony as she stood straighter. *Elliott?*

She peered more closely and saw that it was, indeed, him. His hair glinted in the early-morning sunlight as it bounced across his forehead with each long stride; his fists clenched as he pumped his arms; and the water reflected upward to cast his body in a deep gold, outlining shadows into the ridges across his muscled abdomen. A sheen of perspiration across his chest caught the water's reflection, and his stride lengthened—all style and grace, pulling him rhythmically across the sparkling ocean's edge, following the ribbons of sea foam that seemed to create a path for only him.

Natalie concentrated on closing her mouth and set her coffee cup on the edge of the balcony so she didn't drop it. She couldn't take her eyes off him as he moved like air across the golden horizon.

"Look, Natalie, I'm sorry. I was just—" Paige interrupted the spell, and Natalie whirled around as if caught.

Paige's eyes went over her shoulder, and it didn't take her long to zero in, like some damned submarine scope, on exactly what Natalie had been feasting her eyes on.

"Ah. Is this like taking whiffs of cookies right out of the oven when you're on a diet?" Paige walked to the edge of the balcony and watched him herself. "Your coffee's getting cold."

Natalie picked up her mug and tried to look bored as she sipped it and focused on one of the other beach walkers.

"That woman comes out here and picks up trash every morning, you know," she said, pointing Paige in another direction.

"Uh-huh."

"Aren't you going to look at her?"

"I'm busy."

Elliott had come to the end of the row of cottages—Olivia's was just two from the end—and had turned around and was jogging back the other way, a little slower now. He seemed to be in some kind of cooldown but was still moving at an impressive pace. Natalie and Paige both sipped their coffee and stared. He pulled his T-shirt out of the back of his waistband and mopped his face, then glanced in their direction and did a double take.

He made a sharp turn and jogged in their direction.

Paige's eyes went wide.

"Stop staring!" Natalie whispered.

Paige ignored her completely. "Do you know him?"

"Yes! Stop staring!"

Paige continued to ignore her while they enjoyed another few seconds of his taut chest muscles before he tugged the T-shirt over his head.

Natalie swallowed her disappointment, embarrassed that she'd been gawking for so long. She always hated when men ogled *her*, and yet here she was doing the very same thing.

"Hello!" he finally yelled when he was within shouting distance. "I didn't realize you lived right here."

Natalie couldn't decide if she was mortified or pleased that he'd spotted her and had run all the way over. Vignettes of the previous night—and memories of kisses across the back of her neck—heated her face. What had she been thinking? This kind, shy man needed a friend—and tips on dating, as he was looking for a serious relationship—and she was acting like some sex-starved prairie vole just because she was on a mancation for three weeks. She needed to back off.

But she smoothed her hair anyway and straightened her toast pajamas.

"Yes. My sister Olivia lives here. This is my other sister, Paige. She's visiting, too. But she was just leaving." She gave Paige a little shove.

Paige looked insulted. "No, I'm not! Hi, and you are . . . ?"

"Elliott Sherman." He reached his arm up through the balusters and shook her hand.

"The Sea Lion Man, by any chance?" Paige asked.

Elliott frowned and glanced at Natalie. "Uh . . . yeah, I guess that would be me."

"Sea Lion Man!" yelled Lily, who'd apparently spotted him a minute ago and had hauled the heavy slider to come out and leap across the balcony. At the edge of the balustrade, she squatted so she was eye to eye with Elliott. "How are the sea lions? Did I help them?"

"Lily, his name isn't Sea Lion Man," Natalie said. "It's Dr. Sherman."

Elliott smiled. "It's okay. Sea Lion Man might be easier to remember. And Larry, Curly, and Moe are great. I think they each gained another half a pound. The formula you made yesterday really helped."

Lily giggled and fell to her knees. "Can I help again?"

"If your aunt says it's okay." He glanced up at Natalie.

Natalie felt a warmth ooze through her middle and wondered what the hell was happening to her. Elliott gave her a smile that held a cute combination of embarrassment and hope, and she had a hard time looking away. Their shared intimacy last night—the dark night, the twinkling lights, the medicine, the pajamas, the erogenous-zone kisses—all swirled between them like a huge secret. It seemed to pass between them for just an instant; then he lowered his lashes and looked away.

Natalie finally followed suit and lifted Lily off the concrete. Paige was sipping from her coffee mug and watching the whole exchange with interest.

"Maybe Monday, sweetie," Natalie said, depositing Lily onto her feet.

"Today? Today?" Lily clasped her hands into an exaggerated beg.

"I don't think Dr. Sherman works on Saturdays."

"I do. I work every day." He waved his hand toward the hill where the center was, but then seemed to stop himself when he realized this might not have been the answer Natalie wanted him to blurt out. "I mean . . . Monday is fine, though. Monday is better, probably."

"We're not doing anything today," Paige said, turning toward Natalie.

"Oh, we don't want to impose upon Dr. Sherman for yet another day. I think—"

"It's no problem," he said.

"I'd like to go," Paige said, lifting her eyebrows toward Natalie.

Natalie turned and made her crazy-eyes face toward Paige to get her to quiet down, but she was clearly having too much fun.

"What time would be best?" Paige asked Elliott.

Elliott was glancing at Natalie, realizing, perhaps, that maybe he'd steered a runaway train right off the tracks. "I'll, uh, be there in an hour. Anytime after that."

"We'll definitely see you then." Paige cupped her coffee in both hands and looked at Natalie with an expression of triumph.

Lily started jumping all over the balcony, clapping. "I'm going to bring my Elsa doll!" She ran inside.

"Let's get dressed first, Lil," Paige shouted after her, following inside. She turned once to wink at Natalie before stepping through the slider. "You two behave out here."

Natalie sighed.

"I, uh . . . I'm sorry if that didn't go the way you wanted," Elliott said. "I shouldn't have said that."

"It's okay. I just . . ." She glanced toward the door. "Sisters can be difficult."

"I hear you. This the same sister who was with you at the Shore Thing, right? She was apologizing to you?"

"Yeah. How did you remember that?"

"I have a good memory."

"Must be what makes you a good scientist."

"Something like that."

The ocean waves crashed in the distance, and Elliott shifted his arm along the balustrade. "So you have another sister who lives here?"

"Yes, Olivia."

"And Olivia is Lily's mom?"

"Yes, and she's pregnant with her second, and on bed rest, so I'm here helping out for a few months. Paige is just here being a pest."

"What's she bothering you about now? Earlier it was the mancation, right?"

"It's still that. She thinks she's going to win this bet. I'm sure she thinks you're . . ." Natalie waved her hand up and down in the direction of his torso, but then she didn't know how to explain much further. A flash of how beautiful he was under that T-shirt went through her memory, and she felt herself blush. "You look different today."

"Yeah, no lab coat. Morning run. I run every day at six."

She let her eyes take him all in quickly—roped forearms, trim waist, runner's shorts, muscled legs, and . . . bare feet? "You run barefoot?"

"Always. I used to run cross-country, and we all ran barefoot back then. So your sister thinks I'm what?"

"Oh. She thinks you're"—she flapped her hand toward him again and forced herself to stop gawking at his legs—"tempting me . . . or whatever, in some way, to lose the bet. So how did the rest of the other night go? Did Becky call you again?"

"She did."

"She did?" Natalie was actually a little surprised at that. Becky wasn't wasting any time. "What did she say?"

"She asked me out."

"Really?"

"You sound surprised."

"No. I mean, yes. A little. I'm a little surprised. That she moved so fast. But . . . Well, that's good. Really."

"Thanks again for all your help—driving up there with the antihistamines and then the uh . . . coaching."

Natalie nodded. "No problem." A small heat fired up her neck and ears when she thought about how much she'd enjoyed the coaching, too, but she took another sip of her coffee to look unaffected. "So when are you going out again?"

"Tonight."

The coffee fell with a thud in her stomach. "Tonight! Wow. Okay."

Maybe Becky was genuinely interested in him. And why shouldn't she be? And why should this bother her anyway? This was as it should be, right? Becky was nice. Elliott was nice. Natalie was giving dating advice, and it was actually working. She should be happy.

But she wasn't.

"Well, okay. How do you feel? Are you pumped?" She tried to force some false enthusiasm into her voice.

"Pumped?"

"You know, excited? Happy about it?"

"It'll be okay." He started backing away from the balustrade. "I need to finish this run. But I'll see you today then?"

"Yes, definitely. We'll . . . we'll see you."

He gave her another smile and then turned and started jogging lithely across the sand.

She took a sip of her coffee and allowed herself a good, long look. She didn't like to be someone who ogled another human being, but she told herself it was okay because she truly liked him.

And that thought made her happy. She couldn't remember ever just liking a guy she wasn't sleeping with. It was oddly relaxing, not having to be strategic or play defense. Elliott was just a nice guy. Maybe the first sincerely nice guy she'd ever let herself get to know. And she liked him. And that was okay. And she was helping him.

And that's all this would be.

Elliott flipped on the Bunsen burner, reached for the newest vials of blood Jim had given him that morning, then tried to focus on determining the nucleotide sequence of the capsid protein gene. He was so close to finding homology between these sea lion virus serotypes and some other animals that lived on the island. Thank God Saturdays were filled with volunteers at the center, so Jim had given him the freedom to work on his own projects all morning. He'd stayed up late last night studying the gene sequences of other native animals, and comparing them with what he'd found, and had woken that morning with a slight buzz of discovery.

Well, that and a slight buzz from the memory of touching Natalie Grant on a starlit mountaintop the other night, and pushing the tendrils of hair from her neck, and kissing her there, and hearing the slightest moan slip out from between her lips . . .

Today he was on fire. His thoughts were coming clearer; he was excited about his discoveries; he was feeling confident, and "pumped," as she'd said when he'd discovered her on his run. It had been fun to see her. He hadn't realized she lived so close. His usual shyness had been tinged with just enough confidence now from the brief moaning memory to keep him talking to her with a degree of comfort. And now it was as if his tiny success with her was electrifying him and causing him to live just five bulbs brighter. He'd never experienced anything like this—being so inspired by another human. He wondered if it might be what artists meant when they called on a muse.

Not that it was going any further than this. He knew that. And he needed to switch his thinking to Becky at some point today. But for now, with memories of Natalie on his mind, and excitement from knowing she was coming to the center today, he could enjoy being on fire.

He put the culture tubes he was prepping in a rack and inoculated each tube, then swung back to the lab's side table and furiously typed out some notes onto his laptop.

"Sherm?" Jim's voice came over his shoulder.

"Yeah?"

"You have guests."

Normally Elliott would be irritated or frustrated by the interruption, but this time—knowing who the guests were—he felt a jolt of excitement.

"Give me ten," he said over his shoulder.

He typed out the last of his notes and raced the samples to the incubator, his heart pounding with adrenaline.

Then he headed out to the front area to see his new little friend, Lily; the torturing sister he could relate to; and his new muse.

CHAPTER 14

Natalie held Lily's left hand as the young girl hugged her Elsa doll in the right, and they both stood on the brick path with Paige, waiting for Elliott.

She knew this was an intel trip for Paige, who was ready to gather info on whether she was winning the bet or not. Paige had been pressing Natalie for details all morning about Elliott while Natalie was planting the gerbera daisies outside the back door, where they could be seen from the nursery window. Paige seemed to halfway believe the "just friends" explanation because Elliott was not Natalie's type at all, but she kept peering at her closely and said Natalie had a "funny look" on her face.

Natalie didn't know about the "funny look" part—it seemed embarrassing, really—but she did know she was absolutely *not* going to fail at a mancation. When she remembered her slip from the other night, though, and the shivers from Elliott's instructional kiss, she realized she might have to make the rules explicit.

"So what exactly constitutes a loss, here?" she whispered over Lily's head.

"See? I knew it! I won, didn't I?"

"No. I'm not saying that. I just want to make things clear. A 'mancation' might imply a vacation from all men in general, but I mean it to include only men I'm dating. Dr. Sherman is a friend, not a love interest, but I have been spending time with him."

Paige frowned, clearly unconvinced. The frown remained as she asked Lily if she wanted to go closer to one of the fenced pools. Then she marched back to Natalie.

"Okay, the bet is off if there's a kiss," Paige whispered.

Natalie sighed. That's what she'd supposed. She'd better come clean. "Well, there was a kiss, but—"

"See? I knew it!"

"Two, to be honest."

"Okay, I won."

"Wait, wait. I can explain. He's a friend, and he needed help, and a mutual friend of ours was instructing him on how to end a date."

"He doesn't know how to end a date?"

"He's not very confident."

"So you kissed him?"

"He kissed me. Under the Colonel's instruction."

"The Colonel?"

"He's one of the senior citizens."

Paige looked at her sideways. "A senior citizen was instructing him on how to kiss?"

"The Colonel was instructing him on how to end a date. He was saying, 'If you're not interested, do this' and 'If you're interested, do this.'"

"And which did he seem to be?"

"He practiced both."

Paige shook her head and stared at the baby fur seals' cage for a minute. "So what was the second kiss?"

"Much of the same. Instructional. I just showed him the erogenous zones and let him kiss me on the neck as an example. It wasn't a shared kiss."

"*What?* Erogenous zones? Natalie, a shared kiss is a technicality at that point. Were there closed eyes? Heavy breathing?"

"Paige! Stop! No."

Natalie tried not to think about the goose bumps she'd gotten, or the fact that she hadn't stopped thinking about the kiss since it had happened, but she pushed those thoughts aside and reminded herself of the reality of the situation: "He's going out with Becky Huffington, actually."

"He's going out with Becky? Olivia's friend?"

"Yes. Now hush. Here he comes."

Paige seemed vaguely mollified. Or maybe confused. Or something that made her close her mouth and peer at Elliott more carefully when he came down the path.

As soon as Lily saw Elliott, she lunged for his hand. "I brought Elsa to see Larry, Curly, and Moe!"

Elliott glanced at Paige and frowned in confusion. "Elsa?"

"Elsa!" Lily thrust the doll forward.

"Oh." He laughed. "Well, I think Elsa will like meeting the sea lions."

He motioned for Paige and Natalie, who followed behind him and Lily all the way up the path, Lily gripping his hand and talking the whole way.

Over the next hour, he showed Paige the feeding area, and Lily showed Paige how she made the formula. They went to the private pool where Larry, Curly, and Moe were, and Elliott let them all watch a volunteer named Theresa feed the pups. Eventually, Theresa got Lily into her own apron and gloves and let her help while Paige held on to Elsa for her near the pool.

Farther back along the fence, Elliott leaned next to Natalie. Her heart picked up just at the nearness of his lab-coated forearm, especially when she remembered how muscular it was under that material. She moved away slightly to preserve her sanity and dignity. And the bet.

"We never got to go over the last dating tips you were going to give me," he said so they couldn't be heard. Ahead of them, Lily took the baby bottle from Theresa and held it up.

"No, we didn't," Natalie whispered. "But you should do fine. Becky clearly likes you. And you have your antihistamines, right?"

He dropped his head and chuckled. "I do, yes."

They watched Lily for another few minutes. Her face was lit up with the responsibility and wonder of healing the little sea lions. Suddenly, she turned and looked back at them over her shoulder. "Which one's Larry?" she called to Elliott.

He pointed to a pup in the corner.

"How do you remember which one's which, with nearly fifty pups in here? They all look the same," Natalie said.

"You get to know them. They're also marked, but Larry's the biggest, so he's easy to spot."

"Thank you so much for doing this for her."

"Not a problem. We like when rescuers follow up. I hope you'll keep bringing her."

The comment was a bit vague, but Natalie liked it that way. She pretended he meant he was glad that she herself had come.

"So. You never told me why you're on a mancation," he said suddenly.

The comment took her by surprise, and she wasn't sure how to respond. She hadn't told anyone. Not even Olivia or Paige. The low chain-link fence they were leaning against shook as she shifted uncomfortably and willed her stomach to stop knotting. "I'm not sure I'm ready to talk about that."

Elliott turned and looked at her. She had the sensation of being under a microscope and tried to move away. The sea lions squawked quietly in the background, not strong enough for full barks yet.

Natalie played with the rings on her fingers as Elliott leaned down, as if to encourage eye contact. "Natalie, did someone hurt you?"

His voice was low, tolerant, comforting, indignant. It wrapped around her like a warm blanket, and she wanted to lean into it, or lean into him, and finally tell someone her story. His eyes searched her face as he waited for an answer. She glanced up once and met his gaze. It was so filled with understanding, so filled with compassion, so filled with invitation that she knew she could probably tell him anything right now and he'd listen.

But Paige looked back then, and Natalie remembered that she was supposed to be keeping a distance from Elliott. She could be friends with him, but leaning into the warmth seemed like a line she couldn't cross. She didn't even tell her sisters these kinds of things. Or her girlfriends. Or her mom. Somehow Elliott's offer seemed dangerous—something she'd never allowed herself, and something that would change everything, maybe make her lose herself somehow. She took an additional step back.

"We should be going," she blurted, stumbling just a bit and moving toward the fence opening. "Lily? Paige? Are you ready?"

Elliott dropped his head and stayed by the fence while Natalie and Paige helped Lily give back the gloves, apron, and bottle.

When they were all ready, Elliott ushered them through the next two stations that Larry, Curly, and Moe would be going through, then to the front of the center, where the barks of healthier sea lions filled the air.

"Thank you, Elliott." Paige shook his hand. "You seem to be taking great care of the sea lions. And Lily when she visits. And my sister." Paige winked at him.

Elliott's gaze dropped to his shoes, but he smiled. "I hope you'll all come back," was all he said.

Natalie wanted to shove Paige through the gate. Didn't she already explain that Elliott was seeing Becky Huffington? What was wrong with Paige? Was she just goading them now, wanting to win the bet that badly?

But Natalie tried to ignore the spirals of irritation going through her. She and Paige were always competitive, and that's just how it would always be.

"Where are you and Becky going tonight?" she asked loudly, to remind Paige to mind her manners. She wrapped her arms around Lily.

"The Bars and Barks Event."

"I'm going tonight, too!" Paige said. "And Natalie is. We'll probably see you there."

"I hadn't decided, for sure . . ." Natalie injected.

With a new kind of discomfort swirling between her and Elliott right now, and his insightful guess to the reason for her mancation, she wasn't sure she wanted to be so near him for an entire evening. And she definitely wasn't sure she could watch him on another date. Especially one that would probably end with him leaving with Becky. And she definitely, *absolutely*, wasn't in the mood to have Paige staring her down all night, watching her every move.

"Don't be silly!" Paige said, turning toward her. "You said your senior citizen friends were all expecting you there."

Elliott was watching Natalie with what looked like sympathy.

"Elsa wants to leave," said Lily suddenly, lifting the doll for proof.

Elliott laughed. "I'm sure she does."

Natalie herded Lily through the front gate and wondered how she could get out of going tonight.

It was starting to feel like supreme protection for her heart.

Elliott ushered Becky through the packed Shore Thing bar, waving to several people this time.

The bar was decked out. Elliott had been to three of these events now, and he knew that when the seniors threw their Bars and Barks Events, they always pumped the 1940s music from any nearby jukebox or speakers, heavy on the trumpets and Tommy Dorsey.

This event had a clear USO theme going on, with army-khaki colors everywhere; festive red, white, and blue bunting along the walls; and star fabric covering the tables. Along one wall, a table had been set up with snacks in large tin cans, where guests could use "ration tickets" to get candy, popcorn, nuts, and Cracker Jack—a big part of the fund-raiser.

He handed his ticket to a young woman dressed in USO clothing and bought another one for Becky. The Andrews Sisters sang "Boogie Woogie Bugle Boy" from the jukebox, and Becky swiveled toward the back of the room to the jump-blues tunes.

George approached in a pointed army cap and suspenders and clapped Elliott on the back; Marie had on a USO-girl sharp suit with bright-red lipstick, and she came over and squeezed Elliott's wrist; Doris, in 1940s roll-curls and lipstick that outdid Marie's, rushed toward him and pulled his face down to kiss his cheek.

"This looks great," he said. "Where's the Colonel?"

"He's the guest bartender for an hour," Doris said.

"No kidding?" Elliott peered over everyone's heads.

The Colonel would have to stand on a box or something to tend bar, but he did claim to make a mean cocktail. Through the crowd, Elliott caught sight of the neatly combed tuft of white hair. The Colonel was decked out in a service shirt, with medals hanging in colorful rows from his chest.

"Let's order a martini," he said to Becky.

Becky looked nice tonight. She hadn't dressed for the theme, but she wore a sophisticated, flowing, white-pantsuit thing, with lots of necklaces. Elliott hadn't sneezed once in her presence. He tried to stay as focused on her as possible, even though in the back of his mind he'd thought about work at least fifteen times already. Plus, he knew he was going to react all night to anyone of Natalie's height and hair color that came into his peripheral vision.

He told himself to focus and steered Becky through the crowd to the bar.

Halfway there, Jim and Nell caught his attention from a corner booth with red, white, and blue carnations in the center and waved them over.

Elliott groaned. Nell had been too excited on the phone earlier that he had a second date with Becky. He didn't want to come under interrogation from her, or too much pushing, but Becky had already spotted her and was shimmying over to the music.

"Hell-oooo! How are you two?" Nell asked.

"I thought you weren't coming," Elliott said.

"I found a babysitter, after all, at the last minute."

"After a thirty-minute interrogation and rundown," Jim added, winking.

"It was not an interrogation," Nell said. "You just have to be careful these days."

"I know, love. You're a good protector." Jim scooted farther back in the booth and slapped the seat next to him. "Have a seat, you two."

Becky slid in next to Nell, and Elliott sat across from her. He didn't really want to sit with Nell and Jim. He wanted to be free of Nell's analysis of how he was doing on this date and just have a relaxed time. As relaxed as it could be anyway, with a bunch of sick sea lions in the center. But—on the other hand—Nell and Jim's company might make the evening go by a little faster so he could study his notes tonight.

Within minutes, Elliott spotted Natalie at the bar. She'd dressed for the festivities—a skirt and jacket in soft green, a USO cap on her head, and her hair rolled into 1940s curls. Bright-red lipstick covered her lips, and when she launched into one of her huge smiles at Marie, her lips looked even more delectable than usual.

"So what do you think?" Nell's voice drifted into his ear.

Elliott blinked back at her. "What?"

"What do you think?"

"About what?"

"Elliott, you aren't listening at all." Nell turned to Becky. "He's probably thinking of his formulas again. Elliott is very involved in his work." She said it with a smile, as if it were a selling point, but then she gave him a swift kick under the table that made him know otherwise.

Jim cleared his throat as he followed the point to where Elliott's gaze had been. "Well, we *do* have a lot of things going on at the center," Jim said. "I think we should cut Elliott some slack. Hey, Sherm, why don't you go get us some drinks? Place is so crowded, we'll never get served. Besides, the Colonel is guest-tending for only another ten minutes or so. Tell him I want one of his famous martinis."

"I'll take one, too," Becky said.

"Nell?" Jim asked.

"A margarita for me."

Benny Goodman started up on the jukebox with "Sing, Sing, Sing," and Elliott headed for the bar filled with half dread, half excitement. On the one hand, Natalie was there, and she was like a flame to a moth. But, on the other hand, he was here on a date with someone else. And he didn't want to be an ass. He'd just have to watch himself tonight.

"Hey, you made it," he said cautiously when he squeezed in beside her. She smelled great—some kind of spicy perfume. He tried not to lean in too close.

"Elliott! Hi!" She adjusted the cute USO cap on her head. "You didn't dress up."

"Not this time. I should have, though. I have some of my granddad's old things."

"That's right—the hats."

"Exactly."

"This is my grandmother's." She pointed to the hat on her head.

A sensation of warmth swelled through him at that, but as he tried to formulate the right response in his head, she glanced over his shoulder furtively. "How's your date going so far?"

Elliott scrambled to bring his thoughts back to Becky. "Pretty good," he finally said over the music. "She's back there with Nell and Jim, and—"

"There you are!" growled the Colonel, stepping up on the other side of the bar. His chest barely cleared the row of glasses across the base of the bar top, but Elliott could make out several of his medals, including a Medal of Honor, which he knew was for valor. He'd always stared at his granddad's medals—they were kept under glass in the back room.

"Damn, Colonel, you earned a Medal of Honor?"

"I was just doin' my job. Good to see you, boy. And glad to see you two together."

"Oh, we're not toge—"

"WHAT'LL YOU HAVE, SHERM?" The Colonel leaned closer, clearly having trouble hearing over Benny Goodman's clarinet.

Elliott ordered the three martinis and the margarita. When the Colonel frowned at the order, Elliott motioned his thumb over his shoulder.

"Who are they?" he barked.

"You know Jim, and that's my sister, Nell, who's married to Jim, and my date, Becky."

"BECKY?"

"Yes."

The Colonel looked at Natalie. "Do you know about this Becky?"

Natalie smiled into her gimlet. "Yes, I do, Colonel. She's Elliott's date."

"Do you approve of her?"

"I don't think it matters what I think. It's probably—"

"I'm asking for research purposes."

"Oh. Well . . . " She glanced at Elliott.

He waited for her answer—he was kind of curious, too.

"I think they're both very nice, and they make a lovely couple," she said.

The Colonel stared hard at Elliott, then nodded curtly and turned to make their drinks.

Elliott's brain stalled a little on the "nice" part. She'd called him that once before. "Nice" wasn't a compliment guys liked to hear. "Nice" was dismissive. It was never the guy who got the girl.

"So you think I'm nice?" he asked her.

"Of course."

That explained a lot. He *was* nice. But he'd always finished last that way.

Even though it wasn't the arrangement he'd like, it looked like the arrangement she might need right now, especially after the strange way she'd reacted earlier when he'd asked her about her mancation. Maybe something had happened to her.

"Listen, Natalie, I didn't mean to pry earlier, when I asked if some-one had hurt you, but if you ever want to talk about anything, or—"

"No." She waved her hand as if to dismiss the idea, the words, his apology, his offer. "I didn't mean for that to come up. I'd rather we just forget that conversation." Her hands fluttered over her cocktail napkin and began ripping at its end. Normally Natalie looked like a tough woman who could hold her own, but right now she looked vulner-able—eyes lowered, hands shaking.

A flash of anger swept over him when he realized that this must be the case here. Someone had hurt her. He didn't normally think of him-self as a violent person, but right in that second, he had a strong urge to pound whoever it might have been. He slid a sideways glance at her Good Samaritan face, her intelligent eyes, the lips that had only kind things to say, and her helping hands that were shaking, and he pictured finding this jerk and pulverizing him.

"Whatever you say," he muttered. "But just know that I'll listen."

She turned sharply and stared at him—a hard, skeptical stare. Long eyelashes blinked a few times. But then her features softened and a tiny smile broke out, which she shyly redirected to her gimlet. "You would, wouldn't you?"

That grin was his reward. He wanted to promise her a bunch of things right then—he would promise her anything—if she'd just keep smiling like that. He stood a little straighter.

All the sounds of the bar fell away. He wanted her to open up to him, to tell her what she obviously had trouble with, to trust him, to let him in. If she did that only as a friend, he'd take that. He realized he wanted her company, and wanted her trust, in any way he could get it.

But then a polite, but gruff, cough came over his shoulder. "Uh, Sherm?"

He turned to see Jim.

"The women are wondering why you're not back yet with the drinks. Hey, there, Natalie. It's Natalie, right?"

"Yes." She held out her hand. "You're the one who keeps finding Elliott for me."

"Jim Stout." He shook Natalie's hand, then huddled closer to Elliott. "So can I tell them that you've already ordered, but the Colonel is just taking a while?"

"That's the situation. So yes." Elliott tried to keep the irritation out of his voice.

"All righty then." Jim turned his bearish body. "As you were."

"Who's this?" came a higher voice over their shoulders.

This time it was Natalie's sister, crowding Jim back in.

"Hi, Paige," Elliott said. "This is my buddy Jim. Jim, this is Natalie's sister Paige."

"He's checking on the drinks for his wife and also Elliott's date," Natalie informed Paige.

Glenn Miller's "In the Mood" struck up, and the crowd all seemed to turn in unison to the dance floor. Several talented couples headed out to do impressive swing moves. Much to Elliott's chagrin, he looked up to see Becky coming toward him, her hands outstretched and pointing to the dance floor.

He shook his head, but she kept approaching, with Nell right behind her.

Next thing he knew, Becky and Nell had him and Jim each by the hand and were dragging them across the parquet flooring.

This night was off to a terrible start.

CHAPTER 15

Natalie watched Elliott and Jim being led to the dance floor and felt a little sorry for them. But only a little. It was probably good that Becky was getting Elliott to loosen up a little and maybe have some fun.

"Huh. So he really *is* going out with Becky," Paige said.

"Of course. I wasn't making it up."

"Too bad. And too bad his buddy is married. He's cute."

"Leave them alone, Paige."

The Colonel slid two martinis across the bar. "One more coming up." He looked around. "Where's Sherm?"

"Dancing."

"I don't believe it."

They all turned toward the dance floor, where Becky was sort of dragging Elliott around to the fast swing number. He was all elbows and limbs, but he seemed to be trying.

"Well, he's not going to win any awards now, is he?" the Colonel asked.

Natalie took a sip of her drink to hide her smile. She thought he looked kind of adorable.

"I have one more minute on the clock, then we're going to help that boy out," the Colonel said, shaking his head. "Doris? We have an emergency here!" He motioned her over, pointed at Elliott, then wandered to the other end of the bar to retrieve two more drinks.

A few minutes later, Doris was out there with Elliott, showing him a few basic swing steps, and Becky had swept up poor Jim. Nell had found John-O, and Paige had taken up with George. The Colonel came around the bar and pulled Natalie out, snapping her toward his ribboned chest. He was surprisingly good. He danced slowly but lithely, and always on beat. Natalie tried to match him with some basic Zumba moves she'd just learned. She was doing more of a cha-cha, but it worked with Glenn Miller.

"In the Mood" ended, and the music slowed with an Ella Fitzgerald version of "I Could Write a Book." The couples all stepped back from each other and took deep breaths, wiping their brows.

Natalie saw Elliott breathe a sigh of relief and look up from his feet at his partner, Doris, but then Doris picked up a waltz pose with him and swung him in her direction to Ella Fitzgerald's breathy voice. The Colonel lifted Natalie's hand and swung her the other way. And next thing she knew, Natalie ended up with Elliott, their arms both raised in the air, gripping molecules. Doris and the Colonel sailed off smoothly together to the other side of the floor.

Elliott's eyes widened until he finally rested his hand on Natalie's hip and fell into step. He was only slightly better at the waltz than swing, which wasn't saying much. But finally she stepped closer and let him move to an even slower beat, just barely rocking back and forth.

"Thank you," he said over her shoulder. She could hear the smile in his voice.

"No problem."

They kept a tiny distance between them, moving in a simple circle. Elliott's raised hand felt a little moist in hers, his other warm on her hip. He smelled spicy—aftershave he must have put on for Becky—and

Natalie wanted to lean closer, but she decided against it. Leaning too much into him would be inappropriate. He was the perfect height for her—she loved that her lips came to his chin, and she was so close she could see the stubble follicles along his jaw. She could understand why the seniors always described dancing as a perfect date—standing so close to a man you didn't know, seeing the stubble follicles along his jaw, and smelling the soap he used, which were such intimate, morning-after things, was delicious. Maybe the Colonel and Marie and Doris were onto something when they said they knew a better way to date.

Natalie had a brief, reckless thought of kissing Elliott on that stubble right now. She wanted to put her hands on his chest, just to feel if it was as taut as it had looked in the morning sun today. She wanted to nestle into the warm spot at his collarbone. She wanted to wrap her arms all the way around him and bury herself into the spicy warmth he seemed to offer. But all those things were not hers to have, so she restricted herself to just another inch, leaning only close enough that she thought she could feel his heart beating. Or maybe that was hers.

Becky came into view, searching for Elliott across the floor.

Natalie sighed and stepped back, ever so slightly, and eventually spun him toward Becky.

Her work tonight was done.

Elliott laughed at one of Jim's jokes back at their table and tried not to glance up any more to his right, because he knew Natalie was on that side of the room, and he couldn't seem to know that and focus on any conversation at the same time. Instead, he shifted in his seat so he couldn't look that way. For the rest of the evening, he chatted it up with Becky, Jim, and Nell; put plenty of money into the volunteer pot; turned down an offer of darts because he was worried Natalie might be playing; danced with Becky two more times and Doris once; and thought about the sea lions only five more times. He did okay.

At the end of the night, the Colonel pulled him aside, cleared his throat a few times, and mumbled a request for a ride.

Elliott blinked back at him. "A ride? You're not driving back to Casas del Sur with the others?"

"I'm, uh . . . meeting someone. But I don't want the others to know. I was going to drive myself, but I don't feel like breaking the rules tonight."

"Breaking the rules?"

"I'm not supposed to drive at night. Doctor's orders."

Elliott glanced back at the table at Becky. What was he supposed to do here? "Colonel, I'm on a date. Could I have Jim drive you?"

"Never mind. I'll find a way."

"Wait." Elliott grabbed his retreating shoulder. The Colonel was the type to break rules all over the place, and he could definitely see him taking his own golf cart into the dark if Elliott didn't help out. "It's okay. I'll do it. Let me take Becky home first."

"Thanks, son. I'll wait out front." The Colonel straightened his tie and shuffled off toward the bar, waving to various people.

Elliott sighed and headed back to explain this to Becky. He'd had the sense she was going to invite him over tonight—he'd been getting hints all evening from her. But he didn't know how he felt about it. He liked her and all, but he still felt guilty that all he wanted to think about right now was Natalie. And the sea lions. In that order: Natalie, sea lions, Becky.

But was he letting something good slip away? Natalie was not his. Becky might actually be a candidate. But, then again, didn't Becky deserve better than someone who thought of her as third in line?

"We'll make sure she gets home, Sherm," Jim said.

"But you can come check on me," Becky said with a smile, looping her long necklaces in her finger. Elliott normally wasn't very good at reading women, but that smile was pretty idiot-proof.

He headed for the exit door with a mixture of confusion and dread. He didn't know why he was being so hard on himself—obviously Becky wanted him over, and he wouldn't be hurting anyone if he took her up on the offer.

He loped across the bar floor to Louis Armstrong's sad trumpet in "La Vie en Rose," telling himself not to look around for Natalie, but he couldn't help himself. He glanced once to the left and, like some kind of magnetic response, his eyes landed right on her. She looked beautiful, throwing her head back and laughing at something a big dude—he thought his name might be John-O—was saying.

A flash of jealousy went through him. But jealousy over Natalie was not his to feel. Plus, that was probably the kind of guy she was attracted to.

He decided he hated John-O.

Armstrong's wailing trumpet notes followed him out the door.

Natalie saw Elliott leave the bar out of the corner of her eye and felt a surge of disappointment. She tried to concentrate on something John-O was saying but had a hard time, and she eventually broke away to wander by Elliott's old table. It was weird that he'd left alone. But Nell, Jim, and Becky were gone, too. Maybe they'd all left together but not really together?

Regardless, this was not her business. She checked on the other volunteers, swung by to talk to Sugar for a few minutes, and then ran into Marie, who pulled her aside behind the rations table.

"Dear, can you give me a quick lift?"

"A lift?"

"A ride. I need wheels. I need to . . ." She looked side to side, then leaned closer. "I have a date. And I don't want the others to know."

"Wow. A date. Who's it with, Marie?"

"I'd rather not say right here. But if you can do it, I need to leave soon. I'll go get my purse."

"Okay, I'll meet—"

But Marie had already scampered away.

Natalie smiled, said a few quick good-byes, then headed out to the golf cart.

Elliott pulled straight up the hillside in the Colonel's cart and was immediately glad he hadn't let the Colonel drive himself. Although it was one of the most souped-up golf carts on the island, the road was winding and dark and not paved all the way. It led up to a hotel on the hill—the Castle—which was where he'd guessed the Colonel was going. The Castle was remote and mostly for high-end tourists, and it was the best place to go if you were on a secret date.

"So who's this date with, by the way?" Elliott asked as the golf-cart motor whined in protest.

"None of your business."

Elliott bit back a smile. The Colonel sure never changed.

"But thanks for taking me," the Colonel added gruffly.

Elliott parked the golf cart in the Castle's nearly-empty parking lot and, when the older man hesitated in the passenger seat, decided to walk the Colonel in. Elliott guided him lightly by the arm.

The Castle's dining room was as elegant as they came—the center filled with crystal, glass, and shades of white, while the outside walls created a cocoon of dark wainscoting. Enormous windows opened to views of the town below. Twinkle lights sparkled all the way down, while stars filled the sky from above. A bar sat off to the right through a wide archway. It looked like a small four-piece band was set up, playing to the patrons, which Elliott could count on one hand. Everyone was probably at the Shore Thing tonight.

He and the Colonel took a seat in the center, at an intimate table for two, and the Colonel took some time to rearrange the table setting, laying a lavender envelope against a crystal vase of white flowers.

"Do you know how to order a martini?" the Colonel asked, rearranging the envelope for the fourth time.

Elliott shook his head.

"How long have you been drinking, son?"

"Uh . . . well, I'm twenty-eight."

"Seven years? What do you usually order?"

"Beer mostly, sometimes scotch."

"Well, it's about time you knew how to order a good martini. Here's the thing—you have to make sure they don't pour the vermouth into the glass. You're supposed to pour the vermouth into the shaker, swirl it around so it coats the insides, then pour out what remains. Dry as they come. AND ORDER IT WITH OLIVES. No silly stuff like candy canes and limes."

As the waiter approached, the Colonel turned slightly in his chair. "Two martinis, please. Very dry. Straight up. Stirred, with olives."

The waiter bowed and left, and Elliott leaned closer. "Colonel, I can't stay. I hope you ordered that for your date."

"No, it's for you. I just want you to taste it. Just stay until she arrives. She might stand me up, you know. Though it's not likely." He threw Elliott a grin that shed five decades off him.

"Who is this? Is it someone coming on the night ferry?"

"No, she's someone who lives here. But I just decided I had to ask her out right away. Couldn't wait another day. Time is of the essence, you know."

"You have Senior Prom coming up. That'll be another occasion to ask her out."

"I should have said time is of the essence when you're old. I don't want to wait all the way until Senior Prom."

"But it's only a couple months away."

"*Old*, I said. That's a couple months I wouldn't be with her. And I'm not guaranteed those months. You'd do wise to follow that advice, too, young man, even though you've been drinking for only seven years and don't know how to order a proper martini."

The live quartet struck up a song in the corner of the bar room. Elliott and the Colonel both glanced in their direction.

"Just because you're young doesn't mean you can waste time," the Colonel suddenly said. "When you find someone you're interested in, you need to *move*. Life's too short to waste time drinking bad martinis or being away from the one you love."

The waiter came then and plopped the two martinis down. "Taste that," the Colonel said, pushing Elliott's toward him.

Elliott took a small taste and let it swirl in his mouth a minute. He wasn't usually a fan of gin, but he had to admit, this was delicious. "That's good."

"Always order it that way. None of this sugary crap you young people drink. Chocolate and vanilla! We're not making ice-cream cones here. Martinis should be DRY."

"So tell me about that Medal of Honor."

"Ah, I don't want to talk about the war." He looked away and settled back in his seat.

"I'm just asking about the medal because I admire that kind of courage." Elliott took another sip of his martini. Damn, it really was good.

"That's not courage, son. That's called 'doing your job' when you're in a war. Courage is stepping up when you aren't expected to. You know what the scariest day of my life was?" the Colonel asked. "Asking my wife to marry me."

"No."

"Yep."

"How long were you married?"

"Fifty years."

"Kids?"

"Two. One lives in Virginia, and one's in Florida."

"What happened to your wife?"

"She died of cancer. 1995."

"Did you ever marry again?"

"No. She was it." He took another sip. "Until now. I might have found my second chance."

"It's never too late, right?"

"Actually, it can be. If you don't act. Especially when you're my age. So that's why I'm acting now. But this kind of stuff . . . this first-date stuff . . . this is a kicker. The first time's always the kicker—when you know she's the one, and you ask her out. Terrifying. That takes courage."

Elliott twisted his martini stem and thought that over. "How do you know this one's the one?"

"I know. And you'll know, when it happens to you. She'll make your palms sweat. She'll distract you in ways you didn't know you could be distracted, and you'll wonder why you can't get back to your normal life. She'll make you stupid."

Elliott leaned into his chair. Natalie was a little like that. She made his palms sweat. She made him stupid. At least when he was in her presence. When she wasn't in his presence, he felt strangely alive, just thinking about her. And he'd been more distracted thinking about her in the last five days than he'd been with anyone he'd ever met in his life . . .

"Why do you admire courage so much?" the Colonel suddenly barked.

Elliott glanced up from his drink, startled out of another reverie about Natalie. As his mind tried to wrap around the new topic, he didn't know how much he wanted to admit to the Colonel.

"Most men who admire it feel they don't have enough themselves," the Colonel said.

Elliott looked away. "There might be something to that."

"Something happen in your past?"

Elliott didn't know if he wanted to go there. He never talked about this. The only person who knew the whole story besides him was Nell.

But, for some reason, on this mild night at the top of this hill, with all the city lights below, he found he wanted to tell the Colonel. It felt like talking to his granddad again. Maybe the Colonel could give him some advice.

"I was part of a home invasion," he finally blurted out. "My parents were killed. My sister hid me and her, and she got us out to safety. I was too scared to move."

"Wow. Hard on a kid."

"I was already seven."

"A very young kid."

Elliott shrugged. "I felt like I was old enough to have figured something out. I always wonder if I have what it takes if I'm ever in a situation."

"What kind of situation?"

"Anything requiring courage." Elliott moved his drink in a circle.

"Courage always comes with fear, you know. It doesn't mean you're fearless. That's for fools."

"I doubt you lacked courage when you earned that Medal of Honor."

"Are you kidding? I was scared shitless. Fear is part of a thinking man's life, son. Courage is what you exhibit in the face of that fear. What scares you now?"

Elliott pushed the martini glass back and forth on the white table-cloth as he thought that over. "Not doing my job well enough, I guess."

"What happens if you don't do it well enough?"

"A lot of animals die."

"And there's a possibility you might fail?"

"Definitely."

"In front of everyone?"

"Yep."

"But you're doing your job anyway?"

"Of course."

"That's courage, son." He took another sip of his drink.

Elliott kept moving his glass around. Was that right? Was that all it took? The ability to face your fears? Elliott had enough fears to go around, for certain, but if all he had to do was face them every day, he could possibly handle that.

"I feel like there's something else," the Colonel said.

"Like what?"

"Something involving a woman."

Elliott lowered his eyes. Everyone knew he was on all these dates—Jim, Nell, Natalie, the Colonel—but his heart was yearning for some-one else altogether. The Colonel didn't know that part. Maybe that made him a coward most of all.

"I'm not very good in the love department, Colonel," he finally said, hoping to shut down this avenue of conversation. He looked around the room. "This is a cool place."

"That's why it takes courage."

"What?"

"Love," the Colonel said, leaning back in his chair. "Takes a lot of courage. How long do you think it took me to write that card there and put it out on the table for her to see? Once she sees it, there's no turning back. Takes a lot to put yourself out there on the line, your chest open, your heart exposed, waiting for the bullet."

Elliott took a drink. Is that what was going on here? Was he just scared to put himself on the line? Maybe Natalie was the one for him, but he was too scared to let her know?

"We might start by making sure you know how to dance, though, son. You're terrible."

Elliott chuckled. "I won't argue with that. But I don't usually go out dancing, so I think I'm safe."

"You kids have no idea what you're missing. Nothing is better than dancing with a woman for the first time—holding her in your arms when she's not quite yours to hold, imagining, hoping. I saw you on the floor tonight, and you seemed to catch a little of that."

Elliott wasn't sure which dance the Colonel was talking about—when he was date-dancing with Becky or accidentally dancing with Natalie. But the Colonel was right on one point: Elliott definitely felt something dancing with Natalie. Holding her close, smelling her hair, having his lips close enough to her neck that he thought about kissing her there, just once, for real. He took another swig of his martini and decided to say nothing.

"And you're probably not a good conversationalist—smart, quiet kid like you. Not good at small talk, right?"

Elliott shrugged. "Not exactly."

"Believe it or not, that can work to your advantage. Skip the small talk and go straight to what you want to know—the deep stuff. Ask her about her family, what she wants out of life. You can skip questions about the weather. You know . . ." The Colonel looked toward the entrance. "Ah, here we are." He stood abruptly. "Beat it, kid. I think we're ready to roll."

The Colonel straightened his jacket, then leaned across the table and yanked a rose out of the vase, holding it in front of him.

Elliott turned to see who the Colonel's date was, lifting himself out of the chair, and was surprised to have his eyes light on none other than

Marie, charging through the room in her USO getup, followed by none other than . . . *Natalie?*

Elliott swallowed hard and thought back to the Colonel's use of "we."

And then he wondered just what the hell the Colonel had been telling him all night.

CHAPTER 16

Natalie stopped abruptly when she saw Elliott and the Colonel both straightening their jackets.

What was Elliott doing here? And my God, Marie was seeing the *Colonel?* Marie picked up the pace and covered the entire expanse of white carpeting before Natalie could think of what to ask first.

She smoothed her USO costume skirt and finally followed. The small quartet behind her struck up a smooth violin tune.

"Hello, ladies," the Colonel said with a bow. "Natalie, thank you for driving Marie. Could I have you two fine chauffeurs wait for just a moment in the bar? I already bought Elliott a drink, but, Natalie, what can I get you?"

"I'm fine, Colonel. We'll just wait over . . ." She waved her hand back toward the bar, her mind still swimming about how she'd ended up spending an evening with her greatest temptation. Again.

Elliott followed her into the bar, where she quickly ordered a water from the bartender. Her flesh-colored Mary Jane pumps pinched her toes as she hoisted herself up onto the bar stool. When Elliott seemed to finally settle in next to her, she whirled on him.

"Did you know they were seeing each other?" she demanded.

"No." He moved out of her striking range. "I, uh . . . I didn't know it was Marie who was coming. And I didn't know you'd be bringing her. I can drive them back, if you want."

Natalie settled back down. "No, that's okay." Maybe this wasn't some kind of manipulation. "You're still on your date, aren't you? I can drive them back."

"I think I am." He frowned at his drink. "I'm not sure."

His neck was ruddy again. She took pity on him and gentled her voice. "How did things go?" she asked.

"I think okay."

"Did she invite you over?"

"Yes."

"Then things went well." She tried to put some enthusiasm in her voice. "Sounds good. You should go. I'll wait here."

"I'll just finish my drink."

The four-piece band struck up a new number in the corner. Natalie and Elliott both glanced their way.

"The Colonel ordered me a perfect martini," he said. "Want to try it?"

"What makes it perfect?" She took it from him.

"Dry. Only a little vermouth, swirled around the shaker, then poured out. Only olives as garnish." He watched her carefully.

She tasted it and coughed a little. Strong gin. But not bad. Actually, it was quite good. She took another small sip and then met Elliott's eyes over the rim.

"What are you staring at? Is my makeup running or something?" She took a small swipe around the corner of her mouth. This lipstick was a little much.

"No, I'm just thinking about something the Colonel said. You look . . . you look great," he said.

She had a hard time believing that, with such a harrowing ride up the hill in the golf cart with the fog rolling in and frizzing her hair and misting all her makeup off. She kept rubbing beneath her eyes. "Thank you," she said anyway, because Elliott was still staring. Was her mascara running? She took one more swipe beneath her other eye.

"So, tell me how you think things are going with Becky, generally," she said. "You spent the whole evening with her. Do you feel like you want to spend more time with her? I think you two might make a good couple."

"You do?" He stared at the quartet.

"You don't look very enthused."

"It's the last blind date, at least."

"Tell me what this whole thing is with the string of dates. Why is your sister setting you up anyway?"

The bartender brought her a glass of water, and she was grateful to have something to do with her hands.

"She worries about me," Elliott said. "She just wants me to be set up with someone before she moves to Italy with Jim, so she'll feel like I'm happy. Or taken care of. Or something."

"Do you want those things?"

"Everyone wants to be happy, I suppose. But I don't think that's going to be my source. Even though Nell found happiness with Jim, I don't think that's going to be true for me."

"What? True love?" Natalie couldn't help the little bit of sarcasm that slipped into her voice.

He took a swig of his drink. "That sounded pretty cynical."

"Yeah, I guess I agree with you on this one. People who are in love think it's the right thing for everyone. My sister Olivia is like that. She wants me to have what she has. But they don't see that some of us are fine on our own."

"Right." He moved the olive around his martini.

"I can handle life on my own. I don't need a man to define me or make me whole." Her lines sounded a little clichéd even to her own ears, but it still felt good to say them out loud.

"Your mancation is proving that."

"*Exactly. Yes.* I can certainly handle a mancation for three weeks."

They both nodded into their drinks, lost in thought, perhaps, about how strong they were. Or maybe about how independently they could live. Or maybe how vehemently they were arguing their clichéd positions.

But Natalie reiterated to herself that she *was* strong, and she could definitely last for three weeks. She had to prove this to Paige. She had to prove it to herself.

"My sister thinks I'm some kind of commitment-phobe," she said.

He raised his eyebrows. "Are you?"

She snorted. "Of course not. I'm just discerning."

He nodded, and they listened to the cello ooze out a wistful solo.

He looked back at her. His expression was open, curious, non-judgmental, compassionate. He blinked a few times and gave her just enough space that she could admit anything she wanted, or not say anything at all. She had the sense she could be whoever she wanted to be, and say whatever she wanted to say, and he'd continue to look at her in that same accepting way.

"Paige might be a little right," she finally admitted.

He took a drink and gave her another brief nod that let her know he was listening if she wanted to go on.

She took a deep breath. She did.

"I have trouble committing to jobs. Apartments. Men. I almost couldn't commit to this island. The idea of being so stuck somewhere . . . It just freaks me out."

"What exactly are you afraid of?"

"Making the wrong decision. And being stuck with it."

"I get that. In science, that could be a big fear, too, but we learn to take calculated risks. It's the law of probability."

"Mmm. And what's the probability I'm not going to understand the law of probability?"

He smiled. "Zero. But what's the probability I'm going to bore you to tears with this conversation?"

"Zero. Shoot."

He took another gulp and shrugged. "We assess a situation, and if we're seventy-five percent sure of a positive outcome, we take a chance."

Natalie gave him a sidelong glance. "Are you saying that I should pick apartments and men this way?"

"I'm not saying anything of the sort. I'm just telling you how we avoid getting stuck in the fear of committing to something that could be important, or good."

Natalie stared at her martini stem and traced the condensation. That actually made sense. All her life she'd been afraid of making wrong decisions or committing to wrong things, but lately—with nothing of her own to speak of now—she'd started to wonder if she'd let some good things slip away.

"What's the hardest thing you ever had to commit to?" she asked. "You don't seem to have any trouble."

"Not when it comes to things I believe in."

"Your work?"

"My work, yes. Family—or who's left anyway. My studies."

She nodded. "But no women?"

"Not yet."

"Not even short-term? I mean, everyone wants to have sex."

Elliott's neck went red. "I, uh . . . yeah. I don't know. You want to make sure you both want the same thing."

"Like long-term or short-term?"

"Right."

"Are you looking for long-term?"

He shrugged and stared at his drink for a long time. "Maybe I am. I don't know."

The bartender came over and slid another martini across the bar to her. An olive bobbed at the edge on a bright-pink swizzle stick. "From the gentleman over there." He motioned toward the Colonel. Then he slid a cocktail napkin to Elliott. "And for you." Natalie glimpsed handwriting scrawled across the middle of the napkin.

She looked back at the Colonel, who was engrossed in what Marie was saying, but he glanced over and—when she toasted her glass toward him—grinned before riveting his gaze back to Marie.

Natalie took a sip. "That was kind of him. What's that he gave you?"

Elliott was smiling. "A message."

"What does it say?"

"Time is of the essence."

"Why did he send you that?"

"I think he's trying to tell me something." Elliott folded it in two and shoved it into his pocket. "But I have to talk to someone else first."

"What?" Natalie leaned closer.

"Nothing. So, you don't think you want to fall in love? Have you ever been in love?"

Natalie reeled a little. "No. I mean . . . no. Definitely not. I've never been in love. Not even close."

"More reason for the mancation?"

She decided not to answer that part and instead took another sip.

"Tell me about your parents," he finally said.

"My parents?"

"Yes. I'm not very good at small talk, so I'm just jumping to the parts I really want to know. Your parents—are they still in your life? Do they live nearby?"

"Um, well, okay—my dad—he's been out of my life for a long time. He left my mom when I was two. And my mom—she lives in Los Angeles. She runs an event-planning company for celebrities."

"No kidding?"

"Yeah. This is after she ran a modeling agency. She's very successful."

"You sound upset about that."

"She's pushy. She wants us girls to be successful, too. And I didn't want to be a model, so now she's pushing me into the event planning."

"You didn't want to be a model?"

"I tried it when I was young, but I found it horribly uncomfortable."

"You're very pretty." He threw her a quick smile and then stared back into his drink.

The compliment sent a little heat into her own cheeks. She'd been wolf-whistled at, gawked at, grabbed at, and stared down since she was thirteen, but somehow this shy man, who looked away and turned a deep shade of red when he said "You're very pretty," had delivered the compliment that did her in. Maybe it was because it was clearly uncomfortable for him and yet he said it anyway—a true gift meant for her.

"Thank you," she finally said.

He didn't look up, and she used the opportunity to stare more. She'd grown to love the way his hair fell into his eyes—it looked distracted and messy at the same time, which she found appealing for some reason. Like he was so lost in thought he couldn't be bothered to notice his hair had fallen in his eyes. She also loved his forearms, and she could appreciate them now because he had his dress sleeves rolled up. She loved the way they looked muscled and roped, leading to hands that were strong and gentle at the same time. Natalie remembered the way those fingers had worked that point at the back of her knee, and she felt a residual flush.

She cleared her throat and tried to find her place in the conversation again. "Ultimately, I got out of modeling when I was thirteen. I didn't like people looking at me, scrutinizing every feature."

He finally looked back at her. "They scrutinized at thirteen?"

"Oh, yeah. Your waist is too long. Your nose is too short. Your arms don't hang right, or don't touch your thigh in exactly the right place. It was excruciating. And the men . . ." She shook her head.

"At *thirteen*?" he asked tightly.

She waved off the question. This was too personal. She didn't mean to drag him back into this topic and certainly didn't want to discuss aggressive men with him. "What about you? Tell me about your parents."

He hesitated as if he didn't quite want to leave the last statement alone, but he finally shifted on his bar stool and took another gulp of his martini. "My parents are dead, actually. I lost them when I was a kid. Home invasion and murder. Only my sister and I survived."

Her heart caught in her throat. "Oh, Elliott! I'm so sorry."

Images of a tiny little Elliott and a young sister and their murdered parents floated in front of her and brought tears to her eyes. "How old were you?"

"Seven."

A small gasp escaped her throat. "That's how old Lily is."

"Is she? Lily is seven?"

"Yes."

"She seems so small." He frowned into his drink. "I always thought I was old enough to have figured something out, or acted more bravely, but now that I see a seven-year-old from an adult's perspective . . . I mean, I'd never expect that of Lily."

"Of course not. I'm sure you were very brave. What could a seven-year-old do except survive that kind of horrible situation?"

He seemed to think that over for a second, frowning at the bar top. "I didn't mean to bring the conversation down. I hardly ever talk about it. And here I just told it to you and the Colonel within a twenty-minute time span. Let's move on."

"So who raised you?"

He sighed. "No convincing you to move on?"

"I'm not easily convinced."

He let slip a smile that had a slight sense of admiration around the edges.

"My granddad, mostly," he said. "My grandmother, too, when she was alive, but that was for only a short time. We stayed with them a lot, and when they had failing health, we'd go to other relatives. I spent time in lots of areas of the country—Illinois, Wisconsin, two months in Minnesota."

"This is the grandfather with all the hats and the acorns in his yard?"

"That's the one."

"You were very close to him." She said this as more of a statement than a question, but Elliott nodded again.

"Especially after losing your parents." Tears burned the backs of her eyes at the image of a lost little Elliott, moving from state to state, from relative to relative. "I'm so very sorry, Elliott."

He glanced up but didn't respond to that.

"So, Nell, yeah, I think it's why she feels the need to take care of me," he finally said. "Baseless now, but she stays in that role."

"And that's why she's trying to find you the perfect mate?"

"I guess."

"That's sweet, actually."

"Unnecessary, though."

A swell of empathy expanded in Natalie's chest—that was certainly something she could relate to, having older sisters feel as though you couldn't take care of yourself. But seeing it now, from Elliott's sister's perspective, she could see that it probably stemmed from concern and protectiveness. Maybe her sisters were simply reacting the same way? They were the older sibs, the ones "put in charge," and they didn't know how to relinquish their roles any more than Natalie and Elliott knew how to get out from under theirs.

She drew in a deep breath, ready to ask him more, but just then, over Elliott's shoulder, she saw Marie approaching.

Elliott turned to follow Natalie's gaze. "How are things going, Marie?" he asked.

"Fine," Marie said. "I came over to tell you kids that you can leave now."

Natalie frowned. "Leave? Now? How will you get back?"

"We're staying."

"Staying, yes, of course. But staying for how long? Will you need a ride—" Natalie caught Marie's glance upward at the hotel rooms. "Oh! *Staying.* Yes. Gotcha." Natalie reached for her purse. *Well, good for Marie. Staying over with the Colonel!*

"All righty then," she said, leaping off her bar stool.

"But could you two take one cart back together and leave one for us? He can drive us back in the morning."

"Yes, of course," Elliott said. "I'll leave the Colonel's here."

"Thanks, dears," Marie said, shuffling back to the table.

Elliott looked back at Natalie with raised eyebrows. "I didn't see that coming."

"Me neither."

He took the last swig of his drink. "Can I catch a ride back down with you then?"

"Of course."

Outside, the crickets trilled their spring-evening chirp as Natalie started up the golf cart and began slowly making her way down the bumpy dirt mountain road. Maybe she could talk to him a little more about sisters. It was nice to have someone to talk to who might really understand, who knew how hard it was to prove you were capable of taking care of yourself.

She leaned farther forward, though, to peer through the fog and make sure she knew where she was going. It was scary to be heading down at such a severe pitch in the dark and mist. She tried to ignore the fact that Elliott was clinging to the side rails and sucking in his breath every time she turned a corner.

"Do you want me to drive?" he asked.

"Of course not."

A stroke of heat went over her ears at that. It wasn't as if she couldn't drive. She considered herself a good driver, actually. Most of these golf carts went only twenty miles an hour, but she was good on the brakes and turns.

She picked up a little speed, just to show him how good she was, but the hill was steep and the fog was thick, and the cart began careening. It whirled around the next corner, but the turn was too sharp, the road too slick, the cart too top-heavy, and a rock caught one of the tires. As they flew around the next bend, her headlights cut through the mist to catch the enormous head of a bison, which stood like a monument in the middle of the road. Natalie slammed on the brakes, swung the wheel sharply to the left, and fought as the cart spun top-heavily to the side, then slid toward the edge of a cliff.

Her head lurched forward, and her heart came into her throat, as they skidded to a sickening stop.

A terrible silence surrounded her as she peered up through the swirling dirt.

"Elliott?"

CHAPTER 17

Silence filled the night air as Natalie peered through the dust and faced the overhang of a hillside.

"Don't move," Elliott finally whispered.

Their headlights illuminated nothingness below them—thin night air, with clouds of dust mingling with the fog and swirling in both beams. A gust of wind came up the canyon, whistling through the hills, and the cart wobbled slightly forward. Natalie stifled a scream.

"Okay," Elliott said, low. "Stay calm. I'm going to move a little toward the back, to put some weight back there. Then I want you to come behind me and jump off."

"I c-c-can't move," Natalie whispered. She couldn't feel her legs. She wasn't sure they could even operate. She felt as if she couldn't shift, couldn't move, couldn't even breathe or else the cart would go over. She leaned back as far as possible and tried not to let out a breath.

"I'll help you," Elliott said gently. "Let me get the cart steady. Just . . . stay calm. And stay still."

Natalie wanted nothing less. She wanted to freeze in place. She didn't want even a gust of wind to come up. She certainly didn't want

Elliott to move at all. But before she could give voice to her horror, he slithered his body backward until he turned and moved in three long breaths to the very back of the cart. The cart bobbled up and down. Natalie stifled another scream. The cart seemed to find a more secure resting place, and the headlights rose slightly into higher air.

"Okay, now you," he said.

"I c-c-can't, Elliott."

"Just try. The weight is back here now. You'll feel it as soon as you turn toward me. I'll grab your hand and pull you."

She leaned her body back as far as the seat would allow, shaking with every inch. The feeling seemed to come back into her legs, and she swung them—very, very slowly—toward the back. When the cart didn't seem to shift forward, she finally relaxed some weight onto her right leg, then swung her left and threw her weight in one swift move to the back seats. Elliott caught her arm as she was in motion. She froze when the cart bobbled, and they both waited for it to stop. Finally the headlights rose even farther, level now with the ground. Her heart seemed to start beating again.

"Now step off," he whispered.

Fear seized her again. "What will happen to you?" she said into the still air. She was afraid to turn toward him.

"I'll be fine." His hand gripped her elbow, and he directed her toward the side of the cart. She hesitated, stepping once toward the ground to see if the cart would bob forward. It dipped slightly.

"Elliott, no! You'll go over."

"I won't. I'll be right behind you—I promise."

He didn't look as though he was going to be right behind her. He looked as if he was holding down the back for her. She was so worried the cart would take him over the edge. But his voice was calm, and she decided to trust that he would know the physics of this situation.

"Okay, I'm going to step off now," she whispered.

The crickets trilled in the bushes surrounding the back of the cart, making the night seem so much calmer than it was. Natalie glanced back at Elliott once more. His eyes were steady on her, and he nodded once.

She stepped off slowly, hoping not to rock the cart, but as soon as her last foot left the floorboard, she felt the vehicle teeter. She whirled around to scream, but Elliott was, indeed, right behind her. He threw his arm across her back and brought them both to the ground. The cart groaned forward, stilled for a second, then careened down the side of the mountain. Its fiberglass side was punched in at the first rock. After two bumps, it toppled over and tumbled the rest of the way into the canyon. Branches snapped, dust flew, bangs echoed, and then, finally, everything stilled.

They stood and looked over the canyon in the eerie silence. Finally the crickets started trilling again.

Natalie began shivering uncontrollably. Her legs wobbled. She started to sink to the ground.

"Hey now," Elliott said, dragging her back up. He held her elbows as he let her find her balance. She wanted to lean into him—let him hold her, let herself shake, let his body warmth seep all the way through her until she calmed.

But just as she shifted her weight to allow herself to step into his arms, his eyes went up over her shoulder. His whole body stiffened.

"Easy, boy," he said quietly.

Natalie took three long seconds to turn her head. The bison's enormous woolly-brown head and two half-hooded brown eyes stared in their direction, as if he was watching how the night's events might go. His white horns twisted once, then pointed back toward them. He snorted, and his entire body shook.

"Walk slowly and deliberately, but don't look like a threat." Elliott put his arm around Natalie's shoulders and directed her to the side.

They took long, slow, smooth steps until they'd walked about a hundred feet and around two more bends. Elliott never looked back. After their shoes had crunched the gravel about another fifty paces, he finally looked over his shoulder and brought them to a gradual stop.

He put his hands on Natalie's shoulders and turned her toward him.

As if all the adrenaline had finally slipped away, her legs began to shake. Tears felt like they were pressing against a dam in the back of her head.

"It's okay," he said.

That was all it took—Elliott's soft voice, his reassuring words, his sheltering arms—and her tears burst out as she dove into his shoulder.

Elliott pulled her toward him.

"It's okay. It's okay."

They stood that way for a long time, holding each other in the darkness and the fog, Elliott running his hand down the locks that had come undone, rubbing her back. He pulled her head into the crook of his neck and let her cry.

Her mascara and lipstick left stains all over his shirt, but he felt so good—so safe—that she allowed herself to sniffle for another five minutes, releasing all the fear, all the panic, all the worry she'd been feeling, possibly for fifteen years. She'd always felt she had to protect herself, and had put herself with men who looked as if they could protect her. But they never could, and they'd never had the concern for her that Elliott seemed to have right now. It felt so good to be held this way, by a man who could be gentle with her, who wanted to calm her, who seemed to want her to be truly safe.

He stroked her hair again. She felt him kiss the top of her forehead.

And then she sniffled, hesitated, and caught his lips with hers.

Elliott felt the warmest lips he'd ever known in his life slide across his, and he started at first but then leaned in and welcomed her.

Her body was so pliant, now sliding against his, and his hands felt like homing beacons, quickly finding their way into her hair, holding her close to position her so he could kiss her as thoroughly as he'd been wanting to. He pressed further, taking a step back with her, wanting to absorb her, be inside her, be part of her, protect her, as they backed up against a sharp outcropping. His hand came out to block her from the granite as his lips explored hers, resting her back slowly so he could enjoy this, take her, move his hands down to—

"Wait." Natalie lifted her palms against his chest.

He pulled back, panting, his brain not quite able to catch up with his libido.

"I can't do this," she said, pushing tendrils of hair off her face. "I—I'm on a mancation, Elliott. I can't . . ." She shoved past him and stepped back onto the road, standing there with her arms wrapped around herself.

He took five rapid breaths and sent a slew of curse words through his head.

Natalie looked at him, her eyes filled with remorse. "Elliott, that wasn't . . . I didn't mean to do that. That wasn't a kiss."

"It wasn't?"

"No."

"I'd say it was quite a kiss."

"No. It wasn't. I was just . . . reacting to all that." She waved her hand back toward the bison and the fallen cart. "And my fear was just coming out, and . . . comfort, really. That was comfort."

Elliott took a small step back. His body was on fire right now, his body parts all at full attention. Damned if that was just comfort. But she was saying no.

"And . . ." She waved her hand in a frustrated windmill. "You have your date tonight. You have to get back to Becky."

Damn it. He'd nearly forgotten about Becky. He wanted to stay here. He *would* stay here—on this road, in the dark, in the cool night air—for the rest of his life if it meant he could hold this woman in his arms like that, feel her hair fall out of her 1940s pins and across his forearms, feel her body soften against his, feel her relax into his chest. *Just* like that.

"Natalie," he whispered. He didn't really know where he was going with the next thought. His thoughts were completely muddled, but mostly he knew he didn't want to stop. He didn't want anyone else. And he wanted Natalie with every ounce of his soul.

But she started hustling down the road.

"Where are you going?"

"We have to get back. We have to get you to your date. Don't think that . . . That didn't mean anything, okay? That was just—"

He frowned. "Comfort?"

"Yes. Absolutely."

They walked swiftly down the road in silence, Elliott two or three steps behind her, thinking about what the hell had just happened. He had to calm himself. He had the urge to reach out right now and whirl her toward him, yank her back into his arms, kiss her the way he wanted to—kiss her the way she'd been kissing him.

But no was no.

And she'd clearly made up her mind, given the dust flying off her shoes as she scurried away.

"You know it's two miles down this mountain, right?" he called.

"We'll survive. If we could survive"—her hand waved again—"*that*, then I think we can survive a little walk down a mountain."

They walked another quarter of a mile in silence, Elliott cursing himself a hundred ways through his head, wondering if he'd pushed too much, if he'd not pushed enough, if he was an asshole for kissing this woman he desperately wanted against a rock outcropping on a foggy, deserted road while another woman, whom he didn't want, was waiting for him in her bed.

He shoved his hand through his hair, then slowed as Natalie turned toward him.

"Elliott, we survived *that*." She grinned.

Her sass was back. Her bravado was back. Gone was the woman who'd crumpled in his arms, who'd held him tight. Gone was the woman who was vulnerable to him for a minute. Gone was the one who let him protect her, who brought him out of his worry that he wouldn't be courageous enough in the right circumstances, who made him feel brave and courageous and strong. Gone was the woman who'd kissed him.

But his mind stilled for a second on the courageous part. Who knew that all that adrenaline would kick in and allow him to think straight and stay calm when he had someone he needed to protect? He was relieved and grateful—to God, to the universe, to Natalie herself. He breathed a sigh of relief and felt like a changed man.

He started following her again, following the dust flying up behind her USO shoes. He even managed a smile as she reached back and pulled all the loose tendrils of hair into a twist, shoving them under her cap with some pins.

He'd done that to her.

And damned if that kiss was nothing.

Damned if that kiss was comfort.

Her argument did serve to soothe their consciences—his regarding Becky and hers regarding her bet—but she'd *kissed* him.

But he chose to join her in denial and kept marching down the hill.

CHAPTER 18

"How am I going to explain this to Olivia?" Natalie asked to the crunching of her shoes along the gravel, right next to Elliott's.

They were nearly at the bottom now, and Natalie was exhausted. Her USO costume was rumpled and dirty and torn at the sleeve. Her shoe strap was broken from when they'd fallen in the dirt, and the heel was wobbling. Her hat was falling off, and her makeup was probably all over her face, her lipstick eaten off from chewing her lip all the way down the mountain and wondering how she was going to explain this to everyone.

But, man, explain she'd have to.

She'd have to tell Olivia about her cart. She'd have to come up with several thousand dollars and a plan to pay her back. She'd have to explain to Paige about that kiss and how it wouldn't end their bet. She might have to explain to Becky about that kiss and how she wasn't getting in the way. And mostly she had to explain to herself about that kiss. And what honestly drove it, and how she was not getting attached to Elliott Sherman—tears, hugs, gratitude, return kiss, and attraction to his dancing jaw muscles notwithstanding.

Maybe if she said it to herself enough times she'd believe it.

"We can call an insurance company in the morning," Elliott said.

"We?"

"Or you. I can help. And I can help you pay for it, if you need."

"Why would you do that?"

"I want to help."

Natalie shot him a glance. He probably did. Elliott was too sweet for words, and all she could do was deny everything about him, including how she was falling for him by the minute. Those moments earlier—the moment he'd saved her out of the golf cart, the moment he'd moved her around the bison, the way he'd let her cling to him and cry into his shirt, the way his hand had felt cradling the back of her head, the way he'd kissed with a talent that curled her toes—those were all too close to a flame.

Natalie had felt herself falling—into him, into his arms, into his chest, into a fire of feeling she didn't want to observe too closely because it felt too scary and raw. She'd never let herself be so vulnerable with another human being—and especially a man she didn't know very well—and it was causing all her self-preservation tactics to go on high alert. She felt she'd been too close to another kind of dangerous ledge—not just the one the cart had teetered on but one that would take her heart over the edge, knock it around on some rocks, and dump it into the canyon below. She knew she needed to distance herself.

"I'll handle it," she said.

Elliott was so different from the men she'd known in the past, the dates that had flashed and burned. Those were actual dates, and usually a spontaneous combustion of sorts, with lots of lust fueling them but no feeling. And when the lust ended—the need satiated, the curiosity filled—there was nothing left.

But with Elliott, things were different. It was a slowly growing attraction. She was filled with so much feeling toward him—tenderness, care, the need to protect him from bad girlfriends and bad dates. And every time there was a physical touch, her feelings became more intense, not less. The kinder he got, the sexier he got. Each new feeling, each new thing she learned about him, each new link of connection made him more and more attractive to her. And, from there, each touch came alive with a thousand new volts.

Pressing in with the terror of being too close to feelings she didn't know what to do with, she also felt shame for her earlier driving bravado and the fact that she could have gotten him killed.

She just wanted to get away from him right now and not look him in the eye. Her emotions were all over the place.

"I'm just going to cut through here, at the bottom of the hill," she said.

"I'm absolutely not letting you walk home all by yourself like this. Let's get my cart. It's only two blocks that way."

"I'm fine." She started in the direction she wanted.

"Natalie, stop." He frowned at her. "What's wrong? What happened in the last five minutes?"

She couldn't let her eyes rest on how sexy and protective he looked right now. And she didn't want her gaze to fall anywhere near his lips.

"Nothing," she said, directing her attention to a night-blooming jasmine plant. "I'm just . . . tired. And glad you're okay. And glad I'm okay. And I could've gotten us killed. And I'm sorry. And I just want to go home."

"Please let me take you home."

"But it's right there." She pointed lamely.

"Then we'll both walk."

She rolled her eyes and started for her back alleyway. If he wanted to follow her, fine. He'd have to walk all the way back to his cart if he did, but that was his call.

She stomped to Olivia's place—around the back fence, down the alleyway, past the old tin garbage cans put out for the week, past Mrs. Freeman's cat hiding in the oleander bush, past the trellis of morning glories that were all closed up for the night, past the gerbera daisies she'd planted just this morning. Elliott was still behind her.

She'd never had a man follow her all the way home before to make sure she got there safely. Even though she'd always selected big, tough-looking men to scare off the leering ones, their size and bluster tended to be for show. When it came to truly caring about her well-being—like whether or not she got home safely—they were nowhere to be found. Or they were still in the bar trying to pick another fight, caring more about how they looked to other men than her.

Natalie sighed as she and Elliott arrived at Olivia's back door.

"Thank you," she said over her shoulder. "I'll see you later." She jiggled the handle the way they always did to be let into the cottage, and slipped inside.

She just wanted to get away from her feelings, away from this night, away from Elliott's sincere protectiveness, away from his velvet lips, and especially away from his confused, half-lidded eyes.

Elliott wasn't exactly sure what had just happened, or what he'd done wrong, but he knew it was something. He watched Natalie slide through her sister's barely opened door without so much as a backward glance, noted the gerbera daisies he'd given her that were now planted by the doorway, and turned to stare out into the night.

He headed for his golf cart and replayed the last half hour in his head. Why had she quieted down like that? He hadn't said anything much in the last ten minutes, so it couldn't have been something he said. But, then again, maybe that was the problem—maybe it was something he *didn't* say? But what would that be? How should he have known? Did other men know? Would the Colonel have known? Would John-O? It must be something obvious because she looked awfully pissed.

Damn, women were confusing.

His golf cart was the last one in the Shore Thing parking lot, and he swung himself in and started the ignition, heading up to the other side of town. He had one more task to finish tonight. Another thing that would take some courage. And it was probably waiting for him in lounge clothes with a bunch of dogs locked in a separate room . . .

He was clearly not cut out for this.

After tonight, he was sticking to microbiology.

Natalie woke the next morning and stepped up to the plate in every way she could think of: She told Olivia everything that happened, called the insurance company, met the agent out at the hill to take pictures and show where the cart had gone over and where the bison had been. She came back to discuss a payment plan with Olivia, then took Lily and Paige out on a picnic on the beach so she could talk to her sister.

Elliott had called and left four messages, but she hadn't returned any of them yet. She wasn't quite ready to deal with him, or her changing feelings. But, while running away seemed easier, and the way she would normally have done things, she knew it wasn't the right thing anymore. She finally texted that she was fine and would call him soon. She took a deep breath and told herself she could get through this.

"So how did the rest of the evening go?" Paige asked as they laid out their beach chairs and towels.

"Can I go down?" Lily asked, pointing at the water.

"Yes, but only to your waist."

They watched Lily dancing through the shore break and set up their picnic lunch. Natalie told Paige the whole story, starting with Marie's big reveal, Natalie's surprise at seeing the Colonel at the hotel, and her bigger surprise at seeing Elliott at the table. By the time she got to the part about the bison, Paige gaped at her.

"No!"

"Yes, I don't know where that bison came from."

"So what happened next?"

Once Natalie described her fear and terror, she hoped the kiss would explain itself. But Paige was sharply shaking her head.

"I definitely won," Paige said.

"Paige! No. I'm still on my mancation. I'm not dating him. He was heading down to Becky's house for his real date—I'm sure he's sleeping with her. The kiss meant nothing romantic. And that's the last I saw of him."

Paige looked at her skeptically. "How long did this kiss last?"

"How long?"

"That's right."

Natalie ran it back through her mind, embarrassed that it was on speed dial because she'd already run it back through her mind forty times. "Maybe three seconds?"

"Three?"

"Maybe four."

"Wait, *four*?"

"Okay, maybe five . . ."

Paige sighed and stared out at the ocean. She ran her feet through the sand a few times. "Natalie, you can't keep kissing this guy and telling me you're still on a mancation. You say it's for instruction or comfort or whatever, but the fact is, you've kissed him three times. And five seconds is a long time for a comfort kiss. Bets don't work this way."

Natalie couldn't help but lower her eyes. Paige was right. Her feelings toward Elliott were suspect at best. Damn, did she really just fall so quickly for another man? What was wrong with her? And were her feelings true anyway? Or did she just do that because he was available and yet off-limits? She watched the waves roll into shore and wondered if she'd really become a woman so dependent on men she couldn't even—

"Double or nothing," Paige blurted.

"What?"

"Double or nothing. I think you're slipping, but I have faith in you. I know you're not weak. I know you can do this. I know you can last one season without a man to lean on. You can, right?"

"Of course," Natalie snapped without thinking.

"Then double or nothing."

"Seven hundred dollars?"

"Seven hundred."

The ocean waves crashed in front of them, and Natalie thought that over. Surely she was strong enough to be without a boyfriend for two more friggin' weeks, right? She definitely had feelings toward Elliott, but she could control them properly, couldn't she? It would give her a chance anyway to explore what her feelings were exactly, and make sure she wasn't just using him because he was one of the only twenty-somethings on the island she enjoyed being around. She could cool her attraction and her obsession with his forearms and live independently for that short a time. Couldn't she?

"Okay, you're on."

"Another kiss ends it, Natalie."

"Fine. Another kiss ends it, no matter what."

"And I need your whole three-month stay now."

Natalie stared back at her. "The whole three months?" she asked weakly.

"That's right."

Natalie watched Lily leap through the sea foam as a family of seagulls squawked overhead. The whole three months? That would probably mean she'd never get to date Elliott at all. It's not as if she could wait the mancation out and then go out with him only seconds before she returned to the mainland. That wouldn't be right anyway. If she knew he was waiting on the other end of her mancation, it wasn't much of a mancation, now was it? Paige was right. Either Paige had won right now, and Natalie had to admit she couldn't live without a man, or Natalie should keep betting. If she couldn't keep betting, Paige had every right to win.

"You're a strong girl," Paige said quietly. She sounded almost apologetic. "I want to see you stand on your own. I'm impressed with everything you've done here so far—the jobs you've taken on. You're taking great care of Lily. You're committing to a lot of impressive things with the seniors. But I want you to take this mancation seriously. Prove to yourself that you can be a whole person by yourself. No boyfriend. Three months."

"Thanks, Mom."

"I'm serious. Olivia and I are worried about you. We don't want you to be forty someday and realize you have nothing—no serious job, no serious man, no savings, no home."

Natalie looked away. She had to admit that she, too, had this worry sometimes, much more often as she neared thirty. She knew she had a lot of time, but she was shocked at how fast her twenties were going by—she might slide right into her thirties, playing these same runaway games, and be caught on the end of that decade with nothing to show. She certainly had nothing to show for her twenties.

She shook out her arms and took a deep breath, putting on her new mature, relaxed face. "You don't have to worry about me. I'm very determined."

Paige reached out her hand. "Okay, then. Double or nothing. All three months."

Natalie stared at her hand for a second, wondering again if this was the right thing to do, but then shook. It was. She needed to show her sisters the truth. The new Natalie. She was taking on responsibility, commitment, and making good decisions. She was independent. She'd be fine on her own.

"I need to talk to Elliott today, though—just warning you," she said.

"I don't mind if you talk to him—just no kissing and no sex. Can you do that?"

"Of course."

Natalie decided not to analyze how close to a lie that was. After the last three toe-curling kisses and the sexy new way he looked at her from under his eyebrows, she knew it might very well be a problem. But she'd just have to lie to herself, stay out of his radius, and avoid falling any further to prove she was as independent as she kept saying she was.

"Then talk away." Paige shrugged.

Natalie could hear the smile—or maybe the taunt—in Paige's voice, and she simply ground her teeth in response.

"C'mon," Paige said, lifting from her chair. "Let's build Lily a sand castle before I have to catch the ferry home."

By the time Natalie ended the day, she felt like a real grown-up. She'd owned up to all her mistakes; arranged to pay for them as best she could; had been through several phone trees to talk to insurance agents; found a temporary replacement cart for Olivia; said her apologies; walked Paige and her luggage to the ferry; and even managed to make breakfast, lunch, and dinner for Lily and play five excruciating rounds of Candy Land. If this wasn't being an adult, she didn't know what was.

One thing remained, though: she still needed to talk to Elliott. And she knew another apology was in order. It was rude of her to run away from him the way she had, especially when he'd become freaking Superman last night. It was time to face the music. She would call on her greatest maturity and refuse to fall for him any further. She could do this.

"Elliott? It's me, Natalie," she said into the phone, staring at the sun starting to set out the slider door. "Can we talk for a minute?"

"Uh . . . yeah. Let's talk in person. I'll head down your way."

She smoothed her hair back into its braid and went outside to wait for him.

He looked really good today. He had on beach shorts and a button-down shirt that was rolled up at the sleeves. His hair was a mess as usual, being blown about by the wind, but that was one of the things she was starting to love about him. He had on his glasses today, but he must have gotten transition lenses because they'd darkened into shades in front of the setting sun. She watched him coming up the dune with his hands in his pockets, silhouetted against the sherbet-orange sky, and wondered how she'd ever missed how hot Dr. Sherman was.

"Let's go down," he said, nodding back toward the ocean.

They wandered along the water's edge, the ocean splashing their bare feet, as Natalie assured him everything was taken care of regarding the golf cart and that she didn't need any help.

"But mostly I wanted to apologize," she said in a whoosh.

A small wave overtook their calves. "Apologize?"

"For running away from you last night. I should have left the evening expressing my thanks that you got us through something that was so scary, but instead I ran away and said nothing."

"Why were you running away?"

"I was just . . ."

It was hard for Natalie to admit this. She didn't want to let her feelings out of Pandora's box and let them fly all willy-nilly. She needed to keep them controlled, with names she could handle. It wasn't just the bet money. It was because she didn't know what these particular emotions were. She didn't know what this fear was; she didn't know what that relief was when she fell into Elliott's arms last night; she didn't know what drove her to kiss him when they weren't even dating. She'd had rushes of lust toward many men, but this was something deeper and scarier. It was soft and soothing and vulnerable and raw all at the same time.

She took a deep breath. "It was just an emotional night, and my emotions were all over the place, and then I kissed you, but I didn't mean to. I didn't mean it in a . . . you know, in an attracted kind of way. I meant it in an emotional kind of way. But then I worried that I was giving the completely wrong message. And I'm on a mancation, and I have to win this bet with Paige, so I can't have feelings for you."

He did a double take. "Feelings?"

"Yes, feelings."

"You have feelings for me?"

"No. I can't have feelings for you. That's what I'm saying. We can be friends. But that's it. And you should date Becky. You said you might want something long-term, and you're a long-term kind of guy, and Becky's probably right for that, and I might be a commitment-phobe, and . . . I'm just making a mess of all of this. I'm so sorry I kissed you like that, and I should apologize to her, too."

"That won't be necessary."

"Why not?"

"We're not dating."

"What?"

"I went over last night and told her we probably shouldn't go out anymore."

Natalie stopped in the sand. The ocean roared behind her. "What? Why?"

The wind whipped his hair about his head as he glanced out into the water, then back at her. "Because maybe I'm having feelings for you, too."

She sucked in her breath and backed away slightly. "No, Elliott. You can't have feelings for me. I'm not—I'm on a mancation, and I have to win this bet. And if you have feelings for me, then . . . Please, you can't call things off with her."

She closed her eyes. This couldn't be happening. This was not a mancation. This was falling right back into a relationship. She didn't want to lose the bet money, of course, but mostly she needed to prove to herself that she was strong enough to be by herself for three friggin' months out of her very long life. Elliott was handsome and sexy and smart—he fascinated her on an intellectual level and was starting to make her heart pound every time he looked at her. And he made her feel strong and worthwhile. But she needed to feel worthwhile on her own.

"I truly can't see you, Elliott."

"How about if we wait until the mancation ends—then I'll ask you out?"

She told herself not to look at how cute his smile was when he asked that. Instead, she focused on the misery falling down through her stomach.

"I'm not sure that's how mancations work. If I know you're on the horizon, I'm not legitimately taking a break, now am I? And besides, Paige doubled down and extended it for my whole stay."

He dropped his head. A long silence followed in which he probably realized what she was saying.

"Okay, I can take a hint. Or not so much a hint—a direct request. I'll leave you alone." He started to walk away.

"Wait! You don't have to leave altogether. I mean, we can be friends, right?"

His smile turned wry. "I . . . I don't really know if that's possible, Natalie."

"Let's try. You're such a nice guy. Really. And I like having you as a friend."

"Nice?"

"Of course."

Natalie felt as if she'd lost him. She joked with him the rest of the walk, and he laughed at all the right places, but he seemed distant, as though he'd already moved on, moved his heart out of playing range and into a safe place.

She didn't blame him.

But she'd make this work.

Even if she had to lie to herself the whole time.

CHAPTER 19

On Monday morning, Natalie got up and began her workweek, excited about her more mature life and ready to keep turning over new leaves.

She, Lily, and Olivia fell into their morning routine over the next two weeks, and work at Casas del Sur kept her busy. The only thing she avoided at all costs was driving to the Friends of the Sea Lion center. Being only friends with Elliott—and keeping her heart from pounding like a giddy schoolgirl's every time she saw him—was going to take some working up to. Being a strong, independent woman was harder than she thought.

"Why don't you take us this week instead of John-O?" Doris asked over a bridge hand on the Casas del Sur poolside patio.

"John-O and I have a pretty good system set up," Natalie said, looking at her new hand. "Besides, I like going on the harbor walks with all of you."

Katherine, Marie, and Helen all bobbed their sun hats in understanding.

"Of course, dear, but we miss having you at the center," Doris said. "No trump."

Natalie noticed that Doris didn't mention another certain someone who might miss having her at the center, so she remained silent on that matter.

"John-O and I have worked out a good system," Natalie repeated. "Pass."

"They're going to need lots of volunteers," Doris said. "They're already seeing a crazy onslaught this week. Dr. Sherman seems distraught."

"Distraught?" Natalie snapped her head up.

"He's been very stressed out."

A pang of sadness shot through Natalie. She hated to think of Elliott getting more stressed out about his sea lions. "Are they surviving?" she asked hesitantly.

"The sea lions are doing surprisingly well, although they're getting crowded now. They had their first few releases this week and were able to send fifteen back into the wild. But the numbers keep increasing, and some of the sea lions are getting sicker again. I think they're getting close to a hundred now."

"*A hundred?* All there at once?"

"They could really use your help, dear." Doris swept up the hand she'd just won. "Of course, I told Dr. Sherman and Dr. Stout they need some downtime. They can't keep working at that level of intensity and last all spring. Dr. Sherman said he runs in the mornings."

Natalie stared at her cards. Yeah, she knew that. She'd been setting her alarm a half hour earlier so she could go out on the balcony in the peaceful beach silence and sit with her coffee to catch glimpses of Elliott running along the beach. She never in a million years thought she'd be the type of person to get up every morning at five thirty, of her own volition, but there she was, day after day, sitting on the patio, peering through the bougainvillea. When Paige came in on the weekends, Natalie skipped the ritual, but come Monday morning she was out there again. She told herself she didn't need to. She told herself she just liked getting a jump-start on her day. Some days the fog rolled in and she could barely see him—just a rhythmic, lithe form, moving to the sound of the ocean waves roaring in and hissing out—and it gave her peace: the ocean, Elliott's movement, knowing he was still out there, knowing they were the only two on the beach at that exact moment.

"I'm also giving Dr. Sherman dance lessons starting on Tuesday," Doris said.

Natalie looked up again from her cards. "Dance lessons?"

"The Colonel and I are giving him a dating makeover."

Natalie ignored the pang of jealousy that shot through her and reorganized her cards in her hand. This would be good. If she was going to be a true friend, she should be happy he was dating. He deserved to meet someone nice and long-term. She'd chosen to bow out of that plan. She could barely commit to a phone plan. And she'd never wanted to stay on the island—the idea made her claustrophobic as soon as she thought about it.

She just needed to stay out of Elliott's way for a little while and get her independence established. Then she could possibly reenter his life as a true friend.

"Why don't you come to the center with us this week and maybe lend an extra hand?" Doris pressed.

"No trump," Natalie said. "What can I help with?"

"They definitely need help cleaning the ICU rooms."

The other women nodded over their cards in agreement.

"One spade," said Katherine.

"And they could use more towels, and help washing the towels they have," Doris added.

"Definitely," Marie said. "Pass."

"Actually, that's a great idea," Doris said. "If we all get together, we can probably help with the towels. We have a lot of washing machines here at the apartments—many more than they do. Maybe we can start a rotation."

Natalie nodded. That would have to do. She wanted to help, but she didn't trust herself to see Elliott right now.

"So, did we find a band for the prom?" Katherine asked, laying down one of her cards.

"We found a great big band on the mainland, and they even said they'd let Trummy play along with them," Doris said.

"That's perfect," Natalie said. "Do you need me to arrange anything or take the ferry over?"

"No, you've been doing a terrific job with all your ideas so far—I love everything you've added."

"Thanks." Natalie had been having fun with the planning. She realized she'd absorbed more from her mother than she'd thought, and the organization came easily for her. She was able to find plenty of low-cost decorations, arrange numerous vendors, and coordinate entire teams to take care of things.

"We do need to get the favors we ordered," Doris said. "They're coming on the five o'clock ferry tomorrow night. Can you pick them up for us?"

"Sure." Natalie punched the details into her phone calendar.

"Who are you bringing to the prom, Natalie?" Katherine asked.

"I'm not bringing anyone. I'm on a mancation."

Doris looked at her quizzically. "A mancation?"

"A vacation from men."

"Why are you running away from men, dear?"

"I'm not running away."

Doris and Marie seemed to pass heavy glances at each other.

"That sounds like a good thing then," Doris said. "I would just hate to think you were running away from men altogether. Like Dr. Sherman, for instance."

Natalie's heart pounded ridiculously when Doris said that—she hadn't realized her feelings might be that transparent—but she ignored her heart and moved her aces together.

Doris smiled. "Your mancation sounds like a fine idea, if it's to find your strength as a woman. That's always a good thing. But I would think that a mancation is supposed to be taking a *self-imposed* vacation from men to build that strength, not running away from certain men. I'd say you should spend time with men plenty. Like Dr. Sherman. But simply resist the idea of hooking up with him."

"Doris!"

"Oh, I know you young people move things fast these days. I probably would, too, if I'd been born in your decade. I'm just saying, resist the hanky-panky. Just spend time as an independent woman. He won't bite. If you don't want him to." She giggled with Marie.

"Doris!"

"Anyway, quite frankly, I think he needs a friend."

A slice of panic went through Natalie. "What's wrong?"

Doris glanced up at her and gave her a small, knowing grin. "Nothing's wrong, per se, but you're such a kind girl, and he seems adrift, and I think you could be a good friend to him. You seem to understand and boost him."

"Boost him?"

"You boost his confidence instead of tearing it down. The other women on the island—including his sister—seem to want him to change, to be something he's not. More debonair, more outgoing, more mainstream, more this, more that. But you allow him to be himself. I think he needs someone like you right now. He's a lovely man. A true gentleman, as we used to say. And he needs someone who will let him be the man he needs to be. Anyway, trump for me. We'd better get these cards put away so we can get to swimming aerobics."

Natalie pushed her cards toward Doris and sat in the chair long after the ladies shuffled away.

Trump, indeed.

The following Wednesday, Natalie realized Doris was right. She couldn't run away from Elliott forever. When Steve Stegner asked for a volunteer to drive the cart to the center, she accepted.

As she pulled up the Concierge cart in front of the Friends of the Sea Lion center, she took a deep breath, adjusted her cap, and reminded herself to stay strong.

She dropped each of the volunteers off at their respective jobs, guiding some by the elbow. Her eyes widened at the sheer numbers of new sea lions. Little pups were all over the floors in every ICU room, some in baby playpens, some on towels on the cement. Varying levels of barks came from all corners of the hallways—some strong and sure, some weak and needy. Outside at the pools, there wasn't enough room either, and a few blowup pools had been set up to handle the overflow.

More volunteers than usual moved from one room to another, handling group feedings, medication, weighing, checkups, and "fishing for food" training at the pools.

Natalie glimpsed Elliott outside a propped-open back door waiting on a new rescue. He and Jim were motioning a golf cart in with gloved hands. They both leaped onto the cart bed to haul another cage off, handing it off one to another.

"This is a heavier one," Jim grunted.

"Good news, overall," Elliott said.

"Parasite infection," young Garrett said as he hopped out of the driver's seat, clipboard in hand.

Elliott hauled the cage in one deft movement toward the gurney he and Jim had waiting and glanced up at Natalie, almost dropping the cage.

"Natalie!"

"Hi, Elliott."

Jim came up behind him and grabbed the cage out of Elliott's seemingly frozen hand. "I've got this. You should take a break, Sherm.

You've been at this all morning. *Garrett!* Come help me get this guy into check-in."

Elliott pulled his gloves off and plopped down on a stair stoop.

"Good to see you," he said. "I haven't seen you around in a while." He motioned toward a wooden barrel that was next to the staircase.

Natalie took the barrel and sat beside him. "You've been busy."

"Yeah, it's been a little crazy."

"Doris says you're stressed out."

Elliott gave a tired half smile. "Doris always exaggerates. But I am worried about this epidemic."

"Is it worse than other years?"

"Yeah. I'm in touch with some scientists on the mainland, and they're seeing an influx, too. It's definitely dehydration for the pups. We think the mama sea lions are having to swim too far to get fish to feed their young, and by the time they're getting back, the pups are scrambling toward shore and getting washed up, already dehydrated."

He looked tired. Natalie had an urge to sit by him on the stoop and put her arm around him, but she didn't think they had that kind of friendship yet. With Elliott's admission that he might have feelings for her, and her own libido starting to go into overdrive just seeing him and his tanned forearms again, she didn't know if that would be wise just yet.

"How're Larry, Curly, and Moe?" she asked instead.

"Larry and Curly are doing okay. Moe took a bad turn five days ago and started losing weight. I'm keeping my eye on him."

"Oh no! Lily will be upset."

"Yeah, you might not want to bring her for a few days. Although . . . I mean, I noticed you haven't."

"Elliott . . ."

"Anyway, Moe looks bad, and the whole center looks crazy besides, so I wouldn't bring her this week. We're supposed to get some help from the mainland on Monday, so maybe after that things will look better."

"Can I see Moe?"

"Of course."

He walked her back into the center, popping his head in from room to room, until—amid the hundreds of brown-shaded sea lions in every corner—he somehow spotted Moe across a hall.

"There he is."

Moe was in one of the little playpens in the fourth ICU room, plopped lethargically into the corner on the pink-and-blue play mat, his head down. His large brown eyes peered up at them.

"Oh! He looks terrible."

"I think he may have contracted one of the viruses. Jim's been checking him out. He was sent back here to ICU, where they can feed him intravenously. He'll be okay, though. He's a fighter."

Natalie was pretty uncertain. Moe looked bad. His color had turned grayish again, and his ribs were showing. "Is there anything I can do right now?"

"Do you want to feed him?"

"Yes, I can do that."

Elliott spoke with the volunteer who was handling the feedings and pointed back at Natalie.

Then he returned to her. "Feeding time is in fifteen minutes. Can you wait?"

"Definitely."

"I have to get back to work." He pointed in the opposite direction.

"Yes. Of course."

He lingered in the doorway for a moment.

"It's good to see you, Natalie," he said before finally turning to leave.

Natalie felt her chest fall. He looked disappointed. Maybe he'd felt she abandoned him. Maybe he thought she didn't want to be friends. Maybe he thought she was like all the others Doris had described who wanted him to change first. Or maybe . . . maybe she just didn't know what she was doing, and she really didn't know how to be friends with a man.

She sighed and looked for something else to help with before she could feed Moe.

For the next two weeks, Natalie stopped at the center each day and tried to help where she could. She always popped in to see Moe, and snapped on gloves and did his feedings when her timing was in synch. At other times, she helped at other stations—weighing pups, moving laundry, driving the golf cart down to the harbor landing to pick up supplies, or whatever was called for. The center had been forced to relax its standards on volunteers, no longer insisting on a year's worth of training, as they tried to just get enough people to do all the work that needed to be done.

Lavender Island had really stepped up. Natalie always bumped into Doris, Marie, the Colonel, Sugar, and George at the center, even on their days off. John-O often tried to stay after his Casas del Sur driving was done. Sometimes June came. Tag was often there, and Mrs. Conner from the post office came to help some days, while Mr. Conner often donated his golf cart for extra rescues. Lily couldn't stand to be left out either and begged to come, so Natalie agreed to bring her once a week only. She'd broken the news to her that Moe wasn't doing well. Lily cried the first time she saw Moe in the playpen, but after that, she came back strong, wearing her EMT costume every visit with her stethoscope around her neck.

Like everyone else, Elliott became a full-fledged volunteer, not just a scientist. Gone was his lab coat. He spent most of his days in T-shirts and cargo shorts like the rescue teams.

Sometimes Natalie saw Elliott hauling sea lions from room to room. Other times she saw him in the feeding room, feeding the baby seals with baby bottles. Sometimes he was in the pool area, helping another volunteer haul out heavy buckets of fish, which they threw into the pool and watched to see if the sea lions were strong enough to catch fish to properly nourish themselves. Sometimes he was with Jim, back in his lab coat, soothing a sea lion from seizures. And other times he was out behind the propped-open back door with his gloves on, waving the next golf cart in with new intakes.

The following Wednesday night, Natalie drove home with Lily and realized, right after dinner, that Lily had left her Elsa doll at the center. Natalie called to find out if someone would still be there to let her in and got Tiffany, who assured her she was staying until midnight.

Natalie bounced along in her golf cart back through Canyon Road and parked in the cool night air. The center was mostly closed down, but she could see two lights still on.

The gravel crunched underneath her tennis shoes as she headed in.

"Tiffany?" she called into the silence.

"I'm here," she heard a voice call out to her.

She walked around the corner to where Tiffany was folding donation letters into envelopes.

"There you are!" Tiffany hopped off her stool and motioned for Natalie to follow her down the hall to the feeding room, where Natalie had remembered she and Lily had been earlier. But when they walked up to the chair where Lily had been sitting, the doll was nowhere to be found. Tiffany stopped short. "Where did it go?" She looked all around the seating area. "I swear it was just here an hour ago."

Natalie looked, too—under stacks of towels, inside buckets, inside the boots that lined one wall. "You don't think a sea lion could have grabbed it, do you?" she asked.

"Weirder things have happened," Tiffany said.

They made their way into the next room and looked around there, too, but then Tiffany stopped and peered down the hallway. "I forgot I wasn't alone. Follow me."

They walked down the hall, toward the lab, which had the only other light coming from beneath the door. Tiffany barged in.

"Hey, Tiffany," Elliott's voice said.

The sound sent a warm feeling into Natalie's gut, and she actually had to put her hands over her stomach to calm herself. She took a deep breath and headed in.

"There it is! We were looking for this," Tiffany said, rushing across the room.

"We?"

Tiffany motioned back to the entrance, and Elliott did a double take at Natalie in the doorway.

"Oh, hey." He put a test tube in a small wooden rack with several others, which all clanked together with a soft tinkling noise. "I saw the doll and knew it was Lily's, so I brought it here to return to her."

He wiped his hands on his lab coat and turned to face Natalie. He looked as if he was going to move toward her, but then he stopped and redirected his hands into his coat pockets.

"Here ya go," Tiffany said, bringing the doll back to Natalie and shoving it into her arms. She motioned for Natalie to follow her out.

But Natalie stayed facing Elliott instead, clamping the doll across her middle. He looked terrible—his blue eyes half-lidded behind his glasses, dark circles under both eyes. And his skin looked ashen. It all could have been the lab lights, of course, but his stooped shoulders gave away the fact that it probably wasn't.

He gave Natalie a wan smile and ran his fingers through his messy hair. "Glad you got her back. I'm sure Lily misses her."

"Even after just a few hours," she said.

He tried another smile.

A strange silence welled in which everyone seemed to be waiting on Natalie.

Finally, she turned toward the door. "Tiffany, can you leave us alone for a minute?"

CHAPTER 20

The door closed, much to Elliott's frustration, and Natalie turned back toward him in the silence.

He knew he'd been avoiding her. It had just been easier. After the kiss on Castle Road, her fleeing that night, then her admission on the beach that she really just wanted to keep things cooled down between them, he could take a hint.

He wanted to be friends with her, as she'd suggested, but he wasn't sure how. Every time he came near her, all he could think of was what it felt like to have her in his arms like he had that night, to have her turn her head and kiss him, to have her body become supple and inviting against his. She'd let him protect her, she'd let him save her, she'd let him take care of her. And, since that moment, he knew one thing for sure—he wanted to do that for the rest of his life. He wanted Natalie Grant.

But she didn't want him.

So he was stepping back, trying to determine where the line was: how much he could enjoy her in his life without pushing himself across the boundary she didn't want him to cross.

"You look pretty bad," she suddenly said.

He slid a glance her way. He didn't even know what to do with that information. "Thanks."

"I just figure that's the kind of things friends can say to each other." She thrust her chin in the air. "Right?"

"I suppose."

"You just look tired."

That was probably true. That happened when you worked all the time. When you did your own science work between two and four in the morning. And, of course, when you finally did get to sleep but intense sexual dreams about a woman you couldn't have left you feeling frustrated and unfulfilled.

"Working a lot," was all he said.

"Elliott . . ." Natalie walked toward him.

He stepped back instinctively. Man, he didn't want to have a conversation with her right now—he was way too tired. Way too susceptible to saying something stupid. Way too close to memories of dreams that might let his body betray his wayward thoughts.

Damn it, where was his lab coat?

"I've been wanting to talk to you," Natalie said.

He turned and filled a couple of test tubes. "Now's probably not the best time."

"I won't take up much of your time, I just wanted to say a few things while we have some quietude. It's always so busy here. It's nice to be alone with you for a second."

The test tubes clanked together beneath his suddenly indelicate touch, and he mentally cursed himself. He lifted the rack and walked over to the incubator. "Maybe we could do this another time."

"I just wanted to say I'm sorry."

Elliott froze. *Sorry?* He hadn't seen that one coming.

"For what?" he asked over his shoulder, as casually as possible.

"For creating such an awkwardness that we're now avoiding each other."

He stalled over one of the buttons on the incubator, then finished punching in the correct temperatures. "I don't think you need to apologize for that."

"Just hear me out."

She was right behind him now. Touching distance, he was sure. He wiped his brow and gave the buttons one more try. On the second attempt, he got it right and the machine finally began whirring.

He turned and was immediately face-to-face with her. Or face-to-chin. Or breasts-to . . .

He took a deep breath and sidled away. Where had he put his lab coat?

He fumbled along the countertop for his locker key, put it next to his laptop mindlessly, then pretended he was looking at something important on the screen. "I think I need to wrap things up here."

"We can leave together."

Four hearty cuss words floated through his head, and he bit them all back. *Good move, Sherman. That wasn't very well thought out.* But at least some fresh air might do some good. He grabbed his locker key and strode toward his lab coat.

"I can drive you," she said. "I promise to stay on the road this time."

He pulled the coat out of the locker and shuffled it over his shoulders. He closed his laptop and attempted to straighten his lab desk, almost knocking over a rack of empty tubes, then piled a stack of scientific journal articles he'd printed. As he untangled the paper clips holding the articles together, a small index notecard fell out of one of the stacks and landed faceup on the counter.

"Life shrinks or expands in proportion to one's courage." —Anaïs Nin

It was an index card that the Colonel had given him. The Colonel had left seven in the last week, all in his own linear handwriting—one on Elliott's laptop, one slipped inside. Two had been in his lab-coat pockets, and two had been rubber-banded with his mail. They were always about courage.

Elliott had been realizing the truth of what the Colonel had told him—courage in the face of danger was actually doable. His adrenaline-fueled experience in the cart about to go over the cliff had shown him that. But courage in the face of rejection was where you really needed to pull your bootstraps up. Facing your own feelings—and then laying them bare for someone else to see—was where real courage took place.

Elliott stared at this latest card and took a deep breath.

"Okay, Natalie," he finally said, stuffing the notecard into his pocket. "Let's head home. I have a few things I need to talk about with you, too."

The night air blew through the golf cart as they bumped down the unpaved hill toward Elliott's house. Natalie had decided to forgo the main road and off-road it on a path she knew went directly to his hill. She tried to ignore the fact that he was clutching the passenger doorway with white knuckles and instead focused on driving.

"So what do you think?" she asked.

"About your driving? It kind of sucks. Where's the road?"

"Thanks a lot."

"I figure that's the kind of things friends say to each other, right?"

She swung past the little cottages toward Elliott's place on the ocean. Hardly anyone was out this late, so the narrow path was their own. "I meant, what do you think about my being a good friend or a bad friend?"

"I think you're a fine friend. You're just a crazy driver."

She took a hard turn onto the paved portion, and Lily's Elsa doll flew off the seat between them and scuttled across the floorboard, landing in the street.

"Darn it." She put the cart in reverse. Elliott leaned out and swiped the doll up. She barely let him sit back before she floored it again.

"So anyway, is it because you said you have feelings for me, Elliott? Maybe we should have talked about that more so we could have a more relaxed friendship. I like that you were so honest with me—I really do. I respect that a lot. And I feel like I didn't acknowledge your honesty. And I feel like I'm not being very straightforward or honest with *you*. But friends are honest, right?"

Elliott was gripping the passenger doorway again. "I imagine so."

"I truly want us to be friends. I really like you."

"I like you, too, Natalie."

"But you avoid me."

The wheels bumped over the wooden pier to the other side of Diver's Nook and puttered down a slight dirt hill, then began rounding the cove.

Elliott glanced at something in his lab-coat pocket and then took a deep breath. "Yes, I've been avoiding you."

Natalie looked over at him, surprised he'd admitted that. Although it was true of her, too, it was hard to say out loud.

"Watch the road, please." He pointed ahead.

She refocused her attention and concentrated on the rest of her speech.

"I don't want things to be awkward between us," she said. "I want to hang out with you. I hope you're not avoiding me because I kissed you. Or because you said you have feelings for me. Or because I've recommitted to my mancation, and you think it's something personal."

She turned to stare at him again. He was slumped now in his seat, looking tired.

"If we're going to be honest, here—I'll say that it's probably all of those things," he said. "But mostly I've been avoiding you because I'm attracted to you. I just don't know how to behave, I guess."

His honesty threw a little dart into her heart. She wanted to reach out and touch his hand, but knew that would just confuse things further.

"Oh, Elliott." She let out a deep sigh through the open windshield.

"Road." He pointed again.

"Would it help if I admitted something, too?"

He seemed to think that over. "I don't know."

"Well, I will. I watch you on the beach running every day."

He turned and stared at her. "Really?"

"Really."

He looked back at the road, watching the cliffs go by. "Why do you do that?"

"It makes me feel close to you, like we're the only two out there on the beach, and we understand each other somehow."

He stared straight forward for half a minute, seemingly thinking that over. "You could join me sometime."

"I can't run as fast as you. I'd never keep up."

"I could slow down."

"How slow?"

"For you? A crawl."

She smiled. "A light jog might do. Would that eliminate the awkwardness and allow us to be friends?"

"It might. Or it might not. Depends on how cute you look in your running clothes."

Natalie grinned back at him and steered the golf cart straight up his hill. "You might be shocked to know that my running clothes consist of a man's sweatpants and sweatshirt. Not very exciting."

"We'll definitely be friends then."

She laughed and pulled up into his drive. "Can I come in? I just had a few more things I wanted to say. I won't keep you long."

He seemed to look at something in his pocket again, then shrugged. "Sure."

She followed him through the back door they'd entered with Alice, past the same kitchen, past the same dining table. Nothing looked as cozy or romantic as it had that night, though. Instead of candles and dinner for two, Elliott now had papers strewn all over the dining table—stacks and stacks—along with some empty paper plates. A laptop sat at the head of the table, surrounded by empty coffee mugs, cords, and a headset.

The living room looked similar—papers stacked on almost every flat surface. Natalie could see where Elliott must have carved a small place for himself on the floor in front of the fireplace. Another empty coffee mug sat there.

"What are all these?" she asked.

"Journal articles." He quickly shuffled several of them out of the way, clearing a place for her to sit. "I've been reading up on other scientists' studies of gene sequences for the sea lions in every rookery up the California coast. Plus, reading up on the history of the island and doing some studies on the other animals that live here—trying to see if the environment is affecting them. Here, have a seat."

"Don't mess up your papers. They're probably all organized how you like them. We can go outside."

He looked up, eyebrows raised, papers stalled midair. "Now *that*, Natalie, is being a good friend."

She grinned and wandered out to the patio. The night was warm for June in California—a cooling ocean breeze brushed across the patio and blew across her face. The ice plants on the hill below were ready to explode into their blooms, but the buds were all closed for the night. Natalie pulled her hair from her lips and plopped into a chaise lounge, kicking her legs out in front of her. The ocean rolled out in the distance, the stars rolled out above. Elliott perched on the chaise next to her.

"You don't look very comfortable," she said. "Do you always wear your lab coat at home and sit so stiffly like that?"

"Yeah, well, I don't often have Natalie Grant lying on a chaise lounge on my back patio."

She took in his lowered eyes, his messy hair, and then noticed a bit of a smart-ass smile quirking the corners of his lips. "You're liking this honesty thing, aren't you, Elliott?"

"It is kind of liberating."

"Do you realize you're flirting?"

"Is that what this is?"

"Yeah, and you're kind of good at it. So have fun. But here's the thing—I need to remind you that this has to stay purely platonic."

"Got it."

"I need to finish this mancation thing. For myself, not just for the bet. I need to know that I don't need a man to show or tell me my worth. Can you understand that?"

He nodded.

"I need you to know it has nothing to do with you—I truly enjoy your company. So I'm wondering if we can just put everything else aside—forget about the kisses and the awkward attraction—and simply be true friends for each other while I learn a little more about myself. Doris said you could really use a friend right now who just lets you be yourself. And I know I could."

He looked up at her—the open, accepting expression back on his face. It was an expression she hadn't seen since the Castle, as he'd shut it down right after she'd talked to him on the beach. But now here it was again: compassion, acceptance, concern, and a kind of caring in his eyes she realized she'd missed.

He nodded solemnly. "I'd like that," he said softly.

Relief flooded her. She had Elliott back. And now she needed to be this kind of person to him—the selfless person who acted on what was best for a friend, not what was best for her.

"So now, since you've been so honest with me, I should really be honest with you. You've asked me a few times about the reason for my mancation—do you really want to know?"

His warm smile slowly slid away. "I don't know. Do I?"

"I'm not sure. But it's part of me, and since we're friends now, I'll tell you."

He shifted on the chaise but never took his eyes off her. He wasn't afraid of what she was going to say. He looked ready to fight a dragon for her.

"When I was twelve, my mom's boyfriend at that time cornered me in the kitchen one afternoon and pushed me up against the wall and grabbed me between the legs and called me a cock-tease. I didn't even know what that meant when I was twelve."

She delivered the story the way she always thought back about it—with a nonchalance she'd conjured over time. But she looked up now at Elliott's wide eyes that went from shock to anger in a flash.

"Jesus, Natalie," he whispered.

She lowered her eyes. Spitting it all out like that had felt good—it was like admitting something she'd refused to think about—but now it felt as if a dam were cracking. Her nonchalance had been manufactured. It had just been keeping her from falling apart.

"He didn't do more than that. But he sneered at me beneath all his oily hair and said that I shouldn't walk around the house in shorts like that, or in my pajamas, because did I *want* him to grab me like that? Did I want *other men* to grab me like that? Of course I said no, and he backed off, and my mom broke up with him a week later—probably for an unrelated event because he was a jerk enough to have surely offended her in a million ways, too. But I have to admit, after that, I was always very careful not to walk around the house anymore in shorts, even when boyfriends weren't around. I can't believe that jerk convinced me I couldn't wear shorts in my own house. So anyway, as the years went on, and I found men staring at me, or trying to get me alone in corners, I always had the notion it was my fault. Because of what I was wearing. Because of what he said. So I started wearing big baggy men's clothes just to be safe."

Elliott was very still, staring up at her from under his bangs, his mouth a grim line. "How long did you feel that way?"

"Pretty much forever."

Elliott's jaw danced.

"Is this too much information for you?"

"No," he said. "I told you I'd listen."

"But you look angry."

"I am. I'm angry at him."

A swift gush of relief swept through Natalie—relief and something else, something like absolution—and a warmth settled through her core. Although cerebrally she knew that guy was a creep, and wrong for sending her thinking in that direction all those years, she hadn't ever had someone agree with her. And certainly never had a man agree with her. She'd never told her mom or sisters because she'd been afraid they'd think he was right—maybe she shouldn't have walked around the house in shorts when there was a man there. But saying it out loud right now, and having Elliott look as though he wanted to pummel the guy, gave her a feeling of comfort and solidarity she hadn't known were hers to have. It made her feel as if she could finally tell someone about the most recent events, too.

"I figured out when I was about nineteen that my logic was flawed. But old habits die hard. I still feel more comfortable covered up. The hats help." She touched the brim of hers. "But I still find myself in too many bad situations. The most recent was a boss who I thought was working out, but then he cornered me in his office and became very handsy. When I tried to push him away, he said it was my fault for leading him on."

Elliott's head shook once, and he let out something of a huff through his nose. "Okay, first of all, I'd like to apologize for all men in general. Can I do that?"

Natalie gave a small, reluctant smile. "I suppose."

"And I'm sorry those idiots transferred blame onto you all those years. You should never apologize for simply being a beautiful woman. Unwanted advances are never your fault, Natalie. They're the guy's fault."

For some reason, tears stung the back of Natalie's eyes. A sense of beautiful relief overcame her. "But you can see then how I'm having trouble not knowing what's right with you. I want to give you comfort as a friend, and hug you when you're having a bad day, but now that you've admitted you're attracted to me, I don't know if that's being a . . ." She waved her hand in a windmill. It was still hard for her to say it.

Elliott frowned and filled in for her. "Tease?"

Relief that he got it flooded her again. *"Yes."*

"Natalie, no. You've made things very clear. I just—"

"And then when I kissed you on the hill!" She was on a roll now, her thoughts coming faster. She flung her other hand out in matched exasperation. "I just . . . You can see how I thought maybe something was wrong with me. Because where did that come from? I want to be your friend, and there I was kissing you, and I didn't mean to do that at all. Maybe something *is* wrong with me. Maybe I'm incapable of having male friends."

"You're not incapable."

"You're sure?"

"I'm positive."

"But I was feeling a little attracted to you."

He lifted his head up. "Yeah?"

"But I can't," she said quickly. "I mean I can't be. And it was only a little. And I need to complete this mancation and prove to Paige and myself that I'm as strong and independent as I keep claiming I am."

He sent her a skewed smile. "Just my luck."

Another little dart went through her when she saw the pain in his smile, but she wanted him to know what a kind man he was. He was a good man. A true gentleman, as Doris said.

"You're going to make some woman very happy someday, Elliott. And I do think you're a long-term kind of guy, despite your uncertainty at the Castle a couple weeks ago. And I'm really not. I might be a commitment-phobe, after all. I do tend to do flings. I get bored with men really fast."

He nodded but just stared at his hands clasped in front of him.

"Except you," Natalie said, realizing its truth as it came out of her mouth. "I haven't gotten bored with you at all. Maybe this friendship thing really is best between us."

He gave another wry smile but didn't say anything to that.

"So can we do this? Just give each other the care we need, and be there for the other to talk to, but not move it beyond that?"

He lowered his eyelashes. "Okay."

"And now I need to leave, because you are looking *way* too tired, and as your friend, I'm telling you—you need some sleep."

"I'm kind of hungry, actually. Care to join me for some ramen?"

"Do you seriously still eat ramen, like in college?" She swung off the chaise lounge and followed him into the house.

"It's cheap and easy."

"Not like dating me, right? Yuk-yuk."

"Too soon, Natalie."

She laughed and explored his kitchen with him, looking for some vegetables to add at least, but his pantry and freezer were bare. Finally, at the very back of his cupboard, she found two cans of vegetables. The date stamp said they were still good.

"Those must have been from the previous renters," he admitted.

"You don't eat vegetables?"

"I just forget to shop."

They made the ramen and canned vegetables, then swung up onto the kitchen bar stools to eat them with plastic chopsticks—also from the previous renters—while Elliott told her some of the funnier calls they got at the center from hapless tourists, like the ones who thought they'd spotted a harbor seal who'd been shot through the head, only to find that they didn't know what harbor-seal ears looked like.

At three o'clock, after several stories and even more laughs, she shoved him off the bar stool and told him to get some sleep.

"Would you like me to call the center for you tomorrow and tell them that you won't be in until ten?"

"I can't go in that late."

"If you get a good night's sleep for once, think how much better you can be for the sea lions. And I've kept you up all this time, so I feel guilty anyway. Let me call. Sometimes friends need a little push. Promise me you'll sleep until nine. One night."

He rinsed their bowls and chopsticks. "I can't. I'm used to very little sleep. I'm a bit of an insomniac."

"Try. One night."

He turned off the water. "It would be nice."

"All right then. I'll call Jim for you first thing in the morning. I'll let myself out. Good night, Elliott."

"Sunrises," he said quietly, to the faucet.

"What?"

He walked in her direction and guided her to the back door. "*Sunrises* is something my sister and I say to each other when the other one can't sleep. We started it as kids, when one of us was scared after the murders. We'd say it to remind each other to think of the sun rising the next morning—meaning everything will be fine, and tomorrow gives you a new chance at another day."

"Everything will be fine, Elliott."

He looked at her for a minute too long—searching her face, her eyes, as if he wanted to know that was true.

"Sunrises then," she said quietly, and she stepped off the back porch and hopped into her cart, securing the Elsa doll beside her.

And she thought—as she drove slowly down the hill—that she'd never had a more wonderful, honest, comfortable night with a man.

And with Elliott Sherman.

As friends.

With clothes on.

Who would have thought?

CHAPTER 21

During the next few weeks at the center, Elliott gave her a wide grin each time he saw her. He didn't flinch when she gave him a hug or encouraging pat on the arm, he stopped looking like a deer caught in headlights when she'd approach, and he even started to flirt a little.

She loved having him as a friend.

And helping him was a joy she hadn't expected. She dragged him along when she went grocery shopping for Olivia and pointed to various food options: corn on the cob, broccoli, carrots.

"I don't know how to prepare any of that," he said, with a note of apology in his voice.

"What did you and your granddad eat every day?"

"Nell figured it out after my grandma died, and she'd cook for him and me, but for some reason I never thought I'd need to know any of this stuff."

"It's easy," Natalie said, throwing a few ears of corn into his cart.

"I'm good at some other parts, though."

"Eating?"

"I'll show you later."

Once they checked out, he got a mischievous grin on his face. "Get in."

"What?"

"Get in. This is the part I was good at."

She climbed on the front of the cart and laughed while he raced her through the parking lot. It was wonderful to see him so carefree—grinning like a child—and she felt the same.

They loaded the groceries onto his golf cart, swung down to his house, threw a couple of stalks of asparagus on a baking sheet, and sat on the kitchen counter while it roasted. They had spring salads and asparagus on the patio, staring down at the bright-pink blanket of iceplant blooms that now covered the hillside.

"So, who would *you* invite to dinner if you could invite anyone at all?" he asked one night, as they lay on the chaise lounges eating ribs and watching the sun set over the horizon. He was looking better and better with each passing day—more rested, fewer circles under his eyes, the color back in his face.

"Mmm, good question. Living or dead?"

"Either."

"Mother Teresa. I know it sounds corny, like a beauty-contestant answer, but I'd like to talk to her. I'd like to know her thoughts on forgiveness, and acceptance, and how she just kept it together all those years."

"Forgiveness?"

"Yes, forgiveness is hard."

His intense stare turned into a bit of a frown. "Yes. Well, that request for Mother Teresa sounds about right for you—it fits in with your Good Samaritan gene." A small smile dimpled the sides of his mouth.

"Good Samaritan gene?"

"Yeah, it was one of the first conclusions I came to about you."

She peered at him curiously. "That night Lily and I reported the sea lions to you? You came to conclusions?"

"Regarding that and other things."

"What other things?"

He smiled shyly. "Is this where I come across as flirting, even though I'm just telling the truth?"

"It's okay. I understand you."

"What I thought the first time I saw you is that you were quite a Good Samaritan to travel all the way to my house from the tide pools with a little girl just to borrow a phone to report distressed sea lions. But I also thought you were pretty. And that you had great legs—you were wearing shorts—but I tried not to notice because I was on a date with someone else."

"I thought you said I had intelligent eyes!"

"Intelligent eyes and great legs aren't mutually exclusive, Natalie."

"And here I thought you high-IQ types only noticed things like intelligent eyes and hair the color of the acorns in your grandfather's yard."

Elliott chuckled. "We may be quiet, but we're not dead."

She tried to look prickled, but really it pleased her. Elliott had been careful not to act or say anything very sexual around her, and she'd tried to return the courtesy. But the way he was blushing and looking away right now was really cute. And dangerously sexy. She needed to divert this conversation.

"How about you?" she finally asked.

"How about me, what?"

"Who would you invite to dinner, if you could invite anyone?"

"Oh, we're back on that? Let's see. There are a couple of Nobel Prize winners I wouldn't mind talking to—Emil von Behring, Gerhard J. Domagk, Alexander Fleming—"

"I think you have to pick just one."

"Alexander Fleming, I guess."

Natalie cocked an eyebrow in question.

"Penicillin."

"Ah."

"I admire the people who were able to use science for cures—to contribute something, help someone or something."

"You're doing that, Elliott."

"Not yet, but I'm working on it."

She finished her rib and wiped her hands on her napkin, taking in his focus, his intensity. He even ate ribs with intensity. It was kind of sexy, how singularly focused he was on everything. She wondered briefly if he'd be like that in bed, but she pushed the thought away as soon as it entered her mind. She couldn't let herself think that way about him.

"Work's important to you," Natalie finally said, not so much as a question but to acknowledge she understood this truth about him.

"Yes."

"Is it the most important thing to you?"

He thought that over. "Nell's important to me, too. And little Max, and now Jim. Family. They're all I have now."

"But what about you? Don't you want anything else?"

"Like what?"

"Fame? Success? Money?"

"Nah. None of that's important to me. What am I going to spend money on? Clothes?" He indicated the worn-out, nondescript tennis shoes that he wore almost every day.

Natalie smiled. She'd grown to like Elliott's unassuming way of dressing. His sister was always trying to get him to dress better for dates, but Natalie thought he looked fine. He knew how to match, at least. And when he'd gotten his new glasses, some fashionably savvy optician had talked him into frames that were surprisingly trendy (although he didn't know that). He now had a carefree, modern, hipster look that

Abercrombie & Fitch seemed to be trying to replicate, but it was the way Elliott genuinely looked.

"So what are you doing all the work for?" she asked.

"Self-satisfaction." He frowned as if the answer were obvious. "What about you? What's the most important thing to you?"

Natalie thought that over. Was there anything she had that she was proud of?

"I'm proud of how the Senior Prom is coming together. They didn't have much money to give me to work with—the last assistant activities director apparently absconded with the funds—but I'm happy with the way I'm still pulling it off."

"Does it come easily to you?"

"It does." She thought about that with wonder.

"And it gives you a little high when you get it right?"

She nodded.

"That's how I feel about microbiology. I'm glad you've found something, too. Hang on to that, Natalie. I'm realizing it's a gift."

They carried their plates to the kitchen and ended up in a water fight that had them both laughing the rest of the night.

And Natalie realized she'd been given more than one gift these past few months.

The tide pools became one of their favorite places to spend time together. Elliott liked to go after work to relax and study different animals and algae.

"Look, low tide's in twenty minutes! Let's hurry," Natalie said, pointing to the laptop page he was peering at as they sat on his patio.

They slipped on their "tide pool" shoes—completely caked with mud, dirt, and sand—then sidled down the hillside, jogged across the sand, and climbed over the lava-looking rocks to the very edge of the pools while the low-sitting sun bounced off the water. They'd found a spot where they'd determined the best creatures were—colorful starfish, side-moving red crabs, and tiny hermit crabs moving nautilus shells on their backs. Dark-blue mussels and lavender-pink sea sponges clung to the craggy rocks. Natalie loved the earthy, salty smell there.

"Ooh, what's this one?" she would ask, pointing to a bright-green sea anemone, shaped like a multipetaled flower.

Natalie and Elliott always first scanned the pools for the sea anemones, with their crazy shapes, stripes, and colors, attached to the rocks with bizarre tentacles floating about them, waving with each brush of the ocean.

"That's an *anthopleura elegantissima*," Elliott said, coming closer.

She loved pointing at everything and hearing Elliott say all the names.

"That one clones itself." He bent down beside her. "Splits right in two, and—through longitudinal fission—creates a clone."

The fading sun caught the golden hairs on his arms as he braced himself against his knees. Natalie loved looking at the wonder on his face. He never touched anything—he always treated the tide pools with reverence and wonder, as she'd been taught to do since she was a kid, too. But with Elliott, somehow she guessed he'd never had to be taught such a thing, probably not even as a child. The unwavering respect for Mother Nature simply seemed part of him.

"There's another starfish!" she said, crawling over a rock toward another small pool. She brushed the sand off her palms. "Can they really regenerate lost arms?" She'd been coming to these tide pools since she was a child, but she'd never had her own personal tour guide.

"Some species can. Depends on where their vital organs are."

"What's that one?" She pointed to a beautiful starburst-shaped one.

He leaped down to the other side of the pool and bent closer. "That's an *anthopleura sola*. See its tentacles? Those are acrorhagi—they sting, and he uses them for fighting. These types of anemones sting each other until one moves and the other can claim the territory. Brutal world, these tide pools." He smiled and shoved his hair out of his eyes, leaving little speckles of sand in the strands.

They traipsed along the pool for nearly an hour, carefully stepping around anything that looked living—even the algae—until the sun slowly set and the tide began gently rising, filling the pools a quarter inch at a time until the water began sweeping the toes of their tennis shoes.

At the top of the rocky ledge that led to a drop into the sand for their walk home, Elliott turned to offer his hand. It was the only time he ever touched her—at the tide pools. Natalie didn't like to admit to herself how much she enjoyed these moments: the feel of his hand enveloping hers; the sand granules sliding between their skin; the sight of his forearm flexing as he lifted her from rock to rock; and the salty, manly scent of him when she'd steady herself against his biceps.

At the top, they paused to catch their breath, sitting on the ledge with the view back to Elliott's house. The entire side of his property was a blanket now of bright-pink ice-plant blooms. They watched the waves rush in and out, appreciated the sunset, and stared at the sand crabs until the ice plants closed. When the moon came out, they gazed at the navy waves and talked about growing up, Wisconsin, darts, Humphrey Bogart, and any other crazy thing that came to their minds.

"Do you still have trouble sleeping?" she finally asked when they'd exhausted all their favorite lines from *Star Trek*.

"Some nights."

"My sisters and I used to rub one another's backs to fall asleep. We'd each have to count to ten. It always put us right to sleep."

"I don't want you rubbing my back, Natalie."

"It's not a *sexual* thing; it's a comfort thing." She watched a huge wave splash its sea spray up toward them. The white foam glistened in the moonlight.

When he didn't answer, she glanced over at him. He was leaning back, looking at her from beneath his bangs.

"You ask me to do a lot of things that require my strength, but that might be pushing it," he finally said.

They both watched the waves for another few minutes while Natalie stole furtive glances at him. She had the strangest urge to lay back, let him curl his arm around her, and sigh deeply as they watched the stars and waves. But they were both working hard to keep this relationship in check.

"We'd better get back," he finally said, standing.

She nodded and scrambled to her feet, even as she swallowed her disappointment that this time he didn't reach back for her hand.

The following Thursday, Natalie opened the cottage door to see Elliott with a bag of saltwater taffy, which had become his little custom with Lily. She thought it was sweet that he knew the owner of the candy store and always managed to get Lily the first, freshest batch.

Paige had come in especially early for the weekend and did a double take when she saw Elliott.

"Hey, Paige," he said as he pulled up his usual chair.

"Hey, Sea Lion Man," Paige said, her wide eyes tracking his every move as he, Lily, and Natalie continued their saga of War with the playing cards they kept on the kitchen counter.

When their battle was over, Lily pulled Elliott to his usual spot on the couch.

"You have to see Elsa's movie now," she said.

"I've been promising, haven't I?"

"Yes!" Lily sat close to him on the couch. Whenever they started a movie, she always took off his glasses and switched them with hers, giggling, but this night was too serious with her screening of *Frozen*. As the television flickered its lights across their faces, Natalie found herself transfixed by the growing love between Elliott and Lily. Suddenly all the tapes she'd always played in her head—she never wanted to get married; she never wanted kids—began dissolving right before her as she stared at these two people she'd come to care about so much. She could almost picture being married to Elliott. She could almost picture having a little girl like Lily. She could almost picture staring at her own little family on a couch just like this . . .

A pressing sense of betrayal washed over her. Was she allowed to want that? She glanced up furtively to make sure Paige wasn't walking through the room. All her life Natalie had had the same script to recite—given to her primarily by her mom, edited and honed by Natalie herself—but now here she was, thinking of being part of a . . . couple? Thinking of being a mom? She'd spent so many years conspiring with her girlfriends, conspiring with Paige, about how they were going to live lives of adventure and weren't going to even think about getting married until they were thirty-five, maybe forty. And now, here she was, staring at a man and a little girl on a grandmother's flowery couch in a tiny cottage on a stifling island and thinking it looked . . . *cozy*? She must be losing her mind.

Paige walked through the room for the hundredth time, and Natalie snapped her gaze away from the adorable scene on the couch and pretended to pay attention to the movie.

Halfway through, Elliott fell asleep as usual, but Lily and Natalie just let him snore, smiling at each other over the top of his head.

"We'll have to play Elsa's movie for him again," Lily whispered as the credits rolled.

"I'm sure he'd appreciate that," Natalie said.

She got Lily into bed, then came back to gently shake Elliott's shoulder to wake him, as he'd requested she do anytime he fell asleep on her couch.

He looked up sheepishly and scrambled to the door, giving her arm a tired squeeze good-bye.

Natalie closed the door quietly and returned to the front room under Paige's scrutiny.

"That didn't look like friends to me. You're sleeping with him, aren't you?"

"No!" Natalie was truly shocked. What did she mean that didn't look like friends? She'd never felt like more of a friend in her life. If that wasn't friendship, she didn't know what was.

"You promise?"

"Yes!"

"There haven't been any more kisses? No caresses? He's not copping a feel when I'm not looking?"

"No! Stop, Paige! We're friends, and that's it."

Natalie turned toward the kitchen counter and busied herself with washing their cups and popcorn bowls. She couldn't rectify the heat sliding up through her cheeks and was afraid she was blushing furiously. She felt quite in control when she was with Elliott, but hearing Paige mention kisses, caresses, and touching in relation to Elliott made Natalie picture him leaning toward her, maybe undoing her blouse, maybe smiling a little in that cute way he did, and . . . She needed to stop. It was hot. The idea was hot. That's all there was to it.

She didn't want to think of Elliott that way, but her thoughts were getting harder and harder to resist. Sometimes her imagination drifted when he stood too close at the center, and she could smell his sandalwood soap mixed with the scent that was just all man. Sometimes it happened when he ducked his head after being caught staring at her breasts when they played poker with the seniors at the center. Sometimes she'd have to corral her musings when she'd turn to face him under one of their many sunsets, and he'd be gazing at her with that reverence he sometimes had, lost in thought, thinking things she didn't want to let herself imagine. And tonight the thoughts had gone all the way to marriage? She didn't know what had come over her.

She finished rinsing the dishes and wiped her hands on a dish towel.

Paige watched her over the rim of her coffee mug. "I guess I believe you."

"I do like talking with him," Natalie whispered.

Could she tell Paige any of this? Would Paige understand?

But before Natalie could decide whether she wanted to venture into more revealing information, Paige stood and brought her mug to the sink. "Like I said, I don't care if you talk," she said. "But if I hear of clothes coming off, you'd better be standing at the door when I arrive, ready to hand over my seven hundred dollars. I still think you're going to lose."

Natalie bristled at Paige's challenging tone. So much for sharing. Paige had just ruined the moment.

"I'm not going to lose," Natalie said with a conviction she absolutely believed.

And she was a little surprised to hear the disappointment that lay embedded in that reality.

"We'll see about that," Paige said.

Natalie resisted throwing a dish towel at her. Or maybe a mug. Sometimes Paige could be such a bitch.

The following Monday marked Natalie's last week on the island.

Olivia had only one more week of required bed rest, and Natalie had only one more week of prom planning. It was hard to believe that three months had come to an end already. She thought that the idea of leaving—once it was right on the horizon like this—would give her a feeling of freedom, like a balloon breaking from a fist and floating gently, free, away. But strangely it didn't. Instead of the soaring feeling she thought it would give her, the passing days left her with a sense of enormous, unfathomable loss. By the time Wednesday rolled around, she was actually feeling panicked.

She glanced up at Elliott over the pizza slices they'd just made and were eating out on his patio, and tried to swallow.

"I'm leaving next week, you know," she said.

A shadow crossed over his face as he picked the olives off his slice and nodded. "I know. I'm keeping track."

The sounds of seagulls taking off interrupted them for a minute as they stared at their dinners.

"No chance you'll stay on the island?" he asked.

She'd been thinking all week about that strange reversal of feeling she'd had, and finally came to the conclusion she must have been on a taffy high. The idea of marriage and being a parent this early was insane, clearly brought on by the dim lighting, too much sugar, and the cute way Elliott had been with Lily all night. But now she was thinking clearer. And remembering all her old reasons. Despite how wonderful Elliott was, and how panicked she was at the idea of saying good-bye, she really couldn't live here.

"I can't, Elliott. I admire all of you for being able to do it, but it feels claustrophobic to me."

"But you're not a commitment-phobe." He winked. It had become an inside joke between them.

Natalie sighed. She didn't like that word. She didn't think she was afraid of commitment—weren't commitment-phobes only men who were dodging marriage? She didn't think of herself that way at all. Although, she had to admit, she did tend to gravitate toward unavailable men, as Paige had mentioned. And she did nitpick men until she could find reasons to break up with them. And she did tend to avoid jobs that required long lengths of time or enclosed surroundings with the same people.

But she'd done great with all the commitments she'd made so far these past three months—to the seniors, to the center, to Lily, to her friendship with Elliott. She was really proud of herself. But, then again, they all had an end date. Which made them less like real commitments, perhaps. The idea of staying on for any of these things, especially for an undetermined amount of time, made her want to throw up.

"Hey, do you like snorkeling?" Elliott asked.

Natalie put down her pizza. She suddenly wasn't hungry. "Yes. I used to go all the time when I was a kid—up at Heart's Cove."

"We should go before you leave," he said. "Something you said at the tide pools gave me an idea about an algae. I want to see if it grows over on the other side of the island. Where's a good place to snorkel over there?"

"Heart's Cove would probably be perfect."

"Does it have some east-facing nooks, where algae might grow? Where is it exactly?"

Natalie described the location, and Elliott pulled out his laptop so they could double-check its position.

"This looks perfect," he said, peering at the screen. "Want to go with me?"

"When?"

"How about Saturday?"

"Actually Saturday is Senior Prom, and I was going to ask—"

The doorbell rang and broke Natalie's trajectory. She was finally going to get up the nerve to ask Elliott to go with her, as friends. Natalie had thought perhaps Paige would understand and let her bring a platonic date without sacrificing the bet, which ended the next day. The prom was, after all, part of her job, and what she'd been planning for the last several months. Natalie had thought she could bring Elliott, since the rules were already clear with him, and there'd be no long explanations necessary about the mancation.

When a second, more frantic doorbell ring followed, Natalie lifted her eyebrows. "Hot date?"

He laughed. "I can't imagine."

He left to answer, and Natalie heard voices in the entryway—the other a woman's. Finally, Elliott stepped through the slider.

"Natalie? I'd like you to meet someone."

Natalie turned in her chaise.

"Nell, this is Natalie Grant. Natalie, my sister, Nell."

Natalie scrambled to her feet, thrusting her hand forward. She'd never actually met Nell. She'd seen her at the Bars and Barks Event, of course, and once afterward at the post office, but Nell didn't know her name and they'd never exchanged a word. Seeing her up this close, Natalie could definitely see the family resemblance. She stood before Nell now, expectantly, wanting to make a good impression.

"Nice to meet you," Natalie said, pushing her hand farther forward.

Nell's expression could best be described as perplexed, combined with a bit of wonder, and she shook Natalie's hand hesitantly. "I didn't know Elliott had a friend. Er, I mean, *over*. I didn't know he had a friend *over*."

"It's okay. We're just watching the sun set. Here, have a seat with us." Natalie swept her hand in the direction of the gold-drenched chaise lounges. She truly wanted to get to know Nell better.

But Elliott seemed to have other ideas. "Nell's not staying," he said emphatically, tugging his sister's shoulders back inside the house.

"Elliott, stop!" Nell slapped his hands away. "Maybe I want to chat a little with . . . What did you say your name was?"

"Natalie."

"Huh." The wonder was still on her face as Nell frowned, seemingly trying to make sense of a forest fairy. "Elliott's never mentioned you."

"I'm probably not worth mentioning." Natalie laughed. "I just—"

"Nell's got to be going," Elliott said, pulling at her again.

"Wait." Nell stepped back toward her. "How old are you, Natalie?"

Natalie blinked. That was a weird question. She glanced once at Elliott, who simply looked annoyed and shook his head.

"Twenty-seven," she blurted.

"I see. And what do you do?"

"Nell, I'm sure Natalie doesn't want to be given the third degree. I just wanted you to say hi." He rested his arm over her shoulder and steered her back toward the slider. "Now, where did you have to be? Aren't Max and Jim waiting for you?"

"I'm just curious about your friend, Elliott."

"Uh-huh. Well, she might be curious about you, too, but she's not asking rude questions. Let's do this another time." He directed her back into the house, and although she tried to protest at first, she eventually let him push her inside.

When Elliott came back a few minutes later, he shook his head and plopped down next to Natalie. "She's terrible."

"What was that?"

"She's still looking to set me up."

"Am I a candidate now?" An unexpected smile escaped Natalie, pleased by this endorsement for some reason.

"Actually, no. You're my sister's worst nightmare. She'll call me tonight and ask me more about you."

The smile slid off Natalie's face. "What? What do you mean I'm her worst nightmare? I would be a great girlfriend. I'm perfect for you."

Elliott lifted an eyebrow.

"I mean . . . you know . . . if we were thinking along those lines. Which we aren't. But if we were . . . Wait, why would I be Nell's worst nightmare?"

Elliott threw his arm over his head on the lounge and stared out toward the ocean. "You're too young. Not science-y enough. Not nerdy enough. You don't have a boring, staid career."

Natalie stared hard at him. "Too young? I'm almost the same age as you!"

"She wants me to date someone in her thirties."

"And what do you mean, 'not science-y enough'? Do you mean not *smart* enough? Not cerebral enough?"

"I didn't say that, Natalie."

"And what do you mean I don't have a 'boring, staid career'? You mean I can't commit to a career at all?"

"I didn't say that either."

"But that's what you meant, didn't you?"

Elliott swung his legs over the side of the chaise and faced her. "Look, I'm not going to let you make this into something it's not. I didn't say any of that. And Nell didn't say any of that about you specifically. It's just that Nell told me, a couple of months ago, that she thought I should date women who were in 'in my league,' meaning as nerdy and undateable as I am."

"I think she meant women who were as smart as you, and you know it. You think I'm not smart enough for you, and you know that Nell would think that."

Elliott shook his head. "What are we even arguing about? You and I aren't dating. Your choice, by the way. It doesn't matter what Nell thinks of you. She doesn't get to choose my friends."

Natalie looked away. He was right. But it still bothered her that his sister wouldn't approve of her as a romantic partner. She'd had a long life of being treated with disdain by many, many men, but it never occurred to her she might be treated that way by a woman. Regarding that woman's brother. Whom Natalie wasn't even dating.

She sighed. She *was* being ridiculous.

She reached over and gave Elliott's knee a good-bye squeeze. "You're right. This isn't something we should argue about. So what did she come over for anyway?"

"Nell set me up on a double date with her and Jim for that Senior Prom this weekend. She's flying someone over who she said is 'just right' this time." He made air quotes and leaned back, not looking too happy about it.

The jealousy and possessiveness that zipped through Natalie regarding Elliott's prior dates was something she'd gotten used to ignoring. But this time felt like something she might need to examine.

Because this time it had an ominous sense of foreboding. And she'd need to figure out why.

If she could stop her heart from pounding, that was.

CHAPTER 22

The next day, Natalie had a million errands to run to get the prom organized—so many, in fact, that she was able to keep her mind off her rising sense of apprehension.

As she prepared to leave Casas del Sur that afternoon to pick up Lily, she almost bumped into a closed door at the end of a hallway, then heard a familiar voice drifting out of a door ahead of her.

"Are you sure this is right?" the voice asked.

A smile overtook her for the first time all day as she peeked inside the room.

Elliott was standing in the center, one arm curled around an imaginary partner, the other lifted into the air as if grasping an imaginary hand. He was staring with focus at the floor, waiting for the music to start. Doris was fumbling with an MP3 player at a back table.

"Natalie!" Doris said. "Come help me with this."

Elliott gave her a cute grin as she entered, as if he'd been caught at something.

"I heard you were taking dancing lessons," she said, walking back to the MP3 player.

"I finally admitted defeat."

She fumbled with the cord until the speakers came on, suddenly at the second bar of "Moon River." It jiggled in and out of the song. "I think something's wrong with the cord, Doris."

"Can you hold it for a second, dear?"

"Sure." Natalie held the cord in its precarious position while the music wafted across the ballroom, and Doris met Elliott in the center of the floor.

"Okay, ballroom hold," Doris said. "Shoulder blade, remember?"

Doris only came up to the middle of Elliott's chest, so he adjusted his arm hold to her.

"Now forward with the left foot, side with the right, close," she said as she led Elliott across the floor. "Forward with the right, side with the left, close." The two of them moved in slow, large circles. "Left, side, close," she said. "Right, side, close. Left, side, close. Yes! You've got it, Elliott."

The two of them continued to spin gracefully around the room. Doris was beaming, and Elliott's chin came up into the air. Natalie could have watched these two lovely people dancing to "Moon River" all day.

"Natalie, do you want to come over here and dance with our dear Elliott, here? I'm afraid I'm way too short for him. Elliott, you'll see how much easier it is with someone closer to your height. And age. Come."

Natalie hesitated for a second, but then thought, *Why not?* and went to take Doris's place. The music stayed on, despite the faulty cord.

"Do you remember how to do this, Natalie?" Doris asked, pushing her into position with Elliott.

"I think so."

"Ballroom hold." She adjusted their hands. "Shoulder blade, Elliott." She lifted Elliott's hand higher. "See—isn't that easier? You two truly are the perfect height for each other. Natalie, put your hand on Elliott's shoulder. He has beautiful shoulders, doesn't he?"

"Yes." Natalie smiled, but he rolled his eyes and looked away.

They avoided each other's eyes for the first few seconds, adjusting to the hold, the nearness, the awkwardness, Doris's critical stare. But soon they were floating together across the room, finally looking into each other's eyes. Elliott's gaze stayed steady. It seemed to be filled with gratitude, perhaps for standing in during his lesson, or maybe for being tall enough, or maybe for being comfortable enough for him that he still got the steps right.

But as he continued to hold her stare—the longest he'd ever met her eyes, for sure—she felt an overwhelming sense of gratitude herself. She was thankful for their trust, their friendship, the confidence they gave each other, the laughter they could always share, the months that had been filled with wonder. She stared right back into his eyes and was filled with tenderness, then a wave of sadness at the thought of saying good-bye. As her eyes began to mist, he gave her a small, appreciative smile.

Then everything came back into her awareness: the bright lights, the flickering cord, and Doris's counting "*One*, two, three. *One*, two, three. Good, you two!"

When the music finally ended, Natalie grinned at him politely. "You're going to make a great dance partner for someone."

Elliott cleared his throat and stepped away.

"Why don't we call it quits, too, Elliott dear? You did great today. You walk Natalie out now." Doris all but shoved them both out the door.

They blinked against the sunlight outside the lobby doors and headed across the cobblestone porte cochere.

"I'm going to miss you, you know," he said.

She'd always been rather good with good-byes—she usually approached them with a "See you again soon" feeling instead of a final salute. But maybe that had just been her way of justifying the fact that she liked things to end.

But now, facing Elliott in the warm July sun, she had the sense of dread that she imagined most people felt when they thought of upcoming good-byes. A crushing sense fell through her chest. A sense that she might never see this man again, and that her life would always have a small black hole where he had been. Or a big one. Where he had filled her days with joy. Where he had filled a void that she hadn't even known she'd had. She cleared her throat of the lump forming there.

"So, what else do you need lessons on?" she asked, ready to change the subject. "I assume this is for your prom date?"

He gave a quick snort out his nose. "Everyone's worried I'm going to screw this up. Doris wants me to learn to dance, the Colonel wants me to order the right drinks, Nell wants me to ditch the glasses again, and she's taking me shopping to a place she actually called a 'boutique' on the other end of Main Street. Do guys seriously go to 'boutiques'? That doesn't sound right."

Natalie climbed into her golf cart. "I think it's a thing now. That and manicures for men."

"Oh God, Nell mentioned that, too. And a pedicure? Please. Why bother?"

"You'll just get it messed up again at the tide pools." She smiled and started the engine.

"Right! The tide pools. My hands and feet are in water all the time. Or chemicals. This is all stupid. Do you think this date will genuinely care?" He was leaning against Natalie's driver's-side door rail now.

"Only in bed."

Elliott's smile slid away. He looked at the ground and stepped away from her cart. Natalie felt bad instantly. She didn't mean to razz him. He got so uncomfortable talking about sex. What kind of friend was she, making him feel uncomfortable on purpose? But her thoughts and emotions were all over the place now. She wanted to pull him close and push him away at the same time. And thinking of him and another woman together was making her irritable. She wasn't exactly jealous.

Or so she told herself. She just knew that Elliott needed someone who would let him be himself, someone who would cherish him, and Natalie didn't know if this other woman would be right. Nell had miscalculated too many times already.

"Do you want me to go to your house and teach you a simple dinner you can make?" she asked.

"Sure. Maybe those steaks we made that one night? I can handle the steaks, but could you show me the rest you did?"

"The glazed carrots?"

"Yeah, and the bread. That was awesome."

"Sure. I've got to run now. Gotta get Lily."

"I'm going back to the center. See you tonight?"

"I've got to take care of something tonight, but how about tomorrow? Did you still want to go snorkeling? Maybe after?"

"Snorkeling on a workday?" He smiled. "You're a bad influence."

"I'm off tomorrow. And aren't you snorkeling for work anyway?"

"You're still a bad influence."

"My work here is done, then." She met his smile with a wobbly one of her own. "So cooking lessons afterward?"

He gave her a nod that seemed filled with a host of other emotions: uncertainty, maybe. Or nervousness. Or a little hesitancy that looked not unlike what she was feeling right now. It was a hesitancy perhaps carried over from their dance, that they might need to step carefully now, that they were going to have to say good-bye soon, that there might be deeper emotions catapulting between them, that they might be careening into something that neither of them was quite prepared for. Or that Elliott might be going to the prom with the wrong person.

Natalie puttered away down the hill and breathed in the scent of island eucalyptus to calm her nerves and clear her mind.

Thank God the streets were lined with the stuff.

CHAPTER 23

The next morning, Natalie piled her snorkeling gear into Elliott's golf cart, jumped in behind it, and returned his relaxed smile as they scooted across the island underneath the bright sun.

This would be her first time snorkeling in eons, and possibly her last time gallivanting on a beach with Elliott, so she was prepared to thoroughly enjoy the day. She'd protected herself against the July rays with a wide-brimmed hat, enormous sunglasses, plenty of sunscreen, and a maxi dress covering her from shoulders to toes. She had to admit that she was a little grateful for the sun, and the excuse it gave her to hide behind fabric and straw. Although she knew she didn't need to cover up with the old fears from her past—she was safe with Elliott—old habits just died hard. But she had let her hair loose today, simply tucking it into her hat. It would feel good to let it float around her shoulders underwater today.

As they puttered up to Heart's Cove in the cart, she inhaled the heady scent of saltwater and California sage, staring around her at the beautiful view and pointing out the flora she remembered—the Queen

Anne's lace, the eucalyptus groves. She tried not to think too far into the future.

Heart's Cove was a rocky cliff area off the edge of the town, with a small horseshoe-shaped beach in the center. The scuba diving off this terrain was reportedly some of the best in the Pacific, and—throughout the summer—half of the horseshoe was always filled with scuba divers, scuba gear, instructors, tours, and teams, all diving off the east end into an underwater world of magic.

Not very many people knew, though, that on the other side of the horseshoe, the snorkeling was phenomenal. If you didn't want to invest in the time and equipment to scuba dive, you could simply don a mask and a snorkeling tube and see beauty to your heart's content in the shallow underwater pools. It always felt like an island secret.

She showed Elliott where to park the cart, and they scurried down the hillside, over the lava-rock terrain, and into the sandy horseshoe. There were no footprints in the sand except theirs. The ocean roared in and slapped the rocks around them like their own personal serenade.

"Wow, I haven't done this in a long time," Elliott said, eagerly studying the water. He tossed his backpack into the sand, yanked his shirt over his head, and stared down at the deep tide pools, standing still in his bright-blue board shorts, which hung much lower on his hips than she expected.

Stopped short, Natalie drew in an unexpectedly ragged breath.

Elliott was beautiful. Natalie hadn't been this close to an undressed version of him before. Although he was lean, his shoulders, arms, back, and legs were all sinewy muscle, his skin already tanned from his morning runs. His blond hair brushed along the back of his neck as he planted his hands low on his hips and stared deeper into the pools.

When he suddenly turned toward her, she looked away.

"Yes, very beautiful," she choked out.

She unbuttoned her dress and made a valiant attempt not to look up at his chest and flat abs right now.

Damn. Weren't they wearing wet suits today? She'd brought hers. The sun was warm, but the water hadn't yet caught up. "You're, um . . . you're in for quite a treat."

Natalie turned farther still so he couldn't see the blush that was certainly creeping across her cheeks. With her back to him, she discarded her maxi dress, kicked off her sandals, grabbed her snorkeling gear out of her tote, adjusted the tie at the side of her bikini bottoms, then whirled back around toward Elliott, who was still facing her, hands on his hips.

His eyes widened as she turned, and they swept up and down her body like a touch. Once. Then twice. But—as if he suddenly realized what he was doing—he quickly turned his attention to the sand between them and visibly swallowed.

"I'm sure I am," he said.

He cleared his throat and stepped toward the water's edge.

Natalie panicked for a second. That sexual zing—that sudden awareness, ricocheting between them, here on this deserted beach—was something she hadn't thought through very carefully when she'd accepted his offer to snorkel. They were supposed to be *friends*. They'd *agreed* to that. *He'd* agreed to that. She'd been carefully cultivating that all spring, and—

Oh, please, who was she kidding?

Bet or no bet, she couldn't lie to herself anymore. She'd fallen somewhere along the line. His kindness, his respectfulness, his passion for his work, the code of goodness and honesty he lived by. The way he looked at her, the way he really *saw* her. The way he was so generous with his time and money and attention to the things and people he cared for— Natalie loved all of that.

She loved the way he took her hand in the tide pools; she loved the way he doted on Lily; she loved the way he was polite to her sisters and regarded all the seniors and their histories with the same awe and respect she had. She loved the way he smelled of sandalwood and salt spray; she loved the flirtatious way he'd look up at her from under his bangs; and she even loved the way he separated his food on his plate when they had too many different kinds of vegetables.

Somewhere along the way she'd fallen for Elliott Sherman.

Hard.

And now, here she was, stuck on a deserted cove with no interference, very few clothes, sexual sparks flying back and forth, a pounding heart she couldn't control, a shirtless Elliott who suddenly looked as if he didn't know what to do with himself, and a bet she didn't know if she wanted to keep anymore.

Elliott waded into the cold Pacific and hung his hands on his hips, not sure if he wanted to dive in, pivot to get his wet suit, or turn back around and get another gander of Natalie in that bikini.

The gentlemanly side of him told him to jump into the water. Now. The cold would be a good douse to his libido, which could really use a dousing right now.

But the less gentlemanly side of him told him to turn back around and get another eyeful. Because man, oh man, she was hot. He'd known she was hot—he'd known that all along, of course, ever since he'd first glimpsed her in those short shorts at his sliding door a couple of months ago. But she'd always kept covered enough for him to maintain a sense of decorum and respect her wishes that they didn't move things beyond friendship. Once he'd learned for sure about the lecherous assholes in her past—something he'd guessed at but hadn't been sure of until that night they'd exchanged the Elsa doll—he'd been even more careful not to cross any lines with her. She needed someone who respected her, and respected her boundaries, not just another asshole who was maneuvering ways to get her into bed all the time. So he'd avoided talking about sex, thinking about sex, joking about sex, or even alluding to sex in her presence. It just made things easier to navigate.

But now . . .

Damn. Why hadn't he thought this snorkeling thing through better? He'd brought a wet suit—maybe she had, too.

Another flash of memory of her in that bikini went through his head, and he kept wading forward, still weighing his gentlemanly tendencies against his lascivious ones. He'd grown to care about her so much—developing a feeling of adoration and protectiveness that could only be love. He knew it when he saw it, just as the Colonel said he would. And he ached now with a way to express it physically, too. What if he just turned and marched back toward her, took her jaw in his hands, and kissed her the way he'd been imagining for months? What if he told her he had no interest in any of Nell's blind dates because all he could think of was her? What if he pressed into her, kissing her the way they'd started on Castle Road, running his hand through her hair, down her body, over that bikini string, under it, sliding toward—

His fingers plowed through his hair in frustration, and—mind almost made up—he turned back toward her.

She was tugging her wet suit on. He watched her from behind—watched her body shimmy, her bikini bottom wriggle, her breasts bounce from the side as she jumped and yanked the suit up over her torso. Her arms punched into the armholes, and she wriggled the neoprene zipper up the back with a loop. Her hand flew up to her head, and she twisted her hair into the speediest topknot he'd ever seen, as if her life depended on it.

His chest deflated.

And shame overwhelmed him.

Because she looked scared.

And the last thing he wanted to be was another lecherous asshole in her life.

He turned back toward his backpack and dug his own wet suit out, then tugged it on and carried his flippers and snorkel to the deepest pool in four swift steps.

A cold douse of the Pacific would have to do.

Natalie and Elliott both pulled their flippers on at the edge of the water.

She sidled into the ocean and pushed away all thoughts of him barely clad as soon as they entered her mind—which they did over and over again—and felt a moment's peace that he had the wet suit on now, although it pretty much just outlined the strong, lean shape she now couldn't stop noticing.

"Ready?" he asked.

"Yep." She snapped on her mask and adjusted her snorkel. Her mask nicely kept Elliott and his body out of her peripheral vision.

Underwater, she was able to finally steer her mind elsewhere. The underwater world of Heart's Cove was magical: miles of kelp forests, which swayed beneath and around them, rays of sun from above cutting through the kelp beds like pillars of light. Amid the waving kelp swam neon-orange Garibaldi damselfish, bright-blue angelfish, and schools of gray-spotted calico bass. Elliott pointed to a rock crevice where two spiny lobsters peeked out with suspicious little eyes, and then he took her hand and guided them both toward another set of rocks, where he pointed at a two-spot octopus with fake-out blue eyes on either side of its head.

They swam for what seemed like a blissful forever—Elliott usually ahead of her, looking back often, sometimes smiling behind his mask, bubbles trailing out of his snorkel tube. He was a good diver—possibly better than she was—and they could both stay under for a long time before heading back to the surface to clear their snorkel tubes and dive back down. Often Elliott reached back for her and guided her toward something he wanted her to see—sometimes a nautilus or another colorful octopus, sometimes a color on the side of a rock she couldn't quite make out. She gave him a thumbs-up when she realized it might be the algae he was looking for. Each time he spotted something of interest, they would both float backward for a second, careful to keep their flippers from damaging any kelp or coral, and then slide into another direction, sometimes amid another school of colorful fish. Natalie's hair came loose and floated around her shoulders, making her feel carefree and happy in the quiet, weightless sanctuary, filled with only her, Elliott, his wondrous smile, the bubbles from their tubes, and a world of otherworldly color and motion. She didn't want the afternoon to end.

When it finally had to, she swam up to shore and got her legs beneath her to wade up to dry sand. She collapsed onto a carpet of smooth pebbles and yanked off her mask, laughing and gasping for breath at the same time.

Elliott landed beside her.

"That was outrageous," he said, breathing heavily. "Beautifully outrageous."

"It was." That was pretty much all she could get out until she got her breath back.

Elliott sluiced the water off his face and stared out at the ocean, his ankles crossed in front of him, his chest rising and falling as he caught his own breath. The sun was sitting low in the sky now—heading toward another beautiful sunset—and a sheen of gold illuminated his skin and hair. The peace across his face, the look of wonder, the drips along his eyelashes, the gold highlighting his features made him, suddenly, the most beautiful man Natalie had ever seen.

"You're a champ diver," he said, looking back at her over his shoulder.

"You're not so bad yourself."

"I was trying to keep up with you."

She wasn't sure what to do with the compliment. She didn't quite know what to do with a man like this, who complimented her openly and often. Especially a man who was starting to set her heart pounding at every smile.

"Did you see the algae?" he asked. "I was trying to point it out to you, but it was hard to see. And not quite as cool as the spiny lobsters. Did you see those? I've never seen so many. This is a beautiful place to dive, Natalie." He looked back out at the ocean, and her heart swelled at this newest compliment. It wasn't her island, but it *felt* like her island right now, and she was so pleased that he liked it.

They sat there for nearly a half hour, talking about everything they'd seen together in their underwater wonderland, dripping into the smooth, black ocean pebbles and letting the sun make straw of their hair and tighten their faces with saltwater. Elliott would laugh often, deep and low, his eyes crinkling at the corners, and when it sent a funny fluttering through her stomach, Natalie wondered how she'd ever managed to ignore this guy. She'd been hit hard.

She was truly in love.

It was almost a relief when he stood to get back to their packs.

Back at their spot, tucked at the edge of the cliffs, they stood on top of towels and peeled off their wet suits. Although they were back-to-back, Natalie couldn't resist a peek. She took her suit off quickly, then looked back at Elliott, hesitating with hers in midair.

The golden sun set his body ablaze with orange, outlining all the indentations of his muscles along his shoulders, pecs, and abs. His hair flopped forward as he shoved all his gear back into his bag. He straightened abruptly, dragging his T-shirt up with him, then stalled before slipping it over his head, caught by her expression.

The rays of sun shone brightly between them, like spotlights on their indecision.

His eyes dragged across her body again, this time with less embarrassment, as if he could sense the invitation was now open. He lifted his gaze to hers, staring imploringly into her eyes—questioning, wondering, asking silently what she wanted.

She didn't really know. She wanted him. That she was suddenly sure of. But she also wanted to know she could remain independent for three whole months. And to prove that to Paige. And to Olivia. And to herself . . .

She had only two more days to go.

It took everything Natalie had in her to look away.

CHAPTER 24

Elliott watched Natalie out of the corner of his eye as they chopped carrots at his kitchen counter. She was acting awfully strange. She was so much quieter than usual, and she seemed to be avoiding direct eye contact at all costs.

He wondered if he'd just pushed it too far this afternoon with his adolescent staring at her bikini body. Then her wet-suit body. Then her undressing-back-to-the-bikini body. Then her just-showered body . . . He was a mess.

He should probably apologize.

She didn't need him leering at her all afternoon. She'd made that perfectly clear, that she didn't want that in her life. And he was—

"So you just want to keep these all a uniform length," she said.

He nodded briskly, his hair falling into his eyes. "Got it."

"And you can just put them all into this bowl—then we'll put a little glaze on them."

"Listen, Natalie." He put the knife down and wiped his hands on a towel they had between them.

He took a step closer, but she suddenly pushed herself back into the corner. Shame shot through him. "I'm sorry if I was making you uncomfortable today."

She waved her knife a little. "Could you move back there a little?"

Shocked, he stepped back a few steps. "Am I making you uncomfortable right now?"

"Not really. You're just . . ." She started chopping carrots again. "You're looking kind of good there, with your tight T-shirt and your just-out-of-the-shower damp hair, and I just need you to chop these carrots right now."

He didn't know how to respond to that. He wasn't sure what to do with that information, or how to deal with the undertone of frustration in her voice, or that . . . Was that flirting? So he just did what she wanted and chopped more carrots in silence, glancing over at her from time to time.

"So now we make a glaze." She pulled the brown sugar out of the groceries they'd just purchased, counting out a measurement to him, but he was no longer paying attention. He hoped she was writing this down for him.

"Did you hear that?" she finally asked.

He shook his head. All he could think of now were the terms *tight T-shirt* and *damp hair* and the improbable concept that Natalie might have just told him she found him sexy.

"One-third cup," she repeated.

He nodded.

"And one cup of water."

He glanced up at her, his ears nearly ringing now, and watched her breath quicken, her chest rising and falling, moving her Dr Pepper T-shirt logo in a rapid pace.

"And some butter," she said shakily. She reached for the stick of butter she'd purchased, but suddenly stalled, staring at it against the countertop, both hands pressing instead into the granite.

"I have to call my sister," she said abruptly.

And then she bolted for the hallway.

"Paige," Natalie whispered, gripping the phone. She stepped across the back slider onto Elliott's patio. "Where are you right now? Is Lily with you?"

"Yes. What's wrong?"

"Nothing. Nothing's wrong. I just want to—speak in code, okay? So Lily doesn't know what we're talking about? I just want to call and officially throw the bet. I'll still honor your win. I just want to acknowledge it so maybe you won't lord it over me."

"But you have only two more days!"

"I know. But I'm throwing it anyway."

"Are you with Elliott?"

"Code, Paige."

"Lily's down by the water. She can't hear. So are you with him *now?*"

"He's in the kitchen right now, and I'm outside, but I'm just making this decision. So I wanted to call and preemptively keep you from being obnoxious."

"I'm happy for you, Natalie! I accept your defeat. And I won't even make you pay up."

Natalie's jaw dropped a little. "Did someone hit you with a nice stick this morning? What's with you?"

"What do you mean?"

"You're being so nice to me."

"I'm always nice to you!"

"Not really."

"Do you really think I'm not nice to you all the time?" Paige asked.

"I absolutely think you're not nice to me all the time."

"Name me something I've said that was mean."

"In the last hour? Or over the last few months?"

"Natalie!"

"I'm just shocked at your response. I thought you'd be gloating all over the place that you won," Natalie said.

"The winning wasn't important to me here. Only the end result."

"What are you talking about?"

"I'm talking about you and Elliott Sherman," Paige said. "And waiting three whole months before you so much as kissed the guy—in any kind of seriousness anyway—so you could start a relationship on a proper footing."

"*What?*"

"Abstaining, Natalie. I'm talking about abstaining from sex and any kind of physical relationship and focusing on building a solid friendship first so you have some kind of chance."

Natalie plopped down in one of the chaise lounges. "My brain's a little addled from all the pheromones in the kitchen, so I think you're going to have to explain this to me."

Paige blew a long-suffering sigh into the phone. "The reason your relationships don't work is that they're all destined to crash and burn. They're not even relationships—they're just physical attractions. You see a guy you think is hot, he invariably thinks you're hot, and you throw yourselves at each other. Then you combust and burn out in three weeks. You've done it over and over again. So the idea that you wanted to do a mancation—I liked that for you. I thought it'd be good for you. And I knew if I bet you, and then taunted you a bit, you wouldn't give up. In the past, your follow-through hasn't always been the best, you know."

"See? That's what I mean."

"Just stating facts here."

Natalie rolled her eyes. But she had to admit that Paige was right.

"So anyway," Paige went on, "when I saw Elliott enter the picture, I thought this mancation could be great. Not because I didn't want you to have a relationship, but because I *did*. I just wanted you to find the right guy. And I wanted you to develop a real relationship. And he looked like 'it' all over the place."

"I'm not starting a relationship with him, Paige. I'm just . . . maybe ending one. Maybe I'm saying good-bye. To someone who meant a lot to me this the last few months."

"Why wouldn't you want to start a real relationship with him?"

"I just . . . I don't know."

"Don't freeze up on me now, sis. Here's where you get scared, and you duck like some turtle into a shell."

"I'm not scared. It's just . . . He's not even my type," she sputtered. She knew she was hardly making any sense now. She'd told Elliott herself she was perfect for him.

"Your type isn't a decent, nice guy? Who treats women with respect? Who has a job and a future and is all-around kind and thoughtful?"

Natalie sighed. Paige was right. Elliott was ideal. But she was still terrified. She put her hand over her pounding heart. "It's just with Elliott, things have been different."

"Different how?"

"We're friends."

"See? I think you don't even know what a real relationship looks like. Mom wasn't exactly a good role model. But a real relationship—true love—I think it looks exactly like what you and Elliott have. It looks like a solid *friendship*. Enjoying being together. Trusting each other. Going through life hand in hand, side by side. Together. And each caring enough about the other to want to make life better every day. That's *loving* someone. If you can throw in some attraction and great sex, you've got it made. And correct me if I'm wrong, but I can sense the attraction between you two as if it were laser beams shooting at me. You two aren't exactly subtle."

"I never kissed him, Paige! After you said it was part of the rules—"

"I know, I know. I believe you followed the rules, and I know you almost won the bet. Well, as of Sunday, that is. But you came close. You did great. I thought three months would build something solid, and that's why I extended the whole thing."

It took Natalie a second to catch her breath. "You extended the bet on purpose?"

"Of course. I doubled down because I could see something real between you two, and I thought if I could get you to postpone the physical relationship for once, and let the friendship grow first, you'd avoid the crash-and-burn and have something to build on. You needed a man who respected you, Natalie, and who you respected in return. And now you have him."

Natalie dropped her forehead into her hand. *Paige concocted all of this?* In looking back, she could sort of see where it had happened: Paige's funny glances, her knowing smiles, her challenges that did seem a little pushy.

And maybe Paige was right. Natalie had never had a friendship with a man like this before. And, truthfully, she'd never loved anyone like Elliott before. She'd thought she was just loving him as a friend, but maybe that's what love was—the same kind of love you had for friends who you cared about deeply. She wanted to take care of him; she wanted to be with him; she wanted to make him happy whenever she was in his presence. And she couldn't remember ever feeling that way about a man before. Before she'd always looked for what she could *get* out of a relationship; with Elliott, she was looking for what she could *give*.

"I think he's good for you," Paige said quietly. "And he obviously cares about you immensely. I hope it worked. Your mancation is now null and void. You lost the bet. But I hope you win Elliott."

Natalie could hear the smile in Paige's voice.

"Paige?"

"Yes, sis?"

"This is the nicest thing you've ever done for me."

"I told you—I'm always nice to you!"

"I love you."

"I love you, too. Now go get that guy."

Natalie clicked off the phone and all but ran back into the kitchen.

Elliott had tried to pick up where Natalie had left off and was now staring at the carrots, brown sugar, water, and butter in the saucepan, wondering how high he should turn up the heat. When he heard the slider in the room behind him, he started to turn to ask. He would put these on low, then sit down with her and apologize.

"Hey, Natalie, can we put these on simmer or—"

Before he could finish the question, he felt hands on his shoulders, tugging him around, and then . . . *lips.* Beautiful, soft, sensuous lips, sliding across his, drawing him in, sending a slippery warmth through every extremity.

Soft arms came up around his neck and pulled him in deeper. Before he could think, he had his hands at the sides of her breasts, sliding down her waist, running across the planes of curves he'd memorized underneath her T-shirts. His hands kept moving downward, tracing her shape, grasping her behind, wanting to pull her toward him, into him, wanting her even closer, but then . . .

Some kind of faraway sense came into his head, and he remembered that this was all taboo just a few short minutes ago.

"Natalie?" He grasped for air, for sense, for context. "Wait, what's happening? What about your mancation?"

"I threw the bet." Her fingers were quickening across his chest, his shoulders, his back. "My mancation is over." Her lips found his again.

He couldn't quite process what this meant. His brain had slowed to a stop, the blood now fueling other parts of him as her tongue teased his. He was focused only on her body, and how it felt, and where it met his, and bringing it even closer toward him. But the niggling thought kept coming through that she hadn't wanted this just a minute ago. He forced himself to pull away.

"What happened?" he finally managed to ask.

Her eyes dragged open and finally met his. He forced himself to ignore that beautiful sight for one second—her rosy and swollen lips, her half-lidded eyes, her flushed cheeks—and concentrate on the language coming out of her mouth.

"I called my sister. I called it off. I'm probably leaving next week, and . . ." Her heavy lids dropped again to his waistband, and her fingers followed.

He sucked in his breath and grabbed her hand to try to make sense of this for a second. "Is this a pity offer?"

"*No.* Definitely not. It's—" she sputtered. Her hand waved in the air like a windmill. He watched the whirling for a second and moved out of its way.

"Maybe it's a good-bye. I just thought . . ." She tried again. "I thought it would bring us closer."

He watched her carefully. "Closer?"

She nodded.

"You want to get closer before we say good-bye?"

She nodded again.

He leaned back against the counter again.

"I'm not sure I even know what to do with a woman like you, Natalie Grant." He laughed as reality hit him. "I don't want to be toyed with by someone like you."

Natalie snapped her jaw shut. "Toyed with? Is that what you think I'm doing?"

He immediately realized it was the wrong thing to say.

"No," he finally said, looking into that beautiful face and realizing he might be blowing it. "I don't mean that you're teasing me. Sexually anyway. I mean that I really care about you, and I'm one of those guys who gets kind of attached, so if we have sex right now, I need to know you like me, and you want it, and this isn't some weird thing about a bet anymore."

She looked up at him and wrapped her arms around his neck.

"I'll tell you this, Elliott. I've been staring at you all day, and hyperventilating a little every time you look at me, and remembering every practice and pretend kiss we ever had, and I called my sister in a panic just now to tell her I was throwing the bet because I really, really like you and I really, really want you to touch me. So, no, this isn't about a bet anymore. Now kiss me. Please."

Natalie's heart pounded as Elliott snapped off the burners, grabbed her hand, and began pulling her out of the kitchen.

"Where are we going?" she asked.

"Bedroom."

Her heart continued its erratic pace as he quickened his step across the three oriental rugs and moved forward with a singular determination.

"You're okay with this, then?" she asked breathlessly.

His jaw muscle danced. "I am."

"You changed your mind?"

"I did."

"What changed your mind?"

"If you're toying with me or you're not, or if I can make you happy or I can't, I might as well know I've done all I could and acted courageously."

"Courageously?"

"Yes, courageously."

"It takes courage to sleep with me?"

"It does."

"Why does it—"

Before she could finish the sentence, Elliott turned and took both sides of her face in his hands and pulled her toward him, closing his mouth over hers in a long, silencing kiss. The warmth of his tongue, the warmth of his lips, the warmth of his hands in her hair, sent a hot slide of comfort and wickedness all the way down her center until her legs felt as if they were going to give out from under her. She nearly toppled in her high sandals, and she gripped his chest for balance. He slid his hand down her back to catch her, but kept his warm tongue moving, then brought his hands back into her hair just the way she'd shown him earlier. He ended the kiss with a long, soul-wrenching suck on her bottom lip that turned her limbs to jelly. He moved back, still cupping her face, waiting for her to open her eyes.

When she finally did, she met his.

"How was that?" Elliott asked huskily.

"That was . . ." *Wow*. She caught her breath. "That was fabulous."

He nodded curtly. "Then let's do more."

While her heart pounded in a crazy way, he grabbed her hand again and led her to the bedroom, kicking his shoes off, shuffling papers and journals off his bed and sending them all over the floor. She'd seen him look singularly focused before, but nothing like he did now—he was a man possessed. Once the bed was completely cleared of notes and formulas and pencils and papers, he turned abruptly toward her and . . . stilled.

"Elliott?"

As if frozen, his hands suddenly dropped at his sides. He stared quietly at her body, her face, her breasts.

"Elliott? What's wrong?"

"I feel like this is some kind of test."

"Test?" she asked. "For what?"

He shrugged. "I'm used to learning, and being a quick study, and winning fellowships, and winning awards for my findings. But this . . . I'm not sure what to do here. I feel like if I don't do well, I'm going to somehow fail."

He looked so sweet standing there, unsure, uncertain. She just wanted to throw her arms around him. "It's not a test."

"I don't want to mess this up. What do you like?"

"I think you can figure out what I like."

"How will I know?"

"I'll make noises."

His eyebrow lifted. "I look forward to that. But I want to elicit them correctly. You were supposed to be teaching me, remember?"

She let a smile escape. "That's right—I was supposed to be helping you with the seduction part, wasn't I?"

"Yeah, way to drop the ball, Natalie."

She laughed. "I guess I could pick up from here. Where did we leave off?" She took a step toward him and the T-shirt stretched across his chest. He had no idea how good that thing looked on him, but it truly outlined the physique he rarely showed off.

"Well, the Colonel coached me on dating. Doris taught me to dance. Nell instructed me on how to dress. So what do I need to know from you?" he murmured.

She tugged at the T-shirt hem. "Looks like you've got everything down pat. What more do you want to know?"

"I, uh . . ." He watched her fingertips move under the fabric. "I think you covered the erogenous zones. And, uh . . ." He cleared his throat as Natalie pushed the shirt upward. "I think I understood that. Or most of that. *Some* of that."

He reached over his head and yanked the shirt off for her. Natalie ran her hand across the taut chest and abs she'd seen only briefly before. "Elliott, I'm sure you've done this before. I think you know what's next."

"Yeah, no, technically, I'm fine. I just don't know what you, in par-ticular, might—*oh God.*" He caught her head in his hands as she trailed a kiss down his torso. "Damn, Natalie, that's good, but I—oh *gah.*" He stumbled back a little and cradled the back of her head against his abs, where she'd started to tempt with her tongue, working his waistband undone with her fingernails. He let out a hiss and then lifted her face in his hands. "Okay, here's the deal—I know what *I* like. You're not going to have any problems whatsoever making me a happy man tonight. As you can see, we've already started." He indicated the tent in his pants. "But I want to know what *you* like. What do you want me to do? What do you want me to do to you?"

Natalie couldn't remember ever having a man ask her such a thing in her life. She studied his face to see if he was kidding. But she was met, simply, with a hunger in his eyes—and an absolute determination to please—that shot an ache of want right between her legs.

"Well, first you can undress me," she said.

"My pleasure." He reached for her shirt. "Do you like to be kissed while you're being undressed? Or can I just stare?"

Her breath caught at his husky delivery, then the hungry way his gaze made its way across every inch of her skin as her shirt was tossed to the floor.

He didn't need an answer for that one. He'd decided to stare. And then touch.

A shiver went through her as his hands caressed her, undoing her bra, gazing at her with reverence as if he were memorizing every curve, his fingers tracing the planes of her body. She helped with her jeans and then stood before him in her lacy cheekies. She wished now she'd worn something a little sexier, but . . . On the other hand, Elliott didn't seem to notice. She'd never been met with such a cherishing gaze. All those years in the past, when she'd run from men's stares, she'd never known they could be like this. The element of tenderness stroked her like a fingertip. Her breath came shorter as he held her out slightly and turned her around.

"God, you're beautiful," he said.

She'd never felt more so. She reached up and pulled the loose plaits out of her hair. She wanted Elliott to stare at her this way for the rest of her life—his eyes feasting over her legs, her bottom, her breasts, as he turned her. The adoration in his eyes was coming not just from the appreciation of body parts but every bit as much from how he felt about her as a whole. He truly cared about her. And it shone through.

She reached toward him, but he caught her arms. "I'm not done," he said. His voice was raspy. "So, erogenous zones. Let me see if I can remember." He brought her wrist to his lips and watched her eyes as he kissed gently, then extended the trail of tender kisses up her arm. When he kissed the inside of her elbow, she let out a little gasp, and he brought his eyelashes up to her. "There's the sound."

"Yes." Her voice was breathless and embarrassing.

"I get an A there, then. Let's do the other side."

Another tender trail led up her right arm as her legs became unsteady.

"You said the back of your neck?"

Before she could answer, he turned her slowly, lifted her heavy hair off her neck, and began a trail of sinful kisses across the back of her neck, exactly where she'd shown him before, eliciting the same shivers he had on the rock above the city. This time, though, his other hand was exploring the edge of her cheekies, running a fingertip along the lace, over her hip, along her bottom.

"I like these," he murmured into her neck.

His finger teased the opening where she was already wet, and another gasp escaped her throat.

"Another sound." He smiled against her skin.

"You're . . ." She inhaled some air. "You're a very fast learner."

"One of my strengths," he mumbled. He spent some time there, arousing a series of gasps from Natalie, then lifted his thumb to rub a circle at the small of her back. "Here?"

"Sometimes," she exhaled.

He was on his knees next, dragging her panties down, helping her step out of them, but then he surprised her by running his finger down the backs of her thighs and calves. She was aching for him now, wanting him undressed, inside her, but he stopped at the backs of her knees. "Here?"

"We can skip that, Elliott, let's just—" She had a hard time catching her breath now, and she tried to turn to grab his hair, bring him in front of her, get his clothes off, get him to—

But he grasped her hands to stop her from pulling him, and his tongue warmed the back of her leg in a long, deep suck that seemed to pull at every other sexual organ in her body. She let out a little moan.

"Elliott, please, I—"

"Bend over, Natalie."

"What?"

"Here. Bend over the bed." He motioned toward it.

"Please, Elliott, just get undressed now. I really want to—" She reached for his waistband again, but he caught her hands.

"Am I getting Ds here?"

"No."

"What would you give me?" He smiled. He knew.

"I'd give you an A, but—"

"Then let me continue. We've got a long night ahead of us, and I've got a lot of learning to do about you. I think we've got a few important erogenous zones left for me to explore, don't we? I think we've hit all the before-dinner ones; now let's get to the naked ones." His grin was wolfish. She felt a little light-headed.

In minutes, he had her facedown on the bed, his hands and fingertips running across every square inch of her. He explored, then tasted, then studied, then trailed kisses across her skin, finally turning her to repeat the process in front. When he stalled at her nipples, pulling them into his teeth, she cried out and begged him to enter her, reaching to guide him.

"Elliott! Please."

"I'll get there," he said, pinning her hands back. "I'm learning here."

"I'll give you an A-plus-plus if you'll just enter me now."

He chuckled. "Aren't you enjoying this?"

"I'm enjoying it *immmmm-ensely*. I'm just . . . enjoying it too much. I need you. Inside me. Now."

"We'll get there." His fingertips came down along her pelvis to explore, and she bucked her hips up. "I want to ruin the curve."

She laughed. *"Elliott!"*

He teased her for only a few moments more, stroking her, parting her, inserting a finger, then two, studying her face, smiling every time she moaned, then finally, gloriously, he reached for a condom from his nightstand, kissed her while he put it on, and then slowly, wonderfully, entered her.

"Oh God, Elliott."

She pulled him tighter to her with each thrust, let the wonderful emotion overwhelm her of being *one* with this man—one motion, one body, one mind, one spirit, one feeling, in this one exact moment—and thought how she'd like to meld with him forever. She'd never felt so connected, wanting to envelop him in her, wanting to be enveloped by him, and she pulled him tighter and tighter as they both rode high. Finally, ready for release, she dragged his hand between them, showing him where to stroke—she was definitely one of those clit-orgasm girls, although most men didn't take the time to learn that. But Elliott was eager to learn, eager to please, and followed her lead with mastery. It took him two seconds to bring her to orgasm, which she released with a cry and tears in her eyes. Moments later, he followed, shuddering against her until he buried his head against her shoulder.

Together, they caught their breath, Elliott breathing into her neck. Then she stroked his hair. She felt nothing but tenderness for this man.

"Elliott?"

"Yes?" he mumbled.

"You did it."

He lifted himself up and stared at her curiously. "What?"

"You aced the test," she whispered.

He chuckled and pushed her hair back from her face, then leaned in and gave her the most tender kiss of her life.

CHAPTER 25

In the morning, Natalie blinked open her eyes and tried to figure out where she was. As consciousness rolled in—ceiling fan, white curtains, papers all over the floor—her mind finally landed on the events of the day before. Elliott, snorkeling, making dinner, calling Paige, Elliott undressing her, his smile, and . . . wow, that lovemaking. They'd finally finished making dinner sometime around nine, ate slowly, then headed for the living room for round two. And then the patio, under the stars, for round three. She let her memory slip to his kisses, his care, his touch, his humor and slowly began rolling over as she forced her eyes open. Her hand landed on his empty space and she bolted upright.

She listened for sounds in the front room. Had he left for work? On a Saturday? She looked around the room and let herself sigh over her favorite part of the evening: his very last kiss as they drifted off to sleep together, his arm protectively around her body, his fingers stroking her loose hair until she fell asleep.

Natalie wasn't normally the type of girl to touch during sleep. She normally kicked guys out of her bed so she could sleep peacefully, or she left at three in the morning to get to her own spacious, wonderfully empty bed. "Sleeping over" was not her norm. And cuddling all night was not even in her lexicon.

But last night with Elliott . . . that had simply felt right. Maybe because they already knew each other and were already close. She already trusted him, enjoyed his presence, enjoyed his company. They'd slept next to each other—on outdoor chaise lounges or on separate couches—as friends enough times that sleeping in the same bed with him last night didn't feel stifling at all. It almost felt like wanting to join him at the tide pools—comforted by his hand helping her up, warmed by their legs touching, secure and safe, and always entertained in his company.

She lifted herself out of bed and peeked out the bedroom door, clutching her dress in front of her. Where had he gone? She couldn't hear a thing out there. She snatched the sheets off the bed and pulled them around her.

"He was supposed to be here," a voice said in the front room.

A man's voice? But not Elliott's.

She crept back to the door with her sheet in tow and opened it a crack.

"You need to leave them alone, Nell. It doesn't matter if Natalie was here."

Natalie gripped the sheet tighter. It was Jim. She whirled back to scan the floor for her clothes.

"I can't leave it alone," Nell's voice said. "I'm flying Vanessa in tonight to meet him. Where is he?"

"Maybe he forgot about going out for breakfast today."

Natalie heard pots and pans being loaded into the sink. She wanted her bra but didn't want to leave her eavesdropping space. She stretched her leg across the floor and wriggled her toe to reach for the bra strap.

"Anyway, he's a big boy," Jim said. "I think we need to let him live his own life."

"I just don't want him to get hurt."

"I know, but, Nell, seriously. He's a grown-ass man. He knows what he wants. You need to stop with this."

"But does he really know what he wants?"

"Yes."

"Is it sex? Because I'm sure Natalie can provide that, but I want him to have something more."

Natalie's toe finally caught her bra and she dragged it toward her. Underwear next.

"Look, I don't know. And it's none of our business. And neither are these dishes. Put those down. All I know is that Elliott has been happier in the last few weeks than I've seen him since I've known him. And I don't know how you can be missing that fact."

Natalie had to crawl away for a second to snatch up her underwear, which were slightly under the bed. She scrambled back to the crack in the door and tried to catch up.

". . . tomorrow, and Becky just says that Natalie has always been a screwup, and always irresponsible. I don't want him to get stuck taking care of her. He gravitates toward wounded birds. I want him with a woman who's strong and can stand on her own. And who will stick around. Becky said Natalie can't commit to anything, which is the worst kind of person Elliott could meet right now."

A tiny slice went through Natalie at that, and she dropped her forehead against the doorjamb.

"First of all, you're giving Becky too much credit in this scenario— she has an agenda, you know—and I think you're selling Natalie way short."

"She's only twenty-seven."

"He's only twenty-eight!"

"She has no job. Well, except this temporary job babysitting. And what if she leaves him? When people are afraid to commit to anything, that's what they do, you know. He'll get hurt. He lost our grandfather, and you and I are leaving. He doesn't need someone else to leave him right now."

A silence fell while Natalie's head spun. She wanted to leap out to interrupt this exchange—at least defend herself. But—on the other hand—honestly, the things Nell was saying were true. Natalie *had* been a runner all her life, especially from relationships. She *was* a bit of a wounded bird for Elliott, based on the way he looked at her so sadly whenever she brought up the reason for her mancation. And she *might* hurt him if she started something and left. He did say he was the type to get attached. And she couldn't commit in any long-term way—especially on an island. Even if she stayed just for a short time, what if she did what Paige mentioned and started finding faults with Elliott just so she might break up with him and flee? She stared at the clothes hanging from her fingertips.

"Look, I don't want him hurt either," Jim finally said softly. "Natalie did say she was leaving next week." She could hear the light notes of disappointment in his voice.

"Then encourage him to take this date with Vanessa instead," Nell said. "Vanessa wants a real relationship. She wants a future. And Elliott deserves that."

Another silence followed, where Natalie could hear everyone giving up on her. She let her bra fall to her side.

"We should leave," Nell said softly. "He forgot. Maybe they went out to breakfast already."

After hearing the back door open and close, Natalie sat in silence for a long while. She stared out Elliott's bedroom window at the blue sky and watched a family of seagulls fly by.

She loved Elliott. She was suddenly sure of that. But she loved him so much she didn't want to hurt him. Nell was right—he was in a fragile state with so many losses in his life. And how could Natalie—in good conscience—pull him into a relationship now, knowing she never let them last? Commitment-phobes didn't change their stripes overnight.

One of her flip-flops caught her eye, and she crawled toward it, lifting it off a stack of Elliott's papers and journals. The journal on top was an open suede-bound book, with lined paper inside and what must be Elliott's handwriting. Somehow words leaped off the page at her:

April 16, 7 p.m.: Direct observation: three sea lion pups found alive, washed ashore in Diver's Nook . . .

That was the day they'd met. Natalie tried to look away, but something made her read a little farther down:

April 16, 7 p.m.: Direct observation: met the woman I want to marry. Probably Nell's worst nightmare.

Each scan across the line made Natalie's breath come more and more ragged. *Marry?* The word seemed to grow darker and darker until it looked as if it were written in thick iron letters, ready to lock her up, ready to make her hyperventilate.

Did Elliott think that after their first encounter? How long had he had marriage on his mind? When they spoke at the Castle, he'd said he didn't know if he wanted a long-term relationship—had he been saying that just to appease her? Had he said it just to trick her?

Natalie's breath came faster and faster as she pressed her hand into her chest to calm her heart. She had to get out of there.

She grabbed the rest of her clothes, yanked them on, then slipped down the hall.

Nell was absolutely right about her.

When people were afraid to commit to anything, they definitely fled.

CHAPTER 26

The ocean slapped against the rocks as Natalie sat in the sand and watched Elliott approach. She pulled her windblown hair tendrils away from her lips and rubbed under her eyes, hoping he wouldn't be able to tell she'd been crying.

"Hey." His voice slid through her core like whiskey. The ocean roared before them as he took a seat near her. "There you are. I couldn't believe you left this morning. I went to get us breakfast. Where'd you go?"

She took a deep breath and delivered her message without ceremony. "Elliott, we can't do this."

Elliott blinked a few times. The ocean roared in. "What?"

"A relationship. We can't start one. I had an amazing time with you last night, but we can't . . . we just can't."

He stared at her while another wave rolled up and back, a frown taking over his features. "Natalie, what's wrong?"

"I found a thing in your room—a paper or journal or something."

His forehead crumpled into a scowl. "What are you talking about?"

"I didn't mean to look at it, but I saw that you wrote about rescuing Larry, Curly, and Moe, and then you wrote that you met the woman you want to marry and that she was Nell's worst nightmare. Elliott, did you really think that about me right when you saw me?"

He looked out at the ocean, the frown still in place. Another wave went out and in before he spoke again. "I think I did, yeah."

"Elliott, I don't even want to get married. How could you have tricked me into getting closer to you when you knew—"

"Wait, first of all, I didn't trick you into anything. I was trying to stay away from you, if you'll remember. You kept showing up at the ends of my dates, and I wasn't doing anything remotely like tricking you. It was like the laws of attraction that we just kept gravitating toward each other."

"Laws of attraction?"

"Scientific laws of affinity—likes attract likes. Ocean to ocean. Earth to earth. That kind of thing. It's a chemical thing. Anyway, it was never my intent to end up with you five nights in a row, and end up kissing your neck on a cliff side, and end up in a bar with you at the Castle, and the bison and . . . I didn't plan any of that, Natalie."

"But you wrote you met the woman you want to marry?"

He shook his head. "I can't explain that. I don't know what came over me."

"You said you didn't know if you were even a long-term guy. You said—"

"Natalie, I'm sorry. I'm sorry I wrote that. I'm sorry you saw it. I have absolutely no secret intent here."

"I can't . . ." Her chest started feeling as if it were being filled with lava again. She pressed her hand into it. "I can't be with you—sleep with you or start dating you—knowing you have marriage in mind as the end result. I can't . . ." The lava was flowing around her heart, squeezing it, causing it to beat in an irregular way. She pressed her hand harder.

"We can't start a relationship," she finally sputtered out. "Whoever Nell's setting you up with and flying in for prom—you should go with her."

"But I'm not interested in—"

"I can't offer you anything, Elliott. This other woman quite possibly can. I'm . . . I'm not right for you. I can't commit. And I'm . . . I'm too much of a wounded bird."

"A wounded bird?" The scowl was even deeper on Elliott's face.

"You're probably attracted to those types, and that's sweet—I know you like to care for people—and that's me, Elliott, I do have broken wings. But you need someone who's strong and able to stand on her own two feet."

She thought about revealing everything—the overheard conversation between Nell and Jim, too—but she didn't want to blame this on them. This was her problem. She'd created this situation—letting things go too far with this good, good man, and now not being able to see it through to the conclusion he probably wanted. She needed to back away slowly.

"You're creating a full, rich life here on the island, and you should continue that," she said, her hand still pressing against her chest. "You've got a great group of friends now—all the seniors, Jim and Nell if they come back from Italy. My sister will always be here for you, Lily loves you, and you have the possibility of this new woman."

"But I'm not interested in a new woman. I'm interested in you."

"I can't stay."

The waves crashed in the distance. The truth of her statement hung in the air between them, as impossible to ignore as ocean fog.

"I can't commit. And I can't live on an island," she continued. "You should go to the dance with the woman Nell thinks is right and find someone who can make a life here with you."

The second she heard those words fall from her lips—make a life here with Elliott—Natalie had a brief glimpse of beauty. A flash of a vignette went through her mind, of Elliott, and her, here on the island, dating, walking along the beach, having drinks with friends at the Shore Thing, playing in the tide pools, laying on the chaise lounges under the stars, sitting on the couch with Lily and watching movies. The peace that floated through her at every image was something she'd never known.

But in less than a millisecond, the vision changed. The concept of commitment reentered, crushing all the images and warping them into a tight lava ball that began squeezing her again. Natalie's heart went into overdrive, a feeling of claustrophobia and panic setting in. The ball tightened further with each idea of living on an island, living so close to so few people, committing to a life or job she wasn't ready for . . . She tried to draw a deep breath.

"I can't," she managed to squeak out, pressing her hand to her lungs.

She wanted to elaborate—she wanted to make sure Elliott knew this wasn't about him. He was such a wonderful man, and the man she'd felt closest to her whole life—but her heart kept skipping beats, and she had the sense she might even die right here on the beach. She brought her hand tighter to her chest and took a deep breath. She'd have to explain this to him later. Right now, she'd have to simply survive.

"Did I do something wrong?" he asked quietly.

"No! No. Definitely not." Her heart was going to explode. She needed to get out of here. "You are wonderful. Really, the most amazing man. And someone who's looking for a long-term relationship will be so lucky to find you. But I'm leaving. And you need someone who deserves you." She stood. She had to leave. "I'll see you there tonight, though."

If her heart indeed exploded, she didn't want Elliott to see it.

"Let's talk more later," she added. "I'm going to try to get there early tonight, and I'd love to talk, or at least have a dance with you. But I wanted to make sure you didn't cancel on her tonight."

She began backing up the sand dunes.

"Okay, Elliott?"

He nodded and simply looked confused.

Natalie raced away.

It wasn't her finest moment.

But she had to start breathing again.

Elliott stared out at the ocean for another couple of minutes and uttered curses in his head.

What the hell was that?

He'd thought everything had gone so well last night. He'd thought they were getting closer; he'd thought he'd pleased her in bed; he'd thought they'd made an amazing connection.

But obviously there was something he wasn't seeing, wasn't understanding.

He stared at the waves crashing onshore. He could've told her more about how badly he wanted her to stay here with him. He could've made a case for how much he was falling for her, for how comfortable he felt around her, how much he looked forward to seeing her every day. He wasn't lying when he said he didn't know why he wrote that on the very first night he met her. He barely remembered doing it. But it sounded about right. He'd been hit hard, from the start, and whether it was laws of attraction or magnetic fields or biological chemistry bringing them together, it didn't matter. They were meant to be together.

But he'd chickened out. The Colonel was right: it was easy to be brave in the face of physical danger, like hanging over a cliff in a golf cart, but baring your soul for another human being was terrifying. He'd had so few people to love in his life. He could count them on one hand. And experiencing so much rejection and loss made him terrified of having Natalie reject him, too.

But seeing her recoil so fiercely when she'd had to utter the word *marry*—that told him everything he needed to know. Whether it was about him or not, she was clearly not interested in a relationship. At least not a long-term one. She'd last about a month, probably. And he wasn't prepared to deal with the pain that would bring.

And what the hell was that "wounded bird" comment?

He rose and dusted the sand off his hands. He'd go to the lab today. He'd been right all along—he needed to stick to microbiology.

Relationships and love—they were not his forte.

At the lab, the whirring of the test-tube incubators calmed him immediately. He made the rounds to check on all the sea lions—Moe was doing better, and Larry and Curly were almost ready for release. Mr. Warbler was being released tomorrow, and four others were also on the list. The epidemic was winding down, and even though they hadn't solved the mystery of the influx of dehydrated pups, he was proud of the work they'd done here. It had been a successful three months. Jim's center was definitely off the ground, and they'd have a whole year now to get the last details settled before they'd be hit with any more epidemics. With all the research now going on, hopefully they'd be able to handle anything that came up in the future, and Jim was already talking about coming back from Italy before next spring to possibly settle here with Nell permanently.

Elliott found some of his notes about algae on a clipboard near Moe's area and thought to bring them back to his office to type them up. He'd already been invited to meet with some algae phycologists on the mainland, and several environmentalists were getting together to discuss the warmer waters in the Pacific and see if the lack of fish was the problem. It would be good to throw himself back into work again so he didn't have to think about everything he'd lost here.

The sadness that thought brought down on his shoulders as he moved through the ICU was something he was wholly unprepared for. He'd been used to saying good-bye to people, moving around, pulling up shallow roots. But these past few months, here on Lavender Island, had truly been unique. He'd fallen into a feeling of comfort here, of belonging—from the perfect run along the beach, to the tide pools right outside his house, to the friendly townspeople who made him feel welcome, to the amazing staff at the Friends of the Sea Lion who were truly his people, to having Jim back in his life, to Nell and Max and the feeling of family, to the Colonel who'd been a rock like his granddad in his life again.

Elliott had never felt so welcome in a community before. And of course he knew the person who had made him feel warmest of all—Natalie Grant, who had made the last three months amazing. For once, he'd looked forward to leaving work each day—to seeing her smile, to hearing her laugh. He'd loved walking the tide pools with her as the sun set, and loved watching the waves at midnight with her. He'd loved their talks about all things serious and silly, loved playing darts with her before dinner, loved grocery shopping with her and even stir-frying vegetables in his close-quarters kitchen. He'd loved taking walks with her and Lily, and even loved Natalie's always-exciting golf cart off-roading. And, of course, he'd loved making love to her. He absolutely loved Natalie Grant.

Unfortunately, she didn't love him.

"Hey, what are you doing here?"

Elliott whirled around at the voice to see the Colonel walking toward him.

"Oh, hey. Just checking on the sea lions and getting ready to type up some notes. What are you doing here?"

"Just wanted to check on Mr. Warbler one more time. I had a dream that he took a downturn. But he's looking pretty good. I hope he'll be ready for release soon. But I should go get ready for tonight. You're going tonight, right? You got the girl?"

"What?"

"The girl. Did you get her? Are you taking her to prom tonight?"

The feeling of loss fell through Elliott again—fresh and new and painful and heavy all over again—and his veins suddenly felt filled with lead. The enormity of what he'd just let slip away almost brought him to the ground.

"I might be losing on some of those fronts, Colonel."

"What? Who's your date tonight?"

"Someone named Vanessa, but—"

"*Vanessa?* Where's Natalie? I told you to keep your eye on the prize, son."

Elliott frowned. "Is that who you've been talking about this whole time, telling me to keep my eye on the prize?"

"Of course. Who'd you think I was talking about?"

"I don't know, I—"

"Sherman, don't be so dense. I know men are stupid when it comes to certain women, and you're no exception, certainly, but get your head out of your ass and look around. She wants you. She needs you. You two are meant to be together. So you take that lion's share of courage you've always had in you and APPLY IT HERE."

Elliott ran his hand through his hair. Easier said than done. What did the Colonel know about how Natalie felt? Neither of them knew that. If Elliott could figure that out, he wouldn't be—

"And I know what you're thinking. You're wondering if I even know what I'm talking about. But don't. I'm not senile. *Yet* anyway. I've been around this block a few times, and I've been watching you two, and I know the real deal when I see it."

"Thanks for your vote of confidence, Colonel, but it's not that easy. She just broke up with me."

"Broke up with you? How could she break up with you? You haven't even asked her on a proper date yet."

A rueful smile escaped Elliott's lips. "Yeah, that might have been my problem. But she basically gave me the heave-ho on the beach just now."

"That can't be right. What did she say?"

"She's not into marriage, Colonel."

"MARRIAGE? Damn, son, I'm not talking about marriage. How could you bring up marriage to a woman who's afraid to commit?"

"How do you know she's afraid to commit?"

"She's got it written all over her. Don't be dense. You can't go from zero to sixty with a girl like that. Just baby steps. Don't freak her out. Just ask her out—take it slow. You two are meant to be. Just don't screw it up."

Elliott nodded. Maybe he'd simply been going at it all wrong. He hadn't meant for her to find that note about marriage, but now that it was out there, he'd just have to deal with it—with his true feelings, her true feelings, and lay it all on the line.

"It'll be the scariest thing you ever do, putting your heart out there for a girl you're in love with, but nothing's more worthwhile in the end," the Colonel said. "But you have to tell people how you feel. Don't trade fear of rejection for the possibility of a lifetime of happiness. And time is of the essence, kid. With love, time is always of the essence. Don't waste time you could be spending with her. I, for one, know that. I lay in bed all last night thinking I wasn't going to wake up this morning."

"What?"

"Heart hurt. Probably just heartburn. But I woke up this morning with a renewed sense of urgency."

Elliott reached for his elbow. "Colonel, do you want me to take you to the hospital?"

"Of course not. I have things to do. But you're missing my point. What I mean is—"

"Hey, you two," said a third voice behind them.

Elliott whirled around to see Jim. "You're here, too?"

"Yeah, the Colonel called and wanted me to help him check on Mr. Warbler. What are you doing here?"

"Just getting ready to type up some notes."

"Where were you this morning?" Jim lifted a clipboard from the wall.

"This morning?"

"Nell and I stopped by to get you for breakfast. You bailed on us."

Elliott's mind whirled to remember their plans. *That's right. Damn.* He'd been trying to be better about this plan-making thing with people, but he'd been a bit distracted last night and this morning . . .

"You came over?" he verified, wondering how he'd missed this.

"Yeah, we went inside but didn't see you, and then we noticed your keys were gone but not your phone. Were you running or something?"

"No, I went for bagels." Elliott's mind continued whirring with the timetable on this. If he'd been gone, but Jim and Nell were inside his place, had they seen Natalie? Had she seen them?

Before he could formulate the right question to ask, Jim grinned and elbowed him.

"Looked like you might have had an overnight guest, too," Jim said. "I'd hoped it was Natalie. I saw an extra lanyard and set of keys that I recognized as hers."

"What?" The Colonel snapped his head up.

"Elliott finally scored, Colonel."

The Colonel turned and frowned hard at Elliott. "You're doing everything out of order," he mumbled under his breath.

"I'm glad you got together with her, man," Jim said, walking to the other side of the room. "I really like her. You guys would make a great couple. Nell was a little upset about it, though. She was going on and on about how worried she was for you and how she thought you should focus on Vanessa instead."

Elliott frowned as he continued to put the pieces together. "What do you mean?"

"She was telling me that Natalie was too young and didn't have a job and was too much of a 'wounded bird' for you." Jim made air quotes.

Elliott's back stiffened. "Where were you talking about this?"

"Kitchen." Jim turned to look for another clipboard. "I wanted to stop for a second and talk to her about this because—hey, where are you going?"

"Gotta go," Elliott yelled over his shoulder. "Where's Nell?"

"Home."

"And thanks, Colonel."

Elliott took off at a run down the brick walkway.

The ballroom was decked out from top to bottom in crystal, white and silver, all reflecting the late-afternoon light. The chandeliers sparkled above, reflecting in the mirrored centerpieces within twenty tablecloth-clad round tables stretching across the room, each with a tall crystal vase that rose toward the ceiling. The vases were filled with tall white forsythia branches and a low ring of potted white hydrangeas, surrounded by tiny crystal votive candles that, tonight, would cast each table in an enchanted glow.

Natalie took one more sweep of the room, wiped her hands on her jeans, and decided everything looked perfect.

The whole Senior Prom planning crew had been there most of the afternoon—Doris, Marie, Judy, and all the others—setting out candles, flowers, and mirrored confetti; decorating the refreshments table; and making sure the evening's agenda was memorized. Natalie had finally sent them all home to rest up and spend the remainder of the afternoon primping—getting their hair and nails done, zipping into their new dresses, and welcoming their children and grandchildren. The band would set up the sound system and the dance floor around four, and the catering staff would arrive in the evening to do the last few touches for the fondue fountain, champagne fountain, and lighting.

Natalie wouldn't mind lying down for a few minutes herself. After her embarrassing panic attack that morning with Elliott, she might need a few extra minutes to pull herself together.

"You've got the touch," she heard behind her.

She spun around to see Paige, standing there with the box she'd asked her to bring. "What?"

"The touch—Mom's decorating touch. Everyone's counting on me to be the one to take over her business, but I think it's going to be you. Look at this place—it looks like a royal wedding reception. It's absolutely stunning, Natalie."

Natalie couldn't help but smile at the compliment. It made her feel good to have come through for everyone. It meant the world to hear Paige acknowledge it. Especially when she'd screwed everything else up this morning. At least she got the Senior Prom right. And her time with Lily was something she'd always cherish. And Olivia was thrilled with everything she'd done in the new baby's room.

"Where do you want this?" Paige juggled the box.

"Let's put it on the back table."

Olivia had given Natalie the collection of her grandmother's old pocket watches and small silver clock faces, which Natalie was going to arrange in a silver bowl and use as a decoration next to the cake for their theme "Time Is of the Essence."

"I think it's brilliant to use Gram's pocket watches. She'd have liked that. I'm sure she'll be here in spirit," Paige said, pulling the watches out of the box one by one. "So are you going to go home now and get ready for your big date with Elliott tonight? I can't wait to see him in a tuxedo."

"He's going with someone else."

Paige snapped her head up. "What? I thought he was going with you."

"He deserves better than me, Paige. And his sister seems to think so, too."

"What?"

"She doesn't think I'm good enough for him." Natalie forced a smile, but she knew it came out twisted at best. "And I'm probably not. She wants him with someone who knows how to commit."

"His sister is crazy. You're meant for each other."

Tears started to blur Natalie's vision, and she had to look away.

"I'm serious. You two belong together, Nat."

Natalie tried to smile. This was probably just how things were supposed to go.

A back door slammed, and Natalie looked up to see Doris walking in with an extra handful of napkins.

"These go on the cake table, right?" she asked.

"Doris, you're supposed to be home getting ready," Natalie said.

"I'm about to leave. This looks beautiful. I think it's lovely you're using your grandmother's old watch faces. So pretty. We're all going to *party* tonight, aren't we? I can't wait to see you dancing with Dr. Sherman, Natalie. You two are going to look smashing."

"Natalie's not going with Elliott," Paige blurted out.

Doris's head shot up. *"What?"*

"That's exactly what I said." Paige rolled her eyes. "Personally, I think she's just getting spooked."

"I'm not getting 'spooked.' Elliott and I just weren't meant to be."

"You two are perfect for each other—everyone but you can see that. You're just getting spooked."

The watches suddenly didn't look right, and Natalie shakily rearranged them in the silver bowl. "I'm not looking for a long-term relationship. And Elliott needs that."

"Spooked," Paige whispered to Doris.

Doris took the watches out of Natalie's hands. She laid the bowl aside, then took each of Natalie's hands in her own.

"Now listen here, young lady. Men like Elliott do not come along every day. Men who have staying power, and loyalty, and kindness, and who adore you with all their hearts—they are one in a million. Why would you walk away from that?"

"I just—I hadn't planned to stay here. I can't . . ." Her heart picked up its crazy rhythm again, and she pulled her hands out of Doris's to press against her chest.

"Are you hyperventilating, dear?" Doris asked calmly.

Paige nodded. "She's a commitment-phobe."

"I can tell," Doris said.

Natalie pressed her palms harder. Took deeper breaths. Sank into a folding chair.

"Here, have some water," Doris said, grabbing for a bottle under the table. "How long has this been going on?"

"Just since—" Natalie sucked in some air. "A minute ago, when you said—"

"No, no, darling—I mean, how long have you had panic attacks every time the idea of commitment entered your head?"

Natalie took a few steadying breaths and glanced at Paige. Maybe Paige really had been right all this time. "I guess forever."

"When it first made you nervous, what was it specifically that made you think it was scary?"

The water tasted so good. The parquet dance floor blurred in front of Natalie as she let gulps of water slide down her throat and thought back to other dance floors, other tulle-decked chairs, other catered parties . . .

"I guess our mom," she finally said. "She was always moving in and out of relationships. They never seemed to work. And she told me that I shouldn't marry until I was at least thirty. That I should keep moving, keep exploring myself."

"I'll attest to that," Paige said. "But just because relationships didn't work out for Mom doesn't mean it wouldn't for you. Or me. Or Olivia."

"Exactly," Doris said. "You have to rewrite the script in your head. It's okay to change your mind, once you see that some relationships do work. Being committed to someone can be a very beautiful thing, dear."

"I'm always just worried about getting stuck with someone or something. What if I make a terrible mistake?" she breathed out.

"There are no guarantees," Doris said. "But you can't live your life filled with worry over things that haven't happened. What kind of life is that? Just stay in the present, darling. If you're happy in the present, live in the present. If you're in a relationship or a job or a home or a city that's making you happy right now, simply live in that right now. Don't run away from good things because they may fall apart later. You'll never enjoy them fully."

Natalie kept her hand across her chest as she thought that over; then she took another sip of water. *The law of probability,* she thought. If something were making her happy right now, and had a 75 percent chance of making her happy tomorrow, maybe she should take a chance. She didn't want to keep letting good things slip away.

"What if something else comes along?" she asked.

"There will always be lots of other possibilities that come along, but if you spend your energy on making yours the best—rather than looking at the other possibilities—you'll be happy always. But you have to commit first to feel the deep love there."

Natalie stared at the watches. That did make sense. She'd found that committing herself to staying here on the island for the three months did result in her taking pride and control. And she'd found so many things and people to love here. "Have you ever regretted a commitment, Doris?"

"No. I've always thrown my heart in. During the war, you know, we didn't know how much time we were going to have. So we threw our hearts into everything. I was committed to dancing. I was committed to the studio. I had a wonderful marriage. I have wonderful children. I will leave this world with no regrets. I know I gave them all everything

I had. And you know what? Nothing really is forever. Sometimes the things you commit to leave you before you're ready. My husband died. I had a child who died, too. So you need to take hold of them and seize them and enjoy them while they're yours to enjoy. And give them your whole heart."

The watches blurred under Natalie's vision as she thought about that. Doris was right—everyone was on borrowed time. And when you were given the gift of love, whether from a sister or a niece or a grandmother or a man, you should treat it as such—a true gift. One you might not be allowed to enjoy forever. But one you could decide to enjoy as long as time would let you.

"I have to talk to Elliott," she whispered. "I might have blown it already, pushing him toward some other woman. And his sister still might never approve of me. But I need to at least explain to him what he meant to me. He deserves that."

"Just be open to the idea of a relationship," Paige said. "Don't be scared. This is worth taking a chance on. I admire you, Natalie. And I love you to death."

"You admire me?"

"Of course. I admire your independence, and how you always land on your feet. And how you completed this mancation. And how, no matter what, you can find a passion. And hey, I admire this." She waved her hand across the decorated room.

Doris nodded her agreement.

"Thanks, you two." Natalie stood.

Both women turned and threw their arms around her.

"Now go get that guy," Doris whispered in her ear.

Elliott took the steps two at a time up to Nell's town house and jabbed his finger at the doorbell until it just became obnoxious.

"Elliott! Stop! I hear you," Nell said, swinging the door open.

"I know you're trying to take care of me, and ensure my happiness, but I can't abide by this anymore."

Her eyes widened. "Hello to you, too. C'mon in. And you can't abide by what?"

"I can't come in. I just want to come to tell you to stop."

"Stop what?"

"Butting into my life."

"Butting into your life? What are you talking about?"

"Look, Nell, I love you. Dearly. You've been a great sister to me, and I know you have only my best interests at heart. And I will never forget that you saved my life that day. And that you basically raised me ever since. But I think you've been protecting me for so long, you don't know where your wants for me and my true wants begin and end."

Nell scooped Max up off the entryway floor. "Elliott, what are you talking about?"

Elliott lowered his voice near Max. "I need you to stay out of my love life. And stop with the blind dates. And stop interfering with women like Natalie Grant."

"Natalie Grant? Are we still on this? I thought you were taking Vanessa tonight."

"I was. But I'm canceling."

"Canceling? Elliott, I flew her in especially for this event. I have her staying here for two nights. Can't you just show her around?"

"No."

Nell's eyes grew wide. And then misted over.

Elliott looked away. He didn't want to hurt her, but he had to put an end to this.

"You'll have to show her around yourself. I'm meeting Natalie at the dance tonight."

"You can't just fall in love with the first pretty young thing who pays attention to you. You have to give this some thought."

He blinked back at her. "You think I haven't given this some thought?"

"I just think you're swayed by the first beautiful woman paying attention to you, and you're not thinking properly. Natalie isn't right for you."

Elliott looked away and ground his teeth together. "That's what I'm talking about. You need to back out of this. You think you know what's best for me, but you're not asking me how I feel about it. You want me to have a woman who will take care of me, but you don't understand that what I need is a woman I can take care of. I feel like I've been running all my life—away from fears, away from people, away from getting too close to others for fear they'll die on me. I focus on work because it's easier than facing life, or people. But here's what I know—ever since I met Natalie, I haven't felt fear. In fact, I worry about her fears, and all I want to do is protect her. And protecting Natalie has given me a confidence and a courage I didn't even know I had. Courage, and love, and protecting her, and being a man—they're all intertwined for me now. They're all wrapped up in meeting her. I've never felt so whole and alive as I have these past three months. You have to give me this, Nell. You have to let me go. And stop worrying about me. Let me feel that same kind of love you do for someone else."

She bounced Max in her arms as her eyes glistened.

"I just don't want someone to be taking from you all the time," she said in a small voice. "You're very giving, and I don't want someone taking advantage of you."

"She's not taking from me. She's giving to me."

"What is she giving you?"

"Courage. Love. Laughter. Confidence. A reason to come home every day. And acceptance—a lot of acceptance—she never wants to change me."

Nell looked away. He didn't quite mean that as the barb it probably felt like, but she took it that way. And he didn't correct her.

"She's not taking your money?" she asked weakly.

"She doesn't even know I have money. And the few things I've offered to pay for—she never takes my help. She even wants to buy my groceries all the time."

Nell stared at one of Max's complicated bead toys and thought that over. "She's never asked you for anything?"

"Not once."

She bounced Max once more and then put him down to crawl on the floor. "I can try to give her a chance."

"Give her a chance? Nell, you just drove her away! She overheard you talking to Jim today in my kitchen and heard your 'wounded bird' comment. She's convinced now she's not right for me."

Nell bit her lip and watched Max. "I'm sorry. I'll make it up to you. But could you just finish this date with Vanessa and then—"

"*No!* Nell, no. You're not getting it. I'm in love with Natalie."

As soon as the words left his mouth, he sucked in some air. *Damn.* He hadn't even admitted that out loud to himself yet. And there it was. Out in the open. He was in love with Natalie.

"And now she's leaving," he said. "And I think both of us have blown it. This might have cost me the best thing that ever happened to me."

A silence fell as Nell continued to bite her lip. Max cooed and reached up for her. "What can I do?" she whispered.

He was stunned that she finally seemed to get it.

"It might be too late to do anything," he admitted. "But I want one more chance to talk to her tonight. And I don't want you interfering. If you see her tonight, I want you to be polite. No more meddling."

A tear started to roll down Nell's cheek. Elliott felt bad. He wasn't angry. But he just needed to make things right now.

He reached out and pulled her to him. "I love you, Nell."

She crushed her face against his shirt. "Sunrises, Elliott."

"Sunrises, sis."

They stood that way for several seconds, the setting sun streaming in low across the porch, remembering all they'd meant to each other as kids but knowing they needed to move forward now as adults with their individual lives. Finally, Elliott stepped away and held her shoulders.

"Now I need you to get something for me."

CHAPTER 27

The cool sea air swept her long dress around her ankles as Natalie ascended the steps at the outside entrance to the Casas del Sur ballroom. She wasn't used to attending events solo—she'd always kept a man on her arm to feel more secure, free from other men's leers—but this felt strangely comfortable.

The Colonel had pulled her into his room earlier, made her a martini, and filled her in on his whole outline for how he planned to get Steve Stegner out of his position with a new board of directors the seniors were petitioning for. They'd petitioned the owner weeks ago. And he told her the board was unanimous about wanting Natalie to take Steve's place—they hoped if they hurried, she'd consider staying on the island and taking the job.

The offer took her by surprise. At first, she expected the feeling of claustrophobia to hit her, but it never did. Instead, she was filled with a warmth of being wanted and accepted by this wonderful group of seniors she was proud to call friends. After talking to Doris and Paige about commitment, and how it was so much about living in the moment, a feeling of strength came over her at the idea of committing to a job and an island, instead of fear. She was much more confident now. And, after her mancation this spring, she also knew she truly didn't need a man to help her navigate through life.

Though she did want a man.

A particular one.

One who was standing over by the punchbowl right now, looking a little awkward, staring at the cheese platters with a plastic cup in his hand.

"Elliott!" A smile overtook her as she drew nearer. He gave her one of his sexiest grins. The one that looked shy and mysterious at the same time—as if they had a wicked secret to share, which, given their previous wild night, she supposed they did.

He held her gaze until she had to look away—but only to take in the rest of him. His crisp white collar framed his Adam's apple; the sleek lines of his black tuxedo outlined his strong shoulders. He had his glasses back on, and his new updated frames looked sexy and comfortable on him. His hair was combed neatly, but a few wisps had already escaped down his forehead, and his black bow tie sat just crooked enough to look very Elliott.

He threw her another mischievous grin when he realized she was checking him out.

Natalie reached out to give him a hug. The only thing that stole away from her joy at seeing him look this good was that he'd done it for another woman. And that he very well might hate Natalie right now.

But his smile never wavered as his bright-blue eyes took her in from head to toe. Hate was not part of his repertoire of emotions.

"Wow," he said. "You look . . . Wow." He shook his head.

She'd worn her hair down, letting it cascade down her back. The dress was like nothing she'd ever worn before—true Old Hollywood glamour, fitted against her body from top to bottom, with a layer of long-sleeved lace covering her collarbone and sitting off her shoulder. Her shoes were not too high—she was tall enough—but they were definitely more sparkly and strappy and feminine than she was used to. She felt strong. And happy. And confident.

She pushed a few curls off her shoulder. "Thank you. You look amazing, too."

He gave her a return grin that bordered on relief.

"Where's your date?" she asked, breaking the spell.

He cleared his throat. "No date." He put his cup down.

"No date? But where's . . ." She looked around briefly and tried to remember the woman's name.

"As I said, I have no interest. Can I get you something to drink? Punch is here, or I could go to the bar for a gimlet."

"But what . . ." She tried to put everything into place but had to reframe how she thought the evening would go. But mostly she couldn't help the joy bubbling up that this fine-looking man right here had no lady on his arm.

"I have something for you," he said.

Before she could figure out what he was talking about, he stepped a little closer. "But first I have to ask you something."

She looked up to meet his gaze.

"Would you be my date tonight? No pressure. No commitment except tonight. But I'd love to have you near me all night."

Elliott's manly, salty scent drifted up around her and made her slightly heady for a second, as it instantly launched her back to the memory of being against his naked body. She managed a bob of her head as her voice disappeared.

"Good," he said. "Then let me get the something for you."

He leaned down underneath the punch table and whisked out a pot of light-yellow gerbera daisies that matched her dress perfectly. "I always get the color right. Law of probability," he said with a wink. He handed them to her. "I'm sorry I didn't pick you up at the door. But I'll have you note I don't have on dungarees."

Natalie smiled. "No, you don't. And your shoes are polished, too."

"And may I be the first to say you have sea lion hair?"

Natalie laughed and took the potted daisies. "Thank you."

"Natalie?" Katherine from the prom committee came up behind her, broke the spell, and grabbed Natalie's hand. "It's time to get things started."

Natalie looked up at Elliott with disappointment and apology.

But he simply met her with a proud grin. "It's your turn to shine now," he said. "I'll be waiting for you. First dance."

Natalie kept him in her sights as Katherine pulled her away. *First dance?* Her pleasure. The idea that this man was hers all night settled her soul as she shuffled up to the stage with her arm curled around her potted plant. She was ready to start the party.

Natalie welcomed the families, explained the evening's lineup, encouraged everyone to mingle and enjoy cocktails, and cast furtive glances at Elliott as he made the rounds among his new island friends.

She lugged her potted plant around proudly, explaining to everyone who asked that her date had bought it for her because they both preferred live plants. Hours later—after dinner, soft swing tunes, and making the rounds of hellos—she stood again with the microphone in one hand and the plant in the other and announced the three nominees for Senior Prom king, then the three nominees for Senior Prom queen. The court shuffled forward, and all took their places at the front of the room.

"And your new Senior Prom king and queen are . . ." Natalie announced. "Stanley Koll and Marie Cosgrove!"

The entire place exploded into applause.

The Colonel walked across the front of the room and bowed to ask for Marie's hand. She took it, and the two of them spun out to the dance floor to a slow Tommy Dorsey tune that Natalie had picked out. But as Natalie was clapping frantically through her tears, the Colonel walked up to the band director and whispered something in his ear. The band came to a halt. Natalie frowned. What was the matter?

The band director stopped, turned toward his band, raised his hand in the air, and they all broke out into a modern hip-hop song that Natalie didn't even know, heavy on the bass.

Stunned, she began to march over to see what the problem was, but Doris and fourteen others sauntered out to the dance floor and joined in with the Colonel and Marie—all doing a flash-mob dance. As the music thumped and the base boomed, all twenty seniors swiveled, shook, and clapped their hands in unison, all in a line. The guests—all the seniors' families, children, grandchildren, and friends—went wild, everyone leaping out of their seats and joining in the clapping, straining to get a better view of the Colonel and Marie and the others doing their moves.

When the dance was over, the guests continued clapping uproariously as the Colonel hugged everyone, Marie hugged everyone, and Doris hugged her whole troupe. Finally, the Colonel lifted his hand and struck up the band again into the original tune.

As the Tommy Dorsey tune swelled onto the dance floor, and Natalie stopped clapping and smiling, the lights finally dimmed, and the Colonel and Marie went back to their slow waltz. A few bars in, the Colonel started calling others out. Ballroom dancing for the evening officially began.

"That was great," Natalie heard behind her.

She looked over her shoulder to see Elliott, beaming at both her and the dancers.

"I had nothing to do with that," she admitted.

"Yeah, that had Doris written all over it. I heard the music on her player during one of my dance lessons and wondered what they were up to. Would you join me in this dance?" He held his arm out in a formal pose.

"Wow, you look like you know what you're doing."

"The Colonel and Doris have been pounding this stuff into my brain. Is it working?"

"It must be, because I really want to dance with you right now."

Elliott pulled her out onto the floor. He picked up the waltz rhythm as quickly as he had during their practice and glided her around the floor, his hand firmly at her back.

Natalie enjoyed being in his arms, especially when he brought her closer to his chest than necessary. He smelled delicious—some kind of great aftershave she'd never noticed on him before, something with a musk undertone that smacked of daring and masculinity. He held his chin high, as Doris had probably instructed him to do, but would let just his eyes drop to meet hers and give her a playful grin.

"What did you want to talk to me about?" she finally asked.

"I'm getting up my nerve," he said.

They swung around the edge, moving in their perfect one-two-three, one-two-three, and Natalie closed her eyes and relished the dance while she had it. She'd have to get up a little nerve, too. She needed to tell Elliott all he'd meant to her. And maybe venture into some new plans.

When the dance ended, the couples gathered to clap for the band; then the next tune started up.

"Want to go outside?" Elliott asked.

When she nodded, he guided her through a set of French doors along the side of the ballroom. They walked along the balcony until they couldn't be seen from inside, then Natalie turned and gulped in several deep breaths of sea air. She twisted her dress until she could breathe better. She was nervous now. She wanted to talk to him, too, but admitting how she felt about him, hinting that she'd like to make more of a commitment—it would all take a lot of courage. And she was terrified another panic attack would begin.

And if it did, what was her mind telling her?

She took a deep breath and told herself to take the chance.

Elliott tugged at his collar. Damn, these bow ties were stifling. He loosened the knot ever so slightly just so he could get a little extra air. He jostled the velvet box he had in his pocket—finally secured there after a forty-five-minute hunt with Nell this afternoon. The Colonel was right—they'd done everything slightly out of order, and he might have mucked things up a little, but he had to try.

"So we have some talking to do?" she asked.

She was smiling—so beautiful, so sweet—but Elliott's heart was racing. He was terrified about what he was going to do. And he was terrified at what her reaction would be.

"I do," he said anyway, his throat barely squeezing the phrase out.

And then he got down on one knee.

Natalie frowned at Elliott on the balcony concrete, wondering what on earth he was doing, and then . . . Oh God . . . Her heart started racing again.

"Natalie, I kneel before you as a man of honor, respect"—he glanced up at her—"a whole lot of courage . . ." He laughed. "And most of all as a man of adoration."

The ocean wind ruffled his hair as Natalie watched the crown of his head, and she watched as the moonlight played a circle in his hair. She did know he adored her, and hearing him say it now filled her with a warmth she'd never experienced. It settled first in her brain, then down her spine, then in her heart and stomach as it slowly calmed her.

"I want you to know how much you mean to me," Elliott said, "and how much you've meant to me the whole time I've known you. I used to think I was just a loner by choice—that I threw myself into work because it was easier than being with people—but now I see that I just hadn't met the right people. And I definitely hadn't met the right woman.

"I pretty much needed lessons in everything—how to date, how to dance, what to wear, what not to wear . . ." He glanced up. "But the one who taught me the important thing was you. You taught me how to love, and how to accept love, and how that means that you want to take care of each other and stand up to anything or anyone who gets in the way.

"The Colonel told me a few times, and again just a bit ago, that time was of the essence—he said once you know you're in love with someone, why would you let another day go by without wanting her in your life? So I thought I'd ask . . . and see if you would consider staying here with me on the island, and making a life with me?"

Natalie gasped when he pulled a box out of his pocket. She suddenly felt unsteady on her feet. She waited for the panic to set in. But the box was huge.

"This isn't an engagement ring." He reached out to steady her. "I know better than to mention marriage around you." He grinned. "I thought we'd just take a small step."

He opened the box to reveal the female version of the *Star Trek* TAG Heuer.

"When this prize came to me as a his-and-hers set, I never thought I'd have a wife or partner to share it with. I never thought anyone would understand this kind of thing, or appreciate it like I do." He laughed. "I've never given a woman a piece of jewelry in my life, and I'm so happy the first—and, hopefully, only one—is you. Whatever happens, I want you to have it."

"Elliott, I can't take this. You should save it for—"

"No, it's yours. You were my other half these past few months, and I want you to have it. But I hope we can wear the matching set for a while, Natalie. I know you're a commitment-phobe, and I don't expect you to promise forever, but I'm wondering if you'll give me a chance at a little while. I want to tell you and show you how I feel—*I'm* in this. All the way. I love you, I'm yours, and I'm here to work on making your life better every day."

Natalie stepped back and stared. She waited for her heart to start skipping and the panic to set in. She waited for the crushing sensation, the tight chest, the feeling that she couldn't breathe.

But . . . nothing like that came.

Instead, she looked at the man before her, and all she felt was tenderness toward him, care coming from him, joy at the idea of his company every day, anticipation of more beautiful sex, and—most of all—love, which felt like all those things combined. And, just as Paige said, it felt like friendship with a whole lot of attraction.

"Your sister doesn't approve of me," she finally said in the smallest of voices. She couldn't imagine tearing Nell and Elliott apart. They'd been through too much together.

"She helped me find the watch, actually."

"What?"

"I'd given it to her to save for a niece someday, but I talked to her, Nat, and told her what you mean to me. I told her I would always love her and be grateful to her, but I needed to start my own life, and make my own decisions about who I wanted in it. And when I told her how much I loved you, she started crying. And then she helped me find the watch. It was always meant to be a set."

"Really, Elliott?"

"Really."

"Then, yes," she said when she could finally find her voice.

His eyebrows shot up under his messy hair, which had come undone from the gel and was back to its normal style now, much to her delight. "What?"

She pulled him up to hug him. "I'm saying yes. Yes to the watch. Yes to you. Yes to staying on the island. Yes to starting a relationship with you."

"*Yes?*"

"Yes."

"I can't believe it. I thought you'd . . . Well, forget what I thought. I just . . . Wait, you're saying *yes?*"

She laughed and threw her arms around his neck. "It sounds like you're the one who's shocked now."

"A little."

"I talked to Paige and Doris earlier, and they both convinced me that commitment isn't the scary thing I used to think it was. Doris said you need to stop worrying about possible future failures and just live with what makes you happy in the present. And I can do that with you, Elliott. You make my days so much happier. I fell in love with you a long time ago, I realize. And I can commit to you, and loving you, and making our life together—hopefully a long life together—the best it can be."

"You'll live with me here?"

"Yes. I'll be close to my sister, and my niece, and my new nephew, and the seniors. The Colonel wants me to take the new job opening as activities director. It'll be perfect. You can work at the center. And Nell and Jim might come back someday, and then you'll have your nephew here, too. And we can continue our . . . lessons."

"Our lessons?"

"I'm thinking of even sexier ones."

His smile grew wicked. "You know I'm going to ruin the curve on that."

"I look forward to it."

He pulled her toward him "I'm the luckiest man in the world." His mouth found hers, and he kissed her with a combined fierceness and tenderness she was growing to love about him.

When she finally broke away, they walked back through the French doors to several sets of eyes suddenly on them.

"She said yes!" Elliott announced.

The room let up a collective cheer. Doris hustled over to embrace both of them, Marie gathered them into a group hug, the Colonel saluted, and even George and Sugar and John-O and June seemed in on the plans.

"Did everyone know about this?" she whispered to Elliott.

"I had some support," he said.

Nell approached from the side, beaming with Jim, and held out her hand.

"Can we start over? I'm Nell, and thrilled to meet the woman who finally stole my brother's heart."

Natalie reached for her hand, but Nell pulled her into an embrace.

As Natalie glanced behind them, she saw Paige across the table give her a thumbs-up.

The whole group danced until morning—quite a feat for the seniors in the room, but they were all having a fabulous time.

When the lights finally dimmed after the last dance, Elliott took her hand, touched the watch that now sat beautifully on her wrist, and tugged her out the front door, starting down the hill.

"Where are we going?" she asked.

"I want to walk you home." He tugged his bow tie out of his collar. "I look forward to this good-bye kiss at your door. I want to see how you feel about me."

Natalie laughed. "Oh, I think you'll know."

And they walked all the way home together, barefoot, smiling at each other.

And smiling at the sunrise.

EPILOGUE

The February sun bounced harshly off the ocean waves as Natalie shaded her eyes and tried to see all the figures before her in the sand. She jostled her new nephew, Aaron, in the carrier in front of her.

"Do you want me to take him?" Olivia asked from beside her. She, too, stood shading her eyes and staring out at the sea.

"No, I've got him."

"They sure look sexy out there, don't they?" Paige asked, forming the third figure with her hand over her eyebrows.

They took in Jim, Garrett, the Colonel, John-O, Tag, Olivia's husband, Jon, Elliott, and a new guy named A. J.—all standing with their feet in the sand, lining up crates along the shore, ready for the last sea lion release of the season.

Moe was in this release. He was one of the last three sea lions to make a full recovery from spring's onslaught. It had taken him a little longer than everyone else, but he'd done it. He was almost unrecognizable now—a full year old, nearly three hundred pounds, his coat now a shiny acorn brown like his brothers.

"Well, Moe looks pretty good," Natalie said. "But if you're using the term *sexy* for the Colonel, young Garrett, or any of those married men, we've got to find you a date soon."

"Tag and John-O aren't looking too bad," Paige said.

"There you go."

"And, hey, yours isn't married yet."

"Back off, Paige."

Olivia laughed. "Let's get closer."

They walked another ten feet in the sand along the shore break, picking up Lily on the way, who was doing cartwheels in the wet sand and racing up with a handful of seashells to show baby Aaron.

Natalie, though, kept her sights on Elliott. He turned to smile at them, and, as usual, Natalie's heart wanted to burst with pride. He wore a casual sweatshirt that outlined his shoulders, which had grown even fuller and wider with all the sea lion hauling he was doing and all the eating Natalie was making sure he did. His beach shorts and bare feet were covered in sand as he hauled a heavy crate near the shore break. His hair was still a mess, even though Natalie tried to trim it for him regularly, but the sea air always blew it about his forehead in a way she'd simply come to love.

She handed Aaron off to Olivia and ran up to meet him. She could hardly keep her hands off him these days.

They'd been together about eight months now, and Natalie saw no end in sight. Rather than find him more and more annoying, as she had with boyfriends in the past, she found more and more reasons to adore Elliott. And her love for him—rooted in the deep caring and respect of friendship first—made her want to simply make him happy every day. She never wanted to see him hurt. She never wanted to see him sad. And she did everything she could to make sure he wasn't, focusing on bringing him joy every day.

Of course, he returned the favor. He kissed her forehead every morning. He told her he loved her every day. He brought her potted flowers every few weeks, and he texted her love quotes whenever he thought of them. Normally, Natalie might have found all this suffocating, but with Elliott, she found it endearing. She'd shed the confines of commitment-phobia with this man, and his love warmed her rather than smothered her; it made her feel cherished rather than claustrophobic; it made her feel free rather than chained. And, much to her surprise, it grew stronger every day.

It was the best chance she'd ever taken.

Law of probability, indeed.

"Are they almost ready?" Paige yelled to the men manning the crates.

The townspeople began gathering along the stretch of shoreline in front of Elliott's place, which he'd recently purchased from Dr. Johnson and that Natalie was now redecorating. They all slowed to a stop right before the tide pools.

"LET'S GO!" the Colonel yelled, calling everyone around.

This was a huge turnout for a February. Many of the townspeople had come for this release, as Moe had practically become a Friends of the Sea Lion mascot and town celebrity. He was in the paper almost every week, with detailed news of his slow recovery, and earning lots of donations from island visitors and residents alike, which went back into the center to help feed more sea lions.

The Colonel positioned everyone into two long rows, and Natalie, Paige, Lily, and Olivia joined the lines of onlookers, who formed a sort of tunnel toward the Pacific. Even Paige knew where to stand now, since she'd come to the island almost every other weekend last summer. Natalie and Olivia still couldn't get her to move there with them, but she was starting to crack, her visits lasting longer and longer. Paige's favorite visits were when they had sea lion releases like this one.

Once everyone was in place, Jim held up his hand. He'd come back to the island with Nell for good once their stint in Italy was over. They'd missed all the work they'd done at the center, and Nell wanted to raise

Max in such a close community. They'd bought a cottage just two doors down from Olivia, and Natalie and Elliott had started having dinner with each family once a week. Sometimes Natalie and Elliott just went over to take Max and Aaron out on evening stroller rides after dinner, Lily bouncing along beside them in her new veterinarian costume.

As Jim's hand came down among the crowd, all three crates were opened simultaneously, and the three sea lions popped their heads out.

"Good-bye to Jangles, Toast, and Moe!" Elliott called out.

The crowd all clapped as the three sea lions waddled slowly toward the ocean, first hesitantly, popping their whiskered noses into the air, then—as they instinctively recognized the call of the ocean—faster and faster until all three blubbery bodies leaped together into the waves.

The crowd cheered and yelled as the sea lions dove up and down through the whitewater, their bodies glistening in the sun. Within seconds, they all made short order out of diving down into the Pacific.

"Good-bye, Moe!" yelled Lily, jumping up and down and waving her little hands. "I'll miss you!"

Natalie looked at the pride on Elliott's face—the wind whipping his hair around his head—until he finally glanced back, caught her eye, and smiled.

She wrapped her arms around him and gave him a squeeze.

"I'm going to miss him, too," he whispered into her hair, curling his arm around her back. "We have him tagged so we can keep an eye on him, but—as much as you want them to go back—you realize how important they became to you."

She laid her head on Elliott's chest. "Moe looks so happy out there. He truly found his home," she said.

Elliott squeezed her and leaned down to kiss her forehead. "So did I."

ACKNOWLEDGMENTS

So many thanks go to so many people for helping me bring these books to life.

Thanks, first of all, to the real-life volunteers at sea lion rescue centers throughout California—your constant dedication to helping marine life, and educating the public, is truly heroic and admirable.

Thanks to my very own romance hero, my husband, Chris—he brings me wine, he makes dinner, and he makes me laugh every day. It's a true joy being married to your best friend.

Thanks to my sister-in-law, Denise Sanchez, who has played "roadie," manager, and marketer for me. She's a pillar of strength for our whole family and always offers help and support, no questions asked.

Thanks to friend Barbara Young, who has offered such unwavering support since the beginning of my writing journey—she went with me to my first writers' meeting, threw my first launch party for me, and always offers such wonderful encouragement and cheerleading. You are a true friend, Barbara.

Thank you to my amazing critique partner, Tricia Lynne. You always bring out the best in me and my writing, and always make my books better. Your skill and talent are unsurpassed.

Thank you to friends who read this book at various stages and gave me great feedback: beta readers Debi Skubic, Mary Ann Perdue, Barbara Young, and my mom, Arlene Hayden.

Thanks to friend Michelle Arconti Gordon, who offered some of her own memories of working with sea lion rescue teams.

Thanks to my wonderful Firebird sisters who are always superstar supporters. Especially those who lent a special hand in this book: A. J. Larrieu, who helped with the scientific lingo for Elliott; brainstormers Pintip Dunn, Lorenda Christensen, Wendy LaCapra, Priscilla Kissinger, Sheri Humphreys, Jean Willett, Jamie Wesley, Lexi Greene, Talia Surova, and Pamela Kopfler, who offered great brainstorming ideas; and especially Tamra Baumann, who constantly talks me off ledges.

Thanks, as always, to my terrific agent, Jill Marsal: I don't know what I'd do without you.

Thanks to my editors at Montlake, Maria Gomez and Charlotte Herscher, and to the talented Montlake copy editors and cover designers.

Thanks to my kids for their constant support and encouragement—even from one thousand miles away on college campuses. And special thanks to my youngest—the only one still home—who goes without clean socks many a Monday as his mom is gunning for a deadline.

And a huge thank-you to my parents, Don and Arlene Hayden, who have always been so loving and supportive and are a fine example of a true love story, celebrating their fiftieth wedding anniversary this year. Mom and Dad, this one's dedicated to you!

ABOUT THE AUTHOR

Photo © 2013 Shawn Oudt

Lauren Christopher is the author of the Sandy Cove romance series, which includes *The Red Bikini* and *Ten Good Reasons*, and now the new Lavender Island romance series, which kicks off with *The Kiss on Castle Road*. She has been a 2015 Holt Medallion Award of Merit winner and a 2012 Golden Heart finalist. A professional writer for more than two decades, she has worked on projects from NASA video scripts and restaurant reviews to feature stories on the origins of Santa Claus. A graduate of UCLA with a degree in English, she resides in Southern California with her husband and three children. She loves to chat with readers! Visit her at her website to say hello and learn more about her books at www.LaurenChristopherAuthor.com.